the END of FUN

# the END of FUN

## Sean McGinty

HYPERION

Los Angeles   New York

First Edition, April 2016
10 9 8 7 6 5 4 3 2 1
FAC-020093-16015

Printed in the United States of America

Library of Congress Cataloging-in-Publication Data
McGinty, Sean.
    The end of fun / Sean McGinty.
        pages cm
    Summary: "Seventeen-year-old Aaron is hooked on FUN, a new
augmented reality experience that is as addictive as it is FUN. But
when he sets off on a treasure hunt, left by his late grandfather,
Aaron must navigate the real world and discover what it means
to connect—after the game is over"—Provided by publisher.
    ISBN 978-1-4847-2211-4
[1. Augmented reality—Fiction.   2. Buried treasure—Fiction.
3. Emotional problems—Fiction.   4. Science fiction.]   I. Title.
    PZ7.1.M4352En 2016
    [E]—dc23                          2015017456

Reinforced binding
Visit www.hyperionteens.com

SUSTAINABLE FORESTRY INITIATIVE   Certified Sourcing
www.sfiprogram.org
SFI-00993

THIS LABEL APPLIES TO TEXT STOCK

Tara & Cedar

My continuous word of warning is that you should never be discouraged by failure, and never expect success. Then if you don't find the treasure, you will not be too disappointed, and if you are successful, you'll be able to stand it more gracefully.

—Edward Rowe Snow

# +100 yay!s

# 01.

## MAY HAVE SAVED MY LIFE

Dear To Whom It May Concern Or Whatever,

This is Aaron O'Faolain and I've got some Issues. The directions say I'm supposed to *briefly discuss reasons for Application for Termination of FUN®*. But in order to *briefly* discuss one reason, first I have to explain something else, and before I get to that there's *another* thing, and in order to cut through the crap and get it all straight in my head, it's going to take a little more space than the space provided provides. Which is why I'm doing it here in the YAY!log. I hope you don't mind.

But if you are checking this out and you *do* mind, please understand that I'm not here to troll or anything. I just got a little behind on my FUN®—and that's my second issue. To even be *allowed* to file an Application for Termination, I have to get my YAY!s back up to +100. Which is crazy, but what can you do? So here I am. And if you feel like throwing me a YAY!, that's awesome. Please feel free to YAY! me so hard, and I will YAY! you so hard right back, and we can live out our lives together in peace and harmony forever with eagles and rainbows amen.

OK, here's my rundown:

| name: | already told you |
|---|---|
| username: | original boy_2 |
| age: | 17 |
| region: | america |
| mood: | sleep depraved |
| status: | fail |
| history: | (see below) |

So as for History, that's where it gets kind of complicated. A lot has happened, and it's going to take some explaining. Before I get to the part about the werewolf pills, or the hidden treasure, or the amazing holy wonder, I should probably go back to where it all started, aka my childhood, aka what it was like to grow up in a craphole town in the middle of nowhere, aka Antello, Nevada.

At first it was OK, I guess. Lots of bike riding in the brush. Blue belly lizards. Abandoned trailers. That kind of stuff. The main bad thing that happened was when I was 10 and my mom left town to be with this guy named Hawk. Seriously, that's what his name was. *Hawk*. Mom met Hawk on a dating site, and they bonded over their deep affinity for being irresponsible asswipes and therefore moved to Sacramento, California. The rest of us handled it in our own ways. Dad drank box wine, Evie wrote sad poetry, and I tried to kill myself, which first of all I do NOT endorse, and second of all *** spoiler alert *** I did not accomplish.

Pro tip: do not try to kill yourself at age 10—or any age, really—and especially not by knocking back a bottle of liquid sleep aid and then tossing yourself off the roof of a garage in the middle of a snowstorm. Which, by the way: YAY! for Doze+® SleepStrong™ liquid sleep, and a big shout-out to its gag-inducing harvest apple flavor, which may have saved my life that day, seeing as right after I chugged it, I barfed it all back up on the carpet. Instead of cleaning the mess (a fate worse than death), I decided, *Why not jump off the garage?*

So I climbed the crab apple tree to the roof of the garage and stood there in my jammies with the snow whipping round. And as I gazed down from those lofty heights, I knew—I mean, I just couldn't deny it—those heights weren't even *remotely* lofty enough to kill me. Still, I did in that moment exhibit perseverance and follow-through. I mean, I *did* jump.

But right after I jumped I had this thought—or more like a series of thoughts: *What up, A-dog? Whatcha doin'? You think this is a wise decision? This is not a wise decision at all.*

I swear I was out there for a good ten seconds, just floating in midair with my thoughts, cartoon-style. But then gravity kicked in and I began to fall, and as I fell I managed to make a grab for the rain gutter, which is how I sliced open my hand, and also how I got distracted from my very imminent landing. And as I very imminently hit the snowy concrete, I did detect with my ears a most terrible *POP!* emanating from the general vicinity of my left anklebone area.

Pro tip #2: when your sister finds you on the driveway with blood all over and a foot pointing in the wrong direction, and when she asks what happened, do NOT tell her you tried to kill yourself. If you tell her you tried to kill yourself, she'll freak and tell your dad, and he'll send you to some doctors, and those doctors will medicate you to within an inch of a lobotomy, and you'll lose the next six years of your life in a slightly damp, slightly bitter lavender-flavored brain fog.

Don't do it.

I'm telling you.

Just say you fell.

 ?

# 02.

# YOUTHRIVE®ACADEMY

So that part sucked, and I'm going to fast-forward to my junior year of high school, aka last year, which is the year I finally made the decision to get off the pills, which I'm not necessarily recommending (check with a medical professional and all that), but for me I think it was a good decision—and then, on the other hand, quitting the pills is probably what got me expelled.

The problem was that once the fog was gone, all the feelings came back. Anger mostly. It was like, *What the hell happened to the last six years? Who the hell am I anyway? What the hell am I doing wasting my life in this craphole of a town?*

And I ended up having this "discussion," I guess you could call it, with a certain teacher of mine in a public arena, i.e., classroom. His name was Mr. Danielson, and I asked him in so many words to why not self-administer a paper enema using preferably a nearby rolled-up map of North America (he was my geography teacher). That suggestion resulted in a week's suspension, but what got me booted for permanent was later that same month, on the eve of my seventeenth birthday, when I burned down the gymnasium.

I didn't *actually* burn down the gymnasium—though if you read the way they put it in the police report, you'd think I did. But I didn't. What happened was me and my best friend, Oso, were out in the fields trying to smoke some fake weed he'd got me as a birthday present. It was supposed to be real weed, but it was fake. Once we figured that out, we were like, *In our bored pursuit of cheap fun let us now play with incendiaries.* We had two bottle rockets. Mine was a dud, fizzling out like the saddest candle. So Oso—this is the kind of friend he is—he offered me his.

"Make a wish, bro."

I can't even remember what I wished for, but here's what I do remember: the hiss of the rocket, the silence afterwards, and then a little while after that, Oso tapping me on the shoulder.

"Hey. You see that?"

"See what?"

"The smoke, bro. Where the rocket landed."

And as we stood there watching, the whole place just went up. I'm serious. One second there was this thin plume of smoke, and the next it was like the whole *field* was on fire. The wind came on all howling from the east and blew the flames toward the school, scorching, yes, *somewhat* the steps of the gymnasium—which are concrete by the way, so totally nonflammable—and, long story short, eventually attracting the attention of some police officers and a couple fire trucks and for some reason an ambulance.

Oh, and I forgot to mention: all this was recorded by three separate security cameras.

My dad was not happy. Neither was my sister, Evie. They were even less happy when they got the letter about me being expelled. I'll skip that moment and just say that after they were done murdering me for a while, they informed me that, aside from my mandatory community service, I could not leave my room until I had selected one of two options:

1. Take and pass the GED test

2. Homelessness

I had some time to think about it and in the end decided to lobby for a third alternative:

3. Go live with Mom in Sactown and finish school there

So I applied to this year-round charter school in Sacramento, YouThrive®Academy (YAY!)...and guess what? I got in. I'm not a dummy or anything. After I was accepted, I called my mom. We hadn't talked in months, her preference being a more hands-off parenting approach. I presented my plan like it was some prize, like I'd won a scholarship or something.

"Wonderful!" she said. "I can come visit you at the school."

"I wouldn't actually live at the school."

"Where would you live?"

"With you."

"Me? Oh, you wouldn't want to do that, Aaron. This house is built on a fault line. And don't even get me started on the heat. It's been *unbearable!*"

"I don't mind if it's hot."

"You say that now, but it's just awful. When that sun hits the south end of the house, you may as well just die."

"I could bring a fan."

"Oh, I really don't know, Aaron.... How's Evie, by the way? Did you know she got me a subscription to her newspaper? It comes in the mail. Tell her I read her articles every day. It sounds like she's having fun as a reporter."

"Yeah, she's fine. She's excited for me to go to Sacramento. She and Dad are really excited...."

I let it hang there like that, waiting for her to make an offer, but she never did. She never flat-out said no, either. She just kept dancing around the answer, talking about a bunch of other meaningless stuff until finally I was like, "OK, thanks. I'll talk to you soon, then. Loveyoubye."

But later, when I saw my dad in the hall, I was like, "Mom said yes."

And I remember the next Tuesday just before I got on the bus, Evie pulled me aside. She put her face right in front of mine and spoke to me that way she does, all slow and enunciated like I was just learning English.

"Aaron...for the love of God...try to stay out of trouble, OK?"

"You bet."

But for the love of God what my sister didn't know was I was already *in* trouble for lying to her about going to Mom's. I wasn't going to Mom's. I was going somewhere else. Somewhere far away. I was initiating my plan of thievery and deception. And this—me getting on the bus—this was phase one: Escape from Craphole.

 ?

# 03.

## ZAZZ®

I figured I could make a clean break without anyone knowing anything. Mom never communicated with anyone—it would be forever before anyone had any contact. In the meantime I'd just tell Dad and Evie what they wanted to hear: that I was doing fine in school and hanging with Mom. But what I would *really* be doing— what I *was* doing—was running away to San Francisco with my tuition payment for YouThrive®Academy.

Getting the money was phase two, and it was surprisingly easy. I actually accomplished it on the bus ride to San Francisco. I logged in to my student profile on YouThrive®'s Web site and filed for a cancellation/tuition return. Where it asked for a reason, I wavered between STUDENT HAS BEEN ACCEPTED AT ANOTHER SCHOOL and STUDENT IS DECEASED, and finally selected OTHER. In the part that asked where to send the reimbursement (minus 15% processing fee), I put the routing number to my checking account.

And it worked! The next time I looked, the money was there. This was during the Currency Transition—everyone switching from the dollar to amero—and with all those extra zeros in my account, it felt like I was pretty loaded.

But I wasn't gonna spend it—I'd justified the theft by telling myself that I wouldn't spend it, or not much of it anyway—and whatever I *did* spend I'd make back by panhandling, i.e., phase three of my plan: profit. I'd seen this movie once about some bratty street kids panhandling in San Francisco, and it looked like a cool way to pass the time, but as I stepped out of the BART station on Market Street, I found myself facing a grim reality.

I'd arrived in California just after the first wave of the Avis Mortem, and it was pretty awful. There were dead pigeons all over the sidewalk, plus seagulls and some other birds I couldn't identify. Rotting corpses *everywhere*, everyone in surgical masks, eyes watering from the funky death clouds wafting up from the gutters. It was BAD. And where were all the cool kids? They'd mostly split. Now that currency was digital, the only thing you could panhandle for was food. That hadn't occurred to me earlier.

So now what? I couldn't live on the streets. I needed a place to stay. Maybe I'd just dip a *little* into the money.

But here's the thing: turns out you can't rent a closet *shelf* in San Francisco for under $600,000. I couldn't even cover the first and last month's rent. I looked around for the day and was just about ready to give up—and that's when I learned about hive-houses. Most of the street kids had ended up there—to keep them off the streets. There were a couple openings in a hivehouse on Lombard Street, in the basement of a recommissioned McDonald's, and they said I could have a spot, so I moved in that evening.

I'll say this: pretty much everything you hear about hive-houses is true. There were a hundred of us down there, double-stacked like shipping crates, and aside from my sister's occasional

MathOlympics competitions, I'd never witnessed such a dense concentration of assholes. Even with all the disinfectant, the entire place still smelled like french fries, and I was hungry all the time. I mean *ravenous*. We weren't allowed to bring in outside food, but I kept a stash of Zazz® bars (YAY!) in my cube, and that's how I got my first warning.

 ?

# 04.

## FUN®

The thing about hivehouses is this: as long as they get their money, they don't care who you are or what you do. The warnings are a joke. They really are. You'd pretty much have to murder a resident to get evicted, and even then...they might just give you a warning.

As a result of this lax policy, residents were supposed to work out disputes on their own. What this meant IRL was everyone just ignoring everyone else, silent and alone in our individual cubes. Or sometimes not so silent. Take, for example, when Dulah moved into the cube under mine. He moved in about a week after I'd moved in, right around the time I got snitched on for having Zazz® in my cube, and although the warning didn't mean anything, and although I knew Dulah wasn't the snitch, I was still kind of steamed.

The reason I knew it wasn't Dulah was because Dulah was a drug dealer, so why would he snitch on me for food? The reason I was steamed was because of the reggae. When Dulah moved in, I thought it would be cool to live above a drug dealer, but I hadn't counted on the reggae. Supposedly the units were soundproof, but actually they weren't, and Dulah had a pair of Blastbeats™ going on in his, and let me tell you, he played that shit CONSTANTLY.

After a while I couldn't take it anymore. So one night, it was around one o'clock in the morning, I climbed down to his cube to see if we could work out a deal. Dulah's portal was open, and I found him lying on his pad, staring at the ceiling. His eyes were open wide and he was waving his hands around all loopy and funny like some kind of magician or possibly the victim of a seizure.

"Hey, are you all right? Dulah?" I gave him a little shake. "Dulah!"

He touched something in the air and sat up blinking like he was coming out of a trance.

"WHAT UP, NEIGHBOR!" he shouted over the reggae. "WHEN DID YOU GET HERE?"

We went through that complicated handshake ritual that drug dealers have, and then I told him I'd just dropped by to see—

"SPEAK UP, MAN!"

"—JUST DROPPED BY TO SEE WHAT'S UP BECAUSE IT'S PRETTY LATE AND PROBABLY EVERYONE WITHIN THE BLAST RADIUS IS HAVING A HARD TIME SLEEPING ON ACCOUNT OF THE REGGAE, WHICH, DUDE, YOU HAVE TO ADMIT IS—"

And then of course the reggae stopped and the only sound was my voice shouting out those last few words.

Dulah turned to me. His eyes were all funny. "Say that again? What did you have to admit? I couldn't hear you over the music, man."

"Are you OK? What are you on?"

"FUN®."

"What?"

"I'm having FUN®, man."

"Fun doing what?"

Dulah just looked at me. "The chip in my head. The *lenses*, man. Fully Ubiquitous Neuralnet. That's how you say it: having FUN®."

It wasn't the first time I'd heard of FUN®, but it was the first time I really paid any attention. Dulah gave me the rundown. It had started in Korea and spread from there, and now it was coming to America, but the home version was still in beta, and they needed testers to report bugs.

"Get on while you can, neighbor. My whole world has changed. Like right now? I'm running the *frogskin*, man."

"Frogskin?"

"It makes everyone look like a *frog*. You look like a *frog*, man."

"Oh."

"Ribbit ribbit, *man*. And the best part is, I'm earning FUN®. And FUN® is *money*."

"Actual money?"

"Enough to pay my rent. More than enough."

"How?"

"Bug reports, bonuses, gold mining—but the most FUN® is with YAY!s."

"What's a yay?"

Something flickered across his big, dark pupils. "Repeat after me: *Yay for FUN®!*"

"What?"

"Say it," said Dulah. "Say, *Yay for FUN®!*"

So I said it. "Yay for fun."

And Dulah was all, "BAM! I just earned plus 10 for getting you to say that! If I talk about it, I get even more. This shit is for *real*, yo. Once you're having FUN®, you won't ever want to stop. *Everyday reality is a drag*™, man."

And although he was earning FUN® for saying the official tagline, you could tell that he actually kind of meant it, too.

So the next afternoon I went downtown to see about starting to have some FUN®.

The lensing station was located in an office on Pine Street, sort of like an optometrist's but without the glasses. The lady handed me a pad, and I clicked through the User Agreement.

YES I AGREE

YES I AGREE

YES I AGREE

She took the pad and sent me to a little room in the back. I sat in the recliner. The machine lowered. A voice said:

CONCENTRATE ON THE DOT.

PREPARE FOR CHIP AND LENSING.

The dot moved around in a jittery circle. I felt a prick in the base of my skull. Then everything went pixelated.

And as I stumbled out of the chair and into the light, the world had changed. It was bigger now, brighter, the entire landscape webbed in a shiny digital overlay, bonuses and interfaces just waiting to be touched. I stood at the doorway with the sensory information blowing over me like sand on a windy day at the beach, and a blinking robot face took shape—two eyes, no mouth. When it spoke, a readout appeared at the bottom of my vision:

> hello!
  i am Homie™!
  i will be your guide!
  i will be your very
  best friend!
      r u
      ready
      to have
      some
      FUN®?
      :)

yay! ? boo!

# 05.

## THE SHIT

OK, now I would like to say YAY! for the Shit. And by "the Shit," I mean "anything that is superior in a pleasing way." Like for example fine wines, making out, or Psyke2® IntraCranial graphics chips. FUN® was the Shit. Especially at the beginning. I mean, people are always talking about some new shit, and sometimes it's decent shit, and occasionally it's good shit, but most of the time it's just . . . shit.

Not this time.

*This* time the Shit was for real. You could see it and hear it and touch it—you could hold the Shit in your hands. You couldn't smell it or taste it, but that was fine because it was FUN® and it was everywhere. You were swimming in it. And the other cool part was that not everyone had it yet, so it was like being part of this special club. Of the Shit.

Like, I'd be wandering around the Mission and I'd see a couple exclamation points off in the distance—exclamation points that only I could see—+1 user! +1 user!—and then I'd catch sight of the people under the points, and it'd be a couple cool kids just like me, and as we passed each other we'd YAY! out in our minds like superpsychic adventurers on the hunt for bonus fun.

So that part was cool, and it was fun, and it was FUN®. (Well, duh. It was the Shit.)

But there were some minor issues, though. Bugs and glitches or whatever. Take for example Homie™. It's evolved over time, but back then it was just this pixelated, barely 3D robot face. Bluish on top, orangish on bottom, no mouth, no nose. Two dark, blinking circles for eyes. Pretty much the first thing my Homie™ did was catch a communication virus, the infamous allyourbase_ex, and after that you never knew when the voice recognition was gonna glitch out, or maybe it'd start talking in half-Japanese. Both of which happened when I was trying to final confirm my username.

What I wanted was *the last cowboy*, but when I told Homie™, it blinked and said,

> ok!
>
> i cannot understand u now!
>
> please to speak louder!

"Confirm username: *the last cowboy*."

> ok!
>
> what was that?
>
> u r desire of original name?
>
> is this can be for a person?

"Yes, an original name. For a person. Me. I desire to final confirm my username: *the last cowboy*!"

Homie™ flickered.

> "original boy"?

"No!"

```
    >   i'm sorry!
        that is a name already taken!
        would u like "original boy_1"?
"THE LAST COWBOY!"
    >   i'm sorry!
        that is a name already taken!
        would u like "original boy_2"?
"Start over!"
    >   awesome!
        original boy_2 confirmed!
        :)
```

When I contacted an Admin he told me it was like 800 to unconfirm it, which was total crap, and in the end I was like, *Forget it. I'm not paying.* Anyway, it could have been worse. I could've been original boy_3 or 4 or whatever. Sometimes I still feel a little pang of envy toward original boy_1 and, of course, the *original* original boy. Really, though, *the last cowboy* was what I wanted. Personally, I think that would have been the Shit.

 ?

# 06.

# TICKLE, TICKLE, BOOM!

So there I was, living in SF, having FUN®, free as a bee on the sea. Yeah, the hivehouse was weird, and yeah, I was scamming my family, and yeah, any insect flying over an ocean is bound to get fatigued and crash, but for the moment it was awesome. I'm kind of amazed I got away with it so long, but the truth is this: when people want to believe something, you don't have to work that hard to convince them. Every week or so I called Evie and Dad to give an update on my life in Sacramento. School was fine. California was fine. I was fine. And they bought it! I think they were just happy to have me out of their hair.

As it turned out, I was one of the last people to have FUN® for "free." It was like a week later that they got FDA approval, and people started paying for beta. In retrospect, I should have read the User Agreement, because it was a way crappier deal to get on for "free" than to pay for a contract.

One problem was, they kept changing the rules. Like the YAY!s. At first they were optional, but then they became mandatory, and then you couldn't just YAY! a hot product in the YAY!log to collect points—you were supposed to talk about it, too. It was a lot of work. I started to get a little behind. OK, a lot behind. Because the truth is I hardly even touched the YAY!s.

Here's the other problem: FUN® is *fun*, but it's also got some *really* addicting distractions. Like take, for example, the game *Tickle, Tickle, Boom!* (YAY!). Say what you will about the console versions, the FUN® adaptation is *insane*. You get to the point where all you want to do is play until your eyes fall out. And if you get serious about it, you'll of course want to skip the grind—but you can't skip the grind for free. Or say you want to respawn on a friendly face? That'll cost you, too.

Not gonna lie—I got hooked. Pretty soon I was spending all my time on *Tickle, Tickle, Boom!*, and even though I was doing a decent job earning (so I thought), there was bound to come a day when the roof caved in.

It was a Tuesday, I remember, right after I'd defeated the Boss 4: The Pandacorn on *Tickle, Tickle, Boom!*, maybe three months into my life in San Francisco.

I woke up like any normal day—took a leak, munched some Zazz—but when I went to log in to *Tickle, Tickle, Boom!*, Homie™ popped up and was all,

> access denied!
> user = FAIL!

And I was like, WUT?

And Homie™ was like,

> u r a FAIL!
> :(

So I told it to bring up my account info, and that's when I saw the problem. My balance was at –10,000. How did that happen? The truth is, I knew exactly how it happened. You don't spend a month on your butt playing *Tickle, Tickle, Boom!* and not fall a little behind. But FAIL? I thought that was reserved for, like, egregious trolling or whatever.

I asked Homie™ again if I was truly in FAIL, and it was like,

> i'm so sorry!
> u are truly a FAIL!
> :(

So I took a deep breath and asked Homie™ what I had to do, and it said I had two choices: file a Petition for Return to Normal or an Application for Termination. In order to do either, first I had to earn back all my FUN®, plus catch up on my YAY!logs—100 in all, and they all had to be user approved, meaning I had to get more YAY!s than BOO!s. Plus complete all the regular YAY!s. In the meantime, I was in FAIL:

No mindtalk™.

No timestop™.

No brainzip™.

No unauthorized games.

Basically no real FUN® until I earned back the FUN® I owed. As I sat there reading the terms of my fate, it occurred to me that my rent to the hivehouse was due in a week.

So now what?

How would I have some FUN®?

Homie™ blinked.

> that's easy original boy_2!
> u can go to a party™!

# 07.

## PARTY™ TIME

YAY! for Parties™. In the beginning, they were kind of all right—everyone getting together IRL to exchange YAY!s. But they kept changing the rules and adding more time, and pretty soon no one went unless they had to. Listen: if everyone who is at the party is only there because they have to be, then where you are is not a party—even if there are balloons. Which there were not. Instead, it was 80 people crammed into a dimly lit meeting room in the basement of a building on Pine Street, with a single ironic disco ball dangling from the ceiling.

They'd handed out name tags at the door, like actual name tags—more irony, I guess. The other person in my party pair was this hipster girl named Sasha—username sasha.c8kes—and she was having a lot of FUN® and not paying much attention to IRL. What she did was she accidentally grabbed my name tag and slapped it on her shapely chest without even looking—and now she was original boy_2. So I took hers: sasha.c8kes.

Her mood was WHATEVER, so I changed mine to FLIRT? just to

see what she'd do. She didn't do anything. So I told her a joke, the one about what's long and brown and sticky, the answer to which is: *a stick*. But either she didn't like it or she didn't get it. Not that there's all that much to get.

The reason we were there was to review the latest Animal of Wonder & Light®, the Buffaloon™. I'll say this much: they were getting better with the haptic response. You could almost feel the bristly hairs. But as for personality, I don't know...the thing just stood there flapping its wings...and every once in a while it would whistle. Also: you could give it virtual "hay" and, you know, watch it eat.

> `somewhat docile`

is how I summed it in my review,

> `maybe change head to a lion or a`
> `snake?`

The Party™ planners could see that the Buffaloon™ was kind of a bust, so they announced a double bonus for revised summaries, and just as I was getting started on it, Homie™ popped up.

> `!`
> `time out original boy_2!`
> `u have 1 call(s)`
> `it's from evelyn o'faolain!`

"Send it to voice mail."

> `ok!`
> `here is your 1 call(s)!`

"Aaron? Are you there?"

"Hey, Evie. I'm in the middle of something, so—"

"We need to talk."

"OK, but—"

*"Right now."*

So I filed for a bathroom break and stepped outside. I was certain she'd found me out. My sister is a newspaper reporter and she's got a nose for scandal. Nothing can stay buried for long. It was like, *Oh, shit! Here it comes!* I could feel the sweat beading on my forehead. I was starting to twitch a little.

"Hey, Evie. So what's up?"

"It's Grandpa Henry," she said.

"What about him?"

"He shot himself."

"*Shot* himself? Is he OK?"

"No, he's dead."

"Dead?"

"I'm so sorry, Aaron."

And for a moment there I was just like, WHA—? with that last *T* hanging silently in the air. I hadn't thought about Grandpa Henry in forever. And now he'd killed himself? Old people aren't supposed to *kill* themselves. They're already at the end. It's like dropping out of a marathon at mile 25.

OK, this might sound awful, but I was kind of relieved. Not that Grandpa was dead but that my sister hadn't discovered my lies. I asked Evie what happened, and she gave me the story:

Dad hadn't heard from Grandpa in a while. This wasn't unusual. They didn't really talk. Then there was a snowstorm, and it dumped six feet on Antello and shut everything down for a couple days. So finally Dad called to see if Grandpa was OK out at his place, but no one answered. They found him in the basement on the dirt floor. He'd been there a couple weeks at least.

It was a lot to process. I didn't know what to think. I started walking down the street, weaving through the crowd, everything a little blurry.

"The funeral's next weekend," she said. "You need to come home."

"Home? Who says?"

"Me. You have to."

"No, I don't."

"YES, YOU DO. Talk to your teachers and get all your homework. Take a train. Dad's going to send you money for a ticket, OK?"

"Evie—"

"Aaron. It's your *grandfather*. And there are some things we have to discuss. You're coming home. Got it?"

>   end of conversation
    connection has terminated!

I needed to think, so I just wandered the streets for a while, heading generally downhill as a person will, and eventually I ended up at the piers, and stood there listening to the waves washing against the pilings. A cloud of flies swarmed a seagull carcass. What are you supposed to do when someone dies? It's so weird. One day they're here, and the next they're not, and most of the time you don't even get to say good-bye.

When I got back to the Party™, sasha.c8kes was gone and I'd missed the double bonus. This guy, Dan_Bomb, had taken her place at the table. He was a little guy with big hair, and he was a very serious partier—by which I mean he took the party very seriously—and when I asked him about Sasha, he gave my name tag a funny look and ticked off something on his score pad.

We spent the next hour discussing the tactility and resolution of the Buffaloon™—or at least Dan_Bomb did. But I had other things on my mind. In our coevaluation Dan gave me a 10 out of 10—which he didn't have to do, of course, but actually kind of did, because if he didn't give *me* a 10, I wouldn't give *him* a 10, and then we'd *both* be screwed, quid pro quo–style. Dan wasn't happy about it, though, and in the comment section he wrote:

> unenthusiastic work ethic,
> incorrect name tag, distracted to
> say the least . . . i hope i never
> have to party™ with original boy_2
> again.

# 08.

# A BOY AND HIS ROBOT

I took a train home for the funeral. Sodas were $500 each, and the tiniest packet of Zazz was going for $750. I was still getting used to the new currency—the ever-fluctuating value of the mighty amero—but I didn't need a conversion table to tell me when I was getting screwed. I had two seats to myself until Reno, and then this old dude got on. His name was Cody or maybe Cory, and he was a businessman of some kind, but which kind I forget. He was also a drinker and a talker, and once he got going there was no stopping him. I stared out the window at the smoke factories passing by and thought about my grandpa.

I didn't really know him much, but I will never forget this: he was the first person who ever told me I was smart. OK, maybe he wasn't the *first* person, but he was the first one I *believed*. This was maybe an hour after he told me I was the *stupidest* person to ever walk the earth, but even so . . .

The reason my grandpa called me smart was because I helped him solve this puzzle he was working on. He was always working on these puzzle books, and most of them were way over my head, but this one he happened to be doing... for whatever reason the answer was just instantly obvious to me. I took the pencil and filled in the blanks. Grandpa looked at the puzzle and cocked his head and was like, "Not bad, kid. You're smart."

After he told me that, I got it in my head that I *was* smart, and this was both good and bad. *Good* because after that, other than my anger issues, school was a breeze. School really is easy if you believe you're smarter than it. *Bad* because I also ended up thinking I was a secret genius all the time, even when making—as I have thus far chronicled—some very what might be called *questionable* decisions.

The reason my grandfather called me the stupidest person ever to walk the earth was because I left a shotgun out in the rain. He didn't actually *call* me the stupidest person, but the way he said what he said, you could tell that's exactly what he meant. And I felt it. Though, it's funny that I would believe anything my grandpa said—he was pretty crazy.

I really only have one summer to judge off of—that was the only time I ever spent any real time with him. It was the summer I was 10, the summer after the winter Mom left, which was also the winter I tried to kill myself, and the winter Dad started drinking again. I mean seriously drinking. By summer he needed some time to sort himself out. The plan was for me and Evie to stay with Grandpa, but at the last second I was betrayed. Evie had this friend, Sam Latham, whose family had invited her on a Mormon vacation to Moab.

Well, no one ever said no to Evie. So then it was just me and Grandpa.

He was a big, mean-looking man with a hawk nose, leather skin, and a cigarette forever in his hand. Seriously. You could have walked in on him in the middle of the night and I bet he'd be lying there with a cigarette, puffing away in his sleep. He smoked this weird store brand, Valiant 100s.

I didn't know much about him. Apparently he'd worked thirty years as a slot machine repairman, hating every minute of it, and when it all went digital he got laid off. But he never really talked about any of that. When he talked—if he talked—it was mainly about government conspiracies and other things I didn't care about.

Other than that, he mainly just did his puzzle books. Like *all* the time. He tried to get me interested, but I couldn't get into them. They were either over my head or just plain boring. I mostly stayed in the spare bedroom and played video games. He gave it a try once—I let him be Player 2 on *A Boy & His Robot*. (YAY! Best. Console. Game. Ever.) But Gramps sucked. Every time it was his turn he'd take about two steps and run into a cactus or get eaten by a snatchplant or fall off a cliff—until finally I couldn't take it anymore.

I grabbed his controller and speedran the first level for him, but of course I couldn't stop there, and pretty soon I was going all the way to Level 8, LavaLand, where even the most expert gamer is bound to die once or twice in a fire geyser. When at long last I finally succumbed to the flames, Grandpa only had this to say: "Know what that is? Nothing but a fancy slot machine."

He gave me a book to read, *True Tales of Buried Treasure* by Edward Rowe Snow. There was this weird chubby kid on the cover, and it looked unspeakably lame. I gathered he'd read it when he was a kid or something.

And seriously: What tales, true or not—written in a *book*—could compete with a multilevel interdimensional quest to collect the lost fragments of Robotopia, destroy the evil Fester Cloud, and free all the Sparkles of Joy?

 ?

# 09.

# THE BIRD

But so then one day my grandpa showed up at the bedroom door with something else. Not a book. Not some crosswords. A gun. An actual, real-life gun.

"Come on. Let's go for a walk."

I pressed pause and followed him outside. His place was all by itself five miles out of town—a 90-acre rectangle of sagebrush and cheatgrass, with train tracks running along the southern end. It was a pretty desolate spread, all right. There was only one tree to speak of—a wilted, gnarly Russian olive out by the tracks. That's where we ended up.

There were all these birds in the tree, black shadows darting among the branches. For a long time my grandpa didn't say anything. We just stood there under the rustle of birds. I was starting to get antsy. What were we going to do with the gun?

"They want to cut it down, you know."

"The tree? Who does?"

"*Them.*" He blew a cloud of smoke into the air. "Rats. Human rats. The same ones who built the power lines that gave your grandma cancer. The same ones who imported the birds. And *this*," he said, "is a .410 shotgun. The only rule is never point it at a human being or anything else you don't want killed. Got it?"

He lit another cigarette, put the gun to his shoulder, aimed at the tree, and fired.

*BLAM!*

A dark cloud of birds shot up into the sky, wheeled around, circled us a couple times, then settled in the tree again.

"Those are starlings. Intruders smuggled from Europe by human rats. I'll give you a quarter for every one you kill. But see that bird there? That's a blackbird. Do NOT kill any blackbirds."

This was before the Avis Mortem, of course, before people started wondering if we'd have *any* birds left at all—but even back then at age 10 it was like, *Why would I want to kill a bird? What did it ever do to me?* And for twenty-five cents a pop? Math will tell you that's four birds per dollar. Math will tell you in order to make any real money I was going to have a literal blood-bath on my hands. There was this, too: What was the difference between starlings, which were black, and blackbirds, which were also black?

I still wanted to shoot that gun, though.

So when he handed it to me, I put the butt against my shoulder like he showed me, and I aimed above the tree, closed my eyes, and squeezed the trigger.

*BLAM!*

The kick was a lot harder than I expected, like being punched in the shoulder. When I opened my eyes, the birds were circling overhead.

"Missed. You need to hold it tighter to your shoulder."

But this time the birds didn't come back. The cloud drifted

eastward like smoke in the sky, settling finally at the far end of his property.

"Looks like you're going to have to chase them."

My grandpa sent me off after the birds, and looking back on it now I have to question the wisdom of sending a 10-year-old—who had recently attempted suicide—alone into the brush with a loaded shotgun and a pocket full of shells. Talk about trust. But the truth is by that point I wasn't interested in ending my life—or the life of any birds, either. Clouds were gathering for a thunderstorm, and the air had that kind of jumpy feel to it, like anything could happen.

I ended up on the other side of the train tracks, in the hills beyond the property. The road led to this desert junk dump, the centerpiece of which was an ancient, rusted-out car with tail fins and round holes where the headlights used to be. Just a metal shell. Doors spattered with bullet holes. Broken glass everywhere. Like the aftermath of some terrible last stand. Perfect for target practice.

*BLAM!*, reload, *BLAM!*, reload, *BLAM!*—I painted it in wide sprays of birdshot, adding my signature to the rest. But then, as I was aiming at a rust spot on the fender, something caught my eye.

There was this bird. This little bird. Off to the side, perched on top of a sagebrush. Not a starling or a blackbird—something else. Like a sparrow maybe—but yellow. This little yellow bird, chirping its song into the afternoon. YAY! for the little yellow bird. Next thing I knew, I was looking at it down the barrel of the shotgun. I held it in my sights. Tiny yellow body hovering at the end of my barrel.

And then, I couldn't tell you why, I pulled the trigger.

(*BLAM!*)

When I opened my eyes, the bird had disappeared like some kind of magic trick. I walked over to where it had been. And then I saw it. Yellow fluttering in the brush. I'd winged it. I chased after the bird. What was I gonna do if I caught it? How, in the middle of the desert with only a shotgun and a pocket full of shells, do you repair a broken wing? It didn't matter. Every time I got close, the bird flopped just out of reach, throwing itself around like it was on fire.

And then the bird gave up. It just stopped and sat there on the ground. I walked up to it. It didn't move. It just sat there, looking up at me with a single dark eye. It was breathing real fast.

I looked down at the bird.

The bird looked up at me.

And it's hard to explain, but for a moment I was right there with the bird, lost in that dark tunnel between us...and it was just—darkness. Terrifying. The bird was dying. It was headed to the other side, and it knew it, and I knew it, too. I began to feel like if I looked at it any longer, that bird was going to reach out with its eye and pull me into the darkness, through the window of a bird's eye into the world of the dead.

And that's why I ran. That, and it was really starting to rain. Just pouring down from the sky. I turned around and booked it.

Grandpa was waiting for me on the porch.

"You got soaked," he said.

"Yeah."

"How much I owe you?"

"Nothing."

He eyed me, kind of curious, like he was trying to figure me out. "Where's the gun?"

Right. In my terror I'd completely forgotten about it.

That's when he looked at me like I was the stupidest person ever to walk the earth.

"Never leave a shotgun out in the rain," he said.

So back I went.

Already the storm was starting to pass. The sun had dropped below the clouds, and every sagebrush cast a long shadow, and it was beautiful, but all I could think about was that little yellow bird lying out there in the rain. It was nearly dark when I finally located the gun. As for the bird—I didn't see it anywhere. Not in the brush, not on the ground, not anywhere.

That bird was just gone.

 ?

# 10.

## SMÓKZ™

The train pulled into Antello a half hour early—a first for Amtrak in my experience. I was the only one who got off, and the station was empty. Not really a station. More like a bus stop, with a small Plexiglas awning, some warning signs, and a single plastic bench with a good view of the power lines. I sat down, waited for my sister to show, and started to twitch.

One of the things they don't tell you when you start having FUN® is the part about the twitches. What happens is you get so used to waving your hands around selecting bonuses or whatever that after a while your body starts to have these jerky nerve reactions. Like, you'll just be sitting there and suddenly your hand will shoot up out of nowhere and start waving around.

So I purchased a smókz™.

YAY! for smókz™, cancer-free virtual soothing cigarettes, the best solution for the twitches. The only problem is they cost so much FUN®. But at least they give you something to do with your hands. And the exhale is worth it. The virtual smoke turns into a rainbow or a unicorn or an advertisement for new Hydroburst™ Fruit Bites or whatever, so that's cool.

I smoked my smókz™. It was freezing out there. Maybe my hands were just twitching because of the cold. When I exhaled, a cloud of miniature lambs appeared and mixed with the fog of my real breath and sang to me about new Lambsoft® acne concealer— and then Homie™ popped up.

> what up original boy_2?
 u have 8 new message(s)!

*Eight?* We'd passed through a no-signal zone outside Lovelock, and I'd missed them, all eight—one from my dad and the other seven from Evie.

Here's how they went:

In the first message Evie said she was sick. She wasn't sure what it was, but she felt like crap and she was afraid it might be contagious. In the second message she gave me the symptoms, which included nausea, congestion, fever, fatigue, and itchiness. In her third message she restated the main points of the first two messages, coughing now and again for effect, suggesting that instead of risking deadly infection at her place, maybe I should crash with Dad. In her fourth message she said she'd thought about it some more and she was sure that's what I should do. In her fifth and sixth messages she told me to call her as soon as I got her message(s).

In her seventh message she just coughed and hung up.

Typical. First of all, my sister was and is a flaming hypochondriac. Autoimmune disorders, vitamin deficiencies, tropical diseases—you name it, she's had it. And always at the most opportune times. Like how she got shingles from the German foreign exchange student during fitness week. Or the time she came down with the flu right in the middle of summer, just before swim lessons started.

Second of all, she was always trying to play peacemaker between Dad and me. Maybe she'd set me up—because in *his* message, Dad told me Evie was sick and offered me a place to stay.

So I sent a message to Evie:

> original boy_2: hey evie no prob
> i'm on my way to dads

And then I sent the same thing to my dad, only with the names switched around.

What I thought I'd do was crash with my friend Oso instead. But when I called him, no one answered. Straight to voice mail. So I left a message. And then I started walking.

# 11.

## KING COWBOY

Maybe I'd get a room. Why not treat myself? I deserved it, right? But the train depot was conveniently located at the end of town, pretty much as far from any hotel as possible while still being within city limits. Homie™ suggested I head for the Western Inn by Walmart, but I checked it out on SleepHunt® and the price was ridiculous, so I headed downtown. Which is how I ended up at the King Cowboy hotel and casino (YAY!).

Its glory days were long over, but the King Cowboy still had that crazy casino feel—a jangly labyrinth of lights, mirrors, and games. A thousand chances to win or lose. Grandpa told me that whenever a machine paid out too often or too much, it was his job to "fix" it. Tonight the casino was mostly empty, and no one was winning as far as I could see. As I wandered around looking for the reception desk, I had a funny thought: maybe he was still here in spirit, Grandpa, flitting from machine to machine like a bad luck fairy, dropping the odds by factors of 10.

The price for a room was crazy cheap, so that was good, and they didn't check my age, and that was good, too. The lady swiped my eyes, then gave me a key card and a paper map with room 308 circled on it. It was on the top floor, and I swear I was the only one up there. The room was small and smelly and appeared to have been furnished from items stolen from other motels...but the hot water worked, and for $4,999.98 what more could you expect?

 ?

# 12.

## LUCKY PEDRO'S

After the train ride and motel search I was ready to crash. But first I had to YAY! SleepHunt®, and after that I took a shower, and when I was done I realized how hungry I was. When was the last time I'd eaten? I got dressed and went down to the casino again. The coffee shop was closed for renovations, but there was a Mexican-themed restaurant/bar at the other end. (YAY! for Lucky Pedro's.)

The sign said SEAT YOURSELF, so I did. I took a seat on a padded barstool, lit a smókz™, and turned my attention to the wall behind the bar. It was one of those birthday walls, the ones where if it's your birthday they come out with a big sombrero, plop it on your head, and take a picture. Everyone up there was smiling, having the time of their lives in their sombreros—almost everyone anyway. There were a few who you could tell weren't too thrilled about the situation. Glaring at the camera like: *Just take the effin' picture already.*

Anyway, I was checking out the wall, and next thing you know, the bartender's all in my face.

"Hey, pal, I'm gonna need to see some ID."

"OK. Hold on." I brought up my burner account, the one that says I'm 22.

But the guy wasn't having it.

"Actual, legit, government-issued photo ID. None of this virtual BS. If I don't see an ID, you don't drink. Got it?"

"What kind of place can't check a virtual ID?"

"*This* kind of place, buddy. And if you aren't twenty-one, you can't sit at the bar."

"But I *am* twenty-one. Twenty-*two*, actually."

I gave him the rundown. I was Arnold Hamilton from Uniontown, PA. Age: 22. Birthday: August 1. Height 6'2". Eyes: brown. Hair: brown. Willing to donate organs in case of death.

The dude wasn't having it.

"You can sit at a table and drink a soda pop, *Arnold*."

So that's what I did—but not after putting in an order for some nachos.

"And easy on the onions," I said, just to have the last word.

I sat down at a table just as this girl walked in—or more like a woman. Like in her twenties, maybe.

"Blake," she said. "How long is the coffee shop closed for?"

The bartender considered her for a long moment. "How should I know?" he said at last.

"Because you work here."

"I work . . . *here*," he said. "Lucky Pedro's. I do not work at the coffee shop."

The woman adjusted the bag on her shoulder. She was wearing a long gray skirt and this puffy gray sweater with red stitching.

"Do you or do you not serve coffee?" she said at last.

"Yeah, we serve coffee."

"I will have one coffee, then. Thank you."

The woman sat at a table in the far corner to read a book. The bartender poured a cup of coffee and set it on the bar. He wasn't gonna bring it to her. But the woman wasn't gonna look up from her book, either. It was a Mexican standoff. Meanwhile, the coffee was just sitting there getting cold. And a little voice in my head was like, *Dude, you should bring her that coffee.* And another voice was like,

> what up original boy_2?

u r a FAIL!

u seem maybe agitated?

"Homie™," I whispered, "what's her username?"

Homie™ blinked.

> error!

unidentified!

:(

"Well, bring up her profile, then."

> error!

unidentified!

I thought about bringing her the coffee again, but instead I watched her read for a while. It was actually pretty mesmerizing. I've never thought of reading as being a particularly *erotic* activity, but this was something different. Take, for example, her hair: this one lock kept falling over her eyes, and then a hand would come up and tuck it back behind her ear, and slowly, slowly, slowly, it'd come loose again, and I'd hold my breath waiting for it to fall. And then the hand again. Meanwhile, her eyes didn't lift from the page. Not once.

And her coffee was just sitting there getting cold.

So finally I worked up the *cojones*. I brought the coffee over and set it on the table.

"Here's your coffee."

The woman glanced up. Her face was kind of pink and she had these really blue eyes. "I'm sorry, what did you say?"

"Your coffee was getting cold."

"Oh, right—I didn't really want that."

"No?"

"I just wanted to give Blake a task for being a dick. If I drink coffee, I'll be up all night."

"Oh."

"Do you want it? You can have it if you want."

"No, thanks."

"Go on, take it. It'll piss Blake off."

So I took the coffee. But I didn't want the coffee, I wanted to talk to the woman.

"Whatcha reading?" I asked.

She didn't look up, just kind of shifted in her chair and raised the cover so I could see the title: *Irish Folktales Throughout the Ages.*

"Cool," I said. "What's it about?"

"Irish folktales throughout the ages."

"Ha. I mean, like, what are the tales *themselves* about?"

The woman shrugged. "You know ... it's the same story every time. A young man is in love. He goes on a quest. He wanders around the countryside solving impossible riddles—*find me a song that sings itself, an egg that can't be cracked*—that kind of thing.

He solves the riddles and returns home to find his love has left, and then he turns into a bird."

"He turns into a bird?"

"That's right."

"And then what?"

"That's it," she said. "He turns into a bird and flies away, the end."

"Oh."

The woman looked up, like she was waiting for me to get something. Man, her eyes were blue. Then I got it:

*Flies away.*

Oh, OK. Right.

"Well, I should probably get back to my dinner," I said, and flew away back to my table.

Blake came back.

"Guess what, Arnold? We're out of tacos."

"I didn't order tacos. I ordered nachos."

"Yeah," he said. "We're out of those, too, *Arnold.*"

Awesome. I sipped my soda. It was really turning into a lovely evening.

But then something happened.

Blake went away again, and the woman called over to me.

"Hey," she said. "Sorry about that. He's just being a dick because of me. We have, you know, kind of a history."

"Actually, he was being a dick before you got here."

"Oh, good, then. My conscience is cleared. Thanks—what was your name again? Arnold?"

So I had no choice but to introduce myself as my fake self, Arnold Hamilton, and then I asked her if she was from around here. No, she was from Idaho. She asked me if I was from around here, and I told her no, I was from Uniontown, Pennsylvania. Just in town for my grandfather's funeral.

"Oh," she said. "I'm sorry to hear about that."

She was looking at me now. It was the first time we'd really made eye contact, and I know this is going to sound cheesy or whatever, but OK: first of all, she had these really blue eyes. Like *deep* blue. And there was something strange about them. They were just—*different* somehow. Different in a good way. And then it hit me: this woman hadn't been lensed!

"Hey, you aren't having FUN®," I said.

"No way."

"*No way?* What's that supposed to mean?"

"It *means*," she said, "that everyone I know who's having FUN® acts like a complete *zombie*, and I don't want to be a complete zombie, and therefore I don't want to be having FUN®."

"Hey, I'm having FUN®. Am I a complete zombie?"

"Well, I don't know. When I walked in you were mumbling and staring off into space, waving your hands around in front of yourself—like a zombie."

"I was having FUN®."

"Right," she said. "Having FUN®. Not *actual* fun. Zombie fun."

"Not zombie fun. FUN® fun. It really is fun, too. Most of the time. When you're not a FAIL, that is."

The woman, gave me a look like *?,* because she didn't know what a FAIL was. So I started explaining to her about all the rules and consequences and how I was trying to earn my way back, but I could tell I was kind of losing her, so I stopped.

"How about you?" I said. "What do *you* do for actual fun? Read actual books?"

"Yes, as matter of fact—but this book isn't for fun, it's for school."

"Oh, you're a student?"

"No, I'm a teacher."

 ?

# 13.

## GLITCH-OUT

Technically she was a student teacher—at the same elementary school I went to—but the actual teacher got sick and by this point she was basically doing the whole thing herself. She'd moved from Idaho last fall, sight unseen, to fulfill the rural teaching part of her student loan agreement. She'd been debating between Antello and a place in Texas, and in retrospect she should've chosen Texas.

The whole time she talked I was like, *Yay! She's talking to me!* And I tried to keep it going by peppering her with little questions—I asked her what it was like being a first-time teacher and all that, about the tests and whatnot, but I was having a hard time following what she was saying. I was starting to TSD, aka Temporary Sense Death glitch-out, aka a sudden void of sensation leaving a strange silent hole in your brain not unlike the silence of a Vitamix® Wishspertech2™ risk-free blender (YAY!).

Supposedly they've fixed the problem with more recent versions of the chip, but the chip I have is one of the originals, and even with all the updates and patches I still TSD'd from time to time if I was in an agitated state.

It happened to me then. The woman was talking to me, and suddenly I couldn't hear what she was saying. The audio dropped right out. She was a silent movie. I stood there and watched her talk. God, she had a beautiful mouth. I was really getting into it, just loving the way her lip kind of went up all lopsided and beautiful, and then the audio cut back in.

"Which is why I'm reading this," she was saying, "so I can share it at the assembly tomorrow. It's heritage week at school; we're supposed to present the stories of our ancestors. . . . They told me this was a happening little college town. But the truth is there are approximately ten people here between the ages of eighteen and thirty, and so far let's just say it's not been what you would call stellar. . . ."

"Everyone OK here?" Blake was back. Standing right next to us, actually. "Is he bugging you, Katie?"

"Him?" she said. "No."

I couldn't help but smile a little. It was like, *Suck on that, Blake.*

Blake went away, and I smiled at his receding backside, but then my smile went away because the woman, Katie, was putting her book in her bag and standing up.

"I should go," she said. "It's late. Nice to meet you, um—what was it again?"

And I was like, *Damn, why'd I lie the first time?* and told her again I was Arnold, and she gave me a wave and was gone. I sat there for maybe three minutes before I was like, *You fool! Go get her contact info!*

I got lucky. I found her out in the parking lot. She was leaning against a red truck, smoking a cigarette.

"Hi there."

She fanned away the smoke. "Don't lecture me. I'm trying to quit."

"Lecture you?"

"You know, an elementary schoolteacher who smokes..." She took another puff. "I really am trying to quit."

I reached down into my ballsack for some courage and asked her if she wanted to trade contact info.

"Contact info?" she said.

"Like your username or whatever."

She cocked her head and eyed me with her blue, blue eyes. "Remember? I'm not having FUN®."

"Right." I'd totally forgotten. "Well, you should consider having FUN® sometime. It's...fun. We could mindtalk™ or whatever."

"OK," she said.

"OK," I said.

She didn't say anything.

And normally I would've taken the hint and just left her alone. Of course, *normally* I wouldn't even have followed her to the parking lot. I can't even explain it. But something in me was like, *This girl is cool. Don't just let her go.*

"If not a username, how about a phone number? Do you have a phone?"

"Yes, I have a phone."

"You wanna trade numbers?"

"Just in case I'm ever in Pennsylvania?" she said.

"Right. Or, you never know when I might have to come back for another funeral. People die all the time. Or maybe I'll set out on some kind of quest to turn into a bird or whatever."

She gave it some thought. "Do you have a piece of paper?"

"Just tell it to me. I'll input it in my address book."

"No, that's OK." She took out her notebook, scribbled something on a sheet, ripped it out, folded it up into a tiny square, and handed it to me.

"There. Good night, Arnold. Nice to meet you."

"Good night, Katie."

And good night moon, and June, and beautiful tunes, and the bird of romance, aka the loon. Back in my room, I plopped down on the bed and started unfolding the paper. Hell yes, I'd gotten her number! She'd really folded up that paper. Finally I had it all opened and flattened out on the bed, but there wasn't a number. Instead, there was this:

First you must complete three tasks.

You must bring me:

1. A cloud that makes no rain.

2. A needle that needs no thread.

3. A harp that sings without plucking.

—Katie

# 14.

## MORNING WHEEL

I woke the next morning with Homie™ in my face giving me a special message. I'd been selected to have a spin of the Starbucks® Grand Epiphany Morning Mocha Wheel (YAY!) and possibly win some free crap, none of which actually included an actual cup of coffee—not that I even *drink* coffee—and while I was listening to this message I missed another one. I mean an actual one. From my sister:

> > aaron? i know you didn't stay
> > with dad and you didn't stay here,
> > either. are you even in town? you
> > better be! it's almost 10:00 and
> > dad says you're not at the church
> > so WHERE ARE YOU???

Speaking as a person who's had a lot of experience with running late over the years, it's exactly when you need everything to move smoothly that the most shit goes wrong. I scrambled out of bed and tripped over my bag, the zipper of which I discovered was stuck—and burned five minutes working to get it unstuck, and in the process broke it completely—and when I laid out my funeral outfit on the bed, I discovered that despite the white shirt, brown pants, leather belt, maroon tie, and brown jacket, a critical item was missing: Where were my dress shoes?

I'd forgotten to pack them. So I put on my Osmos™IV running shoes—neon green with the bright white laces—and, long story short, although the church was only seven blocks away, by the time I arrived I was already ten minutes late.

I paused for a moment in front of the big wooden doors to catch my breath and steel myself against the frosty glare of the congregation, and then I stepped inside.

But the church was empty. I mean completely empty. No priest, no casket, no congregation, no nothing—just a milky light filtering through the stained glass windows and good old JC, savior of the world, standing at the end of it all, arms raised up in frustration like, *Hey. Where'd everybody go?*

There was a time in my life when I believed in the Father and Son and the Holy Spirit and all that noise, but around age 10, after my mom left, I pretty much stopped going to Mass. Still, in all my life I hadn't had a single experience with the Catholic Church that clocked in at under an hour. So where was everybody? Had I missed the ceremony?

Homie™ popped up.

>   what up original boy_2?
    u r a FAIL!
    how about for once try to spin
    the morning mocha wheel!
    there is still time!

"Go away. Actually, wait. Maybe I should call Evie. Oh, wait. Never mind."

I saw him now. At the back of the church, near the altar. Blue jeans, gray hoodie, baggy jean jacket with a lot of buttons on it. He gave me a wave. "You made it."

"Where is everybody?"

"Funny story. Who were you talking to?"

"What?"

My dad started down the aisle. "Just now, you were talking to yourself."

"Um, well, yeah. I was just talking to myself. Where is everybody?"

"Like I said. Funny story."

I'll say this: a dad is a big thing. When you're little, you think he's a god. He *is* a god. But really he isn't. He's just a dude with a broken dream. In my dad's case, he wanted to be a drummer in a famous rock band. But that didn't happen. I think it *almost* did, but then it didn't. Then Mom left.

From my discussions with psychiatrists and counselors over the years, I've pretty confidently diagnosed my dad as your classic narcissistic Irish Catholic erratic-cycle semifunctioning alcoholic. I'm not saying he was the worst father in the world—certainly a better dad than my mom was a mom—but then again he wasn't the best, either. I mean, he could have been better, though from what I hear *his* dad wasn't exactly father of the year, either.

"Where is everyone?"

Dad scanned the pews like he was seeing it for the first time. "Yeah. Looks like it's just the two of us."

"What about Evie? Where's she?"

"Sick. Caught a bad case of superpox."

Pretty convenient if you ask me—catching a deadly infectious disease just in time to miss our grandpa's funeral. But Dad seemed to be buying it. Evie just has that power over him. Some kind of special father-daughter bond that remains a complete mystery to me.

He rubbed his eyes under his glasses. "You didn't stay at your sister's last night."

"Nah."

"You should've stayed at my place. I wanted to talk about some stuff. What happened? You were busy with other commitments?"

I shrugged. It was all I could think to do. As for my dad, he just kept on looking at me. There's this one look he has, like, *Oh, right, you're the reason I had to not become the next Johnny McDrummerson* or whatever.

"How's school?" he asked at last.

"Fine."

"You like Sacramento?"

"It's OK."

He nodded. "And your mother? How's she?"

I gave it some thought. At some point I was going to have to come clean and tell him what happened, so why not now? For a moment there, I almost told him the truth. Almost.

"Mom? She's fine. She's, um, you know—fine."

His gaze wandered down to my neon-green Osmos™IVs. "Interesting choice of footwear."

"Where *is* everyone?"

"Funny story. Miscommunication in scheduling. The service was held at nine instead of ten."

"Really? It's over?"

"Not quite," he said. "If we hurry, we can still make it in time to bury the old goat."

 ?

# 15.

# AMAZING GRACE

Now when my dad said, *If we hurry*, what I thought he meant was, *If we hurry...and get in my nice warm car and head on down the road in the accustomed style*. But he didn't mean that. He meant *if we hurry...and jog ten blocks to the cemetery...*

At first I didn't want to do that because I had my bag with me, and although it wasn't very heavy, it was definitely cumbersome. What with the broken zipper, you had to squeeze it to keep everything from falling out, and the whole situation was pretty awkward. I could tell Dad thought it was amusing, but then after a couple blocks the joke was on him, because who was the one wearing running shoes? Then the joke was back on me again because I was the one who tripped on a curb and spilled all my crap on the ground.

Speaking of jokes, we arrived at the cemetery to find three people—a priest, a lawyer, and a cowboy—standing around an unmarked hole in the snow, like the setup of one of those jokes old people tell. It was cold out there, and it looked like they'd been waiting for a while, and that they weren't exactly happy about it.

As we got closer, however, I saw I'd been wrong—for one thing, the hole in the snow wasn't a hole. It was a mound. Of dirt. Second, the lawyer wasn't a lawyer. He was a rep from the funeral home. His lapel pin said NORTHERN NEVADA MEMORIALS, CATERING & FLORAL. The cowboy wasn't a cowboy, either. She was a cowgirl. Or more like a cowoldlady: this tiny little woman in a cowboy hat. The priest was a priest, though, and he was the one who spoke first, thanking us for joining them on this solemn day, etc. When he spoke his mouth barely moved. You could tell he was pissed.

"What's going on?" said Dad. "You already buried him?"

The funeral rep stepped forward. "I'll apologize for that one. We thought you were a no-show."

"A no-show at my father's funeral?"

"It happens more than you'd think."

"What about the rites? Those over, too?"

The priest cleared his throat. "I can do them again."

"Yeah, why not?"

I'm telling you, that guy should've been an auctioneer. I'd never heard a person speak so fast. *Our-father-who-art-in-heaven-hallowed-be-thy-ashes-to-ashes-dust-to-dust-bless-and-console-us-and-gently-wipe-every-tear-from-our-eyes-in-the-name-of-the-father-son-and-holy-etc.-amen.*

But it was freakin' cold out there, and he couldn't go fast enough, and all I could think about was how could some all-powerful god arrange for a day like this? *Why* would he? What's the point? Here's some dude, cold and pissed, talking on behalf of this *other* dude who he probably didn't even know, and definitely doesn't give a shit about, while all these other dudes (+1 old cow-lady) who barely give any more of a shit freeze their butts off. And that's it? That's how you say good-bye to a life? Awesome work,

God. Thanks for mosquitoes, too, by the way. And hey, when are you gonna get around to starving more homeless African kids?

A moment of silence, no tears that I could see, and then the old lady stepped forward. She pushed back her hat, cleared her throat, closed her eyes, and began to sing. It was "Amazing Grace." It's a slow song, and her interpretation was even slower than usual. I mean *crazy* slow. And her voice? How can I describe it? She hit the notes OK, but it was like her throat was full of gravel, and listening to her I realized that this was about the last place I wanted to be, and so I tried to bring up *Tickle, Tickle, Boom!* (YAY!) but Homie™ popped up and was all,

>    access denied!

    u r a FAIL!

Right. I'd almost forgot. So I stood there and listened to the old lady sing. She kept stopping to cough and clear her throat, and it was like, *hurry up, hurry up*—and yet by the end of the song, she kind of had me. I hadn't known him very well, not really, but after all he *was* my grandpa, and now here he was under my feet. It's weird what music can do to you. YAY! for "Amazing Grace." It's a pretty powerful song. One moment I was all, *This sucks I'm cold hurry up let's get it over with*, and then suddenly it was like: *Holy shit, we are burying one of our own.*

After it was over, we walked back to the cemetery gates, and the priest and the funeral rep shook everyone's hand and got into the same car, and it was just me, my dad, and the little old lady. Dad was ready to go, but I told him I'd catch up. I didn't feel like leaving yet, and I didn't feel like walking with him for ten blocks, because then we'd have to talk, and I didn't feel like talking.

He gave me another one of his looks. "How do I know if you're telling the truth?"

"Where else am I gonna go?"

"Just come over, OK? I've got something I need to show you."

"What is it?"

"You come over, you'll see it."

"Just give me a while."

"Fine," he said. "Don't take all night."

So then it was just me and the little old cowboy lady. Turned out she was my grandpa's neighbor. I'd never met her before. Like I mentioned, she was short. Probably no more than 4 feet 9 even with the hat, but otherwise fairly normally proportioned—not like a gnome or anything—except that her skin was kind of gnomelike, all wrinkly like an old glove left out in the sun.

"Do you believe in Jesus?" she said.

The question caught me by surprise. I didn't want to offend her or anything, so I said, "Yeah, sure."

"Your grandfather didn't." She had a voice like a frog, like you might hear a frog singing across the swamp, all low and gravelly.

"He didn't?"

"No. He was a smart man, but he didn't believe in Jesus. I told him he better get himself straight before he died. We used to joke about which of us was going to go first.... I used to tell him, 'Henry, when I die just dump me in the river. Just roll me into the water. That's all I ask. No service, no burial. Let the Lord take me as I am.'" The woman coughed. "Know what he would say? 'Well, what if it's winter, Anne?'"

"OK..."

"If it's winter, the river's frozen. I hadn't thought about that." The woman coughed again. "I told him, hoist me up into a tree and let the vultures have me, then. Know what he said? 'There aren't any vultures in winter, Anne.' He was a smart man, your grandfather. But he didn't believe in Jesus." The woman paused to hawk a speckled loogie into the snow. "Tell me your name again?"

"Aaron."

"I'm Anne," she said. "Anne Chicarelli. And are you Catholic, Adam?"

"Not really."

She nodded. "It's a dead end if you ask me. A husk with no kernel. Tell me, Adam. Have you accepted Jesus Christ into your heart as your Lord and savior?"

"It's Aaron."

"Yes, and have you asked him to come to you and light you on fire so that you, too, may come stumbling out of that cave on the third day, clapping the dust from your hands?"

I try to respect my elders, because they've been through a lot and supposedly know all about life—but mainly because I don't want to deal with their shit. Better to just mumble something and let them go on with whatever it is they're doing, but this was getting ludicrous.

"Can I pray for you, Adam?"

"Pray for me? I guess..."

What I didn't understand was that she meant *pray right now*. She took my hands in hers and bowed her head. Tiny bones squeezing me tight.

"Lord, we thank you for this day and all your blessings. Adam, here, is still young, oh Lord, and thinks he may live forever, but the truth is death awaits us all, and only those who have accepted your son as their savior will live again to see your eternal kingdom. The rest, have mercy on their poor, tormented souls. In Jesus's name we pray. Amen."

Damn, lady. So what did that mean for my grandfather? Endless fire? It was weird that someone who could sing such a beautiful song could also at the same time be so full of it. Join our team! And if you don't join our team, burn forever in hell! Some team. If that's how the game works, I don't want to play.

"Um, thanks," I said.

"No problem. Nice to meet you, Adam."

The woman, Anne, shook my hand one more time, stepped up into a big white truck, gave a wave, and drove away.

So then it was just me out there. Still, I wasn't ready to leave yet. How can I explain it? It was freezing, but I just didn't feel like leaving. The funeral had left me in a strange mood. I wandered back into the cemetery and stood under the oak tree not far from my grandpa's grave. The leaves were gone and it loomed overhead, a giant schematic of a circulatory system, gnarled branches veining a pale sky. A storm was moving in. The first flakes were beginning to fall.

Jesus, it was a miserable day.

 ?

# 16.

# THE DOG

By the time I got to my dad's it had started to snow. I mean *really* snow: gathering heavy on the bushes and the roof and the bare branches of the elm tree he was always threatening to cut down. I was heading in to warm up, but Dad stopped me in the doorway.

"Gimme one of your shoes."

"What?"

"Gimme a shoe."

"Why?"

"Because. Take it off." He was sipping something from an old army canteen, one of those metal ones with the chain on the lid. He aimed the lid at my left shoe. "Gimme that one there."

"No."

"Yes. Just do it." His breath smelled like gin.

Fine. I gave him the shoe, my green Osmos™IV.

"Bones!" he called.

A big gray dog stepped out from behind the recliner. Some kind of Weimaraner maybe. You know the phrase *at death's door*? That's what this one looked like, its front paw wrapped up in bandages, limping over to my dad like a dog in one of those Humane Society ads—one of the real bedraggled ones whose sad orphan hearts have never felt love and whose lips have never once tasted Purina® Ultra all-protein high energy revitalizing dog food (YAY!).

"Hey! Don't give him my shoe!"

"It's a *her.*"

Dad gave the dog my shoe.

She took it in her mouth and limped back behind the recliner.

"Why'd you do that? I don't want her eating my shoe!"

"She's not! Look!"

I found the dog curled up in the corner with my shoe. She wasn't eating it, but she *was* licking it, very delicately, like a tender ice-cream cone. Next to my shoe, sort of nestled up against her belly, were two flip-flops and a pair of my dad's boots.

"What's she doing? Since when do you have a dog?"

"She's playing mom," said Dad. "And she isn't mine. I'm just the one who found her. She was hanging around your grandpa's place—no collar or tags. That neighbor lady, Anne, she said she hadn't seen the dog before. So it's a mystery. No one knows the dog's real name but the dog. Isn't that right, girl? We've been calling her Bones on account of how skinny she is. But technically speaking she belongs to you."

"What do you mean—technically?"

"You always wanted a dog, didn't you?"

"Yeah, when I was like, ten. And you wouldn't let me get one because of your allergies."

"What allergies?"

"You know—how you're allergic to dogs."

Dad blinked. "I'm not allergic to dogs."

"OK, so you lied to me. What's up with the stupid dog?"

"She's been through a lot, Aaron. I should never have taken her to the vet—and especially not that incompetent shit Doctor Aguilar. Well, he *calls* himself a doctor. See, when I found her she was in bad shape. Paw all torn up. Skinny as a rail. Got her here and noticed she was lactating, so I went back to look for the puppies, but I couldn't find any. I took her to the vet to get her paw checked out, and I told the guy he may as well fix her, too, because I didn't want any more puppies . . . *so the doctor fixed her.*"

"I don't get it."

"She was *pregnant*, Aaron. That sonofabitch performed a puppy abortion—and the *only* reason I even know is because he tried to charge me extra for it! I told him, '*When I said "fix her" I obviously meant tie off her tubes—NOT kill her puppies.*' Your sister was profoundly upset. She thinks the dog has PTSD. She went to the vet's and read him the riot act. . . . The point is, like I said, the dog—she's yours."

"Yeah—no. I don't want an old dog."

"Well, hold on. You haven't seen the thing yet."

"What thing?"

"The thing I wanted to show you." He tipped back the canteen and swallowed the rest. "You thirsty? I've got some Sparkl*Juice™."

# 17.

## SPARKL*JUICE™

YAY! for Sparkl*Juice™ but not really, because IMHO it's pretty disgusting actually, and especially the diet kind, which is what my dad had. He poured me a glass and then tipped off his canteen, and then he went to the bedroom to get whatever it was he was going to get, and I sat down on the couch and looked around at the old house.

Same as it always was. Same furniture, same smell. Except there was one new thing—only it wasn't new. It was a record player, like an old ancient cabinet set. Sitting in the corner. There was something familiar about it, but I couldn't put my finger on what it was. There was also something weird: where the record should go there was a pair of women's undies.

Not just any undies, either. Silky red and with black lace around the edges and this sheer mesh—like a screen door almost—in the crotchal area.

Dad came back down the hall carrying a book.

I held up the undies. "This the thing you wanted to talk about?"

"Where'd you get those?"

"I dig the mesh. You wear these when you go jogging?"

"Gimme those," he said.

He took the undies and handed me the book. "Have a look at that."

But I wasn't ready to look. I wanted to talk about the undies.

"How'd they end up on the record player?"

"None of your business."

"Well, it kind of is. I don't know if I want to stay at a place where unsanitary and possibly diseased undergarments are just lying around everywhere—I might catch something."

"Just look at the damn book."

Fine. It was a yellow-and-blue book with a picture of a man and a treasure box on the cover. *True Tales of Buried Treasure* by Edward Rowe Snow. It took me a moment to remember where I'd seen it before.

"Hey. Grandpa was trying to get me to read this when I stayed with him that summer."

"It was on the floor next to him. Look inside."

A folded piece of paper marked page ix of the introduction. Part of a passage had been underlined in black pen:

*My continuous word of warning is that you should never be discouraged by failure, and never expect success. Then if you don't find the treasure, you will not be too disappointed, and if you are successful, you'll be able to stand it more gracefully.*

"Now check out the bookmark."

A scrap of yellow notebook paper folded in quarters. I unfolded it. There was a message, a typed message. I mean like *actually* typed, like with an actual typewriter—and from the looks of it a highly malfunctional one, with a messed-up ink ribbon and a doubled *D* key.

DDear to whom it may concern:

I, Henry O'Faolain, being of soundd mindd andd failing boddy, ddo hereby ddeclare this ddocument to be my final will andd testament as witnessedd by myself here todday in DDecember. If that's not goodd enough for the lawyers, tell them to come talk to me in hell because congratulations that's where we're headdedd, though personally I ddon't believe in hell or heaven either, just a crackedd glass with water pouring out the sidde, andd that's what we call "time." First you have a lot then you have a little.

It looks like I've reachedd my expiration ddate. The ddoctors have informedd me that my lungs are full of cancer, but I ddon't needd someone with a ddegree to tell me what I alreaddy know. So that's that. Time for me to go.

I hereby ddistribute my possessions as follows:

From the 10 acres of property, to my truck, my tools, ddown to the last book of codde on the bookshelf, I leave everything to my granddson Aaron. But please note Aaron that at this stage you are not in possession of the most important thing. This isn't about treasure andd property. When you've finishedd, you'll undderstandd.

I've been here 76 years andd yet I've never stoppedd being surprisedd at how buriedd andd

overrun by rats this worldd really is. Look up,
ddown: levels andd levels of nestedd rats. They
charge us for answers to their rat questions,
andd as we scramble to pay them, keep jabbing
at us for more. Bankers . . . priests . . .
insurance agents . . . businessmen . . . politicians
& other speakers against truth . . . usurpers
. . . lawyers . . . thieves . . . scounddrels . . . Rats,
rats, rats . . .

DDon't worry: I've madde arrangements to
secure the treasure against their rat handds.
Give them a ddime andd they press you for the
whole ddollar. Pause for a moment andd they've
taken your shirt too. Yet I ddo believe Aaron
granddson you are smarter than the average
rat. Got it? Andd when you are stuck, you will
know what to ddo: DDig DDeeper!

Signedd on this dday,

Henry J. O'Faolain

PS As for my remains, I hereby request that
one half (½) of my boddy be buriedd in the
Antello municipal cemetery, rites to be readd
by certifiedd Catholic clergy. The remaining
one half (½) of my boddy to be cremateddd
to ashes, these then to be loaddedd into
shotgun shells andd honorably ddischargedd
from my Remington .410 in the four carddinal
ddirections from some appropriate hill
or vantage point, preferably at ddusk. My
tombstone to readd:

"It Couldd Have Been Wondderful Andd Sometimes It Was"

PPS Ignore the ddouble dd's. But the first clue is this: look behindd the portrait of Mary.

 ?

# 18.

# SHOES

I had to read it twice to figure out what was going on, and even then I wasn't so sure.

"Holy shit. He left it all to me?"

Dad frowned. "I'm the SOB who had to deal with him all my life, but yeah, it appears so. The old man was crazy, and a pain in the ass in both life and death." He plopped down on the couch. "That will proves it."

It *was* kind of crazy. But as I read over the words again, this realization began to sink in. Maybe it *wasn't* crazy. Ten acres, house, truck, tree, every rock and brush—and all of it mine? Holy shit! Problems solved! Wow. You think you're in a hole, and then suddenly you find yourself standing on top of a mountain. And that mountain is made of money. Enough to pay everyone and take care of all my problems. Awesome!

"The old goat was insane."

"You're not disputing it, though, right? I mean, you're not just angry because—"

"Am I pissed I got squat?" My dad was standing again. "I'm happy to be rid of him, not gonna lie. That's my reward. Sorry to say that about my own father, but it's true. But there's someone else we're forgetting in all this."

"Who?"

"Your sister, smart guy. How come she got cut out?"

"How should I know?"

"Well, here's what you need to do. You need to sell his place and give her half. It'll take a while, the market is down, but maybe in a year or so you can get a decent price. . . ."

Right. Of course. Here I was still getting used to the idea that I'd suddenly inherited an entire house + some property + whatever else, and he was already jumping on me to sell it and split it with Evie. But what really got me was how he wouldn't even give me the chance to come up with the idea on my own. Because who knows? Maybe I *would* have offered her something. Definitely I would've. Although maybe not *half.* I mean—come on. He *did* leave it all to me.

My dad continued with his plan: "The reason I say you can wait on putting it on the market immediately is because I think there may be money available now. You know, from the land sale."

"What land sale?"

"The eighty acres he sold to the Coyote Heights golf course. This was maybe five years ago, remember? They never finished it. The whole thing went under when the Restructuring happened. Here's what I want to know: Who thinks it's a good idea to build a luxury golf course in the middle-of-nowhere Antello?"

"So what happened?"

"Well, I know for a fact he got paid. He kept ten acres for

himself. Sold the rest. Didn't trust the banks. And the question is, where did he put the money? I guarantee you he didn't spend it. Which is why I wanted you to come over here in the first place."

He went back into his bedroom and returned with a big framed picture.

"What's that?" I asked.

"Portrait of Mary," he said.

It was quite a picture, actually—there was more than just Mary. But yeah, in the middle it was her, Mary, holding baby Jesus in her arms, and it was a pretty terrifying scene: the two of them were sitting up in a cloud above the fiery flames of hell, tormented souls reaching up for their ankles, and an angel at the bottom right grabbing one of them like, "Sorry, pal, you need an appointment to talk to the lady."

"It was hanging in his living room. *Look behind the portrait of Mary*, right?" Dad turned it over and handed it to me. "Thought I'd let you do the honors. Rip into it. Let's see if we got some money here."

And in my head I was like, *We?*

The backing was wood, and it wasn't easy to rip into. I had to pick it off piece by piece, like taking apart a puzzle. When at last I'd unveiled the back of the canvas... there was nothing there. Zero. Nada. No words. No message. Just the back of the canvas.

"Houston, we have confirmation," said Dad. "The goat was crazy."

"Well, was there anything *behind* the picture?"

"What do you mean?"

"Like on the wall. Like a secret compartment."

"Nope. Just the wall." Dad gazed at the broken pieces at our feet. "It doesn't matter. You and Evie can still sell the property."

"So you keep saying."

He shot me a look. "What's that supposed to mean?"

"He left it to *me*. It's my decision what I do with it or who I share it with."

"You know what your sister would do if it was her name on the will? She'd put it on the market the next day and split it with you."

"Would she?"

"You bet. If you don't believe me, go ask her yourself!"

"Maybe I will!"

But first I had to deal with the dog. When I went for my shoe, her lip curled and she let out a low warning growl.

"Yeah, she gets like that. Your shoe is her new favorite—isn't it, Bones? Give her a couple hours and she'll get over it. You wanna go to Evie's? You can wear something of mine."

"I don't want to wear something of yours."

I reached for my shoe again. Bones growled louder.

"It's either that or go barefoot with a bloody hand," he said.

"Fine. Whaddya got?"

YAY! for my shoes, Osmos™IVs, and BOO! for the cheap, low-cut moccasins my dad offered me, hardly footwear at all. True, it was only a couple blocks to Evie, but even so . . . who offers moccasins when it's snowing? I made it maybe half a block before losing one in a snowdrift.

 ?

# 19.

# HEART TO HEART™

It took me a good ten minutes to find the moccasin—I'm not even exaggerating—and let me tell you, standing on one foot in the snow can really put a guy in a foul mood. By the time I got to my sister's place I'd really worked myself into a lather. *Give her half.* She fakes an illness, skips the funeral, and I'm supposed to *reward* her for that? OTOH, I knew deep down that it was true: Evie probably would share half with me. That's just how she is.

When I banged on the door, my sister didn't answer. Instead, it was Sam.

"Aaron! Why, you're freezing! Get in here!"

YAY! for Sam Latham, whose congenial nature and big heart is like a megadose of the HeartHealth™ lifestyle of Kashi® Heart to Heart™ Honey Toasted Oat cereal. Sam's a big guy with a crew cut, and he's Evie's housemate and also her best friend—and we've always gotten along real well on account of he's without a doubt the nicest guy I've ever known. Over the years he's helped me out with all kinds of stuff, from dating advice, to fashion, to the best way to conceal a fat zit. Basically, he's the closest thing I've ever had to another big sister.

"How's your day going?" he said.

"Well, I buried my grandpa, talked to a weird old lady who told me about Jesus, a dog stole my shoe—and here I am."

"And here you are!"

He brought me in and sat me down on the sofa, told me Evie would be with us shortly, then handed me a blanket, a cup of tea, and a plate of snickerdoodle cookies. I munched on a doodle and he filled me in on the latest news of Evie's disease.

"We spent the morning in the emergency room—as you might imagine, it was an ordeal."

"What'd they say?"

"The results were positive. But there are several strains of Avian Superpox, and only the Zanzibar and Vatican strains have made it over to America, and neither of them is all that super. More like a mild case of chicken pox. She's not even contagious anymore. It's going to be over in a day or two, which is a good thing, because I have to be in Utah in two days to meet my oldest sister's latest baby. Her *third*, by the way. All my sisters are returning to the homeland to spawn. Sandra also has three. Shaley has two. Not even twenty-five years old and I'm already an octuncle. Can you believe it?"

I could believe it. Sam's nine sisters were well known throughout the area for their extreme hotness, desirability, and untouchableness due to them pretty much being Mormon princesses.

Sam's gaze drifted to the hallway. "But what do we have here? Could it be? All fresh and smelling of lavender and calendula and—is that *rosemary*? Honey, you smell good enough to *eat*."

Yep, there she was: my sister, Evie. Scrubbed clean but still looking a little harried in her bathrobe, and also a little hairy—the curse of our family—shower-fresh Evie with unshaven legs and dots all over.

"Hi, Aaron," she said. "No comments about my appearance, please."

"Let me tell you," Sam whispered loudly. "She's been handling the whole thing just *wonderfully.*"

"I have not. I've been a big baby."

"Well, yes, Evelyn. That, too. You're itchy. Who could blame you?"

"Not you."

"Certainly not. Neither of us would. Isn't that right, Aaron?"

"Holy cow, Evie! Look at your face!"

Evie frowned. "Look at my *all* of me. I've even got them on the bottom of my *feet.* I'm not even going to tell you where *else.*"

*"Her b-hole!"* Sam whispered. *"And also her—"*

*"Samuel Latham!"*

So it was true. All of her—at least as much of her as I could see sticking out of the robe—covered in these little red bumps. This was a first. Evie had an affliction that was actually visually verifiable. You didn't have to take her word for it. It was all right there to see.

And I would've expected her to be as smug as a bug in a rug about it, but she seemed more worried than anything else. Would her pristine complexion survive this assault? Or was she going to come out looking like Little Miss Acne Scars? Sam told her she'd be fine. Skin is amazingly resilient. She needn't worry. They were taking every precaution. I got the sense that this was territory they'd covered before. Sam sounded a little weary defending his position.

"Just *listen*. Even right now, *at its very worst*—it isn't even that bad. It's like you've got...freckles. Think of it as your redhead phase, dear. Your face has a new—how shall I say it?—*geography*. Isn't that right, Aaron?"

"More like *topography*."

"Exactly. Little points of interest."

"Mountains and volcanoes."

"Stop!" cried Evie. "This isn't helping."

"Or like little towns."

"Yes, exactly! Proud hamlets with British names: Northmouth, Eastmouth."

"Westforeheadshire."

"Spotford upon Eyebrow."

"You shut your mouth right now," said Evie. "Both of you."

 ?

# 20.

# THE FREEZER

Sam went to the kitchen to make more tea, and after that it was just me and my sister. She *did* look fairly miserable, sitting there with her knees drawn up to her chin, scratch-scratching at the red spots on her ankles, and for a moment I felt my cold heart soften. I was just about to tell her, *Be happy, I'm cutting you in for half the inheritance, so snap out of it already.* I swear—I really was. But then I noticed the furniture: a cabinet of some kind. Or maybe more like a buffet. Some kind of dresser? I didn't know what exactly to call it, but I recognized it. I knew I'd seen it before, and I knew *where*.

"Hey. That's Grandpa's cabinet, isn't it? What's it doing here?"

"Dad brought it here," said Evie.

Then I remembered the old record player back at Dad's place—it was from Grandpa's, too. *Right.* It all made sense. "You guys are already divvying up the inheritance!"

"No," she said. "Dad was worried about someone breaking in, that's all. So he moved a few things. And then I commented that I liked the cabinet, so..." My sister shrugged. "It doesn't matter to me. It's all *yours*, right? That's what you're getting at, *right?*"

"Hey, it wasn't *my* decision. I guess he just liked me."

"He was crazy, Aaron."

"Look, I'm definitely going to cut you in for some of the profits, so don't even worry about that. You want the cabinet, you can have the cabinet."

My sister scowled. "I don't want the cabinet! I just said it was *nice*. I don't want any of it. But you know who could use some help right now? Dad. Have you thought about him? I'd split it with him, if I were you."

"Oh—wait." I held up a hand. "*I* get it."

"Get what?"

"It's all so very clever."

"*What's* clever?" she said. "What are you even *talking* about?"

Yes, it was clear to me now: they'd discussed this. Planned it out. Hatched a clever plot. Evie and Dad would each say they didn't give a shit for themselves and instead ask for a portion on the other's behalf. It was actually pretty brilliant. They could each present their case as if they were only acting out of concern for the other. And here was the *really* clever part: if I refused, *I* was the asshole.

"Wow," said Evie. "Just—wow." She scratched her ankle. The little dots were, like, *glowing* red.

"What?"

"Dad's paying for your school! Or have you forgotten? And now you have the *nerve* to sit there and act like it's somehow *crazy* for me to suggest that you share some of the inheritance with him?!"

Here's the thing about my sister: it's a good idea to avoid pissing her off. She looks harmless and all, but there's a fire burning in that dork. The other problem is, she's usually right.

"Look," I said. "Fine. Whatever. It's cool. I was going to share it anyway. I'm just maybe a *little* ticked off that everyone's always telling me what to do before I even get a chance to think about it. It's like everyone assumes I'm gonna be an asshole about everything."

Sam came back with more cookies.

"No one assumes you're an asshole, Aaron," he said. "Have a snickerdoodle."

I grabbed a cookie. "Everything's just been happening really fast lately. I didn't know what I was stepping into. Also, I don't care what the will says, I'm not taking a retarded dog with me back to San Francisco."

"San Francisco?" said Evie. "Why are you going to *San Francisco*? And the dog's not retarded. It has PTSD."

I told her I meant *Sacramento*, and she didn't seem too suspicious, maybe because she was still so pissed off about me calling the dog retarded.

"Anyway," she said, "I think Dad's going to keep the dog."

"It's been quite a little journey for all of us," said Sam.

"What's that mean?" I asked.

Sam turned to Evie. "Are you going to tell him, or do I get to?"

My sister frowned. "You mean about the vet's?"

"I mean the *freezer*," said Sam.

"What about the freezer?" I said.

"Check it out," said Sam.

"No! Don't," said Evie.

I went to check it out—a Frigidaire® v180 with frostguard™ (YAY!). Inside, where the frozen peas or whatever should be, there was a single yellow bag, and on it was written the word BIOHAZARD in red capital letters.

"You don't want to open that," said Sam.

"Why not?"

"*Because*," said Evie. "When you see a bag that says *biohazard*, you do not open it. Common sense."

"Yes," said Sam, "but is it also not common sense to *not* store biohazardous materials in a residential kitchen freezer? I can never unsee what I saw!"

"Why? What's in there?"

"Puppies," he said.

"Puppies?"

"For the record I did not authorize this. I told your sister that freezer is a public space, and she *knows* how much I like my frozen pizzas and ice creams and bagel dogs. Oh my God—did I just say that? Bagel DOGS? Anyway, yes, after she heard about the abortion mistake, dear sweet Evelyn marched down to the veterinarian's office and demanded to be given the puppies."

"It was so awful! They deserve a proper burial."

"Dear, that's all well and good, but in the meantime—"

"So why haven't you buried them yet?" I said.

"Yes," said Sam. "Why *haven't* we?"

Evie sat up glowing red. "In case you didn't notice, I happen to have superpox. Also, it's freezing cold outside. Also, there's a foot of snow on the ground. But if you clowns want to go bury the puppies, by all means please grab a spoon because, oh yeah, we *also* don't have a shovel."

 ?

# 21.

## AS SEEN ON

No one wanted to bury the puppies in the snow with a spoon, so instead we sat on the couch and ate snickerdoodles. Homie™ popped up to ask if I wanted a recipe. Sam kept teasing Evie about something, but I couldn't follow where he was going, only that it wasn't the puppies—something else she didn't want me to know.

"*Sam...*" she warned him.

"Oh, come now. You can't keep love a secret forever, dear."

My ears perked up. "Keep love a secret?"

"*Sam!* I thought we agreed—"

"Shush. We didn't agree on anything. Why don't you share the good news with your brother?"

"What good news?"

"*Boyfriend,*" he sang.

"Sam!"

"That's right! Evelyn has a *boyfriend*!"

"He is not my boyfriend!"

"Oh, really? Then what *is* he?"

"I don't know. Just a *good* friend."

Sam turned to me. "His name is *Isaac*, and he's about *this* tall, and he's got beautiful brown hair, and beautiful brown eyes, and a beautiful nose, and all his teeth and fingers—and he's an Ivy League–educated *scientist*."

"Environmental impact engineer," said Evie.

Evie getting freaky with a scientist? This was news.

"And they are in *love*," said Sam.

"No! Isaac is just—he's a person I'm becoming friends with."

"Really? *Friends?* Friends don't let friends put their hands where you two friends have put your hands!"

"Aaron," she said. "Don't listen to Sam. Isaac is a very nice person, but he lives in New York and—"

"And he's out here practically every other weekend!" said Sam.

"For his *research*! He's studying the effect of optical radiation on birds, and it's just—it's nice to meet someone once in a while who you have, you know, an intellectual connection with because—"

Sam laughed. "So that's what the geeks are calling it these days. *Intellectual connection.*"

"And what about *you*?" said Evie.

"What *about* me?"

"Mr. International is what, fifty years old? And do you know where they met, Aaron? In some filthy chat room."

"A pox on you, Evie!" Sam touched her nose. "Oh, wait—you've already got one! I just can't fathom where you get your ideas. If you want to know, we happened to have met the old-fashioned way: face-to-face in a ladies' restroom. The men's was out of order. And he isn't fifty—he's not even forty. *Barely* even thirty."

"You distinctly said it was a filthy chat room."

"No. I said we *chatted* in there about how *filthy* it was. The women's side is supposed to be the clean side, right? At any rate, it was a lovely encounter. We exchanged numbers and have been in touch. The only problem is, he lives in Canada half the year, and also he's having FUN®, so even when we're hanging out, it feels like he's only half there.... Sigh. But he *is* beautiful, and he has a cottage on a lake, and I'm going to visit it one day and go rowing through the mist at dawn."

"They've got FUN® in Canada now?" I said.

"Apparently so. It's seems like it's everywhere now...." Sam put his face close to mine. "*You're* not on, are you? But then why do I see a faint flicker around the retina?"

Oops.

"You're on FUN®?!" said Evie.

"Well, they say 'having FUN®.'"

"Since when? Who said it was OK? How exactly are you *paying* for it?!"

What was there to say? I could feel my forehead breaking out into a sweat. I sat there wishing I had some SweatBlok® Clinical Strength Forehead Wipes as seen on Classic Rachael Ray (YAY!), or better yet, a way to tell her everything and just get it off my chest—but I knew that if I told my sister everything, my life as I knew it was over. So instead I just told her a little bit. I told her I'd started having FUN®, yes, but that it was totally manageable. I was earning my way, even making some extra money on the side.

She wasn't convinced.

"What about school? What does Mom have to say about all this?"

BOO! for those questions, and YAY! again for good old Sam, who leapt courageously to my defense.

"Well, but Aaron appears to have control over it. My Canadian friend most certainly does *not*. There's a difference. You don't play games, do you, Aaron? Mr. International spends all day playing *games*. What's that one everyone's always talking about?"

"*Murder Driver?*"

"No."

"*Flower Stomper?*"

"No . . . the one with the exploding panda baby."

"*Tickle, Tickle, Boom!* That's a great game."

"Great? It's like a *drug*. He's on it *all* the time. He wants me to have FUN®, too, but there's no way I'm ever letting anyone mess with *my* eyes. They're the only ones I've got."

"Me either," said Evie. "FUN® is dangerous!"

The tide had turned. Now it was my turn to take some abuse. Sam and Evie lectured me on the corroding forces of modernity and the value of everyday reality, and I gave them both the finger and told them they'd be having FUN® within a year. There was no way around it. In the same way that people used to swear they'd never get a television, or a cell phone, or a wristphone, or goggles, or whatever. It was only a matter of time.

We blabbed for a while, and then it got late, and everyone was tired. Out of pride I'd decided not to ask if I could crash that night on their couch—I would wait for them to ask me. But they didn't, and it got later, and finally I decided to leave. Before I left I got up and rifled through the drawers in my grandpa's cabinet, just to see what was there. There wasn't much. But in the bottom drawer, I did find something kind of cool. Two things, actually. A pair of old-timey snowshoes—the leather ones that look like tennis rackets—and this little silver harmonica.

"I'm taking this harmonica. And these snowshoes."

"Go ahead!" said Evie. "Take it all! Drag the cabinet back to Sacramento if you want."

"I just want the harmonica and snowshoes."

"Take some cookies with you, too. I'm sick to death of snickerdoodles."

Sam wrapped me up a plate, and Evie reminded me to return the plate, and I ate almost all of them on the way home and fed the last two to Bones, who was curled up on my bed with my shoe. She ate the cookies, but she wouldn't trade me a snowshoe for my Osmos™IV—she growled every time I went to make the swap. She did let me sleep on the bed with her, though, so that was good.

"Sweet dreams, Bones," I said.

 ?

# 22.

# LITTLE BAGGIE

When I woke in the morning Bones was gone, and so was my shoe, and so was my dad.

There was a note in the kitchen:

*Went on errand. Be back soon.*
*Shovel the drive if you want.*
<u>*Do NOT touch the thermostat.*</u>

I was kind of hungry, so I tried scrounging up some breakfast, but it was a pretty bleak scene. No toast, no orange juice, no eggs. Nothing.

> how about yay! for naturebite™
  energy cereal?

"Yay."

But no, none of that, either.

I took a bottle of ketchup, a box of taco shells, and a jar of unopened pickles, and combined these ingredients as best I could, but when I was done it didn't look very appetizing, so I left it on the plate. I was hungry, but not that hungry. I was gonna have to get a little more hungry before I ate that thing.

Alone in the empty house I wasn't quite sure what to do with myself. I'm no amateur at pissing away a morning, but the present circumstances threw me off. The snow had left a strange silence and I felt uneasy in my old home. I got up to check out the record player—*my* record player, if you wanted to get technical about it.

I put on a record and laid the needle in the groove. It had a cool sound—not so much the music but the fuzz and pop of the needle, like radio static. As I was listening to it, something occurred to me. A solution to a problem that I'd been turning over in my mind. I stopped the player and lifted the arm thing with the needle on it. It was a tiny, tiny needle, and it took me a second to figure out how to get it off the arm thing...and then I figured it out. I took off the needle and slipped it into my pocket.

I was still sleepy, so I cranked up the thermostat and got back into bed, but just as I was drifting off, a phone began to ring. Dad's phone. He'd left it on top of his dresser. I silenced it and got back into bed, and this time I fell asleep, or almost did, but not for long because then the phone was ringing again. No—more like buzzing. The doorbell. I let it buzz, but it kept on buzzing, so I got up to answer it.

There was a woman standing on the porch. I didn't recognize her at first because of the hat. Or actually, it was more like a bonnet: this gray-blue cloth thing, like what a Pilgrim might wear, with her hair tucked into it so that her ears stuck out in a nice way. In addition to the bonnet, she had on a long gray dress with an apron and lacy shawl thing. A strange getup, especially considering it had to be 10 degrees out, but she was looking at me like *I* was the odd one out.

"Arnold? What are you doing here? Where's Jim?"

*Arnold?* Oh, right.

"Hi, Katie."

Again, I thought about telling her the truth, but then OTOH I was doing pretty well so far as Arnold, so why change it up now? Instead, I told her half the truth:

"Yeah, um, Jim is my, uh—uncle. It was his dad who passed away—my grandpa."

"Jim is your *uncle*?" She gazed at me for a moment, processing the information.

"That's a cool dress," I said. "Very retro."

"It's from wardrobe."

"Never heard of it. Do they sell men's stuff, too?"

"*Wardrobe*—for the play. Don't you know about the play?"

"What play?"

"*Taming of the Shrew.* They changed the final run-through time—didn't he hear? He's the only one with a key, and he won't answer his phone. Right now as we speak twenty people are standing around in the snow in period costume."

"Wait. Slow down. My—*Jim* is in a play?"

"Yes."

"Does he *play* someone in the play?"

"Yes, of course. Tonight!"

"Who does he play?"

"I really don't have time to discuss all this."

"And who are you? Is there like a Pilgrim in the play?"

Katie drew the shawl thing tighter around her shoulders. Her eyes were all icy blue. "I'm the *Shrew*," she said. "Where the hell is your uncle?"

The truth is, I didn't know. He'd just said *errand*. So I invited her inside. She could wait here in the warm. I had the heater going and everything. We could listen to Bob Wills on vinyl and snuggle together on the couch. I didn't actually tell her about that last part, about the snuggling, but it didn't matter. She didn't want to come inside anyway.

"Just tell your uncle to get his butt down to the theater!"

She headed to her truck. Her hand was on the door when I called out to her.

"Hey! Wait! You know those riddles you gave me? I've got two of them figured out already!"

And the woman, the Shrew, Katie—she wheeled around, and it seemed for a moment like she was about to say something—but she didn't. Instead, she got in her truck, slammed the door, fired up the engine, and went rolling down the street.

Dad and Bones showed up maybe five minutes after that. I was sitting at the table contemplating my meal again.

"The hell is that?"

"Pickle taco."

"What's wrong with cereal?"

"You've got cereal?"

"Of course." He rooted around in the cupboard. "Or maybe I don't. But here. I got you something else." He dug into his pocket and pulled out a baggie of white powder, and I was gonna make a crack about it being cocaine, but then he said, "Baked fresh from the mortuary," and I knew what it was.

"Grandpa's ashes."

"It was in the will, remember? He wanted half of him buried and half of him cremated and then shot out of a gun. And by the way, this is the last thing I do. I'm now officially done with the old goat. If you want to shoot him out of a gun, that's on you. Here. Catch."

YAY! for color-coded triple-lock Ziplock® FreshLock™ locking zip bags, which may be tossed and dropped without bursting into a powdery cloud. I picked it off the floor and hefted the strange weight. Half of my grandfather. Weird. Then a question occurred to me.

"Wait—so did the funeral people just, like, saw him in half?"

Dad gave me his one look, the one that says, *What are you, an idiot?* "No—they cremated him and *then* divided him."

"Oh."

He plopped down on the easy chair and grabbed his canteen. "Just gonna catch my breath, then I gotta get ready to go—got another little errand to run."

"Yeah, I think you may be a little late on that one."

I told him about the time change and the key situation, all those actors standing around in the snow, and he popped back out of his chair like a video in reverse. He ran around grabbing different things, swearing and cursing, and just as he was about to fly out the door, I reminded him I needed a ride to the train station.

"Get your stuff, then!"

"Well, I still got an hour."

Dad shoved some papers in a bag. "That's OK! You can be early!"

BOO! for that. Who wants to sit in the cold waiting for a train? I took my time packing, and my dad climbed up and down the walls like a mad spider, and then we got in the car. He backed it out of the garage and we got about three feet before the wheels started spinning in place. Right. The drive hadn't been shoveled.

He slammed the pedal to the floor and the car rocked and shuddered, and finally the old Mazda powered through the drift and went sliding into the street.

We skidded to a stop in front of the Amtrak station. Dad threw me out of the car and shoved my bag in my arms.

"Take care. Have a good trip back. Keep up on your schoolwork."

Standing in the snow in my dad's moccasins, I realized something. "Crap! My shoe!"

But he was late and he didn't want to drive me back to the house and he was already getting back in the Mazda.

"Keep the moccasins and I'll mail you the shoe later! I really gotta go, OK? Say hi to your mom and what's-his-name."

He left me in the station in the freezing cold, and I wasn't happy about it. All these questions kept rushing through my mind. Did I want to leave home again just like that? Did I really want to go back to the hivehouse? What about the inheritance? What about that book, *True Tales of Buried Treasure*? What about *Look behind the portrait of Mary*? Maybe there was *another* portrait. Maybe I could find it. Maybe there was a whole mother lode of money and treasure just waiting for me. And then everything would be OK. I could pay back my dad and get out of FAIL and everything would be cool. It seemed like a reasonable solution.

Also, I really wanted to see some more of Katie in that pioneer dress.

 ?

# 23.

# TAMING OF THE SHREW

I got to the theater early—and a good thing, because the place was already filling up fast. I spotted Sam and Evie in the front near the fire exit and slid into the open seat behind them and gave my sister a punch in the arm.

"Surprise!"

"What are you doing here?" she said.

"How come no one told me about the play?"

"I forgot. Maybe because I was busy fighting off a deadly disease."

Yeah, right. Clearly what we had here was another family conspiracy. Because Dad acting in a play? This was a noteworthy event. Everyone's got a failed dream, and my dad's had nothing to do with the theater. It had to do with being the drummer in a famous rock band. Which, except for the famous part, he'd already pretty much accomplished most of it—the drinking, the carousing, the sleeping with skanks, the shiftless lifestyle, and the inevitable bottoming out. But thespianism? This was new. I scanned the playbill.

*Christopher Sly the Tinker...James O'Faolain.*

And further down:

*The Shrew...Katarin Ezkiaga.*

My sister nudged me. "But really—what are you doing here, Aaron?"

"What's a tinker, like a gnome?"

"A repairman. Why are you still in town?"

"I gotta take care of some stuff."

Just then the lights began to flash, and an announcement sounded over the speakers.

*Audience, please silence your devices as the Silver Sage Players of Antello Community College now invite you to join them for a rollicking journey of intrigue and hilarity...William Shakespeare's* Taming of the Shrew, *set in a 19th-century mining town!*

The lights went out, and the curtains opened upon a dark stage. A single spotlight appeared, and into this light stepped... my dad.

He was dressed like a cowboy: hat, boots, faded slacks, and one of those blowsy tunic things that can also be used in medieval and pirate productions. Also, for some reason, he had a snare drum hanging from his neck. As he began to speak, I felt my grip tighten on the armrests. Here he was, the same man I once saw finish off three bottles of wine at a Christmas party and pass out in the backseat of the wrong car, now standing with his arms upraised, orating in Elizabethan English.

"I am Christopher Sly," he said, I mean orated. "Call me not honor nor lordship. I ne'er drank sack in my life. Never ask me what raiment I'll wear, for I have no more doublets than backs, no more stockings than legs, no more shoes than feet; nay sometimes more feet than shoes." With a flourish he lowered his hands. "Am I not

Christopher Sly? Old Sly's son of Burtonheath, by birth a peddler, by education a cardmaker, by transmutation a bear-herd, and now by present profession a—"

And here the adaptation diverged slightly more from the original because (as I learned later) Dad had requested a change to his occupation—and apparently the Silver Sage Players were so hard up for male actors that they agreed.

"Now a tinker and wandering percussionist!" he proclaimed. "Just ask Marian Hacket, the fat ale-wife of Wincot, if she know me not."

As he delivered these lines he tapped out some grace notes on the drum. He played softly, as background music, but his eyes twinkled under his straw hat with the very real threat that at any moment he might rest one foot upon the little prop fence and take one of those phrases and bust it open into a red-hot ten-minute solo performance of "Wipe Out."

But he didn't. Thank God for that. Just as I was sort of getting used to seeing him up there, the scene ended and Dad exited stage left—or was it right? Depends on your perspective, I guess. Anyway, he was gone, and the lights brightened into a harsh 19th-century sun, and some other actors wandered onto the set—but not Katie.

It was a typical old-timey Western town, the kind where each business is helpfully labeled with wooden signs above the door: SALOON, FEED STORE, HOTEL, BANK, BROTHEL. All of it rendered in convincing enough detail: weathered siding, silhouettes in the lamp-lit windows, hitching posts out in front. But for some reason the buildings were smaller than life-size—like maybe eight feet tall at most—and as a result the actors appeared to be standing a far distance from the town—in a field perhaps, or on a very wide road.

For this reason and others I had a hard time following the action. A lot of the jokes went over my head. I lost track of the plot.

Look, William Shakespeare is The Man—that's what the teachers keep telling me. But The Man can be a little, you know, *rambly* at times. I have a hard time believing even the Elizabethan audiences could always keep up with him.

But when Homie™ popped up in my face asking:

>    yay! for taming of the shrew
>    complete abridged version from
>    elegant glenn® shakespeare library?

I was like, "Yay! Yay!" just to get it out of my way, because suddenly the play had changed: just as it was really beginning to get away from me, just as I was starting to get bored and confused, and right before Homie™ popped up to ask me about Shakespeare—just before that—there was a sound of thunder and Katie, aka Katarin, aka the Shrew, entered from stage right, or left, or whatever it was—stomping onto the stage in her bonnet, dress, and cowboy boots—and suddenly the whole thing made sense again.

# 24.

## SO SOFT

Time slowed to jelly, and I gazed in wonder at Katie and her arms and her belly and her Shrewness and beautiful monstrosity. *That dress.* It was a cool dress, but that wasn't it. It was Katie *in* the dress. She was like a beautiful monster in it, stomping across the stage, kicking over fence posts, raging in her bonnet. What a show! She was somebody else, and yet she was more herself than I'd ever seen before—not that I even actually *knew* her, but her performance made me *feel* like I did. Which is the whole point, right? She was the SHREW.

As the play continued, time started to accelerate until it was shooting forward in a blur—Acts II, III, IV, V—the whole thing colliding in a glorious finale with Katie standing center stage in a brilliant spotlight to deliver her final speech:

"Why are our bodies soft and weak and smooth,

unfit for toil and trouble in the world,

but that our soft conditions and our hearts

should well agree with our external parts?"

That's the Bard for you. *Smooth body. External parts. Soft conditioner.*

> yay! for pantene® spasoft™
> moisturizing conditioner
> original boy_2?

"Yay!"

Good work, Shakespeare. I mean, nice job, man. I couldn't have put it better myself. I stood with the others and clapped, cupping my hands just slightly for maximum acoustic effect. I've never been so turned on by a dress in all my life.

Afterwards, I headed outside to wait for Katie. I hid behind a truck and scanned the lot. Five minutes later, I saw her walking in the snow. Long black peacoat, red scarf, jeans, and carrying what appeared to be a Hula-Hoop. The plan was for me to appear casually out of the darkness like the lead in one of those old black-and-white detective films, but when I stepped out from behind the truck, she let out a yelp and clutched the hoop to her chest.

"Jesus! You scared the shit out of me!"

Which—not quite the effect I'd been hoping for.

"Hi! I was just—is this your truck?"

"Arnold? What are you doing here?"

"I came to see the play. Which was awesome. *You* were awesome. I wanted to tell you how awesome you were. You literally destroyed the place. Is that a Hula-Hoop?"

"No, it's a set of golf clubs."

"Ha. Right!"

"I use it to relieve the jitters before I go onstage.... What are you doing here?"

"Well, like I said—you know, I came to see you. And, uh, my

uncle. In the play. But mainly you. That dress was amazing, by the way."

She gave me a strange look. "And where is this going?"

"Nowhere. I mean, I'm just being honest. If you're wondering where the compliments are coming from, they're for real." I patted my chest. "Straight from right here."

"The esophagus," said Katie.

I *liked* her. I really did. And even if I didn't know her, it was like I already did, like we'd already met a long, long time ago— which doesn't make sense, I know, but at the time it totally did. There was just this electricity. It's like William Shakespeare may or may not once have said: *Whosoever can explain the song that sings when two human hearts meet in the cold, cold night?*

But now she was tossing the hoop in the back of her truck and opening the door.

"Wait. Don't go yet! I've got the answers."

Katie paused. "What answers?"

"Those three riddles you gave me—I figured out the answers."

"There aren't any answers. That's the point."

"No, but there *are* answers! Check it out...." I jammed my hand into my pocket and removed the first item. "Number one: a needle that needs no thread. See? It's from a record player. No thread necessary. One hundred percent threadless." I grabbed the second item. "OK, and here's number two: a harp that sings without plucking...." I gave it a toot and handed it to Katie. "Harmonicas are commonly known as 'harps.'"

"Commonly?"

But she was smiling now, just a little.

"What about number three?"

"You still trying to quit smoking?"

"Yes."

"And how's that going?"

"Same as always: terrible."

"Got any smokes on you?"

She did. I bummed one, plus her lighter, and lit it up and took a puff. Then I blew it into the air.

"There. A cloud that makes no rain."

"A cloud?" Katie eyed the darkness. "That's hardly a *cloud*."

"What? Clouds can be any size! What would you call it?"

"A puff."

"*Puff?* That was more than a *puff*. Here. Watch."

I put the cigarette to my lips, sucked in...sucked in more... sucked in some more...and then *blew*.

"There's your cloud," I said—or started to say, but I only got out the first two words before I started coughing. And coughing some more. I was really having a fit, but that wasn't half as bad as the way the world was spinning and the pukey feeling in my esophagus like I was just gonna throw it all up on the concrete. I put my hands on my knees and waited for the feeling to pass.

"Arnold?" she said. "Are you OK?"

"Oh my God, you gotta stop smoking—those things can't be good for you!"

"Thanks. I'm aware of that."

"So I solved them, right? Does that mean I get your number?"

"I thought you were only here for a couple days."

"Not anymore. I've got business to take care of in town. Want to get a drink or something? Or better yet, you could teach me how to Hula-Hoop. I never learned how."

"You never learned to Hula-Hoop?" she said. "It's easy."

"So you say. The P.E. teacher thought I was goofing around, like making fun of it, but I was really just that bad."

"Arnold—" Katie paused. It was like she was weighing some question. A couple dudes walked past in puffy jackets. She fiddled with her keys. "Look," she said at last. "It's freezing. I'm too tired to go out for a drink. So if I invite you over to my place right now, it just means as friends, OK?"

# 25.

# SHE WAS A SPACE AMAZON

Her apartment was the top floor of an old building not far from the college, and its low ceiling sloped in strange places so that I could stand upright only in an area in the middle. But it wasn't a bad place. In fact, it was pretty nice. The walls were blue and yellow, with twinkle lights strung around a built-in bookcase. The furnishings were kind of spare, though. A small puffy couch, a bookshelf, a floor lamp, a lime-green rug—and that was pretty much it.

"So tell me," she said as she shrugged off her jacket and laid it over the back of the couch. "What's Pennsylvania like?"

The question caught me off guard. "Oh, *Pennsylvania*. Well... there are a lot of trees."

"Trees?"

"Yeah...and no sagebrush, of course. And everyone talks with, like, a Pennsylvania accent. And, I don't know, it's pretty much like anywhere else, only it's *there* instead of here, if you know what I mean."

"I'm not sure if I do."

"Well—"

"Maybe I'm just envious," she said. "I thought this was temporary."

"Thought what was?"

"*This.* This apartment. This *town.* I should probably just give in and get more furniture. But of course the second I do, I'll probably have to move out. That seems to be how my life works. . . . Would you like something to drink?"

"Sure. What do you have?"

"Sparkl*Juice™ and gin."

> yay! for sparkl*juice™?

"Yay."

"What?"

"Sounds great."

"Oh, OK."

While Katie was in the kitchen, I checked out her bookshelf. There was a dusty word-of-the-day calendar on top, several months behind the actual date. I've always liked those calendars, with their unspoken promise to endow the user with the ability to cow rivals through *obfuscation*, which is a word I learned from a calendar, though not Katie's. The word on her calendar was:

*floccillation* (fläk-suh-lay-shun) *1. aimless plucking at the bedclothes as a result of delirium or fever. 2. a sign that a person is approaching death.*

Below this, the shelves were about evenly divided between children's picture books and old pocket paperbacks, mostly what looked like science fiction, with yellowed pages and titles I didn't recognize. *Lunar Horizon. The Daughter Nebula. Omegathon.* I was flipping through *She Was a Space Amazon* when Katie returned from the kitchen.

"Here you go."

"Thanks."

I gave it a taste. It was disgusting.

"Mm," I said.

"You like it?"

"Oh yeah."

God, she was beautiful. You know how some people are just beautiful right away and everyone can agree on it? Katie wasn't like that. She was not absolutely stunning at first, but then, the more you looked at her, the more you saw how beautiful she was. Those pure blue eyes. Which, BTW, were aimed right at me, like, *Why are you staring at me?*

The problem is I was having a hard time finding anywhere else to put my eyes. There was this electricity between us, all in the eyes. I tried looking at the bookshelf, but it was so much less interesting than Katie. It was my turn to say something, but I could hardly get any words to come out.

"Those books are cool."

"Really?" Katie brightened. "That one you have there—*She Was a Space Amazon*? I swear, it was a gift from the universe."

"Yeah?"

"Yeah," she said. "It was the first day of spring and I had this *incredible* hangover. Around five in the afternoon I *dragged* myself out of the house, just so I wouldn't miss the entire day, and as I was walking down the street I saw some people cleaning up after a yard sale. Something told me I should stop to see what was left, and that's when I found the book."

"Huh. What's it about?"

"Inevitability."

"But I mean, what's the story?"

"Well, from the cover you're led to believe it's going to be all about kicking ass, but what it really turns out to be about is how incredibly harrowing this woman's life is. Every time she comes upon a new, mist-covered planet you're like, *No! Don't go down there!* And yet, that's what she does. That's what she was born to do. She's a Space Amazon."

"What's that she's wearing on the cover?"

"I don't know. A bikinotard?"

"I bet she gets cold in space."

"It's strange," said Katie. "Reading that book made me think about my own life. I'm not a fatalist, but I *have* noticed certain patterns in my experiences. It's like, wherever I go, there I am. I can't seem to get away from myself. And no matter how careful I am, no matter how much I plan, I always seem to end up in these very, um, *complicated* situations."

"Like what?"

Katie sipped her drink. "Like now."

"What's complicated about now?"

Two blue eyes watching me over the rim of her glass.

"Not just *now-right-now*," she said. "I mean the *bigger* now. Which also includes the *what-just-happened* and *what-might-happen-next*. Sometimes the last *what-just-happened* ends up, you know, *complicating* the options of the *now-right-now*—because of *what-might-happen-next*."

"You're losing me a little."

"There was a guy."

"Oh. The bartender?"

"Yeah, him too," she said. "And I didn't even like him—but it's *complicated*."

I had no idea what she was talking about. But as our gazes lingered, a little bolt of electricity passed between us, and I could tell she felt it, too—I just could—because it was real. I mean *real* electricity. I hadn't felt something like that since Shannon Boyster gave me a chocolate bar at recess in first grade. But as soon as Katie saw that *I* saw, she sort of jumped back and clapped her hands.

"Time for Hula-Hooping."

"What?"

"I'm going to teach you to Hula-Hoop. Remember?"

We cleared a little stage in the middle of her living room, and she handed me the hoop.

"Let's see what you got."

"I got nothing."

"So let's see it."

I twisted my arms and gave the hoop a swing, which completed 1.5 rotations before falling to the floor.

"Well, you have to at least *try*."

"I *am* trying. Look."

My body would not cooperate. My torso went one way, my ass another, while my hips struggled to maintain some equilibrium between the two. I dry-humped the air frantically. The hoop rattled to the floor.

"Clearly this thing is defective."

"You see?" said Katie. "*This* is what happens when you spend too much time having FUN®. You forget how your body works. Use your core. Imagine you're a salsa dancer."

I tried again and failed again.

"Watch me. Maybe that will help."

But no, that wasn't going to help. Katie was too good. It was like trying to learn how to ride a bicycle by watching a motocross race. I mean this woman was a *pro*. She barely moved at all, just this slight swaying of the hips. Then, with a subtle motion that tingled my groin, she sent the hoop orbiting up over her breasts, to her neck, then slipped her arm up under it and caught it in her hand.

"Here. Try again."

Pretty much I'll try anything once, and probably twice, and probably a couple times after that—but inevitably there comes a point where it becomes pointless. When you have to admit that whatever it is might not be the thing for you. Katie was a good-enough teacher, but as a student I was hopelessly distracted by the method of instruction and general circumstances of the classroom, not to mention the glimpses of pale belly I was getting every time my instructor raised her arms. I mean I was absolutely *floccillated*.

 ?

# 26.

# BONUSES

I gave up on Hula-Hooping, and Katie gave up on trying to teach me. The heater was going now and her apartment was hot, and she set the hoop aside and took off her sweater, revealing a tight black T-shirt with the words *Dirty deeds done with sheep.*

"What's that mean?" I asked.

"*Well, Arnold*," she said in a teacherly voice, "it's an appropriation of the stereotype of my people, the Basques. My sister gave it to me as a joke. I wear it for good luck."

"Basques? Like from Spain? I thought you were Irish."

"*Half*-Irish. My mom is Irish, my papa is Basque."

"I heard a joke about Basques once."

"Did it involve sex with a farm animal?"

"Yeah, pretty much."

"When my papa was a teenager he actually *did* work with sheep," said Katie. "Way out in a cabin in the mountains—but he was doing construction by the time I was born. Now he's retired in Spain. He's coming to America this summer to tell me to get a real job like my sister."

"What's your sister do?"

"Maite? She's a real estate agent in Lake Tahoe. You should see the house she just moved into—it's so obnoxious! But of course *she* was always the chosen one...." Katie ran her hands over her face. "God, I want a cigarette."

We went out to the balcony and she lit one up, and I lit up a smókz™, too, and that calmed me down a little, but when she saw me smoking my invisible (to her) cigarette, she burst out laughing.

"What?"

"I don't know. It's just funny. Like you're pretending."

"I'm not."

But I kind of was. But how could I tell her the truth? It seemed a little too late to do a name change.

I exhaled, and my smoke digitized into a hive of BeeWear® Bee Bonuses and Homie™ popped up.

> yay! to collect bonuses?

"Yay."

"Why do you keep saying that?" she said.

"It's just a thing I have to do for FUN®."

"Ah." Katie took another drag and tamped out her cigarette on the underside of the railing. "There. All done. See? I'm cutting back."

I put out my smókz™, too, and followed her back inside, thinking about how to tell her the truth about everything, how I was actually Aaron O'Faolain, age almost 18, which if you think about it isn't that far from 19—or 21 or 22, for that matter. And as I was working myself up, something funny happened. Back in the living room Katie suddenly spun around to face me, and it was like looking in a mirror—I mean, she was wearing this look on her face like she had something to tell *me*.

"Arnold—" she began.

"Yeah?"

And I knew in that moment that nothing mattered, because she was going to tell me her feelings now, how she liked me, too, how she'd been hiding it all along, and she was going to pull me close and smooch me. I envisioned locking lips like they do at the end of a movie, falling together onto the couch in a tangle of limbs and clothing. I envisioned what might happen after that, but then I pulled back on that vision because no need to get ahead of myself.

But I was already pretty far ahead.

I stumbled into a hug with her like Frankenstein with my arms all outstretched, and as I grew closer her eyes widened, and at the last second the message got through to my brain:

*Abort mission! Subject is creeped out!*

So what happened was, instead of her falling into my arms and locking lips, I sort of wrapped her in this awkward hug. And we just hugged for a moment, and she sort of patted my shoulder, and I patted hers, and smelled the flowery perfume of her hair, and then we drew back and looked at each other.

*Words! Use your words, dude!*

"Arnold," she said at last. "It's just . . . right now my life is . . ."

"Complicated," I finished for her.

And the next thing I knew I was standing at her door, saying good-bye, and a voice in my head was like, *Tell her, dude! Tell her who you are!*

And another voice was like, *No, you idiot! Don't screw it up any more than you already have!*

And a third voice was like,

> hi original boy_2!
> u seem agitated
> what's on your mind?

 ?

# 27.

# ...BOOM!

So that was a failure, but my night wasn't over yet. When I got home, Dad was in the living room, crouched in front of the record player, fiddling with something.

"I could've *sworn* this thing had a needle...." He twisted his head around to look at the space where the needle used to be. "You know anything about this, or am I just going crazy?"

"Who can say?"

Dad looked up at me. His eyes were all narrow. "I have another question."

"Can we talk later? I'm in kind of a bad mood."

"Nah," he said. "I think we should talk now—don't you think, Evie?"

I hadn't noticed her. She'd been standing all statuelike by the kitchen. I noticed her now. Arms folded, glaring at me.

"Evie? What are you doing here?"

"What do you think?" she said.

"Look, if you guys are wondering why I didn't go back to Sacramento, I just wanted to see the play and maybe—"

"That's not what we're wondering, Aaron. We're wondering about this letter from your school."

Dad put his face in front of mine. "What we're wondering is what you've been doing for the last five months."

And I was like, *Oh. Shit.*

And my dad and Evie were like, *This is going to be fun.*

The time had come. The show was over. The curtain had to fall.
What could I do but give them the truth?

I told them about San Francisco, and how I'd reappropriated
the tuition payments (with all intentions of not spending any of it),
how I'd lived in a hivehouse, and how I'd started having FUN®—
and as I listened to myself talk I was actually kind of proud. But
then I got to the part about all the money I'd spent on *Tickle, Tickle
Boom!* (YAY!) and the part about FAIL, and I didn't feel as good
anymore, and Evie and Dad were right there with me. I mean, I
figured they'd be pissed—and they were—but I hadn't realized
just *how* pissed.

Dad did that thing he does where he stomps around the room,
working himself into an anger monkey, and Evie screeched at me
like a hen, the two of them kept roundhousing me with the same
basic point, which was what a deceitful ass I'd been—and it *was*
true, I had been a deceitful ass, and I was angry they'd found out,
and also feeling guilty as hell, like I was gonna start crying or
something, so I excused myself out the front door and took a walk
in the snow to calm down. I called my buddy Oso, but he didn't
answer. Once again, straight to voice mail. I left him a long message about my situation, and then I headed back home.

Dad and Evie were still there. They were still pissed, too.

Dad was like, "We're just so goddamn happy to have funded
your vacation."

"What do you mean 'we'?"

"Half that money came from your sister!"

"What?"

"I chipped in after they cut Dad's hours at work," she said.

"She's been working *extra* hours at the newspaper," he said. "Working her *butt* off so you could lie around and play video games."

I stood there kind of stunned. Taking money from my dad, that was one thing—but taking money from Evie, too?

"Look, I'll pay you both back. With, like, interest or whatever."

My sister just stared and shook her head. "I knew it. I just *knew* something fishy was going on."

"Sure, you did."

"Wow. Just wow, Aaron."

"How about this. How about I go to Grandpa's?"

*"What?"*

As soon as I said it I knew it was the perfect plan. Anything to get away from Dad and Evie. Being around them suddenly made me feel really crappy. "I'll go to his place. I can stay there while I look for the money to pay you back with. Maybe he hid the money somewhere else. Maybe there's another portrait of Mary."

"You need to go back to school."

"Well, I can't. Not to Sacramento, not to Antello High."

"Then you need to take the GED."

"Sure, but in the meantime I'll go out to Grandpa's and find the money."

"Question," said my dad. "How do you propose to get out there?"

"One of you guys can drive me."

"No way my Mazda could make it in that snow."

"What about Evie's CR-V? It's got four-wheel drive. It could make it easy."

"No," said Evie. "I'm not driving you out there. You need to take responsibility for your actions."

"This *is* me taking responsibility. I'm on it. Your car could make it. Tell her it could make it, Dad."

"That isn't the point," he said.

"So basically you guys are trapping me here." I gave it some thought. "Know what? I'll snowshoe."

My sister laughed. "All the way to Grandpa's? That's ridiculous!"

"Says who? I'll go right now."

"In the dark? Are you crazy?"

"Look, I made a mess and now I'm trying to make it right."

I went to my room and returned triumphantly with my grandfather's snowshoes.

"You can't be serious," said Evie.

"Let him go," said Dad. "Let him try to walk ten miles in vintage snowshoes."

I was pretty adamant about getting out of there, but as I was gathering the rest of my supplies, including my broken bag, I realized that maybe they had a point about the whole snowshoe plan.

Ten miles is a pretty long way to snowshoe—especially in the dark, and especially in Grandpa's snowshoes, which were more like clown shoes. I could just see myself tripping over my bag, tumbling down a ravine, breaking my leg, and being eaten alive by coyotes. Dad and Evie would feel so sorry when they heard about that—but not as sorry as I would feel when I was being eaten by the coyotes. I decided to let the snowshoe plan drop. I was going to have to find another way.

The answer came to me later when I was brushing my teeth: What about Katie? She had a truck.

# 28.

## BUNNY_LUVR21

You go to look up a girl's phone number and you end up downloading some porn. It's a tale older than time itself.

I knew her last name from the play: *Ezkiaga*, but when I inputted *Katie Ezkiaga*, and then *Katarin Ezkiaga*, the only numbers I found were these old ladies in Spain.

> u ok original boy_2?
> u seem frustrated!

"I need to find this girl's number."

> ok for sure!
> is there anything i cannot do?

"Give me Katie Ezkiaga's number."

> i already did!

"Those aren't the right ones."

> there aren't any others!

"Fine. Go away, then."

> i know!
> can i show u another girl?

"Nah. Go away."

Homie™ disappeared in a spray of pixels, and it was just me and my thoughts again, but that wasn't any fun, so after a while I was like, "Hey, Homie™!"

> hi!

"Show me another girl."

> u bet original boy_2!
> guess what?
> u have 69 love matches!
> i can show u now!

I scrolled through the profiles, and some of them were kind of cute, but none of them were real, and all of them charged points. So I started searching around until I found one that didn't charge, this hot blond girl with long bangs. Her name was Bunny_luvr21.

"That one there. Open profile."

> warning original boy_2!
> profile is from an unverified
> source!
> r u sure u want to open?

"Yes."

> r u sure, original boy_2?
> bunny_luvr21 has not been verified!

"Open Bunny_luvr21!"

> profile opening . . .

A loading bar appeared, long and blue. Words flickered across in quick succession—

> loading bun_21.vis . . .
> loading bun_21.aud . . .
> loading bun_21.tac . . .

The bar bulged and popped.

> open bunny_luvr21?

warning!

file is from an unverified source!

"Yeah, open it."

Homie™ flickered and disappeared, and another loading bar appeared, and then Bunny_luvr21 popped into view. Not a hot blond girl with long bangs. A rabbit. This shiny white hairless rabbit with big black anime eyes. Its voice was high-pitched and robotic.

> hello sexy original boy_2
> i'm bunny_luvr21 only 99 per min!

"Um. This isn't what I thought it was going to be."

The rabbit bounced up and down.

> lol
> i love when u talk so dirty 2 me
> say yay! and we can start hopping

"Nah. Go away. End program."

> mm can we hop now?
> i want 2 hop so hard
> only 99 per min

"Close Bunny_luvr21. End program."

> lol
> u r so hoppy funny
> i can't end

"End!"

> hop me!

No matter what I tried, I couldn't get it to go away, and I couldn't bring back Homie™, either, so I did an emergency Admin contact and got scolded for contracting an STD and was told to do a hard reboot. I should've known—that's what the Admin always say: *Do a hard reboot.*

You're supposed to lightly touch your fingertips to your eyelids and say the reboot code: *There's no place like home*. But—for me anyway—the self-tactility recognition is pretty terrible, and I practically had to cram my fists into my eyeballs for FUN® to recognize I was touching myself. (Ha.)

"There's no place like home!"

> say yay!

i know you want to hop

so hard

"THERE'S NO PLACE LIKE HOME!"

> oh hop . . .

Bunny_luvr21 flickered and exploded, and everything went black, and after a while in the darkness a familiar face appeared.

> hi original boy_2!

i'm Homie™!

r u

ready

to have

some

FUN®?

:)

 ?

# 29.

## OSO

The next day I successfully avoided my dad and sister (well, they had work) and spent the daylight hours trying to get my shoe back from Bones and brooding over what to do next and executing hard reboots. The stupid Bunny_luvr21 had infected my whole system. Every few hours, Homie™ would flicker and the hairless anime-eyed rabbit would leap into vision and start pestering me some more about hopping.

Evening came. After a tense dinner with Dad and another hard reboot, I finally heard back from Oso.

> unidentified: bro it's oso sorry i can't talk now glad to hear you're in town can u meet me in the ballroom of the king cowboy in an hour? wear a mask if u can don't talk to strangers or reply to this message i'm using a burner tell u about it later

Awesome. It was kind of a confusing message, but I was happy to have an excuse to get out of the house. Just before I left, I tried one more time to retrieve my shoe from Bones. I went to snatch it from her, and she snapped up and bit my hand, and I yelled and dropped the shoe, and she leapt back like I'd hit her. She cowered on the floor.

"Hey," I said. "*Easy.* You're the one who bit me. See?"

Little pinpricks of blood were rising to the surface of my skin. It wasn't bleeding all that much, but it still stung. I washed it off in the sink and wrapped a towel around it, and when I got back to the bedroom, Bones was there, ears flat against her head, all sad and angry at the same time. And she still had my shoe. I decided to let her keep it a little while longer.

I headed to King Cowboy in my dad's mocassins. The snow had melted some during the day, but now it was all an icy slick. I fell down four times. When I finally got to the casino, I saw what Oso meant about wearing a mask. It was a party. Not a Party™, but a *party*, a real party, with real balloons and everything, like some kind of Mardi Gras celebration, everyone dressed in feathers and beads and these glittery masks.

The music was thumping and there was a fog machine going, and I wandered around looking for Oso, and then a big woman in a bird mask grabbed me by the elbow.

"How do you know Tawna!" she shouted.

"I don't know Tawna!"

"You don't know Tawna?!"

"I don't think so!"

"You gotta meet her! That's why we're all here, right? IT'S HER FRICKIN' BIRTHDAY!"

I told her I was looking for my friend, but either the birdwoman didn't hear me or she chose to ignore me. Instead, she dragged me through the fog in search of Tawna. But Tawna was not going to be found. Not that night. From what I could gather, Tawna had run out the back door with a guy named Maury, or maybe it was Clarence. Terrence? Opinion seemed split fifty-fifty as to whether this was a good idea, seeing as it was in clear violation of her parole—and then in the other corner you had True Love.

Eventually I peeled away from birdwoman to continue my search for Oso, and just about the time I was getting ready to give up, this dude in a bear mask put his hands on my shoulders.

"Oso!"

"Hey, bro!" He wrapped me in a big bear hug. "Anyone know you're here?"

"Just you and some woman in a bird mask. She wanted to introduce me to Tawna."

"You saw Tawna? Where is she? I been looking everywhere for her."

"I don't think she's here. I heard she left with some guy."

"What?" Oso whipped off the mask. Dark eyebrows all bunched together.

"She went out the back with some dude."

"Lawrence? Was it LAWRENCE?!"

"Maybe?"

"Come on!"

YAY! for Oso Sandoval, whose real name is Angel—*Angelo*, actually—and who is known among friends as El Oso, the bear, on account of how big he is. But being big isn't what makes Oso cool. It's his creative mind, positive energy, and mad art skills, which

I'm sure would easily give him star status at any one of the more than 150 Art Academies™ of America, whose unique programs and flexible learning options make it the first choice for aspiring creative professionals. (YAY!)

Here's just one example:

When we were in fourth grade, our teacher handed out these worksheets with a picture of a glass of water on it. And next to the top half of the glass it said *50% Air*, and next to the bottom half it said *50% Water*, and on the bottom it said, *Technically, the glass is full.* And what we were supposed to do was color in the water. That was the entire assignment. Maybe we were learning fractions or something. Mrs. Carlyle was nice, but she was a pretty crappy teacher.

Anyway, while the rest of us fought over blue markers like a bunch of monkeys, Oso crossed out the word *full* and wrote *imaginary.* Then, where the water was, he drew a dragon in scuba gear eating its own tail and blew everyone's mind. The guy has talent.

I followed him through the crowd, down a hallway, and out the back door. We ran up and down the alley looking for Tawna. But Tawna was gone.

"Well, she wasn't the one I really needed to talk to anyway," said Oso. "It was that sonofabitch Lawrence. They're probably halfway to Reno by now."

"Who's Lawrence?"

"A shape-shifting son of a bitch."

"What?"

"An evil spirit in human clothing, bro. He stole my pills. Swapped them out for duds. Now I'm wanted by a Mexican biker gang. I'll tell you about it later. You wanna see my new truck?"

I followed him down the alley to where his truck was parked. It wasn't just any truck. It was like this giant almost-monster truck with skulls painted all over it.

"That's yours?"

"Not bad, right? Dude I know gave it a twelve-inch lift. Then this OTHER dude, he works at a body shop out by Walmart, he let me use his airbrush. I was gonna put another creeper on the hood, but I didn't have the time. Whaddya think?" He ran his hand lovingly along the hood of the truck. "Feel how *smooth* that gloss is. I buffed that shit with a *diaper*."

It was pretty nice all right. Oso had done it up in blue and white with his signature creeper skulls, which had evolved since the last time I'd seen them. They were even creeper-ier now.

Oso grabbed my wrist. "What happened there? You get bit?"

So I told him about Bones and my shoe. Oso nodded. "That's awesome. Know what the Apache say?"

"The Apache?"

"The tradition is, in order to become a medicine man, you have to be attacked by a snake, an eagle, or a mountain lion!"

"...And?"

"And you got attacked!"

"By a dog!"

"Hey, it's the modern world, bro! We do with what we have. Snake, eagle, dog—it don't matter. That right there." He pointed to the tiny bite marks. "That right there is a *sign*, bro. Big changes are coming your way. Mark my words."

# 30.

# INFINITE WEIGHT

We climbed into Oso's big truck and started down the road.

"You were saying something about a Mexican biker gang?"

Oso glanced in the rearview mirror. "Right. Los Ojos de Dios. The Eyes of God, bro. They want to find me and hit me with a big stick. They may be following us now. Who can say?"

I twisted around to look behind us. No one back there as far as I could see. Unless they weren't using their headlights. It also occurred to me that we were not riding in the world's most inconspicuous vehicle, a lifted Chevy with skulls painted all over it.

"What happened?"

"I got scammed, bro. The old switcheroo. I was slinging some stuff on the side for Los Ojos, just to make a little money, then they said they were getting a kilo of VPHPs. I didn't have the money for that, but I had a buyer—Tawna—and so they loaned me the money. But then Tawna wanted to have Lawrence test the VPHPs for potency, so I stupidly let her have all of them for a night—that was my mistake and I will admit to it—and when I got the

VPHPs back, they were no longer VPHPs. They were aspirin! And whaddya know? Tawna no longer had the money to buy them."

"Dang."

"Dang is right! Now Los Ojos de Dios say the money is due. There's really only three of them—three brothers—but you do not want to be late with their payments. It's part of the whole biker gang thing. But it doesn't end there!"

"No?"

"Nuh-uh! My aunt, she works at the police station, and she said someone called the anonymous hotline and said I was slinging VPHPs for Los Ojos. So now I'm a person of suspect."

"What are VPHPs?"

"Very Powerful Hallucinogenic Pills, bro. Tawna swears she didn't switch them out, but I know they got switched. It was Lawrence! I knew he was of the darkness the first time I laid eyes on him. But my real issue is the bikers."

Wow. Oso had really stepped in some shit. But maybe I could help him.

"Hey! I know what we can do. You've got a truck—let's go to my grandfather's. I think there's money there. I can give you some to pay off the bikers."

Oso waved my words away. "No worries, bro. I don't need your treasure. I'm gonna be fine. Los Ojos de Dios got nothing on me. I'm El Oso de Dios. I can outsneak and outlast them. On the other hand, I'm always down for a treasure hunt." He turned us left toward the edge of town. "Let's see what we can dig up."

At first the road was fine, but then we got to the part where they'd stopped plowing, and there were just these two tracks going off into the snow, and Oso's truck began to fishtail. He stopped the truck and shifted the short stick.

"Four-wheel drive, bro."

There was a grinding sound. Something was stuck. Oso grinded it some more.

"Huh. Never made that sound before."

"What is it?"

"I think it's the four-wheel drive, bro."

It was true. Something was stuck or broken or I don't know, but Oso couldn't get it to work. He put the truck back in two-wheel and stomped on the gas and we swerved in a wide arc and slid off into a snowbank. Thunk.

"No worries, bro."

He slammed it in reverse. The wheels spun, and the truck rocked up and down.

"OK, hold on," said Oso. "We need some weight in the back to get traction. You wanna be the weight?"

I climbed into the back and he showed me where to kneel. "Yeah, right over the axle just like that. Here's what I want you to do, bro. I want you to take a deep breath and summon all the matter in the universe across all space and time within yourself. Just take it all in. Got it?"

"All the matter in the universe?"

"Suck it all in like you're a giant black hole, bro. Yeah, like that. You are now infinitely heavy. BELIEVE IT. Here we go...."

Oso got back in the truck. The wheels spun and the engine whined. The body rocked back and forth. I knelt in the back, in the cold, trying to imagine myself as a black hole, just sucking everything all around me, the very light itself. And it was strange, because the longer I was out there, the more I actually began to feel lighter, like I was actually *losing* weight, like I'd been enrolled in the WeightWatchers® Infinity Loss™ weight loss program (YAY!)

or whatever, which isn't a diet exactly but rather a healthy way to live.

The wheels stopped and Oso's face appeared out the window. "Got good news and bad news, bro. We're gonna have to dig."

"What's the good news?"

"That *is* the good news: I know how to get us unstuck. The bad news is I don't have any shovels."

So instead of digging for treasure, we dug out Oso's truck with our hands. In the freezing cold. For an hour. I didn't really mind. It was just good to be doing *something*, if that makes sense. I kept looking off into the distance. Way out there, out in the blackness somewhere, was my grandpa's house. *My* house. Huh. With money or treasure or—who knows? Just sitting out there. Just out of reach. Just waiting.

 ?

# 31.

## LOOT

We gave up on the truck idea, and I got home late and slept in late the next day, successfully avoiding my dad, and then in the afternoon I worked up the nerve to go ask Katie about her truck. The sun was out, the snow melting, everything glittery and full of promise.

But when I got to Katie's apartment no one was there. Well, duh: it was two o'clock in the afternoon. She was still at work. There was only one elementary school in town—good old Antello Primary—and it was only a couple blocks from her apartment, so that's where I went next.

It was weird to be in my old elementary school again, although not much had changed. It still looked the same and sounded the same, and the smell took me right back to being a kid again: glue, disinfectant, and the faint lingering odor of puke. I checked in at the front office and got a visitor's badge and a complimentary ChocoLoot™ chocolate coin (YAY!), but I forgot to ask where Katie's room was.

There were these three boys loitering in the hallway, so I stopped to ask them.

"You guys know where Katie—where Miss Ezkiaga's room is?"

The boys were dressed up in animal costumes. Two of them were birds, with paper beaks on their faces and felt feathers around their necks and under their arms, and the third kid had on these fake elf ears.

"Miss Ezkiaga?" I said again. "Youngish blondish woman with real pretty eyes? Whoever can tell me where her room is gets this chocolate coin."

"Chocolate coins are gross," said the first bird.

"They make you barf," said the second bird.

"I ate one once," said the elf, "and it made me barf gold."

"So 'no' on the coin, then. Do you know where her room is?"

The first bird raised his beak. "Are you Miss E.'s boyfriend?"

"Not really...not yet...I'm working on it."

"Did you kiss her?" said the second bird.

"Did you touch her *boobies*?" said the elf.

"Boobies? Look, I'm not really comfortable having this conversation with you. I just need to know where her room is."

"Miss E. doesn't have a room," said the first bird.

"Miss E. has a *portable*," said the second bird.

"Her class is out back where the *portables* are," said the elf.

"Great. Thank you. Anyone want this coin?"

But none of them did, so I slipped it back in my pocket and headed out to the portable classrooms. There were four of them where the tetherball courts used to be. I found the one that said MISS DERADO & MISS EZKIAGA and stood by the door and listened in.

"Take a little time," Katie was saying, "and think about Dress As Your Favorite Animal Day, and everything you learned about animals and each other, and how important it is to respect everyone's personal space bubble and—"

A bell began to ring and I couldn't make out the rest. After the ringing stopped there was a brief moment of silence like someone drawing in a breath, and then all around me kids began to pour out of the portables. They swarmed the scene, a waist-high tide of children dressed in animal costumes, and when there was a break in the swell, I ducked into the trailer.

I must not have made much noise, because when she turned and saw me she jumped a little.

"Jesus! You scared me."

Once again, not quite the reaction I was going for.

She tugged the hem of her T-shirt down around her hips. It was pink, with a picture of an otter on the front.

"Hi! I was just in the neighborhood and thought I'd drop by.... Here. I brought you something."

I handed her the chocolate coin. She looked at it for a second, then dropped it in a bowl of identical chocolate coins on her desk. Then she aimed her blue eyes at me like, *What are you doing here?* I started telling her how I felt weird about how we'd left things.

"Look, I know you said things were complicated, and that's cool. But I wanted to ask you something."

"Arnold." She sighed. "You're nice and all, but... it's the Space Amazon, OK? The rule is: no new planets until the old planets are out of sight."

"Is that your rule or the Space Amazon's rule?"

"Both."

"But rules are meant to be bent, aren't they? Like, take Dress As Your Favorite Animal Day. I saw a kid back there dressed like an *elf*. Or take you, for example. *Technically* you're not dressed as a favorite animal—you're just wearing a shirt with a picture of an otter on it."

*"Sea lion,"* she said. "And there's a big difference between Dress As Your Favorite Animal Day and my personal life."

"Yeah," I said. "But what if it wasn't personal?"

"What?"

"What if it was purely business?"

I told her about the will, the treasure, and the snowy road. How I needed a ride. How she had a truck.

Katie bent to scrub a glue smear from the table. It was like she was working through that same old question. "And when do you need this ride?"

"The sooner the better. I was thinking tonight."

"I've got P.T.A. tonight."

"Tomorrow, then."

"I have to get my journal grading done on Wednesdays."

"Thursday."

"You're very persistent."

"Or Friday?"

"Friday is Pilates."

"All night?"

"No, not all night."

"Look—it's not a date or anything. I swear. I just need a ride. Send me on another quest. Tell me to get you something. A knife that needs no sharpening. A drink that has no calories."

"You mean like water."

"Sure. I'll do anything."

Katie scrubbed at the table, and I could see her working through that question, whatever it was.

"Fine," she said at last. "I should be done with P.T.A. by seven. Meet me at my place at seven thirty and I'll give you a ride."

 ?

# 32.

## ZAZZ® II

On my way to Katie's that night, Homie™ popped up and was like,

> warning!
>
> u r not having FUN®!

Which, no duh. I was in FAIL. I told Homie™ to go away, and it did, but then it popped back up again.

> warning!
>
> u r not having FUN®!
>
> warning!

And I couldn't get it to shut up, so I took a five-minute Irish Heritage™ Dairy Quiz, which actually took twenty minutes on account of how I kept missing the number of nutritional benefits a heritage cow gets while grazing on pure ancestral Irish pastureland. (It's more than you'd think.)

> warning!
>
> u r not now having FUN®!

I tried to YAY! some stuff, but Homie™ said I'd already used up all my YAY!s. I couldn't YAY! again for another eight hours. I tried to take a quiz, but I was out of quizzes, too.

```
>   warning!
    u are not now having FUN®!
```
"What can I do for FUN®?"
```
>   eat a zazz® bar!
```
"I don't have a Zazz® bar."
```
>   buy a zazz® bar!
```
"Homie™, I'm broke."
```
>   u have enough for a zazz® bar!
```
"Go away, please?"
```
>   ok
    :)
```
Homie™ disappeared/popped back up again.
```
>   warning!
    u r not having FUN®!
```
So I looked up the nearest place I could buy a Zazz® bar ... and that's how Katie and I ended up at the GameCage® Gaming Center in the old strip mall on the edge of town.

The Zazz® bars were behind a little glass case with other candies and plastic trinkets—glow-in-the-dark dinosaurs and parachute men and mood rings—and they weren't for sale. The dude behind the counter said you had to win them with tickets from playing the games, and to play the games I had to purchase tokens.

"I can't just buy one?"

"Sorry. It wouldn't be fair."

I turned to Katie. "You mind if we win some tickets real fast?"

She looked at me. "You planned this, didn't you?"

"What?"

"You planned to come here and play these games. Is this like a date?"

"No, no—I didn't—I swear—"

But then from the expression in her eyes... It's kind of hard to explain, but I wondered if she was actually kind of maybe hoping it *was* a date. Like maybe she was warming up to me.

So I bought some tokens and we headed into the game room.

The guy had said Skee-Ball was our best bet, but on our way to the Skee-Ball games I got distracted. The low ceiling and tile floor created an echo chamber, reiterating and amplifying the jangly electronic soundscape. There was this one video game, *BattleBorn II* (YAY!), the very same one I used to play after school at Oso's house when we were in grade school.

"Wow! I haven't played this one in forever. Want to give it a shot?"

"I don't know," said Katie. "You can't earn tickets from it. And I'm not really into fighting games. I can never figure out the moves."

"Well, then you haven't played *BattleBorn II*! Come on. Just one game. It's not complicated at all. I'll show you what to do." I dropped a couple tokens into the slot. "Here, hit that button. Now choose your character."

Katie scrolled slowly through the faces as if scrutinizing them not for fighting ability but moral character, and when the timer ran out she was resting on Xoti the Deer Sorceress—actually not a bad choice. I'd selected Long Mop, mainly for his grappling technique, which is always fun to try out on a beginner. The arena was a Shinto temple set on a precipitous mountain ledge, and as our characters stood there glaring at each other across the mist, I explained the basic controls—high kick, low kick, jab, uppercut, jump, duck—and gave her a moment to practice.

"Ready? Watch out! Here I come!"

I double-punched Xoti in the face, snapping her head back and sending a spray of blood over the mountain ledge. Then, while the stars circled above her head, I kicked her in the shin, grabbed her horns, and threw her to the ground.

"You need to block. I forgot to mention that. Here, hold back on the joystick. Right, like that. But if I crouch I can still hit you—see? So if I do that, then you have to crouch *and* block. But when you're in a defensive crouch, I can then stand up and bop you on top of the head...like *this*. To avoid that, option one is jump over me...but if you *do* jump, then I can snatch you out of the air for a body slam, see..."

"You said this wasn't complicated!"

"It's not! Hold *back* on the stick. *Back*."

PUNCH!

"See, you have to block that."

It's not polite to just beat the crap out of a total noob, but the adrenaline was flowing in my veins, and even with Homie™ popping up in my face to warn me I wasn't having any FUN®, I was actually kicking straight-up ass, all the moves coming back to me like I was 10 again: Thunder stomp! Fire flash! Century fist!

"Check this out. If I remember right, there's this move where I grab you by the horns and just start *wailing*..."

Xoti crumpled to the bamboo floor, energy meter depleted, and I walked up and kicked her over the ledge. She fell screaming into the river below and was skeletonized by a passing school of piranhas.

"That's a secret that you can do that. It only works in the Shinto temple."

"Yay. What a blast. Getting murdered by proxy."

So her turn was over, and the next opponent was Psychonaut, and because it was the first computer opponent, the AI was turned down low and it was no big task to bring him down—and yet I don't need to explain the joy in beating an opponent before an admiring audience—and as I rammed his head into the floor of the murky dungeon, I wondered if this was how the Knights of Yore felt as they fought in their tournaments: crowds cheering their violence, whipped into a frenzy. And on a raised dais a maiden stands waving her kerchief. . . . But as I finished him off with a final eye gouge and turned from the console in triumph, I saw that Katie was no longer standing beside me.

I found her at the Skee-Ball machines, munching on some popcorn.

"You missed some real action back there."

"I got hungry." She aimed the bag in my direction. "Popcorn? By the way, I'm going to kick your *ass* at Skee-Ball."

She wasn't kidding. Truth is I'd never played Skee-Ball before—just never had the desire. It's a pretty simple concept, the objective being to send a ball up a wooden ramp and jump it into one of several holes labeled with different point values. You take one object and hurl it toward another object and hope for the best. No special combos, no zooming camera angles, no instant replays—you don't even get to kill or maim anyone.

Which maybe explains why I sucked at it so bad. It's difficult to say what I was doing wrong, exactly—or maybe it was just that I was doing *everything* wrong—but anyway, every approach seemed worse than the last. First I rolled the balls too hard, bouncing them off the backstop and sending them cascading down the tiers into the gutter, then too soft, dropping them off the lip of the ramp and out of sight. Katie was no expert, either, but going off of point totals, she was easily twice as good as me.

And whereas during *Battleborn II* I had been careful of her feelings, she had no problem giving me her honest assessment of my performance.

"You're terrible at this."

Another ball bounced into the gutter.

"*Aim.* You have to *aim*, Arnold."

By the time we were done we had enough tickets to purchase two Zazz® bars with a little left over, and I told Katie she should get something for herself, and without hesitating she picked out a little silver mood ring.

"Thanks! I always wanted one of these. Now I can always tell how I'm feeling."

I ate my Zazz® bar and Homie™ shut up, and we got back into Katie's truck. The evening was actually turning out pretty nice. Almost like a date or something.

"Look at that," she said.

"What?"

Katie held up her hand. "The ring. It was green—but now it's yellow."

"What's that mean?"

"I don't know," she said. "It didn't come with a chart."

 ?

# 33.

## DARKSIGHT®

It was snowing again—not hard, just lazy: these big, fat feathery flakes touching down on the windshield of Katie's truck. We were near the edge of town, almost to the road to my grandpa's, when I remembered something. My toothbrush—I'd forgotten to grab it out of the bathroom.

"Can we go back and get it?"

"Back to your uncle's?" The truck slowed to a stop. "Arnold..."

"Look. I'll be so fast. It'll just be a second."

Katie started to say something and then she stopped herself. She turned the truck around and drove us back to my dad's house.

"I'll just wait here if you don't mind."

And now I'd like to mention a problem I have with FUN®, which is this: night vision. In that there isn't any. I don't know what it is about the lenses, but you can hardly see in the dark. So often you find yourself standing there in a blurry haze wishing you had a pair of DarkSight® Night Vision Goggles with duel-spectrum infrared illumination and adjustable comfort straps (YAY!). I'll also admit that, yeah, my dad had a point about shoveling the driveway.

Here's what happened: as I was heading up the driveway, I slipped on a patch of ice.

It happened fast: one second I was walking, the next—WHAM!—I was on my back looking up at the sky. I lay there watching the snow falling from the darkness above. I sat up and dusted off my arms, but as I was going to get up, something stopped me. My left ankle. The weak one. The same one I broke when I jumped off the garage roof. It kind of hurt.

"Are you OK?"

Katie was standing over me. She knelt and felt my ankle. I could put a little pressure on it, but not much. And it was too much. Not the pain, but Katie. The way she was touching my ankle. The way she was looking at me. My hands were beginning to twitch, and then my whole body was, and I could feel it coming: a full-on TSD glitch-out.

My vision blacked out, then flickered back on.

A car was pulling into the drive.

Katie's face was right in front of mine. Her lips were open.

Black again.

Then back on again.

She was right there. Illuminated in the headlights of the car.

"Arnold?" she said.

"Yeah?"

"Arnold, there's something I need to tell you."

And then everything went black again.

# 34.

# EVIL, HAIRLESS RABBIT OF TRUTH

I came out of the glitch-out to the sound of a strange, high-pitched voice.

> ```
> hello stud
> would u like to hop with me?
> only 99 per min
> ```

Then Katie's voice:

"Arnold? Are you OK? You had a seizure or something."

> ```
> mm we can hop so much
>    in so many different ways
> ```

"Yeah, I'm fine. TSD. Hold on. I gotta do a hard reboot."

But then I saw that she wasn't alone. My dad was standing there next to her.

"What's going on?" he said. "What are you doing here, Katarin?"

And Katie was like, "Arnold fell and had some kind of seizure. I was making sure he was OK."

And my dad was like, *"Arnold?"*

And Katie was like, "He was only out for a second."

And I was like, "It's no big deal. Just a TSD glitch-out. Just a little more than usual but nothing—"

> yay! now for bunny_luvr21

"It's nothing big. Hold on." I jammed my fists into my eyes. "There's no place like home!"

And my dad was like, "Who the hell is Arnold?"

And Katie was like, "*Him.* Your nephew."

And the bunny_luvr21 was like,

> oh please hop me

"THERE'S NO PLACE LIKE HOME!"

With a *pop!* the rabbit disappeared, and it was just Dad and Katie, and they were both looking at each other strangely.

"Aaron is my *son*, Katarin. His name is *Aaron*. He's seventeen! He's in *high school!*"

Katie spun to face me. "What?! Is this true? But *why?*"

I was too stunned to think of anything but the truth.

"Because I wanted you to like me."

"So, wait a second," said my dad. "You two know each other?"

"Yes!" I said. "Duh! Of course!"

The cat was out of the bag—or more like the rabbit. The evil, hairless rabbit of truth.

But that wasn't all. What I hadn't realized was that there was *another* rabbit—or, I don't know, maybe there was another bag. But anyway, there was more to it. Because why should he care whether we knew each other? And why did he keep calling her *Katarin*, so formally?

I'm sure genius is a burden, but what about those of us with only slightly above-average intelligence? So often you find yourself in these situations where you're smart enough to realize something's going on and yet you're too dumb to figure out what it is.

But I was beginning to figure it out.

As I looked up at them looking down on me, I remembered something—the thing that Katie had said to me right before I glitched out. *There's something I need to tell you.* Clues cascaded through my brain.

The play.

"Complicated," she'd said.

*The undies on the record player.*

Their shared love of Sparkl*Juice™ and gin.

Oh, wow. Oh, *shit.* Oh, YAY! for the stab of truth, the way it scratches with a flurry of claws, the way it bites with bunny teeth, the way it lays waste to everything you ever thought you knew.

 ?

# 35.

## ROMEO AND JULIET

But how? When? Where? *Why?*

For God's sake, *Why?*

I had a lot of questions, but I didn't get a chance to throw any of them at Katie. She was getting into her truck now. She was slamming the door and cranking the ignition.

"Wait! Holy shit, just hold on a sec!"

But the windows were up and the engine was going and she didn't hear me—or anyway she didn't answer me—and then she was driving away.

So then it was just me and my dad.

No one said anything, not at first, because where do you even start? Suddenly all I could think about was that pair of undies I'd found, the ones with the see-through crotch. How exactly did they end up on the record player? What sordid scene unfolded before that? It was too much to think about. I had to get it out of my mind. I had to leave. But I couldn't leave until I knew.

"What happened between you two?"

"Between *us*?" he said. "How about *you*? How do you even know her? Why was she calling you *Arnold*?"

"She thought that's what my name was."

"So you lied to her just like you lied to me and Evie."

"What happened between you two?"

"None of your business."

Ever wonder if you could take your dad in a fight? Me too. All the time. Usually the answer is no—but this time I was just angry enough to give it a shot and see what happened. Definitely I could get in one good hit before he knew what was going on—the element of surprise. The question was, how hard would he come back at me?

"Just tell me!"

Finally Dad gave a shrug. "We were in a play together last spring. *Romeo and Juliet*."

YAY! for the play and the movie and the pizza franchise—but not really. *Romeo and Juliet*?

"What happened?"

"I guess you could say there were some sparks."

"Sparks? What's that mean? You're like twice her age!"

"And you're half!"

"Not even!"

Dad laughed. Suddenly everything was funny to him. "Know what? It's over between me and her anyway. You have my permission to see her."

"Permission?! I don't need your *permission*!"

He stood there smirking.

"I don't need your *permission*!"

Sometimes when I'm mad I can't think of anything to do but repeat the same stuff over and over.

"I don't need your *permission!*"

"OK, I get it! You don't need my permission. Fine. All I'm saying is she's old news to me anyway, and it's too freakin' cold to argue out here. Can you walk on that ankle, or do you need help?"

No, I didn't need help. I wasn't going in his house anyway. I was going to Evie's.

 ?

# 36.

# PRIDE ≠ COURAGE

On my way over to Evie's I had some time to think. One thing became clear: mad as I was, it was probably best not to tell my sister. She didn't need to know about the whole weird love triangle—things were screwed up enough already without adding her expert testimony.

My sister answered the door in her jammies.

"It's time," I said.

"Time for what?"

"Time for Grandpa's. I need a ride."

"I already told you, I'm not giving you a ride."

"Come on, Evie! Help me out, here."

"Are you OK? You seem...agitated."

"I'm fine!"

Evie gave me a look. "What time is it, anyway?"

"I already told you—time to go to Grandpa's."

"It's late, Aaron. I've got work in the morning. Do you need a place to sleep? You can have the couch if you want. But I'm not giving you a ride."

So I crashed there and spent the next morning begging my sister for a ride, but she wasn't having it. She had work to do. I tagged along while she chased down a lead on some story about the spring motorcycle jamboree, but all I could think about was Katie and Dad and how weirded-out angry I was. Even if she'd thought he was my uncle, she could've told me *something*. Just given me a hint. Just to soften the blow.

Late in the afternoon, after all the reporting was done, Evie gave in.

"Fine! I can't stand the moping any longer. I'll give you a ride, but first you need supplies—food and warm clothes and toilet paper—and if the road is even a *little* bit sketchy, we're turning right around. Got it?"

The first problem was I didn't have my bag. Katie had it. It was sitting in her truck when she peeled away from Dad's. Without explaining, I borrowed a sweatshirt and some long underwear from Sam, then we got some food and headed out.

It had been a warm day and the road was clear—dry in places, even—but even so Evie still went at a crawl, and nearly turned around twice, and by the time we got to Grandpa's it was dark and starting to snow again. And as we pulled into his drive, I had to wonder: Was nighttime really the best time to be breaking into my grandpa's house?

In all her worries about supplies, Evie hadn't thought about bringing a flashlight, and I hadn't either, so I had her put on the brights and wait while I checked it out. There were a couple chairs on the porch, and an old charcoal grill. The door was unlocked, and I pushed it open and set my grocery bags down. The light from Evie's car spilled into the living room, and I could see the outlines of furniture: his reading chair, the floor lamp, a table. I reached in and felt around the door for a switch, but when I flipped it, nothing happened.

Back at the car, I explained the situation to Evie.

"Power's out. How about you drive me back in the morning before work?"

"What, so you're afraid of the *dark* now?"

I knew her tactic—the appeal to my manhood—but unfortunately pride does not equal courage in the same way that, say, cleaning a dirty grill with a balled-up wad of tinfoil does not equal the ease and satisfaction of watching a KitchenTech® Advanced Grill-Cleaning Robot (YAY!) do the job for you.

I stood for a long time deciding what to do next.

"Fine. Leave the lights on while I see if there's a flashlight."

Back at the doorway, I paused for a moment to look at my shadow on the far wall. Then I stepped inside, and the shadow took a step nearer to me, drawing closer as I headed toward the kitchen, growing smaller and smaller until as I rounded the corner it disappeared.

It was quiet in the kitchen, and there was a chill to it—or maybe I was just imagining things. There was a smell, too—there was definitely a smell. Stale cigarette smoke and just...staleness. I tried another light switch. It didn't work, either. I stood there, listening to the sound of my own breathing, wondering what to do next:

> what up original boy_2!

u r a FAIL!

u seem a maybe little tense?

"Go away!"

Feeling along the countertop, I edged my way around the kitchen until I got to the drawers by the sink. They were empty.

*All* the drawers were empty. I crept back out into the living room and down the hallway. There were two doors at the end of it—one open and the other closed. I opened the closed door and peered at the darkness inside the spare bedroom. I could just barely make out the outline of the bed in the corner.

I went back to the car.

"Keep the lights on. Give me a couple minutes so I can see my way into the bedroom. Then you can go."

Evie looked up from her comfy seat. She had the heater on and was warming her hands. "You sure you're going to be OK in there?"

"What—so suddenly you care? I'll be fine."

"Check in with me tomorrow morning, OK?"

"If I make it through the night."

"Now you're just being dramatic."

I headed back to the house. The handle was jammed on the door, and I'd barely stepped inside when I heard the tires crunch on gravel. As Evie backed away, the last of the light receded like water down a drain, and I was plunged into darkness.

My whole body tingled, and my eyes were doing swirlies from straining to see into the darkness—and it's strange, but it was like the darkness was looking back at me, like the eye of that bird all those years ago. I just stood there. I could hear myself breathing. I stopped breathing and just listened. The darkness listened back. But there was no one there but me.

 ?

# 37.

## MORNINGSUN™

It was a long, cold night. There were barely any covers on the guest bed, and I kept shivering myself awake, and then I had to pee, but there was no way I was getting out of bed until I had a little light on my side.

When I did sleep, I had dreams. More like nightmares. First it was my dad and Katie, the two of them mashing their faces together on a velvet couch while I pounded on a bulletproof window. Then the window shattered and I found myself standing alone in a big field. It went on forever, just this gigantic field lit up under the stars with the silhouette of a tree at the far end, this big tree standing out there alone in the brush.

I started walking toward the tree, but then I remembered how bad I had to pee. I paused under the stars to unzip my fly, but just as I was getting ready to go I felt something brush against my ankle. I looked down to find a hand—a *bloody* hand—reaching up from out of the ground like some kind of monster in a horror movie, just ready to grab my tender ankle and pull me down into the netherworld and eat me alive and—

> happy morning original boy_2!
  welcome to another day!
  yay! for morningsun™ muffins?
"Yay."

The darkness was gone. I unballed my fists and took a breath. I really had to pee.

The water in the toilet bowl was frozen, but I didn't realize this until after I started to go. My pee hissed on the ice, little tendrils of pee steam wafting into the air. But when I tried the sink, it worked, so that was good. At least I had water. There was a single green bar of soap, and as I was holding it I saw something outlined on the face of it—a small, intricate coil: my grandpa's fingerprint. I rubbed my hands across the bar. The fingerprint disappeared.

I threw open the curtains in the living room, and the light poured in on the floating dust. Even in the light of day it was strange and kind of creepy being in my grandpa's house. Not much had changed since my last visit all those years ago. The green couch, the brown recliner, the corduroy ottoman, the chipped coffee table—it was all still there. But it was different. Without my grandfather, it was just—it's hard to explain. It was just a place.

And it occurred to me—*Aaron, dude, this place is yours.*

And yet as I stood there in the middle of the living room I knew it wasn't true. This was *not* my house, it was Grandpa's house. Even if he wasn't here, even if it was just a place now, even so—it was all still his. This was *his* living room. *His* recliner. *His* reading lamp *his* table *his* television *his* woodstove *his* green coffee mug sitting on a table.

And there was the place where his cabinet had stood, the one Evie jacked. And there against the wall, next to the space, was his bookcase—his crosswords, Sudoku, word jumbles. I took a book out and flipped through the pages, looking at the answers filled out in his neat block print. *His* handwriting. Somewhere, in one of these books, he'd penciled in his last answer.

Puzzles. *Right.* I reminded myself why I was there: to find the portrait of Mary. If there was one. In the living room there were three things hanging on the wall—a washed-out brown painting of deer in a field, a smaller painting of a steamship on a stormy ocean, and a Northern Nevada Auto Parts calendar turned to December.

So I moved on to the kitchen.

No portraits of Mary there, either, but here's the strange thing: the kitchen was practically empty. In the sink I found a plate, a knife, a fork, and a spoon—but beyond that, there wasn't hardly *any*thing. The cupboards were completely bare, no silverware in the drawers, not even a toaster on the counter. Where had it all gone? Even the fridge was empty. I stacked my food on the empty racks, and then I went outside.

The property was all glittery—morning sun melting the last of the snow on acres of sagebrush—but the house itself wasn't much to look at. A squat brown box, dirty windows, black chimney pipe poking up from the roof. Peeling paint, crooked door, sagging porch—one of the carved wooden posts had been replaced by a 2 × 4. OK. Even if it wasn't much, it was something. A little outpost in the brush. Things had happened here. My grandma had grown tomatoes. My grandfather had raged at the world.

Out by the shed sat his blue Ford Ranger. There in the distance was his tree, the single Russian olive, bare branches holding up snow. In the other direction, up the valley, I could see another, newer house with a corral and two horses, one white and one black, and beyond this stood the remnants of Coyote Heights—the luxury golf course development he'd sold his property to, the one that had failed after the restructuring. The source of the money I had yet to find.

It was a pretty crazy sight. Like something out of an apocalypse. Houses half-finished. A road that went nowhere. The luxury hotel, tall and square, standing alone in the snow, windows boarded up, Tyvekked walls rippling in the wind.

# 38.

# VINTAGESHACK™

There was one room left to check out. I'd been avoiding it, but I couldn't any longer. His bedroom. My whole life, I'd been in his bedroom maybe once. The floor creaked as I made my way to the window and opened the shades. The bed was neatly made. The clock on the bedside table was dead. There was a chair, a dresser, and a desk with a typewriter on it. His typewriter. The one with the messed-up *D* key where he'd hammered out his final will and testament.

> u like that original boy_2?
> want to see more like it?
> yay! for vintageshack™ decorative
> housewares!

"Yay."

I checked his closet. It was weird. The pale, short-sleeved cowboy-style shirts he used to wear—they smelled like him. The whole closet did: a mix of leather and smoke and old man. I made a quick search—no Mary—then returned to the living room and thought about my next move.

Maybe I'd take a shower.

A quick, hot shower to help me think.

But as the first icy blast hit me—and as I shrieked and jumped out onto the linoleum, and in the moment of clarity that accompanies a shock of cold water—a few things were suddenly very clear. First of all, you gotta have hot water. Second of all, water heaters need power to run. Third, there was one more place I hadn't checked.

The basement. I hadn't checked the basement. But then I remembered the basement was where he'd shot himself, and I wasn't about to check it without light, plus now I was freezing, so I called the power company to get the power turned back on, but the lady had no record of the address on file. I argued with her for a while that this couldn't be true because I had been to his place when there was electricity, and although this was decades ago I was pretty sure he'd lived out the rest of his life with power—and the house had the outlets and light switches to prove it.

"I'm sorry," said the lady. "You're not on file."

I called Evie, but she didn't know the answer. She told me to call Dad. I told her I didn't want to call Dad. She asked me why not, and I said because I was mad at him.

"What happened?"

"Nothing. I don't want to go into it."

"You two need to learn to get along."

"Thanks for the advice. Hold on, I'm writing it down."

"I'm serious," she said.

"Me too. I *seriously* want some power and light, or I *seriously* want a ride back into town."

"I told you. Call Dad."

 ?

# 39.

# FLASHLIGHT

So I called Dad.

"The power's out. I called the power company and they said they don't have a record of this place. I called Evie and she said to call you."

"You sound upset," he said. "Is this about the Katie thing?"

"No. It's about power and light. I want the power back on. No one told me there wouldn't be any power. Do you or do you not know what the solution to this problem might be?"

"Sure," he said. "It's easy."

"What is it?"

"Your grandpa wasn't on the grid. He used a generator. My guess would be that's where your problem is."

"Where's the generator?"

"In the basement."

"The basement?"

"Yeah. Go down there and I'll walk you through the trouble-shooting."

But that was the whole problem. I couldn't go down to the basement until I had some *light*. That was the whole point.

"So get a flashlight," he said.

"There isn't a flashlight. I just searched the entire house."

"Nah, I know where you can find one."

"Where?"

"The basement. There's one on the fuse box. I left it there after they took his body out."

Ugh. I opened the storm door and headed down the concrete steps, feeling along the cold walls until I came to where the fuse box was supposed to be.

"It isn't here. There's no fuse box."

"Yeah, there is. Don't you see it?"

"I don't see *shit*, Dad! Remember? It's dark down here."

"It's right there on the eastern wall . . . maybe ten feet from the door? About chest level? It seems highly unlikely to me that an entire fuse box would just disappear."

Finally I found it. And YAY! for the flashlight on top, its thin, milky beam nowhere near the piercing candlepower of a Maglite® XL 1000 LED flashlight with patented FocusBeam™ technology (YAY!)—but anything was better than darkness.

I followed the hazy beam to the little room in the corner and ran it across the generator, the wires and hoses and pipes and other things I didn't have names for, the product of thousands of years of accumulated knowledge—and yet the whole thing was a mystery to me.

"Don't worry," said Dad. "It's easy. Designed by geniuses to be run by monkeys. Look to your left. You should see a control panel. There are three settings: OFF, AUTO, and TEST. What's it on right now?"

"OFF."

"Well, there's your problem right there. Flip it to AUTO."

So I did. There was a clicking sound—*click, click, click*—and then a ragged cough like it was trying to start—and then nothing. I toggled between AUTO and OFF a couple times, but whatever was supposed to catch would not catch.

"It's broke."

"Nah, diesel engines don't break like that. The odds that you're going to have some major mechanical malfunction are pretty slim. The design as a whole is way more simple than your common gasoline engine, and—"

"Dad! I don't need a lesson on generators! I'm not trying to *build* one—I just need it to *run* again."

"Well, that's just the problem, isn't it? Nobody wants to know how anything works anymore. They just want everything to magically run when they flip a switch."

"Yes. Exactly."

I just wanted it to *work*—and clearly the switch was not working. Clearly, the whole thing was beyond my abilities, and if we were ever going to get it fixed, Dad needed to make a trip over to Grandpa's place. But no, he wasn't having it. He was enjoying this, his foray into tech support. He walked me through a series of steps to troubleshoot the problem, and at the end of it I flipped the switch again. The generator coughed and sputtered. And then—nothing.

"It's broken."

"It's not *broken*. There's something we're missing here. Hold on. Let me think. You checked the fuel drums?"

"Yes! They're full!"

"And the fuel filter?"

"I took it off and shook it out like you said."

"And put it back?"

"I screwed it on tight."

"But not *too* tight—you don't wanna bust that seal. Hmm. There's gotta be something I'm not thinking about here."

I didn't like being down there, what with the flashlight casting strange shadows every which way, and I was on my way back up the stairs when Dad spoke again.

"Ha! Wait! I bet I know what it is! You see the fuel line? Where it connects with the engine? There's a butterfly valve there, right? Check to see if the valve is closed. Turn it so it's parallel to the line. You get what I'm saying?"

I followed his instructions, and this time, when I flipped the switch to AUTO, the whole thing came roaring to life. Incredible. And noisy. I closed the door, but even so I could barely make out my dad's words at the other end of the line.

"Great," he was saying. "Problem solved."

I felt along the wall back to the fuse box and I flipped on the light switch. A flicker and then, lo and behold, the whole place was illuminated. Power! Hot water! I took a couple steps and stopped.

There was something there. Something dark. A stain on the earth at my feet.

Holy shit.

Here it was, ground zero. The place where he'd taken his last breath before pulling the trigger, the spot where he'd fallen, where he lay on the ground with the blood pooling out of his head.

I scrammed right out of the basement.

 ?

# 40.

# BUCKET MOUSE

So that was day one. The sun came out the next day and melted the snow while I continued my search for the portrait of Mary, doubling back on everything I'd already checked over. The bedrooms. The dressers. The closets. The living room. The washed-out brown painting of deer in a field, the smaller painting of a steamship on a stormy ocean, the Northern Nevada Auto Parts calendar turned to December.

Where was the portrait?

Back in the kitchen, under the kitchen sink, I found something else.

A bucket.

A white plastic paint bucket, half-full of water.

And swimming in the water? A live, real-life mouse.

Yech!

You'd think that after seeing my grandpa's brains all dried up on the floor I'd toughen up, but—I don't know. Mice are just so—how can I even explain it? *Shiver.* That's all I can say. *Double shiver.* And there it was, doing laps in the water in the bucket. I'm serious. It was swimming *laps.* Around and around and around it went. How long had it been in there?

I couldn't just set it free—everyone knows the first thing a mouse is going do when it escapes a bucket is head straight for the nearest human, climb up that human's leg, and, if that human is male like me, take a big ol' bite out of his sack of Planters® special mixed nuts (YAY!). That's the nature of mice. It's just what they do. So instead of dumping the bucket, I took it outside, set it a ways from the house, and draped a towel over the edge like a big, fuzzy escape ladder, then leapt back out of the way so the mouse couldn't get me. I squatted behind the porch and waited.

I was squatting there, my whole being on highest mouse alert, MouseCon 10, when Homie™ popped up.

> u have 1 call(s) from unidentified
   original boy_2!

"Send it to voice mail!"

> yay! here it is!

"Hi," said Katie. "It's me. I got your number from your dad. You left your bag in my truck."

"No, you drove away with it."

"We need to talk."

I told her sure, that was fine, and she asked what I was doing at the moment, and I said at the moment I was at my grandfather's, hiding behind the porch, waiting for a mouse to crawl out of a bucket and hopefully not chomp off any of my bits.

Katie was quiet a moment. "OK," she said. "Well, maybe I'll just head out there.... Is that OK?"

"Sure. See you soon."

I resumed my crouch behind the porch, eyeing the bucket and the towel ladder from a good safe distance, but after, I don't know, another ten minutes, the mouse had not emerged, and my fear was beginning to give way to impatience. *Come on, you stupid mouse. It isn't that hard. You grab onto the towel with your disgusting little claws. You climb out. How hard can it be?*

Finally I worked up the courage to check the bucket again— and guess what? The mouse was gone. When I was distracted by the call from Katie, it had climbed out—no doubt heading right back to the house to set up camp under my bed.

Katie showed up with my bag, and we sat on the porch.

"You know," she said, "*Aaron* is a lot better than *Arnold.*"

"I guess so."

"Look, I want to apologize. I should have said something about your dad sooner. I really should have. Only—I didn't know Jim was your dad. I thought he was your *uncle*. But that doesn't matter. I should've said something. And I tried—I really did. When you were at my place that evening, I *tried* to tell you. But it was just so complicated. You know—the Space Amazon and all that."

"Space Amazon, my ass. You could've said *some*thing. How hard could it be?"

Katie pinned me with her blue eyes. "Well, *you* weren't exactly up front with me, either. What about all the *Arnold* stuff? What about your *age*? I served alcohol to a *minor*!"

"Yes, and I called the police, so you better watch out."

"All I'm saying," she said, "is you could have told me, too."

"Fine. OK. So tell me what happened between you and my dad. You slept together?"

Katie's eyes widened. "What? No!"

"Well, what about the undies on the record player?"

"The undies?"

"The black undies!"

She blinked. "What are you talking about?"

"The lacy red undies with the see-through crotch!"

"Wait. You mean from the play?"

"So, they are yours!"

"They're from the play!" she said. "They were a prop!"

"So, you didn't sleep together."

"No! God, no!"

I took a breath. OK. "So, what happened, then?"

She just looked at me. Two blue eyes. "You really want to know?"

"Yes!"

"Fine. We . . . made out a couple times."

"*Made out?* Oh my God, I'm gonna throw up!"

Katie just sighed.

"A couple times—that's like twice, right?"

"Um, more than that."

"More? How *much* more?"

"I don't know—maybe twenty."

"*Twenty?!*"

"It was part of the *part*, Aaron."

"What part? What are you talking about?"

"The play! *Romeo and Juliet!* The guy who was supposed to play Romeo got put on house arrest, and your dad was the next youngest guy in the cast. I'm telling you, this town is *geriatric*. So there he was—and I was Juliet. Let's just say having a forty-five-year-old Romeo really added an unintentional dimension to the play. To top it off, two days before opening night, Tybalt quit and was replaced by a sixty-five-year-old woman. The whole thing was a shit show."

"So, that's all it was? You made out in the play?"

"Well, and he asked me out for dinner."

"And you said *yes*."

"It's a small town! I was lonely! There's no one here my age! We had dinner. I thought it was as *friends*. But at the end of the night he kissed me and it was just so—*awkward*. I had to tell him I just wanted to be *friends*, and it was all just so awkward, OK?"

"I'm gonna throw up. I really am."

Suddenly she was glaring at me. "You think this is *easy* for me? I thought you were someone else! Look." She was standing now, pacing around in the gravel. "Can we just agree that we both screwed up? I don't have a lot of friends in this town, and I'm just—I'm trying NOT to be the Space Amazon, OK? So, can we just be honest with each other?" Katie paused. "You shouldn't have lied to me about your age. And, yes, I should've told you about Jim. I'm sorry. If you want, maybe we can figure out how to be friends."

"Friends?"

"Yes. You've got my number. If you decide that works for you, then feel free to give me a call sometime."

After she was gone I sat there on the porch thinking about what she'd said. Funny how quick things change. Like at first I'd thought they'd slept together, and would've given anything to make it not so—but now that it was not so, I was still pretty skeeved. *Making out. Twenty times.*

But the worst part was the part about friends. Friends? I didn't want to be *friends*. One second I'm Arnold and I'm 22 and everything is cool—and the next second I'm just me again and it's all a huge mess. What about the way our eyes had met? What about the electricity I'd felt? *Friends?* I sat there, mind swimming around and around in circles at the strangeness of it all, around and around in an endless loop with nowhere to go, around and around like, you know, a mouse in a bucket.

 ?

# 41.

## RMS MARY

I woke the next day with Katie on my mind and spent the morning doing not much of anything except thinking about what she'd said. *Friends.* I tried logging into *Tickle, Tickle, Boom!* just for the hell of it, spent an hour half-assing another search for the portrait of Mary again, and then to top it off, Homie™ popped up with a newsflash on the Avis Mortem.

> yay! big news!
> scientists release new projections!
> according to latest computer
> models avian extinction rate has
> been upgraded to 54.4 percent over
> the next decade!
> :/

*Upgraded?* That was one way of putting it. Faced with the oncoming dead-bird disaster, the great scientific minds of the world had gathered in a race against the clock—not to offer a solution but to see who could bum out the most people the fastest. It was like, See you at the apocalypse, mofos.

I sank deeper into my mood. I tried taking a nap, but I couldn't get to sleep, and finally, with the loneliness pressing down like a pile of bricks, I called Katie.

"Hi. Listen. I thought about what you said. And, well, OK."

"OK, what?" she said.

"OK. We can be friends if you want."

Hell, it was better than nothing.

"OK," she said. "Great! Friends it is."

"You wanna come over or something?"

"Now? I'm at school."

"Maybe after school, then? Maybe you could help me look for treasure. I'm really at a loss here."

She showed up later all bright-eyed in her school clothes like everything was OK. Friends. Why is it that women always think you can be *friends*?

"So, what's going on?" she asked.

I handed her the will, and she read through it a couple of times.

"Wow. Cool. A real live treasure hunt!"

"Not really. So far it's just a bunch of dead ends."

"Well, are you sure you've searched *everywhere*? It's got be *some*where, doesn't it?"

No. Not really. It didn't have to be *any*where or mean *any*thing—except that the old man was crazy and the birds were all going to die and Katie was going to be my *friend*. I sank into the recliner and kicked up the footrest. "I've checked everywhere. There's no portrait. Look around for yourself. There's a picture of deer, and a picture of a boat, and a calendar. And that's all there is."

"Well," she said, "I don't know much, but I do know this: whenever a hero sets out on a journey, there's only one thing that sustains him to the end."

"Nachos?"

"*Faith*. You've got to have *faith*, Aaron."

"Screw faith. I just want the treasure. He didn't have to make this so frickin' complicated."

Katie paused. "Look," she said delicately. "Before we go any further, you've got to understand something: *treasure* won't make you happy."

Yeah, I'd heard that one before. I wasn't buying it.

"It isn't about *treasure*," she said. "It's about the *journey*."

"Right. And you would know."

"I *would*. Remember how I was telling you about my dad? When I was little he was making all kinds of money. We were rich. Well, not *rich* rich—but it felt like it. And I've never been so miserable in my life. Papa was never home, and when he was, my mom and he were always fighting—and it wasn't until he lost it all in a real estate scam that he finally got his priorities straight."

"No," I said. "This is different. I *need* the money. To pay back my dad and sister. To pay off FUN® and get out of FAIL. And maybe, yeah, to buy some cool shit. And once I get the money and do those things, it will make me *happy*."

Katie just laughed. "Believe what you want. But I'm serious, Aaron. I've seen it—it's like there's a hole in all of us, and whatever you try to fill it with, that hole has no bottom and can't be filled—"

"A hole that can't be filled," I said.

"Right. Exactly."

"Sounds like another one of your riddles."

She ignored me and started looking around the living room. The picture of deer. The boat. The calendar. Then back to the boat. Her gaze lingered there, and then she started looking up something on her phone. She stayed there a long time, looking back and forth between her phone and the picture on the wall.

"Hey! I think I've got it!"

"What, the boat?"

"It isn't just a *boat*—it's a steamship!"

"So?"

"So I think it's the RMS *Queen Mary*! It was, let's see, an ocean liner in the twentieth century that sailed the Atlantic Ocean."

She showed me her phone, and the picture there, and the boat in the picture was *exactly* like the boat in the painting—dark hull, white top, three big smokestacks. YAY! for the RMS *Mary*, flagship of the Cunard Line, roamer of the oceans, whose home is now a permadock in Long Beach, California, and whose stately Art Deco compartments serve as a full-service floating hotel, one-of-a-kind fine-dining experience, and wedding/events venue, open seven days a week.

"*Faith*," said Katie triumphantly. "It was here all along."

 ?

# 42.

## LOAD ALL

Crazy how something can just stare you in the face and you don't even know what it is. But now I did. The RMS *Mary*. No need to rip away the backing or anything like that, because when I lifted the picture from its nail on the wall and flipped it over, it was right there, a small envelope taped to the back of the canvas, a single name written along the flap: *Aaron*.

It was a thin envelope, no wad of cash stuffed inside—but maybe a cashier's check? As I tore open the flap, I mustered all the faith I had. Faith in treasure. Faith in success. Faith in—

But no. Nope. Nada. There wasn't any treasure. There was just a note, a short one, five words written out in my grandpa's neat block print:

THE WILL IS THE KEY.

And that's all it said.

"*The will is the key?* The hell is that supposed to mean?"

Katie examined the paper. "Maybe he's talking about *will* as in *willpower*? As in, *you've gotta believe*? Or maybe"—she paused—"maybe he's talking about the will itself? Like his final will and testament?"

"But the will told us to look *here*, and now you're telling me that this is saying to look at the will again? That doesn't make any sense!"

Katie ignored me as she read through the will, tracing her fingers along the words.

"What about this?" she said at last.

"What?"

"This part. Right here." She put her finger on it and read: "'*The remaining one half (½) of my boddy to be crematedd to ashes, these then to be loaddedd into shotgun shells andd honorably ddischargedd from my Remington .410 in the four carddinal ddirections from some appropriate hill or vantage point, preferably at ddusk. My tombstone to readd: 'It Couldd Have Been Wondderful Andd Sometimes It Was.'* If the will is the key, maybe you need to think about fulfilling it. It *is* part of the contract, after all. Get it?"

I didn't.

"Well, a will is a contract, right? Between the living and the dead. And before your grandpa fulfills *his* end, maybe you've got to fulfill *your* end. Maybe *that's* why you haven't found any treasure yet."

"You think he's holding out on me? Like, from beyond the grave?"

"Well, I don't know."

"That's crazy! Now you're getting into some mumbo jumbo hocus-pocus crap. How could me shooting his ashes off lead me to the treasure?"

"I'm not sure. It's all I've got right now."

It wasn't much, or anything at all, really, but after she left that afternoon I couldn't get it out of my mind. Fulfill his last wishes. I couldn't just inscribe a tombstone—that would take time—but I could shoot him out of a gun. No way was it going to lead me to the treasure, but OTOH, it *was* his last wish, and what else did I have going on? Not a whole hell of a lot. But where was the gun?

Back down to the basement I went, doing my best to keep my eyes off the dark stain on the floor.

And there it was. Leaning up against the wall behind the door. The same .410 I'd held as a child. Dad must've set it there after he found Grandpa. I cracked it open, and a single, empty cartridge popped out.

Here it was. The fatal bullet. Cartridge. Whatever. I looked at the empty cylinder where the payload went, all those tiny pellets he'd fired through his brain.

There was a metal cabinet in the corner, and in it I found the other thing I needed—a box that said LoadAll. Back when I was 10, he'd showed me how it worked, how to load the shells with powder and shot—and I wished I'd paid a little better attention because after I took it upstairs and got it clamped to the table, I couldn't figure it out. YAY! for the LoadAll—an ancient, rickety contraption, nothing like the smooth precision of a Sharpshot® Precision II shell reloader with comfort handle and convenient carrying case.

But eventually I got it to work.

Most of the work was already done for me, actually. Inside the box were some empty shells, already primed, plus some wadding, powder, and shot. I replaced the shot with my grandpa's ashes. That was the tricky part: as I was working I spilled some of the ashes onto the table. I tried sweeping them into my hand, but they got all mixed up with the dust on the table.

Working as carefully as I could, I loaded my grandpa's ashes into four shotgun shells—and then five, because there was enough of him left over. I held the five shells in my hand. Hefted them up and down. Felt the strange weight of them. You never expect to hold your grandpa in your hands. You just don't. And yet here he was. Half of him, anyway.

 ?

# 43.

# COYOTE HEIGHTS

So once again, like back when I was 10, I took my grandfather's .410 and a pocketful of shells and started out into the brush. I headed toward Coyote Heights, in the same general direction I'd headed all those years ago. Only, it was different now. The junk pile was gone, the brush was gone, and it had become a failed golf course development. The snow had melted—the weather was really weird that spring—but it hadn't done much for the grass, all yellow and matted like the back of some mangy dog. Abandoned. I stood on the paved path, looking up toward the hills, with the sun low at my back.

I hadn't quite realized the extent of it. I mean I knew the golf course was *big*, but this thing seemed to go on *forever*, spreading out along the contours of the land like some ancient god had come and dumped out an enormous bucket of yellow paint. Once, this had all belonged to my grandpa. Before that, it was the railroad's, and before that it was probably the Paiute Indians'—except they used to say no one owned the land.

Well, I'll tell you what: this land had been *owned*. A couple model homes sat vacant—For Sale signs and fluorescent stakes divvying up the bulldozed, quarter-acre lots. To the south, the rectangular buildings of the unfinished resort towered above the flat like a sad castle.

YAY! for Coyote Heights. Its 200-room luxury hotel, 18-hole PGA-level golf course, and fine dining options would surely have been a sight to behold, like for reals, had they ever finished them.

OK.

*Preferably at dusk*, he'd said.

We were getting pretty close to it.

*Some appropriate hill or vantage point.*

I climbed the tallest hill I could find, out by the 14th hole. The sun was lower now, not quite dusk but pretty close. I opened the gun and loaded a shell.

*Four cardinal directions.*

I raised the gun to my shoulder and aimed the barrel in a more-or-less southerly direction, toward Arizona. I squeezed the trigger, or tried to, but it wouldn't squeeze. What? *Right.* The safety. I pressed the little button and aimed one more time....

But before I fired him off, it seemed like I should say something. I wasn't normally one for prayer, but in that moment prayer is what seemed appropriate, though it took me a while to think of what to say.

*Dear God,*

*Hey, it's Aaron O'Faolain. I'm out here today fulfilling my grandpa's will. My catechism teacher once told me that people who commit suicide don't go to heaven. I don't believe in heaven, so I didn't really care, although it did seem kind of cruel to me. Like,*

*I knew this guy in junior high who killed himself, Greg Carlton—remember him? He was a good guy, but he was gay and had really bad acne and people gave him endless shit for it. You wouldn't believe how cruel kids can be. Or maybe you would.*

*And then you've got all these OTHER people saying you don't make it to heaven unless you've accepted Jesus into your heart. Well, IMHO people just like to make up stupid rules to put other people down. We're all just looking for a little guidance down here. . . .*

*What I'm saying is, if there IS a heaven, I just want you to know that I humbly submit that you let my grandpa in. And Greg, too. He was a good guy, my grandfather was—and so was Greg. You've got to understand: life here on Earth is pretty crazy. Everyone's running around pretending like they know what's going on, but the truth is, we're all just scared. No one wants to die . . . except I guess sometimes they do. We're just looking for, like, a little meaning, you know? It's confusing sometimes, being a human.*

*Anyway. Thanks for your time.*

*Amen.*

I raised the gun again, aiming south, and pulled the trigger.

*BLAM!*

The recoil punched my shoulder, a cloud of dust erupting from the barrel and hanging in the air for a moment before the wind took it. Ashes to ashes, dust to dust—that's just some shit they say at funerals—you forget that it's *true*. I opened the shotgun to remove the empty shell—or tried to, but for some reason my hands were shaking. I took a couple deep breaths. *Calm down. It's just, you know, YOUR OWN GRANDPA.*

I loaded the gun, turned east, toward Utah, and raised the gun again. Far in the distance, pale blue mountains rose to the sky.

*BOOM!*

More dust in the wind. Somewhere, way off in the distance, a dog began to bark.

I loaded another shell, aiming north this time, toward Idaho.

*BOOM!*

The cold wind blew in from the west, scattering my grandpa's ashes, and I waited for it to die down, then fired off a shot toward California, aiming high to avoid any blowback.

*BOOM!*

The explosion echoed into the distance, the sound fading until it joined the wind. Dust floated, vanished. There was one shell left: the odd, fifth shell. Where was it supposed to go? I wasn't sure. I aimed at the sky, where God the Father and Mary and Jesus and all the rest of them sit upon their thrones of glory or whatever, but for some reason I couldn't bring myself to fire again, so I just slung the .410 over my shoulder and headed back to my grandpa's.

 ?

# 44.

## LIGHT IS LIGHT

Back at the house it was getting dark, so I turned on the lights and sat back down again—and YAY! for Philips® full-spec Illumiwatti™ Soft White Light Bulbs—which is not what my grandfather had in his floor lamp, but nonetheless he had some kind of bulb in there, and light is light, and as I was holding up the will to examine it again, I noticed something.

Holes. There were these little holes—these, like, little pinholes— scattered throughout the paper, as if it had been blasted with a tiny shotgun. Dozens of holes scattered around the paper, with the light pouring through, like stars. And then I saw that the pattern wasn't random. The dots were positioned in line with the text, each one above a word.

Some kind of code! It had to be!

The first thing I did was call Katie.

"I think I found something!"

"What, the treasure?"

"No. Some kind of code."

"A code?" she said. "What is it?"

"I don't know. I haven't worked it out yet. There are all these, like, little pinholes. In the paper. Like some kind of code."

"Cool. Want some help? I like solving codes."

"Come on over. I'll wait for you."

By the time Katie arrived I'd underlined all the words with holes above them:

> I, Henry O'Faolain, being of soundd mindd and failing boddy, ddo hereby ddeclare this ddocument to be my final will andd testament as witnessedd by myself here todday in DDecember. If that's not goodd enough for the lawyers, tell them to come talk to me in hell because congratulations that's where we're headdedd, though personally I ddon't believe in hell or heaven, either, just a crackedd glass with water pouring out the sidde, andd that's what we call "time." First you have a lot, then you have a little. . . .

> . . . ddown to the last book of codde on the bookshelf, I leave everything to my granddson Aaron. But please note Aaron that at this stage you are not in possession of the most important thing. This isn't about treasure andd property. When you've finishedd, you'll unddderstandd.

> I've been here 76 years andd yet I've never stoppedd being surprisedd at how buriedd andd overrun by rats this worldd really is. Look up, ddown: levels andd levels of nestedd rats. They charge us for answers to their rat questions, andd as we scramble to pay them,

keep jabbing at us for more. Bankers...
priests...insurance agents...businessmen...
politicians & other speakers against truth...
usurpers...

DDon't worry: I've madde arrangements to
secure the treasure against their rat handds.
Give them a ddime andd they press you for the
whole ddollar. Pause for a moment andd they've
taken your shirt too. Yet I ddo believe Aaron
granddson you are smarter than the average
rat. Got it? Andd when you are stuck, you will
know what to ddo: DDig DDeeper!

And then I wrote them out on a separate piece of paper:

*Goodd congratulations crackedd the first codde but this stage isn't finishedd yet I've buriedd levels of nestedd answers as insurance against usurpers ddon't press pause yet Aaron granddson got it? Ddig ddeeper!*

Katie was pretty stoked. "Holy wow. That's *amazing*."

I read the message again, proud of myself for cracking the code. But then the reality began to set in—now what? The code— it wasn't actually all that helpful. The only instructions were to "ddig ddeeper." Which is the same thing he told me in the original will. Ddig ddeeper. What did it mean?

"Dig deeper..." said Katie. "It means we've got to keep searching."

"Well, but it's the same clue as before. How is that helpful? This thing just keeps going in circles."

She looked at me. "*Faith*, remember?"

"Yeah. Sure. But now what?"

"I'm not sure."

We spent the next hour reading over the message, considering the possibilities. Maybe the treasure was buried somewhere—but where? I needed a location. Some kind of x-marks-the-spot-type thing. It was starting to get late, and I was sure she was going to leave soon, but then she noticed something else.

"Check it out! Some of the words have more than one hole above them. Like the word 'insurance'—there's a hole above both the *i* and the *s*. 'Usurpers,' too. It's got a hole over the *u* and the *r*. That's it! I bet we're supposed to look at the individual letters. *Levels of nested answers! Dig deeper!* The clue itself is another clue!"

She wrote out the letters with holes over them, and it looked like this:

DDTEEFDDTHGIEEVILODDNAISSURDDRAENDDGIDDD

"That's a lot of letters, I said. "So many *D*s..."

"Yeah," said Katie. "But look—it says in the PPS you're supposed to 'ignore the double *DD*s,' so let's take those out." She crossed out each pair of *D*s and rewrote the code:

TEEFTHGIEEVILONAISSURRAENGID

"OK," she said. "Let's see.... In the middle there, we've got the word 'evil.' Or actually 'evilonaiss,' kind of like mayonnaise, but evil. The most evil condiment of all."

I gave her a look, like, *Really? That's what you got?*

"And what's 'aengid'?" she said. "That's kinda creepy, don't you think? Aengid, the evil angel. And there at the beginning? 'Teef'? That's, like, how a baby would say 'teeth.' A creepy demon baby. It's like one of those books."

"What books?"

"Or movies."

"What movies?"

"You know—one of *those ones.* Where the hero finds a mystical object and meddles where he shouldn't and ends up opening the gates of hell."

"And the evil angel comes out."

"Yes! Or a demon baby, or a plague of wild rats, a rainbow of fruit flavors...I don't know...." She looked at me with wonder in her blue eyes. "Aaron, it could be *any*thing."

 ?

# 45.

## PENCIL VS. FUN®

"Anything. How is that helpful?"

"I don't know!" she said. "But isn't it *fun*? *My* grandpa never left *me* a hidden treasure." She grabbed a piece of paper and a pencil from her bag, "Let's crack the next code!"

Huh. I hadn't really thought of it that way. It *was* kind of cool— and not just because of the treasure. I mean here we were, me and Katie, hanging out together, having fun. Like *actual* fun. Together. The together kind of fun. Which is maybe the best kind of fun.

We spent the next hour hard at it, arranging and rearranging the letters according to a dozen different schemes. We wrote out every other letter, every third, every fourth. We wrote the corresponding letters that came before and after in the alphabet. Nothing. Strange to be using actual paper—the process was so slow. Something occurred to me.

"The solution—it's so simple!"

Katie looked up from her work. "You figured it out?!"

"I'll ask Homie™! There's got to be a program out there for cracking codes. I'm telling you, ten seconds and we'll have it!"

"Wait. But doesn't that kind of take the fun out of it? Don't you want to figure it out on your own?"

I gave it some thought. "But see, that's what you're not getting—this *is* me figuring it out."

"Give me a little more time. I want a shot at it before you go using technology."

YAY! for the pencil in her hand, a good old-fashioned Dixon® No.2/HB—because wasn't that technology? "A pencil is technology, too."

Katie begged to differ. "It isn't the same thing. At least this way we're using our brains."

"Hey, FUN® is *in* my brain."

"You know what I mean. . . . Maybe we need to try a different approach. Maybe there's some other clue we're missing."

"Like what?"

"Like I don't know. Tell me about your grandpa. What was he into?"

"Well, codes, obviously."

"But what kind of codes?"

"I don't know. Everything." I directed her attention to his bookshelf: crosswords, Sudoku, word searches, anagrams . . .

"Anagrams," she said. "Maybe that's it. Maybe it's an anagram!"

"You think?"

"You got any better ideas?"

"Yeah. FUN®."

"Come on," said Katie. "Just give it a shot on your own. *Without* FUN®. Humor me, Aaron."

# 46.

## CODECRACKER™

Over the next hour or so we worked on anagrams without FUN®—
and I gotta say, Katie was pretty good at it. A real natural anagram
machine. As for me, I pretty much sucked a butt. I could barely
make a word. Mostly I just watched Katie work. It really was a
beautiful sight, the way she hunched up under the lamp, hard at
her studies, the way her hair kept falling down.

"OK," she said at last. "I've got a couple leads here. How about
this? *A teenager is grief.* Or how about this? *Soft reggae is eerie.*
That's kinda true, isn't it?"

"I don't really like reggae."

"But is it eerie? When played softly?"

"I doubt he put in all this trouble just to tell me about *reggae.*"

"Fine. So what do *you* have?" She grabbed my paper and read.
*"Aaron rules?* Come on! *Virgin ogre? Riven filth? Sloven thug?* What
are these, death metal bands?"

"Maybe he got me tickets to a show."

*"Aaron."* She was using her teacher voice. *"You have to take
this seriously."*

"First you said to humor you, and now you want me to take it seriously. Which is it? Look, we could have this done in five minutes using FUN®."

Katie didn't answer. She was examining my paper.

"That gives me an idea. Maybe we need to set aside the most likely words. Like your name, for instance. That makes it easier. Is it possible to make the word 'treasure,' too? Or 'money'? No—there's no *m*." She looked up from the page. "Go ahead and use your FUN® if you think it's so great. I've got my brain. Nothing beats good old-fashioned human ingenuity!"

Just out of principle I knew I was going to have to beat her—if not for the sheer joy of winning, then just to demonstrate the superiority of FUN®. It was John Henry versus the steam hammer all over again, and I was the steam hammer.

I found this free upgrade, CodeCracker™ by LiteTouch Industries® (YAY!), that said it could do anagrams. But when I went to download it, Homie™ denied me.

> oh so sorry!

FAILed users may not download

upgrades without permission!

"So give me permission."

Homie™ flickered.

> permission denied!

:(

"Aw, come on!"

"Trouble with FUN®?" Katie sang.

Homie™ popped back up.

> guess what original boy_2?

i will be your best friend!

> i know how u earn temporary
permission for download a free
upgrade!

"Great. What do I have to do?"

> learn the bramburry farms® new cow
boogie™!

"What?"

> it's the hottest craziest dance!

Which, no, it wasn't. What it was was a rip-off of the New Bronx Boogie, and a good nine months too late to be relevant. Homie™ wouldn't let me do it sitting down, so I got up and danced around like an idiot, with Katie laughing her head off.

I completed the Bramburry Farms® New Cow Boogie™, including the YAY! at the end, downloaded the anagrammer upgrade, inputted the letters TEEFTHGIEEVILONAISSURRAENGID, and Homie™ flickered for a second....

> error!
unable to display results!
insufficient image space!
987,665,098,765 possible
combinations!
:(

"Seriously?"

> seriously original boy_2!
987,655,098,765!
:/

"So show me SOME of them. Five at a time. And make it have meaning."

> sorry!

"meaning" cannot be derived from
given letters!

"No—I mean give me something that makes *sense*."

> ok i can make word "sense"!
>
> :)
>
> TEEFTHGIEEVILONAISSURRAENGID =
> "i hogtie fragile SENSE and
> virtue."
>
> "duh go SENSE a vigilante tire
> fire."
>
> "dough SENSE: fritter a genii
> alive."
>
> "digital giver of SENSE a unit
> here?"
>
> "ugh i SENSE a fad: lingerie over
> tit."

"Wait—no. You don't understand. The word 'sense'
doesn't have to be in it. Take the sense back out. Make it *mean*
something."

> of course!
>
> i can take *sense* out and make
> something *mean*
>
> TEEFTHGIEEVILONAISSURRAENGID =
> "inane devil egg, ur testis r
> oafish."
>
> "get a sieving retina, horse flu,
> die."

I glanced over at Katie to see how she was doing.

"Hey. No peeking!"

So I told Homie™ to subtract the letters A, A, R, O, N and give me some sentences starting with that.

```
>   u bet!
    TEEFTHGIEEVILONAISSURRAENGID -
    AARON =
    (AARON) "the gift is elusive in
    greed."
    (AARON) "i live thus in fried egg
    tees."
    (AARON) "the fun is rigged see it
    live."
    (AARON) "i lied if i ever hit
    gene's guts."
```

I scanned the next four, and the next after that. I was getting nowhere fast, and then Katie shouted out that she'd gotten it, so I picked the best one I could find in the vast sea of crap data and said I had it, too. Maybe.

"Yeah?" she said. "So what is it?"

"Show me yours first."

"Fine." She handed me a paper, and there it was, written out in her neat, schoolteacher's handwriting:

*Aaron, evil heirs get suiting feed.*

"What's that supposed to mean?"

"Well, I don't know," she said. "It's like, 'Be a good boy or you might get screwed.'"

"You think *that's* what he spent all this time trying to say?"

"Well, what did *you* come up with?"

So I wrote it out for her:

*Aaron, I give hugs, i.e. 'el friend test.'*

She started laughing. "Oh. Right. That makes a *lot* more sense. 'El friend test'—what's *that* supposed to mean?"

Both solutions were admittedly lacking. That much was evident. We searched a little longer, but without the same fire as before, and then Katie said it was time for her to go.

# 47.

## ANSWER CRANE

I thought about her all night long. I *dreamed* about her. She was sitting on my grandpa's recliner teasing me about how she knew the code. And when I woke the next morning to the sound of knocking at the front door, I was sure it was Katie with the answer. It wasn't. It was the little cowboy woman from the funeral, Anne Chicarelli, the one who sang "Amazing Grace," dressed in a long gray coat and a beat-up old cowboy hat to match.

"Adam," she said in her gravelly voice.

*"Aaron."*

"There are two kinds of people in this world: those who believe it will end in fire, and those who believe it will end in ice. Which kind are you?"

What a weird question. "I don't know. Isn't the sun expanding into a red giant or whatever? So maybe fire?"

Anne raised the brim a little to gaze at me with dark eyes. "There is a third option, you know."

"Asteroid?"

"There is a great land, Adam, beyond the horizon. Few people in this world ever get there anymore. And yet some do. *Never again will they hunger; never again will they thirst. The sun will not beat upon them, nor any scorching heat.* Do you know what I'm talking about? I'm talking about heaven, Adam. And do you know what the key to heaven is? Jesus Christ."

"I see."

"Have you found him yet?"

"Um, I wasn't really looking."

She smiled. "Your grandpa, he was the same way. Stubborn to the end. Oh, he let me talk—I could talk and talk and talk—but he always had that same smirk on his face. Very similar to the one you're wearing now, I might add. I will tell you the same thing I told him. You want to know where Jesus is?" She patted her chest. "He's in your heart. But that's not what I came to talk to you about today. Did you know I have a twin sister? Not identical—fraternal. She lives in Phoenix, and if anyone got the better genes, it was Georgia. She's a foot taller than me and never smoked a day in her life, yet her insides are riddled with cancer. Now, you tell me this, Adam: If Harriet is dying, what chance do I have?"

She hawked up something and spit it out.

"I came here to ask you a favor, Adam. I have to go to Arizona soon to visit her. I was wondering if you could watch Cain and Abel for me."

"Who?"

"My horses. Do you like to ride horses? Your grandfather sure did. He'd go out into the hills with Abel and be gone half the day. You're welcome to ride Abel. He's gentle as a breeze. Cain, on the other hand . . . I wouldn't recommend Cain unless you really know what you're doing—and even then he's likely to surprise you."

"I don't really ride horses, but I could watch them for you, sure."

As soon as I said that I kind of regretted it, though it seemed the quickest way out of the conversation. But Anne Chicarelli wasn't done yet.

"Wonderful. Shall we pray?"

She took my hands in hers and we prayed again. I mean she prayed and I pretended to listen very reverently because, again, why rock the boat? She talked about Jesus and God the Father and all the things they would do for us, how they would move mountains for us—or maybe *we* were supposed to move mountains for *them*? I was a little distracted.

I'd just gotten one new message(s):

> katie_e: call me when u get a
> chance!

After the amens, Anne said she would let me know in the next week or so when she was leaving for Arizona. I said that was fine.

Then I called Katie.

"Guess what?" she said. "I think I cracked it!"

"Cracked what?"

"The code! It's so easy a child could figure it out! Which, to tell you the truth, is exactly what happened. I wasn't the one who solved it at all. One of my students showed me. I can't *believe* I missed it the first time. Look, I've only got a couple minutes, so I just wanted to tell you that the message is—"

"Wait! Now, just hold on."

Funny, but suddenly I kind of wanted to figure the answer out on my own. Because if Katie just handed it over, what was the fun in that? Especially if it was easy. Shouldn't I at least take another stab at it? After all, it was from *my* grandpa.

"Maybe you could give me a hint."

"A hint?"

"Yeah, so I can figure it out myself."

"A hint," she said. "Fine. OK. Look in a mirror."

"What?"

"That's your hint. *Look in a mirror!*"

It was a terrible hint. I mean, here's how a hint should work: a hint should lead a person gradually across the long bridge from question to answer; it shouldn't just lift you up with a Manitex® Series S Tandem Axle crane (YAY!) and plunk you down on the opposite shore. It shouldn't be like that. The transition needs to be gentle.

You probably figured it out already, but anyway, here it is—here's what I saw when I held the letters up to a mirror. The letters were all backward now, but I could still read the message. And here's what it was:

ⴄIⴖⱯƎЯЯUꙄꙄIⱯⴖOⵑIVƎƎIⴄTⱧƎƎT

 ? boo!

# 48.

## KOMBUCHA

Finally! An actual, workable clue!

I was all ready to head out to the Russian olive and start some digging, but then Homie™ popped up with a message from Evie. She and Sam were hosting a barbecue for Sam's little sister Shiloh, who was visiting and would stay through the summer. OK, then how about offer me a ride or something? I wasn't going to walk ten miles, but there was another solution. My grandpa's blue Ford Ranger. *My* blue Ford Ranger. I found the keys and got inside—and it was the best smell ever in there. All warm with stale cigarettes. Like a man's truck. And whaddya know? It fired right up.

I found Evie and Dad relaxing at her dining room table with some iced tea. Bones was there, too, and scattered around her were about a dozen stuffed animals—ducks and otters and bears and lions. She was pacing back and forth between them, picking one up and dropping it next to another.

Dad took his feet off a chair and pushed it my way. "Your sister got an e-mail."

"From *San Francisco*," said Evie. "From the *hivehouse*."

"The hivehouse? Why are they writing you?"

"Apparently you never gave an official notice of vacant occupancy. Apparently you owe five months' rent. Apparently you signed my name as your cosigner on the lease."

"Crap. Right. I had to because I was a minor."

"You didn't *have* to forge my name! They threatened to send the bill to collections! You're going to ruin my credit!"

Dad sipped from his canteen. "You really outdid yourself this time, buddy."

"OK, so we write them a letter or pay them back or something."

"I already did," said Evie.

"You already paid them?"

"Yes."

"You owe your sister," said Dad. "That house needs to go on the market pronto. Either that or we rent it."

"If we rent it, where do I go?"

"Stay at my place. Finish up your GED from there."

"No way. That's not going to work. I need to be at Grandpa's to find the treasure."

"Treasure?" said Evie. "Aaron, has it crossed your mind that maybe Grandpa was—"

"'Crazy' is the word for it," said Dad.

"But that's just it! He wasn't! Look at the will!"

I spread it out on the table. I showed them the pinpoints. And the first code. And the second. And I was like, *Take that!*

"*Dig near Russian olive eight feet.* He buried something out on the property! Some kind of treasure. There's *some*thing out there, and until I find out what it is, the property is NOT for sale. *Or* rent. But you know what? Eight feet is a pretty small area to work with.

I bet I can find it within a week. And when I do find it, I'll pay you both back, and everything will be cool, OK?"

They just looked at me. I looked right back, holding my ground as best I could.

"You *really* think there's something there?" said Evie.

"Yes! Did you not read the code? It's buried by the tree!"

"You ask me," said Dad, "the old man was—"

"Crazy. I know—you already said that. Listen: there's money there. I know there is."

All this bickering was making me thirsty. "I'm thirsty. What are you guys drinking?"

"It's called *kombucha*," said Dad. "Your sister made it. Know what kombucha is?"

"Iced tea for hippies."

"It's a symbiotic relationship between bacteria and yeast," said Evie. "There's a pitcher in the fridge. I guess you can have a glass. You might want to add a little honey and ginger."

"Ah," said Dad. "Is that what the zing is? Ginger? I was wondering." He turned and gave me one of his looks, like, *Ah, my sweet Evie doth fill me with such pride—and then there's you.*

I went into the kitchen and got some kombucha—not delicious RiverEarth™ Kombucha, but nasty homemade kombucha—and then I saw that my dad had brought a bottle of gin over, too. I dumped half of it out in the sink, and then on second thought poured some in my kombucha, and then filled the bottle up with water until it was at its previous level.

My drink needed some ice, so I opened the freezer, and there was that yellow BIOHAZARD bag again—the one with the puppies—staring back at me. I slammed the door shut, fought off a shudder, and using what supplies I had, I mixed myself a warm kombuchatini.

But the truth is I'm not much of a drinker, and there are reasons why kombucha isn't commonly used as a mixer. It was even worse than the Sparkl*Juice™ Katie had served up. I took one sip and just about dumped it out in the sink. But I was starting to twitch a little, and I needed something to do with my hands.

Back in the dining room, conversation had moved on to other things. Dad was getting his band back together. Nothing new there. He was always getting his band back together. I didn't even know that they'd officially split. They were a Christian rock band now— or as Dad put it, *a band that just happens to be Christian*—and they were calling themselves "The JC Wonder Excursion." Or at least that's what Dad wanted.

"But Manuel, our bassist? He wants the JC Wonder *Experience*. I keep telling him, Hendrix already used *Experience*. That name is taken. You tell me, which is better?"

"I agree," said Evie. "*Excursion*, not *Experience*. How about you, Aaron?"

"Have you considered *Riven Filth*?"

"*Risen Filth*?" said Dad. "Are you kidding me?"

"Not risen—*riven*. It's cooler that way."

The door flew open and Sam appeared.

"Greetings, all! The arrival of sister Shiloh is imminent! I just got a call from mile marker 108! Fire up the barbecue!"

Let me tell you, the dude was amped. He unpacked the groceries and flew around the house, tidying as he went—moving a plant one inch to the left, rearranging knickknacks on a shelf, that kind of thing. At one point he lifted the glass out of my hand, took a chug, and came up coughing.

"Whew!" he said, wiping away a tear. "That is some *strong* kombucha!"

"Isn't it?" said Dad. "It's got a zing!"

"It's the ginger!" said Evie.

 ?

# 49.

# SUNFLOWERS AND STARS

I already mentioned the legendary hotness of the Latham sisters. Well, Shiloh was no different. She was a year older than me, and I knew *of* her—I mean I'd watched her and her sisters from a distance—but I'd never really spent any time with her on account of the Lathams—all except Sam—had been homeschooled. She was dressed in a tie-dyed tank top and jean shorts, and she had new LCD MotionNails® (YAY!)—they can be cheesy, but they sure looked good on Shiloh: sunflowers and stars dancing along the tips of her fingers.

Sam was stoked to have her home, and stood her in front of us and gave us her life story. Her full name was Shiloh Marie Latham and she was a freshman biology major at the University of Nevada, Reno. Also—and against her parents' explicit wishes—she'd recently started having FUN®. According to Sam, he and Shiloh were the black sheep of the family—Sam for obvious reasons, and Shiloh because she was the first of eight children not to attend BYU.

"Word on the street is, she even drinks!" Sam said. "I'm just so very proud of her."

"*And* I almost failed Intro to Chemistry," said Shiloh.

"Well, *I* came out at a family reunion. Top that."

His sister gave a faint smile like, *I could, believe me, but you don't want me to.*

And yet despite their boasts, when you got down to it, Sam and Shiloh were pretty much wholesome to the core. You could just tell. The fact could not be concealed. Something to do with their sturdy Mormon heritage, I guess. All those years of selective breeding. Like Labrador retrievers.

"I'm trying to convince her to come back here for school," said Sam. "Shiloh had a little bit of a run-in with—"

"It was completely unfair!" she interrupted. "I didn't even have a sip! I was the designated driver!"

"Apparently campus security disagreed, and now she's on academic suspension."

"Academic probation."

He gave her a hug. "Sweetheart, either way I'm just so proud of you. I think it's a sign. Come back home and live with me!"

"I don't know...." she said. "I'm still thinking about it.... I moved to get *away* from the hicks."

"Slander!" said Sam. "Libel! Heresy! Isn't that right, Evelyn? Is not that right there the very textbook definition of heresy?"

"No," she said.

"And yet how can Shiloh stand here, before this town's finest citizens, and compare them to hicks?"

"Well, I didn't mean any of *you*, obviously," she said, and her eyes flickered over mine.

It was time for dinner. We sat out back and ate hamburgers, and let me tell you, that girl was having FUN®. I mean *really* having FUN®. Username: shiloh_lilly. Unlike me, she wasn't in FAIL—in fact, she was working on her Seventh Star. I watched her with envy. She wasn't rude about it or anything, but you could tell—I could anyway—that while she smiled and nodded and answered questions, she was doing ten other FUN® things at once.

I kept stealing secret glances at her—she really knew how to rock a tie-dye. She was a pretty quick eater, too, but this turned out to be because she was in a hurry to meet up with some of her friends. Sam was going, too. The rest of us were invited, but only out of Mormon politeness, and we all said thanks but no thanks. Dad had to leave for band practice, and so then it was just me and Evie.

"I know a good Realtor," said Evie. "But first we need to get someone out there to appraise it...."

"Hold on! Slow down! Before you just give away the inheritance, I need a little time, OK?"

"I'm not talking about *giving* away anything. I'm talking about making prudent financial decisions."

"All I know is, it would be ridiculous to sell a house with money buried on the property—not to mention disrespectful to Grandpa. We gotta have, like, a little *faith* in his will before we just auction off all his property to the highest bidder."

Evie sighed. "You really think there's something buried out there?"

"No—I *know* there is."

"How much time do you think you need?"

"A week," I said. "Tops. OK? Then we can talk about selling."

# 50.

## BOO! FOR MATH

I woke early the next day (for me anyway), grabbed a shovel and a digging bar from the basement, and rooted around in my grandpa's closet for some work gloves. I found a pair of leather ones, all gnarly and stiff. Also a hat. ANTELLO PROPANE, it said. The red had faded to pink, with a dark ring of old sweat circling the inside. It didn't quite fit. Just a little too small. I hesitated before undoing the plastic snaps in the back. Gloves are one thing, but there's something personal about a man's hat.

What a trip. My grandpa had worn the hat and now I was wearing it, and standing on the ground he'd stood on, under the thin shadow of the same scrawny Russian olive. In the distance I could just barely make out the two horses, Cain and Abel, standing in Anne Chicarelli's corral, still as statues. The only thing giving them away, the occasional swish of a tail.

The snow had completely melted now. The obvious thing was to look for disturbed earth, or places where the brush had been cut, or maybe some kind of an X. But as far as I could tell, the ground around the tree looked the same as everywhere else—sagebrush, cheatgrass, rabbit brush, dirt. I stood with my back to the trunk, took eight paces due east, and stuck my shovel in the earth.

As I dug deeper the gloves softened, fitting themselves around my hands. The earth became cooler, with the faint smell of water, and after a couple feet I found these moist cords of rope veining the soil—roots—branching and diminishing into finer and finer strands, until the fibers became like human hair. They were springy and gave me trouble until I figured out I could slice through them with the shovel. I cut them and tossed them out into the sun, where they dried up like sea snakes washed onto a beach.

*Shit,* I thought. *This is going to be easy.*

But two feet down the earth began to change, topsoil giving way to hardpan clay. I traded the shovel for the digging bar, raising the heavy iron and ramming it between my moccasins. With each soft *whump* the earth lifted and split in a muffled detonation. Sweat trickled down my temples, along my cheeks, to my neck. I fell into a new rhythm, breaking up the ground with the bar, scooping it out with the shovel...breaking earth...scooping it out...It was kind of good to be working. At least I had something to do with my hands.

Around 11:00 I hit something hard and the bar rang out like a tuning fork. Metal? Some kind of lid? I fell to my knees and scraped away the dirt, revealing...a rock. About the size and shape of a dinner roll, or maybe a large muffin. There were more. I dug them out, one by one, and by the time noon rolled around the hole was maybe up to my chest.

Then Evie showed up.

"How's it going? Any luck so far?"

"Not unless you count rocks. I'm starting a new hole."

She peered into the one I'd dug. "And how deep would you say that is?"

"I don't know. Four feet? Five?"

"But it needs to be eight."

"Eight? No, I think you're misunderstanding. *Dig near Russian olive eight feet.* The hole needs to be eight feet from the tree."

"Really?" My sister gave it some thought. "Are you *sure*? I thought it needed to be eight feet *deep*."

"Eight feet *deep*? You know how deep that is?"

"Ninety-six inches."

"If I was standing in the bottom I would barely even be able to touch the top."

"But listen to the sentence, Aaron: *Dig near Russian olive eight feet.*"

"Yeah? And?"

"*Dig near.* It's saying you need to be *near* the tree. But the hole's supposed to be eight feet *deep*."

"No—what it's saying is you gotta dig eight feet *near* the tree. Depth isn't specified."

"Eight feet *near*?" she said. "That just sounds weird. *Near* is the wrong preposition. You'd say *out from.* Dig eight feet *out from* the Russian olive. The way the sentence is constructed, you are supposed to dig an eight-foot hole. *Near* the tree."

We argued about it a little longer, and then Evie left, and I was like, *Thanks for all your enthusiastic support and positive vibes.*

Because eight feet deep? Really? That was a lot of digging. Like, exactly how much digging? As a general rule I try not to bring math into things, because precision can be a real bummer, but I was already tired of digging, so I thought I could use the distraction.

I brought up Homie™ and worked out an equation. Not an equation like Equation™2 Trifold Lenspoppers (YAY!), but a regular old equation:

```
>   area of a circle = πr²!
```

With eight feet of diggable ground radiating out from the base of the tree, that would give me

```
>   π x 8 x 8 = 201 ft²!
```

But of course that was only surface area. So suppose Evie was right and the *depth* was also eight feet? Then we had to figure out the volume.

Volume of a cylinder = $\pi r^2 h$, with h in this case being the depth of the hole. Assuming a radius *and* depth of eight feet, that would give me

```
>   π x 8 x 8 x 8 = 1,608 ft³!
```

According to Homie™, one cubic foot of earth could weigh anywhere from 80 to 125 pounds, depending on water and clay content. Assuming a weight somewhere in the middle—say, 100 pounds—then:

```
>   1,608 cubic ft of earth x 100 lb
    per cubic ft = 160,800 lb of earth!
```

Wait. What?

I ran through the calculations again, but the answer came out the same: 160,800 pounds of earth to move. And I'd told my sister I would get it all done in a week.

So like this:

```
>   160,800 lb ÷ 7 days in a week =
    22,971 lb per day!
>   22,971 lb ÷ 10 working hours in a
    day = 2,297 lb per hour!
```

> 2,297.14 lb ÷ 60 minutes in an hour =
> 38 lb of earth per minute!

OK, so thirty-eight pounds *per minute* for ten hours a day for the next seven days—so basically I would have to be a nonstop whirling robot machine of digging excellence like the earth had never seen. Except that I didn't have seven days left. I'd already started! Day one was almost done! Had I moved my quota of earth? How much time was left? What was it in minutes? Seconds? How did that alter the equations? How much did the shovel weigh? How much weight can a seventeen-year-old human male reasonably expect to lift per minute?

There's no end to the math that can be applied to a given situation, but that doesn't change the fact that at some point you've actually got to do the work. There was no need to calculate any further. I had been led down a dark and dangerous path, and it was time to turn back.

The lesson here was clear: *Screw you, math.*

 ?

# 51.

## BLISTERS

Even with mathematics itself against me I kept at it, and as I dug the next day my thoughts meandered here and there, touching lightly on different subjects like a rabbit grazing in a wide meadow. I thought about my grandpa, who'd stood out here on this same land, digging in this same earth. I thought about how he'd told me I was smart. I thought about the ashes and the gun. I thought about my dad and my sister and all the money they'd thrown my way. I thought about Katie, and what it would be like to walk up to her and say, *Guess who just found the treasure? You want to check out Belize?*

As I dug, the leather on the gloves wore down to a smooth, steely gloss from the bar, and taking them off at lunch I found a bloody blister on the inside of each of my thumbs, and learned about new Griffin® Antibacterial Anesthetic & Disinfectant Skinsafe™ Safety Gel (YAY!).

The next day, day three, my shovel broke, right where the shovel part connects to the handle. The thing just snapped in half. I tried scooping out the dirt using just the blade, but it was foolishly slow, and eventually I drove into town to snag one of Dad's shovels, and by the time I made it back the sun was going down.

And that was day three.

Day four was slightly better, in that I got some digging done. Even so, it didn't amount to much.

When I'd first laid eyes on the excavation site, I could see it real easy in my head: take out a chunk there...a chunk there... and *KAPOW*! Treasure. Only, it doesn't work that way in real life. It comes out one shovel load at a time, and each of those loads has to be lifted out by *you*.

Day five is when the fatigue hit. I woke and thought about sitting up—and that's about as far as I got for a while. I was sore. I mean *really* sore. I mean sore *every*where. Shoulders, back, arms, legs—entire muscle groups I hadn't thought about in years.

Eight feet deep? Insane. I climbed down to the bottom of the first hole and started digging again. But the last two feet were straight hardpan. Every inch had to be broken with the bar and then scooped out above my head, and by the time I got it to the surface, only about half the dirt was still in the shovel.

Near the end of the day I brought out his tape measure to check out the depth of my holes—I had three now, and they seemed pretty deep to me. But as they say, "the tape does not lie," and in this case the tape said 5 feet 9 inches in the very deepest one—5 feet 10 if I really fudged it.

*Screw you, tape.*

On the sixth day of digging I just about gave up. Pathetic, right? I'd been so sure that I could find the treasure in a week, and here I was on my ass scratching pictures in the dirt.

Homie™ popped up with a message from Katie.

katie_e: hey are u at your grandpa's?

original boy_2: yeah i'm here

katie_e: something terrible happened!

original boy_2: what is it?

katie_e: can i come over?

original boy_2: of course!

It was late afternoon, sun shining down full force, but the thought of Katie coming over perked me up, and I decided to get some real work done. I dug through the heat, dug until the sun sat in a ball of flame on the horizon, shadows stretching long and thin across the desert. The light bled from the day and still no sign of Katie, so I dug on, dug until it was too dark to see what I was doing. The ground was black, the horizon a dark shadow. Looking back toward my grandpa's house, something caught my eye. A little glow in the darkness. Two little glows. Headlights. A pickup truck.

 ?

# 52.

# HAZMAT

I found her on the porch steps, frowning in a yellow jumpsuit. Yellow jumpsuit? Not a yellow jumpsuit, a Chemstop® hazmat chemical protective garment, to be exact, with double storm flap, attached chemical-resistant gloves, and durable TuffWeave™ outer layer (YAY!).

"Hi, Katie. What's going on?"

She thrust out her arm, slid back her sleeve, and lifted a piece of gauze. "What's that look like? Be honest."

It was pretty gross, all right. This reddish, necrotic sore on her forearm.

"What is that?"

"A leper mite bite. I've got leper mites! But you didn't answer my question: What does it *look* like?"

"I don't know. It's, um, big and sort of webby and—"

"A puckered butthole!" she blurted. "That's what one of my students said. And I was like, *Puckered? Nice vocab word, Taylor.* I thought it was just a mosquito bite, but it kept getting worse. So I went to the doctor, and he tested it for leper mite saliva, and now my whole building's under quarantine!"

"Quarantine?"

"The extermination squad showed up this afternoon. The whole place is under plastic wrap! They wouldn't even let me take my grade book! I had to stand in the chemshower for fifteen minutes and then they burned my clothes! I've been trying to reach Olivia all afternoon, but she won't message me back!"

"Who's Olivia?"

"The P.E. teacher. We're not, like, great friends, but I know she'd at least give me something to wear and let me sleep on her couch. *If* she would answer my messages! I don't think I rinsed long enough. That stupid chemshower is burning up my skin. God, if I ever needed a sign, this was it. I'm not supposed to be in this stupid town. Do I look red to you?"

Kind of hard to tell under just the porch light. But I knew the answer to her problems. She didn't need to leave town.

"Stay here."

"What? No. I just need to get in touch with Olivia."

"Really? Why not just stay here?"

Katie looked at me like, *You know why not.*

"There's a spare bedroom and everything. I wouldn't even—" I paused. "Just think about it anyway."

"That's OK," she said. "But could I use your shower? And maybe borrow some clothes? This stupid jumpsuit is *itchy.*"

While Katie was in the bathroom, I dug through my bag and got her something comfortable. I knocked on the bathroom door, and it cracked open and an arm appeared. I handed her the clothes.

She was in there a long time, and meanwhile I strolled around the house humming to myself. I couldn't help it. Because here she was! And who could say—maybe this Olivia the P.E. teacher was a real flake and the only option would be for Katie to stay here with me. She probably hadn't had a chance to eat in a while, so I figured I'd make her some food. My cooking skills are pretty limited, but I can do toast and eggs OK.

Homie™ was bugging me about taking a cooking quiz, so I did that, and then Katie appeared. Her skin *was* pretty red, and kind of shiny, too, but at least she seemed a little more relaxed now, standing there in my sweats and old plaid shirt.

"Nice threads."

She sniffed the air. "Hey, do I smell something burning?"

The eggs!

I couldn't find a spatula to scrape them off. In that whole kitchen there was barely a utensil, I swear.

"No spatula?" she said. "How did he cook?"

I didn't have a clue. I'll say this, though: it was almost too much, Katie standing next to me in the sweats and shirt. Almost like jammies. She was helping me with the eggs now, scraping them off with a fork. Brushing up against me as she reached for the salt and pepper.

"Katie."

We were looking into each other's eyes now. I was asking her a question. A silent kind of question. She tried to hide the answer, but I swear before she pushed me away I saw it. I swear I did.

But then she blinked and drew back, and the answer changed. Shook her head a little, almost imperceptibly. It was like, *Aaron. Friends. Remember?*

# 53.

# ASS MOUNTAIN

I didn't sleep very well that night. I just kept thinking about Katie. What does age matter? In the end, what does it even *mean*? A couple more years on Earth, that's all. A little more experience. I was still thinking about her the next morning, my seventh day of digging, as I trudged out to the Russian olive tree. I just didn't get it. I did and I didn't. I pounded the earth with the digging bar and scooped out the dirt. Then around noon I just sat down and looked out at Ass Mountain, with its big white rock *A*.

If you've ever driven through Nevada, you've probably noticed that the towns all have their initials spelled out in white rock on some nearby mountain or hill. As far as I know, the mountain they're on takes the letter as its name. Thus, you have "*E* Mountain" in Elko and "*C* Mountain" in Carlin—and let us not forget Battle Mountain's massive *BM*—but as for the town of Antello, the name "*A* Mountain" has some obvious issues—like you can imagine a scene with out-of-town visitors quickly devolving into a hick Abbott and Costello routine:

"Which mountain?"

"*A* Mountain."

"I know, but *which* mountain?"

"*Witch* mountain?"

"No—WHICH mountain?"

"I told you: *A* Mountain."

"But what's the *name* of the mountain?"

"No—*A* is the name of the mountain."

"Buddy, I'll kick your teeth in."

The name has some problems, so to avoid confusion the locals have referred to *A* Mountain by a number of different names over the years. At one time it was Ant Hill, which was then bastardized by a generation into Panty Hill, and by their cruder descendants—my generation—into Ass Mountain.

And YAY! for its lofty heights—loftier even than the 400-foot, max-flight potential of an AirWind® AlphaFlight™ expandable stunt kite, with triple-stitch construction and convenient storage sleeve (YAY!).

I mention the hill because that's where I was looking when Oso called.

"Hey, bro. Can you see me?"

"Where are you?"

"Up on Ass Mountain! Right below the *A*. See?"

I couldn't. It was just a little too far.

"Here's what I want you to do," he said. "Get two shirts, one white and one black. Drive out here and park in the turnaround. If the lot is empty, put on the white shirt. If you see anyone else around, even just a parked car, even if it's *my* car, put on the black shirt. Got it? Empty lot: white shirt. Otherwise: black shirt. Next order of business: hike up the mountain. On the top, just outside the fence, you will find a communication, directing you as to—"

"Hold on a sec, Oso."

"You're not comfortable with the shirt idea. OK. We can work out something else. A different type of signal. Some kind of semaphore? The sneakier we are, the better. I don't want you out there standing on one leg waving a blanket above your head. That just attracts unnecessary attention. Los Ojos de Dios are closing in, bro, I can feel it."

"It's just—I'm in the middle of something at the moment."

I told him about the will, the code, the treasure.

"Well...huh. OK, maybe I'll just head over there, then."

And I swear it wasn't fifteen minutes later that Oso showed up in his creeper truck. He got out, slung a green duffel over his shoulder, and headed over to the Russian olive. He jumped and caught a low, springy limb. The tree swayed under his weight, leaf shadows simmering in the dirt.

"So get this. I'm at El Capitan, waiting for them to make my number seventeen double chicken enchiladas to go, when the bell rings and the hottest girl I've seen in like *forever* walks in. I don't even know the *word* for it. Wearing short shorts and a tie-dyed T-shirt, bro. This little tie-dyed T-shirt."

"El Capitan, the restaurant? I thought you couldn't be seen in public."

Oso dangled there from the tree limb, knees bent, hairy belly peeking out from under his shirt.

"I'm standing there by the fountain drinks, getting some Sparkl*Juice™. And when I look back I see that she's coming over to the drinks, too, and it's like, *Oh, crap, here she comes! What's she gonna do?! What am I gonna do?!* So I put my lid on my drink, bro, real smooth, and I say to her—I say, 'The Sparkl*Juice™ is a little flat'—and she looks at me and doesn't say a word, she just

smiles. But, bro, it was the *best* kind of smile. And talk about…"
He cupped his hands gently in front of his chest, like a man cradling two baby bunnies.

"Enchiladas at El Capitan! And you wanted me out in the desert with semaphore flags?"

"Same thing happened last week. I was at Mass, and there was this *other* woman sitting in the next pew up. The reading was from one of Paul's letters to the Corinthians—I remember because I was thinking, *Dude can really talk some shit when he wants to.* He was going on and on about the providence of God, just laying into them Corinthians. And then I saw the woman. When she got up for communion, you should've *seen* the jeans she was wearing. That rose on the back pocket must've been stitched to her butt cheek. As she's coming back down the aisle and I'm pretending to pray, she does the same thing—smiles at me. What's up with that?"

"You've been going to *church*, too?"

"No one's going to beat me in the house of God, bro. Not even Los Ojos de Dios." Oso peered down at my labors. "Nice work, by the way. I hope you're prepared, though. Because this whole enterprise is about to get a lot more *fun*."

"Yeah?"

"Oh yeah. The paradigm is about to shift, my friend."

Oso knelt, unzipped his duffel, and extracted three black metal objects: two lengths of tubing, and a sort of a plate thing.

"By the way," he said, "you know that gesture I made a second ago?"

"What's that?"

"The *gesture*, bro. Two scoops of vanilla ice cream." He held out his palms. "How long you think guys been doing this for?"

"I don't know. A long time?"

"You bet your ass! I bet they did it in pioneer times. And the Renaissance. Bet you could bust it out for old Saint Paul and he'd know what you were talking about. *Cavemen* probably did it. It's a universal gesture."

I tried the gesture out. "Yeah, I guess so."

Oso stood there, scrutinizing my hands. "But see, bro, I like to do it a little different. I like to give 'em a little bounce, like they've just fallen out of her bra."

 ?

# 54.

# LATHAM SISTER ARCHETYPE DILEMMA

Oso finished assembling the device and held it up for me to see.

"Belongs to my little cousin. *Belonged*, I should say. My aunt was going to throw it out, so I took it. I had a feeling that someday it might come in handy. And here we are! Know what they call that?"

"A metal detector?"

"*Providence*, bro. But yeah, it's a detector of metal, all right—let's see what it can do!"

He flipped the switch to ON, and the machine began to emit a loud, high-pitched squeal, a harsh mix of overtones, like:

*EEEEEEEEEEE!*

He twisted the knob—there was only one knob—but no matter how he tuned it, or where he aimed the plate, the squeal did not change in pitch or volume. It just went *EEEEEEEEEEE!*

"Does that mean it's found something?" I asked.

"Not sure."

"Is it broken?"

"Don't know. First time."

*EEEEEEEEEE!*

"Can I do something? Can I help? Maybe the batteries are low?"

"Nah, bro. The batteries aren't low."

Oso swept the machine over the ground, down into the holes, around the tree—but the sound would not stop.

*EEEEEEEEEEE!*

"How do you know the batteries aren't low?"

"Because I just put some in!"

*EEEEEEEEEEE!*

Oso paced around the tree, sweeping the machine here and there, adjusting the distance from the earth, but still the sound would not stop. It was *terrible*—some kind of electric banshee. He walked further and further into the brush, and pretty soon he was dancing, stomping his feet and turning in a circle and swinging the thing like a ribbon around him. Like a Mayfair jig. He danced up a rise and down the other side until I couldn't see him anymore— and when he returned, the sound had stopped.

The little plate dangled from a cord. He walked up to the Russian olive, raised the detector to his shoulder, and swung it through the air a couple times like a batter warming up.

"We got three options here, bro. Option A: there's high metal content in the soil. What's the ground like around here? You run any tests?"

"No—but I don't think it's any different than anywhere else."

"OK, option B: there's a psycho-magnetic disturbance, like we're standing in some vortex. Have you looked at a compass? Does it spin in a circle?"

"Um, not to my knowledge."

He nodded. "Of course, there's always option C."

"What's option C?"

Oso took a couple more practice swings, and for a moment I thought he was going to bang it against the tree, but at the last second he swiveled his torso around and hucked the detector out into the air. Oso is a big guy, and he has a good arm on him. The detector arced high into the sky, diminishing in lazy somersaults, and for a moment it seemed to pause against the blue—frozen at its apex—before dropping to the earth and landing with a *thunk* in the brush.

"Option C, *mi amigo*, is that that thing is a piece of shit. How about I help you dig for a while?"

There was only enough room in the hole for one person. I shoveled up the dirt, filled a bucket, and Oso lifted the bucket out of the hole. It went fast with two people, and before long we had a pretty good-sized hole. From the bottom looking up it was impressive—if you squatted down and got the right angle, that is.

But still no treasure. We took a short break, which turned into a long break, and ended up shooting the shit for the rest of the afternoon.

I had a question:

"Hey, you know that girl you saw at El Capitan? You said she had on a tie-dye? Did she have long brown hair?"

"Yeah! That's right! You know her?"

"Well, maybe."

I told him about Shiloh.

Oso's eyes widened.

"The legendary Latham sisters! You telling me I spotted one in the wild and didn't even know it?! Wow. But now that you say it, yeah, it *was* one of them. I'd say the hottest one of the bunch. Definitely hotter than Savannah."

"Really? You think? Savannah's the oldest one, right? What about Shawna?"

"Shawna? You serious? Shawna is near the bottom of my list, bro."

This was territory we'd covered before. The old Latham Sister Archetype Dilemma—like the dilemma you feel when opening a package of new QuadStuff™ DoubleStak™ Oreo Cookies (YAY!)— like which delicious cream-filled wedge are you going to eat first?

It's like this: growing up in Mormon country you begin to notice that with large families, certain genetic traits become more evident with the repetition of children. In the Lathams' case, there were two basic templates. First, you have the more angular but also mousier model, who takes after Sam's mother, and then there's the rounder-faced, wide-eyed model, who I tended to favor. Both were beautiful in their own way, and I guess you could imagine it as a bell curve, with the middle portion— the averages—being debatable, and either end of the curve—the extremes—being more or less beyond dispute. Like, Oso and I could both agree that Shiloh was hot. And then at the other end you had poor Sally.

But I wasn't interested in Sally or Shiloh—or Savannah, or Shaley, or Shawna, or any of them. I told Oso about how Katie had come by, our little moment in the kitchen.

"There was a spark. I felt it. I know I did."

"The light in the monkey," he said.

"What?"

"It's something my uncle says. 'There's a light in the monkey.'"

"I don't get it."

"Me either. It's kind of like a Mexican zen koan. I think it maybe has to do with you being the monkey and that spark you felt could be the light. Or maybe you are both the light *and* the monkey? There's room for interpretation, bro. But you kind of know it when you feel it, right? Like you and that girl."

"Yeah, I guess so."

 ?

# 55.

# DAILY INTELLIGENCER

So ended my seven days of digging. Where was the treasure? Seven days gone. Seven days nothing. In seven days God created everything, all the planets and stars and birds and trees and monkeys and people. And me? I dug three holes.

The next day I drove into town to see my sister.

YAY! for the *Daily Intelligencer* newspaper, whose award-winning, in-depth coverage of quilting circles and traffic accidents is delivered twice weekly to the greater Antello County area. The offices were in an old building downtown, and when I got there Evie was doing a phone interview, so I had to wait. There were a couple back issues of the *Daily* on a table, and I flipped through them. It was strange. A real, physical *paper* newspaper. The news was kind of interesting, though—like for example, this thing they were calling "Jamboree-gate."

Personally, I would've called it "Motor-gate" or "Moto-jambo-gate," because either of those has a better ring to it, but then of course I'd be too lazy to write the actual article—which is why my sister is a reporter and not me. Basically, the gist was that the city council, a scandalous nest of weasels if there ever was one, was in danger of completely destroying the upcoming fourth annual Antello International Motorcycle Jamboree yet again.

To begin with, they'd botched the vendor licensing contract to the point that the state sent in an auditor. Also, they'd scheduled it on the same weekend as Lovelock's own *tenth* annual Harley Fest, so now there was direct competition. Finally, the cleaning and sanitation committee had awarded not one but two no-bid contracts to the mayor's brother-in-law. OTOH, there was going to be a Battle of the Bands. Dad's band, the JC Wonder Excursion, was already signed up to play. I read all about it in the article Evie wrote.

As I flipped through the pages, I noticed that a lot of the stories contained my sister's byline. Like over half of them. From the looks of it, it was just Evie, one other dude, and the Associated Press.

The office door opened and Evie appeared.

"Hey," I said. "Are you, like, the only reporter or what?"

My sister looked at me. "You didn't know that? They let everyone go but Brian and me. It's insane. When I started out we had six reporters. SIX, Aaron." She fanned out her fingers and added a thumb. "Now it's two!"

"You're doing a good job."

"No, I'm hanging by my fingernails from a ledge. And do they thank me? Oh, they *thank* me all right, and then they ask for more. *You're doing a good job, Evelyn. You're keeping us afloat.* No, I'm drowning here."

"I thought you were hanging from a ledge."

"Both. I'm hanging and the water is rising and I just know they're going to walk in here one day and turn off the lights and shut the whole thing down. It's only a matter of time. Journalism is dead, Aaron. This, what you see here, is the death rattle." She threw herself into a chair and let out a sigh. It was weird to see her like that. Most of the time with my sister it's about 80% for show, but here she seemed truly bummed. I tried to cheer her up as best I could.

"You're doing a good job. The articles are cool."

"You don't get the paper out at Grandpa's, do you? I'm signing you up, OK? It'll, like, double our subscription rate."

I was on my way out the door when Evie stopped me.

"Hey," she said. "Wait. So why did you come here anyway?"

I reminded her about the dig and my promise to find something in a week, but she was so wrapped up in her own stuff, it almost didn't register.

"Right," she said. "And did you find anything?"

The way my sister was looking at me, it gave me pause. The truth is I'd kind of been thinking about telling her I was done, we could sell the house. But that wasn't going to cut it. "I haven't found anything—*yet*. That's what I came here to tell you, I just need a little more time. There's something there. I'm really close. Just a little more time, that's all."

 ?

# 56.

# PIZZAZILLA™

And then came the heat: 98 the next day, 99 the next, then straight up to 104. Evie had signed me up for a subscription to the paper, and on Thursday the latest edition arrived. The heat wave wasn't quite yet enough to break any records, so the *Daily* went looking for another angle. A chiropractor had passed out in his attic after trying to fix the swamp cooler. He was driven by his wife and daughter to the hospital and revived, and the three of them made the front page under the headline HIGH TEMPS CONTINUE, which I would've changed to DEATH TOTAL FOR HEAT WAVE HOLDS STEADY AT ZERO.

Given the heat, I decided on a new, more efficient approach. Instead of digging blind pilot holes here and there, I'd approach it more scientifically. I tied a string to the trunk of the tree, measured out eight feet, and walked it in a circle, dragging my bar in the dirt to trace out the circumference. Within this circle I'd dig down an inch at a time, as in an archaeology excavation.

The top layers were much softer than the hardpan underneath, so for a while—until I'd extracted the top foot or so—my work would be easier. Or so I thought. But I hadn't factored in the heat effect or the fact that digging is still digging no matter how you dig it—which is to say: WORK.

It took the better part of two days to dig out that first foot, and my hands were blistered pretty bad by now, and I could feel my resolve slipping. The only thing that kept me going was the thought of my sister, and how hard she was working, and how nice it would be to walk up to her with a couple gold bars tucked under my arm and say, "Take it. Go treat yourself to a day at the nerd spa or whatever."

Anyway, three days into my new approach and I was about ready to give up, and then something happened. I was digging out the perimeter on the western end when I heard a sound. It was like: *tink!*

By this point I knew the sound of a rock, and this did not sound like a rock. I set the shovel aside and knelt on the ground to brush away the dirt, and there it was, looking me right in the eye. I'd found something. Holy shit. I'd FOUND something!

It was . . .

( . . . Drrruuuuuuuumrolllllllllllllllllllllllll . . . )

A fork.

A *fork*?

Yup, that's what it was. The pattern on the handle matched the set in the kitchen.

*OK, a fork.*

I polished it with my shirt and set it against the tree. It sat there looking back at me. I dug some more, and not much later I found something else.

A spoon.

*OK, a spoon.*

Were they silver maybe? I brushed the dirt off the spoon and read the inscription. *Stainless steel.* Great. Wonderful. What next?

Two more spoons and another fork. Then a pair of butter knives, another fork, and two more spoons. I tossed them over to where the fork and spoon were. They clanged off each other as the pile grew. Along with the forks and spoons and knives, I also found a cheese grater, a pair of tongs, and that spatula Katie had been looking for. Oso's metal detector had been correct. There was metal junk everywhere. But that was the problem. That's all it was: junk.

After all the clues, this is what he'd buried? I kept digging, but the more kitchen items I excavated, the more I began to doubt the whole enterprise. What next? A toaster?

And yet every time I heard the shovel hit metal I was hopeful, like it might be something *more* than a fork or a spoon or whatever—but it never was.

Around noon, clouds began to gather—thunderheads—blotting out the western sky. The gray washed overhead and the wind began to rise. The air cooled, and my shadow began to fade, then disappeared altogether, soaking into the ground like water. In the distance, Anne Chicarelli's horses were becoming agitated in their corral. They charged the perimeter, necks outstretched, plunging through the cooling air. I could feel it too: something was coming.

And then it came.

I was chucking another spoon at the pile when I saw a flash. Lightning branched up the sky, a fiery tree, quickly burning itself out. A moment of silence, then a deep rumble began to gather at the far edge of hearing. It rolled across the land in a low, crackling chorus, and then the crackle opened into a giant *BLAM!* that shook the very ground beneath me.

I made it inside just as the first raindrops began to spatter across the windowpanes.

> yay!

said Homie™,

> let's stay inside and play pizza
  trivia challenge! yay! for new mega
  pizzazilla™ from pizza barn®! can u
  name the 12 meats on pizzazilla™?
  name the meats for FUN® original
  boy_2!

"I don't want to."

> come on!
  no one can resist to name the
  meats!

Just to get it off my back I took the challenge, but I didn't really try, and in the end I could only get nine meats.

> ouchers!
  u got a C+ at pizza barn® academy
  of pizza™ studies! u missed
  pancetta flecks prosciutto flakes
  and summer sausage slices! yay! u
  will receive +1 for each correct
  answer! say yay! for collect!

"Yay."

I stood at the kitchen window. Now that the rain was here, the horses had settled down in their corral, resigned to getting wet. But their trials weren't over yet. It began to hail. Just like that: rain one second and hail the next, tiny white stones boiling over the earth, bending the rabbit brush and grass. The metal roof tinked and panked overhead. Still the horses didn't move.

Where would they go? I watched the hailstones bouncing off their backs—tiny from my vantage, but not so small when you were up close, I'm sure.

Sometimes it must really suck to be a horse.

 ?

# 57.

## MEG WIG

I woke the next day feeling bummed about the dig and called Katie to see if that would cheer me up. I told her about what I'd found buried under the tree.

"The whole thing is a joke," I said.

"Are you sure?"

"If it isn't, feel free to tell me what it is."

"I don't know—I've been dealing with my own problems."

The quarantine had been lifted, but when the extermination squad was taking care of the leper mites, they discovered all these code violations in the foundation, and now her building had been condemned.

"What are you gonna do?"

"Well, I'm packing up my stuff right now."

So I drove into town to help Katie. What are friends for, right? Anything = better than digging up more stupid forks. When I got there, her place had changed. Where before it had been kind of spare, now there was crap everywhere, books and boxes and clothing, like a packing bomb had exploded.

Katie had changed, too. She had on this big gray wig that went down over her ears like a helmet.

"What's with the wig?"

"It's for the play. Harold Pinter's *The Birthday Party*. I'm 'Meg, a woman in her sixties.' The director wasn't happy I'd be in Tahoe for a week, but he really doesn't have much choice. I've actually done this play before, so I pretty much know all the lines: *Is that you, Petey?* Pause. *Petey, is that you?* Pause. *Petey?* And then Petey says, *What?* and *I* say, *Is that you?* There are a lot of pauses. That's what Pinter is known for: the 'Pinter pause.'"

"You're going to Lake Tahoe?"

"My dad's visiting from Spain. We're staying at my sister's for a couple weeks, then he's coming back here to see the play. God! I didn't realize how much crap I had until I started going through my boxes. I guess it's a chance to simplify. They said to just leave what we don't want. And when the workers come in they'll be like, *Hey, Tom, I wonder what kind of person lived here.* Pause. *I don't know, Bob.* Pause. *But she sure had a lot of crap.*"

It was true. Katie had a lot of crap. It was going to take *hours*. The working conditions weren't great. They'd had the place sealed, and it was stifling hot in there and smelled like burnt rubber. Our progress was slow. Every time I tried to do something I just made more work for Katie. Like, I'd fold a sweatshirt and catch her five minutes later unfolding and refolding it, or I'd fill a bin with bathroom supplies and she'd dump it out and replace it with socks.

Mostly I just sat and sweated and watched her sort through her stuff, while a stunningly inefficient box fan whirred on HIGH in the window. The sound was like an airplane engine, but the breeze was just the faintest whisper. I stuck my fingers through the dusty grill and let the plastic blades whap at the tips.

As I watched Katie pack, a question began to worm through my mind. *Why?* Why just friends? Why not more? The spark was there. I'd *felt* it. The light in the monkey. So she was a little older, so I was technically a minor—what did it matter in the face of the spark? I changed my mood to LOVESTRUCK, but of course she couldn't see it.

As for Katie's mood, it was fairly breezy. She flitted from pile to pile, practicing her lines as she packed. It was confusing. I could tell she liked me, she really kind of did, but OTOH she acted like we were just two good friends hanging out in a sweaty apartment.

At some point I had the bright idea that she could store it all at my grandpa's place—anything to buy a little more time—and at first she was hesitant, but then she agreed, so we drove the boxes out there and stacked them in the other bedroom. It was almost dark by the time we were done. I walked her to her truck.

She thanked me and gave me a little hug, and there was that spark again, and I couldn't keep it in anymore.

"Katie. Can we talk?"

She looked at me in the twilight, and I could tell she knew exactly what I was going to say, even if *I* didn't know exactly—something about the spark and all that—and I watched the recognition flash across her face like lightning, and I watched her face change, and when she answered me, it was in her Meg voice. "*The caretaker had gone home. So he had to wait until the morning before he could get out. They were very grateful.* Pause. *And then they all wanted to give him a tip. And so he took the tip. And then he got a fast train and he came down here.*"

"No, but seriously."

"Wrong line. You say: *Really?* And I say, *Oh, yes. Straight down.* Pause. *I wish he could have played tonight.*"

"I'm done playing. Can we just talk?"

"We *are* talking. You say, *Why tonight?* And I say, *It's his birth-day today.* And you say, *His birthday?* And I say, *Yes. Today. But I wasn't going to tell him until—*HEY! OW!"

She looked up at the wig dangling above her head. I'd scalped her.

"That was fastened to my *hair*, Aaron!" The Meg voice was gone.

YAY! for the Meg wig, manufactured by PrettyJane® Charm Accessories, with durable synthetic weave and adjustable com-fort hooks. Katie grabbed for the wig, and I flung it into the brush.

Two blue eyes glared at me. "You go pick that up."

So I did. I handed her the wig, and I said, "Katie."

And she said, "What."

And I took a breath and said, "I like you and . . . I think maybe you like me, too."

Katie blinked. "Oh, Aaron. What am I supposed to do with that?"

"It's the truth."

"No, it's—the truth is complicated. It's the Space Amazon. Don't you get that?" She tried to smile. "Come on, you're seventeen. You've got, you know, a little growing up to do."

"Sure. Everyone does."

She closed her eyes and sighed again. "Can't we just be *friends*? What's so hard about that? Or like sister and brother."

"I've already got a sister."

"Then a friendly younger aunt."

And I was like, "Give me a chance. I'm gonna be eighteen pretty soon. A legal adult. Old enough to buy cigarettes. Old enough to go die facedown in a ditch on the field of war or whatever. So why not old enough to be with you?"

"Aaron—*please.*"

"Look inside your heart. At least just *think* about it." It was some pretty cheesy shit to say, *Look inside your heart,* but I meant it. I really did. I meant it so much, I couldn't shut up about it. "It's like, there's a light in the monkey. That's what they say. There's a light! Just give it some thought, OK? When you're in Tahoe. Take as much time as you want. Meanwhile, I'll be here. Just growing up more and more."

"Ugh!" she said. "Why do you have to—"

"Just look in your heart, Katie. That's all I ask!"

 ?

# 58.

# ECOG33K

The next day I changed my mood from LOVESTRUCK to LOVESICK and returned to the dig, not hoping to find anything, just to distract myself from the feelings I was feeling. The Russian olive was shiny after the rain. The water had washed away some of the dirt, and I saw something gleaming in the sun. Not a fork, not a spoon—something else. Something made of glass. A bottle.

And I was like, *Yes! A message!*

But no—it was just a bottle with some dark liquid it. And as I lifted it out of the earth I knew then that the old man was crazy, he just was, and everything up to this point had just been a colossal waste of time. Light in the monkey, my ass. I unscrewed the cap and gave it a sniff. Some kind of booze. Dead man's liquor.

Homie™ popped up.

> what up original boy_2?
> u r a FAIL!
> u have 1 call(s)
> from evelyn o'faolain!

"Guess what?" she said. "Isaac surprised me—he came to town a week early!"

"Who?"

"My b—" She stopped herself. "My friend from New York. He got in last night. We're going tubing and we need a fourth. Want to come?"

"When?"

"Right now. We're on the way." I heard a muffled sound, like she was covering the phone, then my sister hissed at me: *"Be nice to him, OK, Aaron?"*

Sure. Why not? Anything was better than digging.

Five minutes later, her CR-V pulled into the drive. It was just the two of them. Evie and her new special friend.

"Aaron, this is Isaac. Isaac, this is my little brother."

The guy smiled and thrust out his hand. "Wow! Nice place! I'm really thrilled to go tube with you today!"

He was a tall guy with dark hair, and he had on short khaki shorts and a safari shirt, plus one of those weird baseball caps with the flap in back to keep the sun off your neck. Also, he was having FUN®. Username: ec0g33k. YAY! for Isaac. Coming from New York, I'd expected more of a, I don't know, sophisticated hipster kind of dude, but this guy was pretty much a big dork. I could see why my sister liked him.

"Where's Sam?" I asked.

"Sam has work. We're meeting Shiloh out by the river."

I changed into my swimsuit, grabbed the bottle of dead man's liquor, threw it in a bag with a towel, and piled into the backseat.

Isaac was driving, and as we turned down the road, he caught my eye in the rearview mirror. "Hey, Aaron, you eat any breakfast yet? You hungry?" He held out his hand. "Purple Jolly Rancher. Don't worry—it's sugarless."

Now, when someone says *hungry*—I'm never really *hungry* for candy. Especially not for breakfast. Especially not sugarless Jolly Ranchers™.

"No, thanks."

"Sure?" After a moment he withdrew his hand, unwrapped the Rancher, and popped it in his mouth. I could hear it clicking against his teeth as he drove down the road. "Breakfast of champions."

Evie craned around. She was wearing this big, goofy smile. "Yeah, Isaac's got a bit of a sweet tooth."

She said it the same way you might say: *Yeah, Isaac likes to skydive.* Or: *Yeah, Isaac is an MMA fighter.*

"Aaron," he said. "I have question. Earlier, when I said, *'I'm thrilled to go tube with you today'*—was that correct?"

"What?"

"He means," said Evie, "is that how you'd *say* it?"

"Exactly," said Isaac. "Can a person quote unquote 'tube'?"

"Isaac's interested in local vernacular and native customs. Which is one reason we're taking him tubing."

"Well, there we have it! You said tu-*bing*! Is that the correct way, then? *Tubing* instead of *tube*?"

"Gosh," she said. "I don't know. I think one could also say *tubed*. It's acceptable either way—don't you think, Aaron?"

I tried to play along. "I don't know. It's like boonie stompin'. You wouldn't say *I boonie stomped*. You'd say, *I went boonie stompin'*."

"That sounds intriguing," said Isaac. "What exactly is *boonie stomping*?"

"*Stompin'*. Just some shit you do in high school when you're bored."

"It means to drive a truck around in the brush," said Evie.

"Ah," said Isaac. "*To drive a truck around in the brush. Does that mean we are boonie stomping right now?*"

"I guess it does!" she cried.

"Well, hey. All right!"

Actually we weren't, because for one thing we weren't *in* the brush, we were *on* a gravel road going *through* the brush. And second of all we weren't going fast enough, just barely moving at a crawl. Third, there wasn't any alcohol or firearms involved.

"Hey," I said. "You know there aren't any speed limits out here."

"Actually there *are* speed limits," said Evie.

"I like taking it slow from time to time," said Isaac.

"That's just Isaac's way."

"What can I say? I prefer to exercise caution."

"Mm," said Evie. "You know I like caution."

Isaac chuckled, and my sister leaned over and put her mouth to his ear and whispered something. I couldn't hear the words, but I could see her lips moving, and what I thought I saw her say—it kind of shocked me. "Caution makes me wet." That's what it looked like from my angle. It was like, *Evie didn't just say that, did she? No way!* But then why were Isaac's ears suddenly all red?

 ?

# 59.

# FOREIGN LANGUAGES

I asked if we could maybe listen to the radio or something, and Evie put on NPR because of course. It was some kind of quiz show about the news. She and Isaac kept shouting out the answers and laughing together at the same parts, and it was sort of cute and embarrassing and confusing all at once—confusing because there wasn't anything to laugh at. I'm telling you, *none* of that show was funny. And yet every once in a while they'd just bust up. Not ironically, either. They were really into it.

We headed leisurely in a southeasterly direction—15 mph tops—tracing the eastern slope of Ass Mountain out past the mobile homes, turning finally up the dirt road that parallels the Humboldt River. One of the panelists on the NPR quiz show was being supposedly hilarious about some movie I hadn't seen, and I was starting to get kind of sleepy, but then we rounded a bend and there was Shiloh, leaning against her red Jetta, in a tie-dye shirt and jeans. We stopped to let her in, the plan being to drive up to the turnaround in Evie's car, tube back down to Shiloh's car, and then drive it back up to retrieve Evie's.

"Morning!" She slid into the backseat.

"Purple Jolly Rancher?" said Isaac.

"Um, OK."

Shiloh took it and opened the wrapper and popped it in her mouth. I watched her suck on it. Then I was like, *Dude, stop watching her suck on that Jolly Rancher™.* The car shuddered over a cattle guard, scaring up a pair of crows from the brush. Around the next bend the land opened upon a wide flat area, ringed by aspen, where the cows had been. This was our spot. We got out, and Isaac began inflating the tubes with the little electric pump he'd brought along.

"How much pressure do we want here? Forty P.S.I.? Fifty? We are aiming for a fine balance of buoyancy and resiliency. I imagine there are pointy objects lying in wait."

"Truly," said Evie. "Prickers and thorns. How's that one look, dear brother?"

"What, the tube? It looks fine."

"There we have it! Confirmation from the master himself. Now everyone gather round—it's sunscreen time!"

My sister squirted a fat dollop on my hand, then Isaac's, then Shiloh's.

"Be liberal in your application. For the sun's rays do burn the flesh."

"Truly," said Isaac, smearing lotion over his ears.

It was pretty embarrassing, this loverspeak of theirs, like some kind of foreign language, like the kind you'd have to study using Rosetta Stone® (YAY!), the gold standard in computer-based language learning.

Shiloh and I looked at each other and kind of simultaneously rolled our eyes—and that was kind of cool.

Then it was time to float. But Evie wasn't ready yet.

"You men travel onward. Shiloh and I must tarry here a moment to discuss...lady things."

"Verily," said Isaac. "We will travel slowly that you might apprehend us."

"We would be honored."

So then it was just me and Isaac and the river traveling verily slowly. The current was lazier than I'd seen it in a long time. We drifted side by side like two widgets on the world's slowest conveyor belt. It was going to be *hours* before we made it back to the car. I suspected Evie had put me out with Isaac so we could "get to know each other," and I gave it my best, but I have to say we were on two different levels. The river drifted in a lazy S and widened, and we found ourselves stopped at a shallow spot, a sort of sandbar made up of little rocks. We sat in our tubes and waited for the ladies to catch up, and I unzipped my backpack and took out the booze. "Want a drink?"

"Um, OK." He took a sip, made a face, handed it back to me. "What is that?"

"Dead man's liquor."

"Never heard of it. Regional brand?"

"Pretty much."

I gave it a sip. It was pretty nasty, all right.

"So Evie said you're a biologist?"

"Environmental impact engineer. I'm studying the Avis Mortem."

"Bummer."

Isaac nodded. "The Avis Mortem is very distressing. My firm has been contracted to investigate the possibility of electromagnetic radiation as a contributing factor. So far, results have been inconclusive, but there's some promising evidence. Our suspicion is that the specific waveform utilized by full immersion reality generators—like, for example, FUN®—may have something to do with it."

I felt obligated to ask a question, so I was like, "How's that work?"

"Well, in order to transmit information safely to an embedded subcutaneous receiver, the F.C.C. required an extremely low frequency and modulation signal. All well and good, except for the fact that it's beginning to look like the migratory navigation system evolved by birds may utilize the *very same signal*."

He paused for dramatic effect, and I knew I was supposed to say something at this point, so I did. "Huh. Interesting."

"Isn't it? Our hypothesis is that the signal-to-noise ratio is being raised to the point where certain vulnerable groups are unable to maintain a cohesive migratorial integrity. We aren't sure of the exact mechanism, but based on autopsies in the field, we believe it has something to do with a low-frequency signal and the avian nictitating membrane."

At which point the dude basically lost me as far as details went. But I understood the overall point.

"Basically, the birds are getting lost and dying because of FUN®."

"Yes. Exactly. I was being unnecessarily abstruse, wasn't I? You know, we sometimes jokingly refer to the field as 'Chinese algebra,' which is actually relevant, as the majority of the research is out of China. At any rate, if you aren't acquainted with the jargon, it can seem pretty convoluted. But yes, exactly what you said: we think the birds are dying because of FUN®."

# 60.

# PURE RADIANCE

So that was a bummer of a thought, but then Evie and Shiloh drifted into view. They bumped up onto the sandbar, both of them grinning and wiggling their legs. The tie-dye was gone. Shiloh had on a bikini now. The top was yellow and the bottom was blue with yellow polka dots, and my eyes traced the acute angle where it disappeared between her legs. Above this, streaming upward were a series of tattoos. Stars. This series of inky blue stars, 10 of them, like a map of a distant galaxy. A tattooed Latham sister! It was hard to not look.

The river was low, and we kept bumping up onto sandbars, or more like mudbars, and then at one point it widened into another giant field of rocks, all glittery with water around them, and it looked like *miles* before the river might be floatable again. We waded across the rocks, carrying our tubes over our heads like refugees from a water park. Evie kept apologizing, but it really wasn't necessary. Everyone was having a good time. I kinda hung back to take in the view. Blue sky and sparkling water. Sagebrush and fence posts. Shiloh kept sliding her fingers under her bikini bottom to adjust it on her butt.

Funny. It was kind of turning into a beautiful day.

The river narrowed again, though still not quite enough that you could float it. The rocks were gone and it was all mud now, or more like *muck*, river muck, and at some point Shiloh's flip-flop was sucked into the muck and I stopped to help her dig it out—and by the time we made it to where you could float again, Isaac and Evie had drifted away on a current of love and river water.

As we floated down the river I could tell Shiloh was having a lot of FUN®, skin all glistening in the light, so I left her alone and YAY!ed Sunsoft® PureRadiance™ moisturizing sunblock. After a while the current became a little less slow and we came to the cool part of the river, this wide ravine with sandstone cliffs, where people had spray-painted their names. Way up at the top where eagles soar, and partially covered by a newer tag, you could still see Oso's old signature, the creeper skull. I turned to Shiloh to point it out, but her gaze was blank, hands gliding through the air, off in her own little world.

As the walls rose above us, the FUN® began to flicker and Homie™ popped up to say,

> oh no!

no more service!

Shiloh blinked in the light like she'd just woken up.

"You lose the signal?" I asked.

"Yeah—you?"

"Yeah."

"How are you sitting like that?" she asked. "Like, all the way in your tube? This valve thingy keeps getting me. No matter how I sit, it's either jabbing me in the butt or in my back."

"Flip the tube over so it's facing down."

Shiloh laughed. "Duh. *Flip it over.* I'm so dumb sometimes! I guess I'll just have to wait until it's shallow again."

"Nah. You could get out and flip it right here. I mean, it's what, two feet deep at most?"

"You think? We're going kinda fast now."

Not really. But she had the twitches pretty bad by this point, and when she got out of the tube, she wobbled for a second, then plunged butt-first into the water. Squealing, she righted herself and emerged dripping out of the water like some kind of sexy swamp creature. I guess I had a smirk on my face.

"That was *not* funny," she said.

"It was *kinda* funny."

She put her hands on my tube, pushed, and flipped me into the icy water.

"There! Now we're even!"

It was a pretty exhilarating feeling, being dunked by a Latham sister like that, and now that we were both wet and shivering and twitching, we started to have fun. Like, we just started talking about stuff. She'd heard about my little school escapade and asked me about living in San Francisco, and what the hivehouses were like, and if I missed my friends there.

"I didn't really have any friends. It was actually pretty lonely."

"Oh. Really? I just thought because your last two moods were LOVESTRUCK and LOVESICK that there was maybe like a special someone...."

"Oh. Right. No, that was just—I was just goofing around."

"Oh," she said.

We floated down the river, twitching and chatting until we were back in service again, and then around the next bend was the parking area. I had a message from Evie. We'd just missed them. She and Isaac were driving Shiloh's Volkswagen up to get Evie's car.

We set our tubes on the grass and waited by the creek. Lazy current drifting by. Soft murmur. I unzipped my bag.

"Want a drink?"

"Um, I don't really drink."

"Oh. I thought—"

"Well, I've *tried* it. But I didn't really *like* it."

"OK. Fair enough." I took a sip and coughed.

"But hey," she said. "Just because I don't drink doesn't mean I don't do *other* things."

"Yeah? Like what?"

"You know," she said. *"Other things."*

"What, like you smoke weed?"

"No!"

Then what was it? Cigarettes? Pills? Shoplifting? What was she getting at?

Shiloh's brown eyes watched me with amusement.

And finally I was like (to myself in my head):

*Holy shit! You idiot! Don't you get it? This girl—this Latham sister—she's hitting on you!*

I couldn't believe it. But another look confirmed it. There was that electricity again, the spark, the same one I'd felt with Katie, only this time *I* was the one kind of holding back. Funny how that works. Well, but she was Sam's *sister*. And what about Katie? Did I not just give her a big speech about how much I liked her? But did I also not just say I was only goofing around with all the love stuff?

There was still time to pull back.

There was still time to end the fun.

But then Shiloh's hands were on the back of my head and I was touching her shoulder and the hormones were taking over and we were almost kissing and it was almost too much, the guilt and hesitation and desire. But then we *were* kissing—soft lips, sweet breath—and I forgot about all the other stuff because that wasn't me, *this* was me, and I was a signal-to-noise ratio and I was a cohesive migratorial integration and I was as hard as Chinese algebra.

 ?

# 61.

# ARSE

It was decided that Evie and Isaac would take their car and Shiloh would give me a ride to my grandpa's. When we got there I gave her the tour—living room, kitchen, bathroom, spare bedroom, and then my grandpa's bedroom where Katie's stuff was stacked in boxes. *Katie's stuff!* What was I doing?

Back in the spare bedroom we sat on the bed and made out. Mashed faces. Smooched in mutual duration. My hands were shaking—my whole *body* was shaking—but not from the twitches.

Shiloh drew back and touched her hand to my leg. "Hey," she whispered. "Wanna doink?"

"What?"

*"Doink."*

"Doink?"

"Don't tell me you haven't *doinked* before."

Wow. Here I'd thought she was this goody-goody Mormon girl. But this was really direct. *Doink?* I'd never heard anyone call it *that* before. It made it sound like a brief collision or something.

"Yeah, I haven't ever really..."

She smiled. "So you're a doink virgin!"

"Um, pretty much."

"This is going to be fun! Wanna give it a try?"

God, she didn't beat around the bush.

"Oh, and don't tell my brother. Sam teases me about being a black sheep, but really he's got this, like, way-too-perfect image of me. Are you OK? You've got this look on your face."

"Um, there's one thing.... I don't really have any protection."

"Protection?" said Shiloh. "Like *condoms*? Hold your horses, pal! I said *doink*—not *do it*."

"What?"

"You know—*doink*. With our ARSES."

*"Doink with our arses?"*

"ARtificial Sex Emulations—an avatar of yourself. You can get them from the FUN® Shop."

YAY! for ARSES, but when I logged in to the Shop and tried to download one, I was denied.

> users in FAIL not allowed!

"That's OK," she said. "I'll just scan you. You won't be able to do any upgrades—a lot of guys, you know, *upgrade*—but it's OK with me if it's OK with you."

"Um, OK."

"Good," said Shiloh. "Take off your clothes."

"My clothes?"

"I have to scan you, right?"

So there I was, butt-naked with my arms outstretched like a T as she ran her gaze over me—and I mean *all* of me—and my mind kept jumping back and forth between these two thoughts, and the first was, *Wow, this is like kind of clinically erotic.* And the second thought was, *No, buddy. This is two steps beyond weird.*

My only consolation was that when she was done I would get to scan her—but when I asked her about that, Shiloh just laughed again.

"I'm already scanned, silly. Look. There I am."

And there she was, standing in the corner of the room. Shiloh's ARSE. The resolution was actually pretty good. It looked the same as her—same face, same body, same star tattoos—only with blue hair, bigger boobs, and a raccoon tail.

"I'm sending you your ARSE," she said. "Load it when you get it."

>   new message original boy_2!

I loaded my ARSE, and there I was. Me, Aaron O'Faolain, naked and pale, no upgrades or enhancements. I raised my hand—my ARSE raised his hand. I touched my lip—so did the ARSE of me. I examined this strange mirror of myself, and it examined me, both of us thinking the same thing: *Do my balls really look like that?*

And then Shiloh's ARSE was in my arms, boobs and hair and raccoon tail and all—just like I'd imagined it might be, except completely different, and crazy weird. We sat down on the bed—me and Shiloh's ARSE on one side, Shiloh and my ARSE on the other—two couples facing different directions. As the four of us were making out or whatever I kept catching glimpses of her, the actual Shiloh, and I longed for something real. Real skin. Real hair. The worst part was the eyes of the ARSE—all big and brown and dead in the middle. Like looking into the eyes of a fish. They never quite manage to get the eyes right.

So we did the thing, the four or us, two real and two not,

and it was crazy weird but also better than anything I'd ever done before—sort of—and after it was over I heard the lonely cry of the train whistle way out by town. Our ARSES faded into the walls.

Shiloh lay on the bed, typing something in the air. She finished it up and smiled. "I rated you nine point eight stars."

"Rated me?"

"Yeah. I took off a little because you're a noob and you seemed kinda, um, distracted. I expect you'll do the same or better when you rate me."

"Yeah, OK."

She rolled lazily on the bed. "You should probably do it now before you forget."

"Do what?"

"Rate me."

"Right. Of course."

So I gave her 10 out of 10. I wasn't going to be the one to mess up her perfect score. I left the comments blank, though, because what was there to say? I couldn't think of anything. The right words just didn't exist. The silence pooled around us.

Someone had to say *some*thing, so I asked her about the stars on her hip.

"What's the story behind those?"

"What? The stars?"

"Yeah, the stars."

"There isn't really a story."

"No? It's not like a constellation or anything?"

"Not really."

"Oh."

"I just like stars."

Huh. *I just like stars.* From the tone of her voice it sounded like she'd heard the question before. Maybe she had. Maybe more than once. Maybe all the guys who made it this far asked about the stars.

 ?

# 62.

## ♥LESS™

Shiloh came over again the next day, and we doinked again, and then she came over the next day, too. And the next. Every time I almost ended it, but a little voice inside my weiner was like, *No, you idiot!*

Crazy. Here I was, finally, after all these years, after all the false starts, having real, actual, *almost* intercourse. I should've been stoked. But I wasn't. So why'd I do it? Why'd I *keep* doing it? Maybe because it was like a game, and this was the crazy part of the game, and maybe I could make it out alive. Maybe everything would be OK.

But in the back of my mind I knew it wouldn't. Every time we were done with doinking, in the clarity that followed, a little voice shouted from inside my skull—*End this!* And I almost did, I really almost did, but then one day when we were done and our ARSES were fading into the light and Homie™ was asking me to YAY! new ♥less™ face accessories, she turned and sort of snuggled up to me.

"You're getting better," she said. "I'd say you're almost ready for the next level."

My ears perked right up.

"Next level?"

Shiloh sat up on her elbows. "We've been spending a lot of time together, haven't we?"

"Yeah."

"And it's been—*fun*, right?"

"Yeah, it has."

"So, OK." She tilted her head. "Does this mean we're kind of a thing?"

"A what?"

"You know—a *thing*. You and me."

"I don't know—does it?"

"I'm asking *you*," she said.

And I couldn't stop myself, the words just came out: "Sure. Yeah, I guess it does."

And then we kissed, only it was a different kind of kiss, a deeper kiss, and when we were done, Shiloh put her lips to my ear. "I've got protection."

And my whole being instantly snapped into a single exclamation point like: *!*

And then we were kissing again.

And then we did it.

Only, we didn't *really* do it. We *almost* did it. We almost really actually did it.

I think.

The whole thing was crazy. I was so amped up I was practically floating outside of my body, looking down on myself and Shiloh, thinking, *Holy shit! I can't believe this! This is a thing that is happening!*

And then just at the crucial moment, something else happened.

There was a flash, and the audio dropped out and the visuals dropped out and everything went black. And it took me a moment in the nothingness to realize what was going on: full-on TSD glitch-out! I couldn't believe it! Robbed of my shining moment by FUN®!

And then I was back, and it was over, whatever had happened was over, and Shiloh was sitting up looking at me all kind of like she was embarrassed for me, because it had clearly ended before it had even really begun.

In the moments after, with the excitement all gone, the terrible feeling crept in again. What was I *doing* here? I liked someone else. I liked Katie. I just couldn't help it. I think that's how you know if you really like someone, if you can do it—or almost do it—with another person and not be happy about it. Shiloh was hot, but all I could think about was Katie. But when Shiloh snuggled against me and told me we could maybe try again tomorrow, I put my arms around her and was like, "Yeah, sure." And that sounds kind of ♥less™ of me, and the truth is, it was.

 ?

# 63.

# THE CHEESE

This all happened right around the time of the next big wave of the Avis Mortem—thousands of seabirds washing up on the coast of Oregon. I remember because when I was at the store that night I had to watch and give a YAY! for CNN Action IU™ Important Update. It was a pretty bleak scene, all right: waves white with birds, bulldozers crisscrossing the sand, smoldering incineration piles—a stunning ecological collapse to be sure, but I had other things on my mind.

Katie was coming home soon. She was coming home in a week, then she was coming home in a couple days, and then she was coming home tomorrow. Never in my life had time passed so quickly. It was like standing in a freakin' wind tunnel.

Instead of telling her the truth, I told her I'd come down with something and it was probably contagious, and then I decided to go see what other kinds of trouble I could get into—which is how I ended up at the King Cowboy Casino that night, sneaking shots of dead man's liquor into my jumbo iced tea, watching the Lakers get their asses handed to them by the Jazz in the second game of the Western Conference play-offs. I was waiting for Oso to show up. He'd sent me a message earlier:

> unidentified: hey bro i got some
> stuff meet me at king cowboy if u
> want to go on an adventure

He arrived in the middle of the third quarter dressed all in black—black turtleneck, black jeans, black shoes—and holding in his hands what appeared to be a block of Valu-Best® medium cheddar cheese (YAY!). He draped an arm over my shoulder.

"It's the birds, right?"

"What?"

"The melancholy pose, bro! The slumping shoulders. It's the whole bird die-off thing, right? I know just how you feel. That shit will drill a hole in the middle of your head and suck out all the fun."

"Yeah, the birds."

I didn't feel like telling him about Shiloh or Katie. I just didn't.

"Maybe this will help." He dug a hand into his jeans and came out with a fistful of something and held it under the bar where only I could see. Resting on his palm were eight little pills—four green and four yellow.

"What are those?"

"Those are Rectrine, bro. And those green dudes are Follicol."

I've never really been all that into pills. I guess my experience on medication kind of put me off the scene. But I was feeling edgy, so I figured, why not?

Oso handed me my share and I drank them down. Then I asked him what Rectrine and Follicol were.

"You don't know Rectrine?" he said.

"I don't think so."

"Really? You don't remember the ads? 'The all-natural solution'? This was maybe two years ago? There was a blond lady in a wheat field? And some pictures of clouds?"

"Doesn't ring a bell."

"Well, here's the thing. On its own, Rectrine is merely a colorectal stimulant—but you mix it with plain old over-the-counter Follicol hair growth for men, and it's a freakin' howl. That's why they call it *werewolfing*, bro!"

"Werewolfing?"

"Also because the Follicol makes you grow hair. *Side effects may include hair growth, auditory hallucinations, nausea, dry mouth, memory loss, spine tingle, ghost limbs, and severe equilibrium deprivation.*"

"Those are just the *side* effects?"

"Yeah, bro! But they pale in comparison to the main event: random energy bursts and creeping euphoria."

"What the hell is a rectal stimulator?"

"*Colorectal stimulant*. Like a laxative. Thus the cheese."

"The cheese?"

"The *cheese*, bro! The cheese will plug up our digestive systems and counteract the laxative effect. The cheese is *key*."

I wasn't so sure about that. Wouldn't the cheese just make it worse? Oso didn't seem to think so. He said that's what everyone who werewolfed did: they ate the cheese. He ripped open the plastic, tore off a big orange hunk, and slapped it into my hand.

"Eat up and hold on, because in forty-five minutes to an hour we are going to be bigger than Jesus."

Fine. I ate the cheese. In twenty minutes, however, the pain was too much—not the pills, but the loneliness of the bar, the wickedness of man, and the inadequacy of the Utah Jazz, who no matter how good they get will always be from Utah—and that just ruins it somehow, even when they beat up on the Lakers.

Oso was fidgeting around, making a dirty, thumb-printy wolf-man action figurine out of the remainder of the cheese—the dude is an artist—but I was in a dark mood. I asked him if this was what he'd meant when he'd said an adventure, sitting in a bar making cheese men. He said it was a part of it, then he bit the head off the wolfman and handed me the rest.

"Come on, bro! It's action time."

 ?

# 64.

# INTERACTIVE CHEMISTRY

Twenty minutes later we were standing in the shadows of a tree in the yard of a dark split-level house.

"What is this?"

"*La casa de Pedro*," said Oso. "The home of the leader of Los Ojos de Dios."

"What are we doing *here*?"

"Going on an adventure, bro."

This didn't answer my question, but I let it ride for a moment because Oso was busy looking for something in the flower bed. Then he found it. A rock. A fake rock. With a little sliding door on the bottom. And inside the door, a little silver key, gleaming in the moonlight.

"You can't call it breaking and entering if you got a key, bro."

"I'm not so sure about that."

"What we're doing here is merely *entering*."

Actually, the word for it was "trespassing." But my question was, What were we doing here in the first place?

Oso pulled an envelope from his back pocket. "See this? This here is my exoneration, bro. I'm tired of running. Inside this envelope is the title to my truck, plus a key, plus instructions as to where they can find the truck, plus the rest of the money I owe, plus a note explaining in so many words that this is my final offer and that if they choose to pursue me further, I am taking my story to the cops, where I will sing like a little bird about their multitude of nefarious activities. Pedro and his bros are at the Winnemucca biker festival this weekend. I'm gonna leave this on his pillow for when he gets back."

"Why not just hand it to him in person?"

"Nah, I want him to understand I'm serious. Imagine the look on his face when he finds out I've been inside his home."

"Oso—man—are you sure this is a thing you want to be doing?"

"Absolutely, bro. I've got it all planned out. Here's how it goes: with stealth and werewolf-like reflexes I will deposit this exoneration on the pillow of his bed. Next, you and I will drive up to Ass Mountain—one last ride in the creepermobile—hike up to the white-rock *A*, and howl at the moon. Look at it. Have you ever seen anything more freakin' glorious?"

I looked. It was true: a big, fat yellow moon hanging in the sky over Antello.

"And *then*, bro, just as we're peaking, the first golden ray of dawn will *ping* over the hill like a laser, and the light will scour us clean and leave us pure as children, with the white *A* shining on the hillside like a passing grade from God. How's *that* sound?"

I couldn't deny it. It sounded pretty good.

"I'm going in," said Oso. "You're the lookout. You see something, you give a howl, OK?"

He disappeared into the house, and I took up my post in the yard. It had a bad feeling to it—I mean, the yard did. The grass was too neat, the juniper bushes trimmed into cubes, with little stone statues in the flower beds—the kind of yard that belongs to a person with a home security system.

There was something else, too. I was just beginning to notice it. The air had a strange buzz—or more like a crackle, like someone had turned up the volume on a dead radio station.

Homie™ popped up.

> hey original boy_2!
  u have 1 incoming call(s)!
  from katarin ezkiaga!

"Send to voice mail."

> i don't understand
  when u whisper!
  please to speak louder!

"I said, *Send it to*—"

> ok here is your call(s)!

"Aaron?"

"Oh, hi, Katie."

"Hi. How's it going?"

"Um, you know.... How about you?"

"Well, I'm back. *We're* back. Papa and me. We just got into town. We're staying at the Best Choice Inn out by Walmart."

"Oh. OK."

"He, um, kind of wants to meet you."

"Who?"

"My dad. It's not anything bad. He just gets really, um, *excited* about things.... And so I was wondering, what are you doing in the MMMOOORRRNNNNING...?"

Katie's voice had gone real low and slow. Not soft—*low*. Like someone playing a church organ underwater, with lots of slow vibrato. Like *wub wub wub wub wub*. I brought up the equalizer and messed with the levels. It didn't help. What was going on? I slapped Homie™, and the sound reverberated into the night. I scratched my head, and that reverberated, too.

My hand had reverb. Why the hell did my hand have reverb?

*The pills*. Right. THE PILLS. YAY! for Follicol™ hair growth for men and BritLabs® Rectrine™, and their potent interactive chemistry tingling up my spine.

Silence now.

Katie was done talking.

It was my turn to reply.

"Tomorrow morning?" I said. My voice sounded like a muted trombone, just *wah wah wah*. "What time again?"

"*Wub wub wub*," she answered.

"OK, cool." (*Wah wah.* ) "Talk to you later." (*Wah wah wah.*)

```
>  end of call(s)
```

The nausea was hitting me hard as I flopped to the lawn. Everything was swirly. The trees wouldn't stand still. I thought about puking, and even tried a little, but nothing would come up. My retching sounded like a squeak toy.

Then suddenly the nausea passed, replaced by something else. Something different. It took me a moment to figure out what it was—and then I figured it out. I had to use the bathroom. I *really* had to use the bathroom. What about the cheese? Screw the cheese. I *really*, *REALLY* had to go—and that's when I noticed the light.

 ?

# 65.

# THE SOFTEST ROLL

There was a light on.

In the house.

Just this light.

A little light in an upstairs window.

And for a moment there I was filled with immense envy—because was that window not a bathroom window? Was Oso not perched up there upon a cool porcelain bowl with a *Better Homes and Gardens* magazine and the softest roll of new Charmin® SofterTouch Double Strength toilet paper (YAY!), while I clenched in such agony on the lawn? But then I noticed something else. I'm always noticing things.

The window—it was too big to be a bathroom window. It was more like a bedroom window. And I had to wonder at Oso's tactics. If you're all about stealth, why turn on a bedroom light? It was almost as if there was someone else on the premises....

And then came a crash—this big, long crash—from inside the house. Like someone tripping over a stack of pots and pans. There was a shout, another crash, and then *all* the lights came on at once, every single one of them, even the outside lights, like the eye of God opening up.

And it was like, *Bingo, you dumb shit!*

A moment later, Oso rounded the corner, heading at me in a sprint, a package in his hands. He was saying something, shouting to me, nostrils flaring like a horse, but I couldn't make out the words—just *wub wub wub*—and yet I knew what the message was anyway:

RUN!

There was just one tiny, little problem. My limbs weren't working. Or, it wasn't that they weren't *working*, per se, it was that there were suddenly so many of them. *Ghost limbs.* Until I sorted out which were real and which were not, I wasn't going *anywhere*. It couldn't happen soon enough. Whoever or whatever was after Oso was probably after me as well, and any second now he, she, or it was going to turn the corner and find me rolling around on the ground like some kind of whacked-out centipede.

Sure enough, as I was playing Twister on the lawn, a figure appeared from out of the dark. I curled in a ball, protecting my soft underbelly against whatever was coming at me, but it wasn't the beast—it was Oso. He took my arm and tugged me to my feet. I could understand the words now:

"Off your ass, bro! We gotta GO!"

And then we were running. The pills were hitting hard now, and I began to understand why they call it werewolfing. Suddenly I was feeling OK. I mean, I was feeling better than OK. I was feeling like I could *run*.

You should've seen us, me and Oso. Talk about speed. Talk about endurance. Down the block, past the cemetery, the high school, the old abandoned hospital, then up into the tree streets, down another hill—I chased after my friend, and the only reason he didn't get away was every so often he'd look over his shoulder and slow down for me. I was moving. I was going. I was feeling such sweet, sweet relief—but then I had a thought that slowed me right the hell down. *Wait. Relief? Didn't I really have to go? How come I don't have to go anymore?*

A quick inspection in an alley confirmed it. It was true. I removed my undies and flung them over a fence into the darkness in disgust—and it was only then that I realized I needed something to wipe with, and that's how I lost my favorite pair of socks.

Oso was gone now, but I was able to locate him by the sound of his voice. He was standing at the entrance of the Old 65 gas station, pounding his fists against the big glass doors.

"Let me in! Let me in or I'll blow this house down!"

Behind the glass, two attendants were staring back at him from the counter. One of them was holding a mop stick like a baseball bat, and the other guy was speaking very purposefully into a phone.

"Oso! Let's go! They're calling the cops!"

Oso wasn't listening. He was pounding on those doors, the glass wobbling, ever so slightly, with each impact.

"Guys! I just want the key to the bathroom! Gimme the key!"

"Oso! We gotta go!"

I grabbed his arm. My friend turned to face me. His eyes big and yellow. It was like he didn't recognize me.

"Oso. Come *on*!"

He growled and shoved me away. "I need the key!"

Look, you never leave a man behind. I know that rule. I KNOW THAT. But what was I supposed to do? Stand there and fight him until the cops got us both? As I was heading across the parking

# ᏏᏏ.

# NANOBUBBLE

I woke the next morning with a splitting headache and a vague feeling that I'd committed myself to some kind of obligation, but what it was I couldn't remember. I scraped myself out of bed and crawled to the bathroom. Homie™ popped up.

```
>   hello original boy_2!
    it's 10:08 a.m.!
    the weather is: sunny 78
    u r a FAIL!
    yay! for banana boat® ultrabloc
    nanobubble hydrating waterproof
    sunscreen yay?
```

"Go away."

```
>   yay!?
    i will be your best friend!
    :)
```

I swatted it aside and took my first pee of the day, where I was surprised to discover that my urine was electric blue, although that didn't concern me as much as the way it foamed. I was heading into the kitchen when Homie™ popped up again.

> sup original boy_2!

"Go away."

> u have 2 missed call(s)!

One was from Shiloh, the other was from Katie. Neither of them had left a message. It didn't seem like a good sign. Then Homie™ was back.

> u have 1 incoming call(s) right now!

from katarin ezkiaga!

"Thank God you answered," she said. "I tried earlier, but my battery ran out before I could leave a message. We had to go back to the hotel to find my charger, so that's why we're late. But anyway, we're here."

"Where?"

"The pool."

"The pool?"

"We just got here. Sorry we're late. Are you here?"

"Am I at the pool?"

"We're *meeting* here, remember? You, me, and Papa. Like I told you last night...remember? You're still coming, right? Please tell me you're still coming. He's starting to drive me insane. I could really use some company."

"We're meeting at the pool?"

"Yes! He wants to meet you, remember? Look, it's nothing serious. It's just...well. I've got to warn you. My papa, he's kind of... I don't know...*enthusiastic*."

"What's that mean?"

"He may ask you some questions...."

"Questions? About what?"

"I don't know," she said. "Just, you know, questions."

 ?

# 67.

# DECODER

The truth is, I've never liked swimming pools, and not just because I'm a terrible swimmer and don't enjoy hanging out with a bunch of strangers and their bodily fluids in a big tub of chlorine—but now that I think about it, those are some great reasons right there.

There were two pools: indoor and outdoor. The indoor one was the more popular one, at least with the kids—when I got there it was a boiling froth of children, flotation devices, and actual froth. Shrieks echoed off the concrete walls. Chlorine fumes burned the air. At the far end, through the dirty aquarium windows, I could see the outdoor pool, all glittery in the sun. Two figures were paddling around in the water: Katie in a purple swimsuit, and this big hairy dude who I took to be her papa.

So out I went. The hairy dude climbed out of the pool to greet me—this short, barrel-chested man with blue eyes, a mustache, a smile like Katie's.

"My name is Aitor Ezkiaga," he said as he pumped my arm up and down. "But you may call me 'Mr. E.' I am from the town of Errenteria in Gipuzkoa, Euskadi. Do you know this place? Not Espain—*Euskadi*. Basque Country. Katie has told me much about you. I am so pleased we can finally meet."

"Yeah. Nice to meet you, too."

Mr. E. looked me up and down and smiled bigger. "It is nice to be here, no? Swimming pools are places of happiness. And yet, my nipples, they are sore."

"Papa!" said Katie from the water. "I keep telling you, that expression doesn't translate into English!"

"Well, but it is true. Can you not both see how sore they are?"

When I woke up that morning pretty much the last thing I expected to be looking at was Katie's papa's nipples—and yet here there they were, just chilling out on his chest like some kind of weird sea creature.

"Why are my nipples sore?" he said. "Because I am saddened. I see her so rarely, and yet now my daughter will not race me in a swim. I have come all this way, across the ocean, and yet my dear youngest daughter refuses—"

"Papa! No one wants to race! Can't we just hang out?"

Mr. E. winked at me. "Maybe together we will convince her for a race later, eh, Aaron?"

"I gotta tell you, I'm not much of a swimmer."

"Nonsense! Follow me!" Mr. E. raised his arms, bent his knees, and knifed into the water with barely a splash, a perfect 10-point dive, resurfacing in the middle of the pool. "Come! Join us!"

I jumped in and we paddled around in the water for a while, and Mr. E. asked me a bunch of questions. Apparently Katie *had* told him about me. He asked me about my grandfather, and the treasure, and what I wanted to do after college. And I was like,

*College?* But then I caught Katie's eye. She'd been acting strange ever since I'd got there, which made sense—the whole swimming pool situation was nothing if not strange. But now she looked alarmed.

"Papa, you don't have to *interrogate* him!"

"What? This is not an interrogation! I am simply asking some questions!"

She began to speak to him in a foreign language, and he answered her in it, and I couldn't understand what they were saying, but then FUN®'s Universal Language Decoder (YAY!) detected their speech as Basque and began translating it for me:

> mr.e: daughter i am most pleasant!
> not an embarrass of you! can this
> allow me chat with special fellow/
> suitor?
> katie: papa can it not be we
> simply to enjoy nice day?
> mr.e: yes i am of course!
> furthermore yet i must hold
> special desire for a competition of
> swimming.
> katie: papa no one will be special
> desire for a competition of
> swimming. please rather to enjoy
> the sky of yellow sun.
> mr.e: already it does daughter
> but the belief holds true a
> competition of a swimming is
> outrank idle pastimes as evidence

of for example here. i am restless
agitation for swim!
katie: dear papa we communicate in
outrageous length. is time arrival
for english? he may apprehend our
discourse.
mr.e: special fellow/suitor may
apprehend our discourse? this can
be possible?
katie: yes! have you not observed
he is at present having computer
simulation eye of amusement/joy?

The two of them snapped their heads in my direction. I very casually examined my fingernail.

"So," said Mr. E., "you are probably wondering why I have asked to meet you here, at a swimming pool? All my life I have loved to swim, but that is not why. Did you know, I helped to build this swimming pool!"

"You built it?"

"Incredible, no?"

"Um...yeah." You don't really ever think about anyone ever *building* a swimming pool. I don't. I looked around the pool at the sparkling water. "I really like the tile stripe around the edge there."

"That we did not do. That was added later."

"Well, and the slide."

"Also later." He ducked under the water and rose back up, dripping like a fish. "Aaron, I come to America age of eighteen with ten dollars in my shoe. After working with sheep for almost no pay, I ask my friend Kepa, I say to him, 'Where can I find a good job?'

He replies, 'I am going to build a swimming pool. Do you know how to build a swimming pool, Aitor?' And I say, 'No, Kepa. But I will *learn*.'"

Katie rolled her eyes.

"Together, we built swimming pools all across this land and Idaho. We sold that business and started other businesses. The restaurant. The shoe store. Later, we sold these, too. You see, this is how business works. Always one thing leading to another. Now Kepa, he lives in Las Vegas in a house with three swimming pools."

"One's a hot tub, Papa. And one's a fish pond."

"THREE pools! I told him, what do you need all these for? One is enough. But that is what I have discovered about life: if you tell a man that he cannot have something, that is exactly what he will want, no?"

"Um, sure."

"It is so good to meet you, Aaron. You are a gentleman of honor, I can tell."

*"Papa,"* said Katie.

Mr. E. clapped his hands together. "OK, then. If not talking, time to race!"

"Papa, no one wants to race!"

"A friendly swim, then. We go down, we touch the other end, we come back. What does Aaron have to say about this proposition?"

They turned to me, the deciding vote.

"I gotta tell you—I'm *really* not much of a swimmer."

"You have said this already, Aaron! But if this is true, you are honest, and if it is false, you are humble, and either way it is very admirable." He winked at his daughter. "Now get out and stand on the edge with me and show me that you are brave. We dive on the count of three."

So there I was, trying to remember the last time I'd swum an entire lap across a pool. Ever. The wind had picked up, and it was cold against my skin, but the pool looked even colder. A woman was moving swiftly along the far end. I watched her smooth, even strokes as if I might memorize and repeat them.

"One!" said Mr. E.

"Papa, do we really have to—"

"Two!"

I took a breath.

"Three!"

The water was colder than the air—like 10x colder—and the first thing I did was inhale a noseful of it and blow it out in two shoulder-length draglines of snot—only that wasn't what was holding me back. Terrible form, lack of buoyancy, fear of drowning: that's what my problem was. I splashed along with Katie and her papa for maybe four strokes, and then I was looking at their feet— and that was the last I saw of them until they were coming back the other way.

The whole thing was pretty weird. Afterwards, in the men's locker room with Mr. E., it got even weirder. I'm talking about when he whipped off his trunks like it was no big deal and tossed them on a bench. Suddenly I was trying to not look at a lot more than his nipples.

"My daughter, Katie," he said. "She is a special person."

"She, uh, she really is."

He nodded. "She told me about the ring of promise. It was a very special gift to her—you should know this."

*What?* There he was, all his parts hanging wrinkly and low, and I couldn't think of anything to say, so I just nodded like, *You bet!* and when he hopped in the showers, I scrammed out of there.

Katie was standing in the lobby. It was our first moment alone together all day.

"What's up with your dad?"

"Yeah, he's pretty crazy all right."

"He asked me about the ring of promise."

Her eyes widened. "Oh God! Sorry. He gets so confused about things."

"I don't get it."

"The mood ring. I lost it when we were swimming at Tahoe. And I was looking for it, and he asked about it, and I told him it was a *mood* ring. But things can get lost in translation with him."

"Like how he thought I was in college?"

"Yeah. And, um, he may also think you're twenty-one... and..." Katie shifted the bag in her hand. "He may also have gotten the idea that—"

"Hello, you two!" Mr. E. came bursting through the doors. "Ah, I do feel refreshed after a swim! So now what is next on our agenda?"

"I've got rehearsal, remember?"

"Yes, of course! And you, Aaron? Would you like to join me for a late breakfast—my treat?"

"He can't, Papa. He was just telling me about the work he has at home."

"Right," I said. "All the work."

"Good for you, Aaron. Work is good."

 ?

# 68.

## HAPPYTIMES™

Back home in my grandpa's recliner, I sat with my heart all fluttery and confused. What was going on? Katie appeared to have told her father—or at least led him to believe—that I was kind of like her boyfriend. But *why*? That meant there was some truth to it, *right?* Maybe she'd thought about things. Maybe she'd searched her heart. You don't go looking for a lost ring unless it's special, right? And if *it* was special, *we* were special.

Right?

> hey original boy_2!
> u r a FAIL!
> u have a call from user
> shiloh_lilly

"Send to voice mail!"

For once, Homie™ did what I asked.

I let out a breath.

Right. Shiloh. What about Shiloh?

Up to that point in my life I'd always thought of the sacrament of confession to be just one more weapon in the Catholic Church's arsenal of guilt-making and shame. But now I understood. I really needed someone to talk it out with. Someone who wouldn't judge me too harshly. Who would listen and empathize. Who could offer a way forward.

Instead, I told Homie™.

It hovered patiently while I gave it the story, then it dipped in the air and displayed a single exclamation mark.

> !

Then:

> yow!
   u should please totally doink her!

"Who, Shiloh? You didn't hear me right. We already *did* doink. Remember? You were there. And now I'm feeling like crap about it."

> u r feeling the crap!

"No. I'm feeling *like* crap."

> be cool!

"I AM cool."

> that's right!
   u r cool!
   so very awesome cool happy!
   yay! for happytimes™!
   a coolest new game!

"You aren't exactly helping."

Homie™ spun in a circle.

> i can help!
   tell me what u want!
   what it is that u want?

Good question. What *did* I want? "I don't know, someone to tell me it's all gonna work out OK."

> it's gonna work out all ok!

"And to, like, tell me I didn't screw it all up."

>   u didn't screw it all up!

"And, I don't know, to like hold me or something."

Homie™ hovered there.

>   :(

    i don't have any arms!

# 69.

# INTELLIGENCER AGAIN

Days went by and I kept to myself. With Katie it was easy: she was either hanging out with her dad or she had play practice. But as for Shiloh, it wasn't so easy. She messaged me, asking how I was feeling and if I wanted to go to the motorcycle jamboree with her. But no, I couldn't go to the jamboree with her because I was going with Katie. Only that isn't what I told her. I told her I had to help my friend Oso.

This was true. He did need my help. The latest edition of the *Daily Intelligencer* (YAY!) arrived, and when I sat down to read it—anything to distract myself—I saw something from the police blotter:

Angelo "El Oso" Sandoval was arrested on charges of breaking and entering, resisting arrest, and possession of a controlled substance.

Oso! I'd been so wrapped up in my own worries that I'd completely forgotten about him! I called his number and got voice mail. But then after a minute he called me back from a different phone.

"Hi, Aaron."

"Where are you?"

"Jail, bro."

"Jail?"

"Three squares and a bed, bro. This is the right thing for right now. Everything's been simplified. It's just me and these four walls. Eat some food, do some push-ups, meditate... My energy feels more in balance than ever! I was just talking to my lawyer. His name is Peter Juliet, and he's in love with my aunt Rita so he's going pro bono. He might be in touch with you—he says he wants to involve you in the trial."

"What, like as an accomplice?"

"Nah, bro—character witness."

 ?

# 70.

## DANGER IN SLOW MOTION

And then came the day of *The Birthday Party*. It was a day of much significance. Not only was it opening night of the play, it was also the first day of the Antello International Motorcycle Jamboree, and also Katie's actual birthday. She was turning 23. Nearly a quarter century. I met her that morning for the jamboree—there was no other way around it. I was on full alert for Shiloh. But if I saw her I wasn't sure what I would do. Run?

Katie was in a pretty good mood and kept talking about what a beautiful day it was. It wasn't bad. Blue sky, wispy clouds, sun streaming down, cigarette smoke wafting on the breeze. That kind of thing. You could hear the music from three blocks away. I thought we'd be early and beat the crowd, but I was wrong— not even 10 o'clock yet and already the place was wall-to-wall motorcycles.

A lot of it was a weekend-warrior/suburban-dad kind of vibe, but on the other hand some of these people were the real deal. Anyone can put on a leather vest, and anyone can get a face tattoo, and anyone can smoke meth until their teeth fall out—but not everyone does. I'm talking about the locals. In a weird way I was kind of proud of my hometown. Grandmas in leather. Teen moms with Heinekens. Fat dudes in T-shirts with slogans designed to cut through the courtship crap and get right to the heart of the matter:

FREE BREATHALYZER

BLOW HERE

↓

Predictably, the line for kettle corn was about a half-mile long, but it was Katie's birthday, and that's what she wanted for breakfast.

I'm not kidding about the line. *Endless.* The good thing was, no sign of Shiloh. We stood there with the sun beating down, and after a while Katie took my arm. "Help me. I'm an old woman now."

"Yeah, right."

"But you! So young, so innocent. You don't know what it's like to ache and putter about."

Was she flirting? Teasing? It felt like a little of both, and I didn't want it to stop, but I felt a darkness, too, because it was all so tricky, and what about Shiloh? After we got our popcorn, I convinced her to check out the Gold Angels, a synchronized precision riding ensemble (YAY!). They were in the Bud Lite® Action Arena, which was also the convention center parking lot, which was a couple blocks from the main action, which is why I wanted to be there. The better to avoid Shiloh.

A square, maybe half the size of a tennis court, had been cordoned off with yellow caution tape. Four large men on Honda Gold Wings wove noisily around each other in painfully slow circles while a woman in leather narrated over a P.A.

"...Every move choreographed down to the last second.... Right now, if you were to look down on this from above, like from some kind of scaffolding, you would see they are presently tracing a beautifully symmetrical four-leaf clover. . . ."

I crammed my face with popcorn and watched them go. The men were fat and they wore outfits color-coded to their motorcycles—red, white, blue, and gold—so they would never forget who owned what bike. Then it was time for doubles. The motorcycles stopped and four women emerged from the crowd— red, white, blue, and gold—and stepped onto the back of their corresponding machines, which then rolled on forward to trace more complex patterns at even slower speeds.

"Wow," said Katie. "Like danger in slow motion."

 ?

# 71.

# FLAMEPROOF

After the Gold Angels there was a demonstration of a Duratek®
T101 Flameproof Suit (YAY!), and then some kids on minibikes
who, even if they weren't on fire, were still pretty cool, and for a
moment I almost relaxed. Almost. Then, thank God, Katie had to
go get ready for the play. After she was gone, I allowed myself a
breath of relief. I'd made it! No Shiloh in sight! But on my way out
of there I ran into my dad.

He was sitting on a bench sipping from his canteen and talking to someone on his phone. Bones was there, too. I thought
maybe I could sneak by, but the dog saw me and let out a sharp
bark. Dad put up a hand, signaling for me to stop. He finished his conversation and returned his phone to his pocket.
"Saw you over at the fire demo with Katie. Looked like a good
time."

"It was OK."

Dad leveled his gaze at me. "Looks like you got a choice to
make, buddy."

I was like, *What? How did HE know?* "Who told you about Shiloh?"

"Shiloh?" he said. "What about her?"

"What are *you* talking about, then?"

"I'm talking about your scheduling conflict—the play and the Battle of the Bands."

He opened a schedule of events and tapped on the part about the Battle of the Bands. His band, the JC Wonder Excursion, was scheduled to play at 7 P.M., the same time as the play.

The man has his flaws, but one thing about my dad—I remembered this now—was he always showed up to my high school basketball games. Which was pretty cool of him, considering most of the time I didn't even play. Not saying he was always sober when he showed up, and I remember more than once turning around and seeing him straight-up snoozing. But he *did* come. And this Battle of the Bands thing was kind of like *his* game, wasn't it?

"Damn, I didn't realize. Maybe I can go to both?"

"They're the same time!"

"Yeah, I see that."

Dad folded the schedule. "So now what's this about Shiloh?"

"Nothing."

He scrutinized my face. "Interesting..."

"I've gotta go, OK? I've got some stuff to do."

I could hear his voice behind me. "You got a choice to make, buddy!"

It was true, I did. The world is full of choices. All kinds of choices. Too many choices. I thought about my choices as I hightailed it out of there. There's just so much crap to choose from in this world. But then sometimes you don't have a choice. Time keeps moving. Stuff keeps happening. You've got to just keep on going on, flamesuit or no flamesuit, as you head on into the fire.

 ?

# 72.

## THE BIRTHDAY PARTY

My next stop was the GameCage® Gaming Center, and it was a good thing I had some time on my hands, because I had to play nine million games of Skee-Ball until I got enough tickets for the prize I wanted. But the prize seemed so small on its own, so on the way over to the theater I picked some sunflowers from a vacant lot and made her a bouquet.

When I got to the theater I found a gang of biker chicks having a discussion in the lobby.

"Well, *whose* party?" one of them was saying.

"I'm not sure," said another.

"Someone who thinks they're pretty damn important," said a third. "To rent out a place like this."

"Oh, I don't know. It has a certain charm...."

"But where are the decorations? Where's the *cake*?"

"How should I know? The guy just handed me the tickets. He didn't give me *instructions*."

"Tickets to a birthday party! Who raffles off tickets to their own birthday party?"

I headed down the back hallway to where the dressing rooms were, but Katie wasn't there, so I wandered further until I came to a pair of metal doors and a thin shaft of sunlight. One of the doors was propped open with a woman's sandal.

There was a little covered walkway between buildings, and Katie was out there in her bare feet Hula-Hooping in full-on Meg regalia: skirt, blouse, shawl, makeup, Meg wig. They'd done a good job aging her—wrinkles, creases, bags, and even a bit of a jowl effect—and it made for a pretty jarring contrast between that and the smooth gyrations of her hips. I watched her, my brain struggling to put together the conflicting visual information.

"Oh, hi, Aaron."

"Happy birthday." I handed her the flowers. "There's another thing, too. I'll give it to you after the play."

She sat down on the curb and pulled a cigarette and lighter from her apron pocket.

"Still smoking, eh?" I said.

She took a drag and looked up at me. "I'm just nervous. I think it's my dad. I forgot how much I hate performing in front of him. He's *way* too enthusiastic. Hey. If you see him, could you like sit next to him and, you know, make sure he doesn't clap at the wrong parts?"

"Sure. OK."

But by the time I got to the seats, they were already flashing the lights and telling everyone to dim and silence all electronic devices. I don't know how many people that theater holds—not a lot, and it wasn't even half-full. It made sense, I guess. I mean what piece of theater, even a Harold Pinter masterwork, can compete with a couple hundred motorcycles?

Right before they turned the lights out, I spotted Mr. E.

I started down an aisle, but it was the wrong one and I ended up below him, about 10 feet away. It would have to do.

The curtains slid open on a darkened stage. A spotlight illuminated a table and two chairs. Behind this, a bare white wall with a single door. The door opened and a man walked onstage. He sat down at the chair and unfolded his newspaper and began to read. After a moment, a woman's voice called from offstage:

"Is that you Petey?" Pause. "Petey is that you? *Petey?*"

"What?" said the man.

"Is that you?"

"Yes, it's me."

The door opened and Katie appeared. From somewhere in the darkness behind me came a sudden burst of clapping.

YAY! for *The Birthday Party* by Harold Pinter, whose Broadway revival production is available on FT formats. As a play it was dark and perplexing, but Katie was the shit in it. There's nothing better than watching a person doing what they do best. There really isn't. The effortlessness of it. The grace. The drama. The sexiest old lady I'd ever seen. By the time it was over I'd grown old and died with her six dozen times.

Afterwards, I found Mr. E. in the lobby by the drinking fountains, surveying the crowd, such as it was, with a big grin on his face.

"A triumph, no?"

"Oh, definitely."

"We must celebrate."

"Yeah, of course."

He stood there for a moment savoring it all, then leaned in with his voice low.

"But tell me—here is what I did not understand. Why was everyone so cruel to one another? And why did they speak so slowly?"

# 73.

## NO ESCAPE

Mr. E. insisted on taking us out to a birthday dinner for Katie, and that's how we ended up at Lucky Pedro's Bar & Grill again—the same place I'd met her all those months ago. The place was packed with bikers, and we had to wait at the bar for a table, and then a waitress came to tell us our table was ready. In order to get to the dining room you had to pass through a short hallway and a pair of hinged, saloon-style doors. So that was what we did, and that's when I saw what was waiting for me—for us—on the other side.

In the far corner there was a table.

And seated at the table there were five people.

And those five people were Evie, Dad, Sam, Isaac, and Shiloh.

Oh, God, no.

But it was true.

There they were, deep in conversation, and at first they didn't seem to notice us, and no one seemed to notice them, either, and I squinched up my eyes and started to pray that we might all continue on in our lives without the knowledge of each other's presence—and I was almost to the "amen" when I heard someone call out my name.

It was Sam, waving us over. "Howdy, strangers!"

The next thing I knew we were standing there with them, introductions were being made, and everyone was talking at once—Katie, Evie, Dad, Mr. E., Isaac—all except Shiloh, who wouldn't look up at me. I checked her status, and as I was doing so it flashed from PARTY DOWN to UNAVAILABLE.

Now, for some reason Dad and Isaac were getting out of their chairs, and for a brief, wonderful moment I thought they were getting up because they were leaving, but then I saw that they were just getting up to move the next table over to theirs.

Then incredibly we were seated, all eight of us wrapped around two tables: Evie, Isaac, Sam, Dad, Mr. E., Shiloh, Katie, and me. For a moment I felt nothing, just sat in a daze, slowly remembering myself, and I note here as a matter of medical interest that I experienced the return of sensation as a physical thing first—in the form of perspiration, then cotton mouth, detumescence, and finally my butthole shrinking down to the size of a poppy seed.

After that, everything got really vivid. Shiloh's silver necklace, the touch of Meg eyeliner Katie had missed, the reflection of candlelight in Isaac's glasses, it was all there in glorious 3D, with the contrast way up and the brightness, too—my napkin white as a road flare—everything and everyone glowing around me with a radiant finality like it was appearing for the very last time. And yet nothing happened. I mean, nothing out of the ordinary. No one stood to denounce me, or lunged at me with a knife, or burst into tears. Instead, the waitress came and took our orders, and after that I excused myself to the bathroom.

It was a dinky little room with a small, screenless window that could be reached only by standing on the toilet. The latch had been painted over—but not enough that I couldn't get it undone. I pried the window open and found myself looking onto a dark alley. An unattended motorcycle, a white Harley-Davidson Road Queen® Special Edition (YAY!) was parked near a blue Dumpster. Painted across the saddle in blue script was a single word: *Escape.*

From somewhere down the alley came the sound of laughter. High, musical: a woman's laughter. I never saw her, but I knew she was the owner. You could just tell—a laugh like that just *had* to have a white Harley to match. I dreamed of our escape. How she'd come laughing to her steed, and how I'd squeeze out the window and hop on behind and wrap my arms around her big leather jacket. And how she'd gun the engine and we'd ride off into the sunset to begin a new life together somewhere out west. *Way* out west. Somewhere like Japan.

 ?

# 74.

# THE OTHER BIRTHDAY PARTY

Back in my seat, and everyone was talking, the conversation raging around me like a river. It was insane. There were so many horrifying things. Mr. E. was talking up Katie's birthday with my dad, and Evie and Katie were laughing like old friends about some biker they'd seen, and Sam was gabbing with Isaac about the Battle of the Bands, and everyone was just chattering away—everyone except for Shiloh, who was sitting there with a vague smile on her face, like she was remembering some old joke.

So I messaged her:

original boy_2: how's it going?

And she messaged me back, just one word:

shiloh_lilly: guess

"Second place," Sam was saying. "Did you hear that, Aaron? The JC Wonder Excursion got second place!"

"We should've got first," said Dad, "but the power went out."

original boy_2: did you go to the biker jamboree?

"You guys should play at the Cowboy Poetry Festival," said Sam.

"Cowboy Poetry Festival?" said Isaac. "That sounds interesting."

shiloh_lilly: does this count?

"Yeah, not really," Evie explained. "Most of them aren't real cowboys. They're all originally from New Jersey or Wisconsin or *New York*—no offense. And they talk about, you know, *ropin'* and *ridin'* and *the range* and *critters*."

"And the hardscrabble people," said Dad.

original boy_2: are u ok?

"Right," said Evie. "The hardscrabble people. Who work hard all day and then look out on the land and feel the world deeply."

"Now, hold on, honey," said Sam. "I've looked out on the land and felt the world deeply—well, I *have*."

shiloh_lilly: yay! for
birthdayexpress® party supplies?
original boy_2: yay!
shiloh_lilly: guess what?
original boy_2: what?

"Question," said Isaac. "What's a *critter*?"

"Skunks," said Dad. "Porcupines, raccoons. Unwanted varmints people shoot."

"So is a rabbit a critter?" Isaac asked.

"But why would you shoot a rabbit?" said Sam.

"I'm not saying *I* would," said Dad. "People do, though."

shiloh_lilly: u r an asshole

"The Nevadans shoot rabbits," said Evie. "The 'cowboys' from Wisconsin write poems about them. So it all kind of evens out."

original boy_2: i should have said
something
original boy_2: i'm really sorry
original boy_2: i didn't mean to
hurt anyone
shiloh_lilly: lol right

"*I* wouldn't shoot a critter," said Sam. "What on earth did a rabbit ever do to anyone?"

"They'll eat your garden down to the nub—I've seen it."

shiloh_lilly: i hope you're having
fun

"In Spain there are no more rabbits," said Mr. E. "They have all died. Once, they were everywhere. Now?" He slashed his hand through the air. "Gone."

"But look here, Sam," said Dad. "What about some mouse that's getting into your kitchen and pissing in your butter dish? Would you shoot one of those?"

original boy_2: i'm sorry

"Mice DO that?" said Sam. "Now, hold on. Why would a mouse pee in a butter dish?"

shiloh_lilly: u already said that

"Look," said Dad. "*Butter dish* is just one of an endless number of options. You have to realize that once you're asleep, a mouse—or *mice*, which is more likely the case—has six to eight hours of free rein in your house. Think about THAT."

"We keep our butter in the fridge," said Sam.

original boy_2: it's all just kind
of complicated

"Oh, goody," said Evie. "Here comes the food."

shiloh_lilly: don't message me
anymore

"Huevos rancheros?" said the waiter.

original boy_2: shiloh, i'm sorry

"That was me," said Isaac.

"And the beef tacos?"

shiloh_lilly: don't message me
anymore

"Over here," said Dad.

original boy_2: ok but can we at
least talk?

Homie™ popped up between us.

> ouchers!

user shiloh_lilly has blocked u
original boy_2!

:(

send white flag?

What was the point? She didn't want to talk. It made sense to me. After dinner the waiters and waitresses brought out the big sombrero birthday hat and stuck it on Katie's head, and we all sang the birthday song. We sang it in Spanish and then in English, and no one sang it louder than Shiloh, or at least that's how it felt, and all the while smiling at me with that look on her face.

Katie closed her eyes, made a wish, and blew out the candle. Everyone clapped and cheered.

 ?

# 75.

# BEST CHOICE

Later that night I ended up in Katie's hotel room, the one adjoining her dad's room, just the two of us sitting on her bed. (YAY! for the Best Choice Inn®, with business-friendly suites far superior to anything I ever experienced at the King Cowboy.) It was time to give Katie her present. I took the little box out of my pocket.

"Got you something else. Happy birthday."

"Aw, you shouldn't have." She looked at the box in my hands. "I wonder what it could be...a Crock-Pot?...A pony...?"

But before I gave it to her, I had to say something.

"Hey, Katie," I said quietly.

"Or perhaps a single delicious cigarette, just waiting to be—"

"Katie, I need to know something."

"Yeah?"

"Is this a thing?"

"A thing?"

"You and me...is this a thing or not?"

"Oh, Aaron," she said. "Do we have to—"

"Well, yeah. Because your dad, for one . . . he seemed to think we were a thing . . . and I thought that if *he* thought we were a thing then maybe it was because you *told* him we were, and if you told him, then—"

"Look." She shifted uncomfortably. "I probably shouldn't have let him get so excited about you and me, but you *are* my friend, and it just made it easier if you were twenty-one and—everything else he just assumed. That's just how he is. He goes bananas about everything."

"So we're not a thing. This isn't serious."

Katie sighed. "Can we please just not get into this conversation again? How about we just have fun? I was having such a nice time before you started in on all the questions. . . . So what's in the box? Don't keep me guessing."

And the way she talked, like I was just annoying her with my feelings, I guess it kind of pissed me off.

"Well, about us being a thing or not—there's another reason I wanted to know."

And Katie was like, "Yeah?"

And I was like, "Because when you were out of town, I started hanging out with this girl."

Katie blinked. "Oh?"

And it's funny how a person's expression can change so fast.

"Well, that's probably good, then." Her voice was real casual—but not really casual. There was like this wobble to it. "Who is it? A friend from high school?" She picked a plastic cup off the table and started unwrapping it.

"No, someone else."

"Oh."

"It was Shiloh."

"From dinner tonight?" She was standing now. "*That* Shiloh?!"

"Yeah, pretty much."

"So the whole time at dinner...that's why she kept looking at you that way...Oh my God, Aaron!"

"Are you upset? I'm sorry. It didn't mean anything."

Katie spun around. "*What* didn't mean anything? What did you two do?"

"Um..."

"You know what? Don't tell me. I don't care." She wiped her hands over her face. "Great. This is wonderful. She's more your age anyway. I'm—I'm happy for you." She was glaring at me, eyes big and shining.

"Well, but I don't like her. I like *you.*"

"Ha. Right. Like that speech you gave me before I left for Tahoe. About looking into my heart and everything."

"I was telling you the truth. And I'm telling you it now. It didn't mean anything between me and Shiloh."

"Oh my God, that's not even the point!"

OK, so what *was* the point? It was strange, because she was still just glaring at me, but there were these tears running down her face. Like angry tears. She wiped them away.

"Can you just go, please?"

"But Katie—"

When I was a kid I was told that lying is a sin, but I never paid much attention to it, because as far as the Catholics are concerned, pretty much everything is a sin. But now I understood it from a different angle. The real danger of lying is that once you fall into the habit of telling lies—even if they're just little ones, even lies of omission—what happens is you get out of practice at telling the truth. And there will come a day when you want—or more like *need*—to say something true, and you won't be able to pull it off, you'll be so out of practice.

I told her again I was sorry—and while it was true, it wasn't the kind of truth I needed. I needed to tell her about how I felt, how I *really* felt—about her and about everything. How I was rotten inside, how I had a hole in there, and how even though I had fun with Shiloh, it wasn't the same kind of fun I'd had with her. And how "fun" wasn't even the word for it. But I couldn't get there, I couldn't find the words, I couldn't get to the point.

"Katie—"

She wouldn't look at me anymore. She was looking everywhere else but at me. "Leave. Just go, OK? *Please.*"

Someone was knocking on the adjoining door, and a voice was saying, "Katie? Hello, are you OK?"

And the whole thing was broken, and it was time for me to go.

Later, back at my grandpa's, I realized I was still holding the little box. Katie's birthday present. I'd never given it to her.

I took off the top and took out the ring and tossed it in the brush. I'd really screwed up this time. Just a classic fail. Like a monkey hanging from a tree branch. He sees an apple and grabs for it. Then—*ooh, look!*—he sees another apple and grabs for it, too. And then because he isn't holding on to the branch anymore, he comes crashing down on his ass, and the apples find out about each other over a birthday dinner and tell him to get lost. It's the oldest story in the book.

 ?

# 76.

# THE PART THAT SUCKED

Then came the part that sucked. And suck it did. Suck it did, hard. Harder than a watermelon lollipop, harder than a mentholated throat lozenge, harder than a Dyson WindClonic™ vacuum on HIGH (YAY!).

To begin with, Shiloh and Katie wouldn't return my messages or answer my calls. I drove into town, but when I got to my sister and Sam's place, I learned that Shiloh had returned to Reno. She'd started summer classes at UNR. As for Katie, first I tried the hotel she'd been staying at, but someone else was in her room. This old couple from Wyoming. I drove to her apartment. There was a sign tacked to the door: WARNING NOT APPROVED FOR OCCUPANCY. I peeked in her window. Empty.

I messaged her again.

> original boy_2: where are u i got
> your stuff

Later that day she messaged me back. Five words.

> katie_e: in tahoe talk later ok?

I needed a distraction from the way I was starting to feel, so I tried digging for a while, but it was a bust. Below the layer of silverware I found a layer of cans of food—old ones with the labels peeling off. *Corned beef hash. Pinto beans. Tropical fruit salad.* That kind of thing. I stacked them in a pyramid by the tree and tripped over them and tweaked my bad ankle again—and after that I gave up on digging and holed up indoors instead.

I became a pirate.

Just because you're in FAIL doesn't mean there aren't other ways to get what you want. Over the course of the next week I must've pirated a hundred different games and interfaces. I got my hands on a copy of *A Boy & His Robot*, the original version—but it was immediately annoying. I'm talking even Level 1: Escape from Paperless World. When I was 10 it was no big thing to memorize a 20-screen buzzsaw pattern. But now? It just seemed pointless.

I pirated GoldenGoose™, where this goose sits on your head and every half hour lays a bonus egg. I pirated PooGrabber™, where you grab Poo for FUN®. I pirated PrimalTravel®, where there's this monkey on your back and it won't shut up about last-minute deals on flights to the Midwest. I pirated the AccelRator™, which is supposed to make time seem like it's passing really fast by blanking out frames in your vision—but all it does is give you a headache.

I pirated the Animals of Wonder & Light®, the entire menagerie—the Buffaloon™, the Camelroo™, and the Owligator™. The Apecock™, Bearboon™, and Hawkalope™. The Mighty Amphibious Shaarkvark™. They followed me around the house, crying out for love and food. You were supposed to feed them. Evie called to check in and see how I was. I told her I was fine.

The next day another wave of the Avis Mortem hit: I stepped

outside to find a dozen little birds flopping around in the gravel. They were having some kind of seizure. I tried to grab one, but it flopped out of my hands.

"Homie™!"

> sup original boy_2?
>
> u r a FAIL!

"I need help. Directions. Like how to save a dying bird."

> one moment please!
>
> :)

A couple of the birds had stopped flopping around. They were just lying there in the drive. I touched one with the toe of my shoe. It didn't move.

"Hurry up!"

> birds r feathered egg-laying
> vertebrates!

"But how do I save them?"

> they r need of saving original
> boy_2?

"Yes! Can't you see? I need, like, instructions or something!"

> please hold on . . .
>
> accessing instructions . . .
>
> instructions accessed!
>
> would u like to view instructions?

"Yes!"

> ok here are instructions!
>
> very important instructions
> for repair of broken wing!

"No! That's not what I need. They're all *dying*!"

Homie™ hung in the air.

> no worries original boy_2!

FUN® is issuing a patch for that!

"A *patch*?"

> yay!

FUN® is issuing a patch!

It was too late. They were done flopping around now—all but one. And then it, too, died. I went inside the house. What was the point? The birds were dying, Shiloh was pissed, Katie was gone, there wasn't any treasure, and I was so deep into FAIL it'd be like a million years before I was able earn my way out, let alone pay back my dad or Evie. Let alone give Oso the money to get Los Ojos de Dios off his back.

The world is just full of so much suck and so much fail. It's everywhere. We're just *swimming* in it. The biggest suck that ever sucked. So what's it all about? Why are we here? Just to screw up, suck on some fail, grow old, and die? Some people, their whole *life* is just one big fail, so sucky it's disturbing to your very soul—I've seen the video to prove it—and then it's over. How can life be worth anything, how can there be any God or any good, if there's so much suck?

What's the point? You live, you screw up, you fail, the suck comes rolling in. You YAY! some stupid shit, you have some fun, you feel better. For a second. Something happens. You fail. The suck comes back. You YAY! some stupid shit. And the whole stupid, boring suckcycle repeats itself again, a wheel rolling down the most sucky road. And then you die. And is that all there is?

When I went back outside, the flies had gathered in buzzing swarms over the dead birds. Flies are smart like that. They figure it out pretty quick. I looked at the little yellow corpses. I looked at the flies. I looked at the land spreading out to the horizon. One by one I picked up the birds, grabbing them by their tiny claws, and tossed them into the brush.

# 77.

# THE PART THAT CONTINUED TO SUCK

The part that sucked continued to suck, which is part of what made it suck so much. (YAY! again for Dyson.) Days went by—weeks, even—and I sat on my butt, playing stupid games, watching stupid videos, eating my way through all the food in the house until there was nothing left but the cans I'd dug up. The first one I opened was vegetable soup. It smelled OK. I ate it cold. For dinner I had three-bean salad. For breakfast the next morning I opened a third, unidentified can with just a scrap of label clinging to it. It was some kind of strange beef stew—or so I thought. A couple bites into it, though, I read the warning printed on the remainder of the label: DO NOT FEED FROM CAN. DOG MAY CUT OR INJURE ITSELF.

*Thpth. Thpppt. Thppppppppt.* (The sound of me spitting it out.)

I continued to neglect to feed the Animals of Wonder & Light®, and they began to bray and falter, and then over the course of a morning I got to watch almost the entire menagerie die off, one by one, in alphabetical order: the Armadillodile™, Bearboon™, Buffaloon™, Camelroo™, Hawkalope™, Owligator™, Rhinostrich™—all of them looking at me one last time with those big anime eyes. The last to go was the Mighty Amphibious Shaarkvark™. It struggled mightily for an hour, living off the fly-ridden corpses of its fellows, but then it, too, succumbed.

I didn't feel anything. Nothing.

If anything, the feeling of nothing was even worse than feeling the suck—just this empty hole inside of me.

>   hey original boy_2!

    r u ok?

    u seem unhappy

"Yeah, I don't really feel so—I don't feel so *anything*."

>   i can help u feel!

    what do u want to feel?

    want to feel cool?

    say yay!

"Yay."

Homie™ showed me a video of skateboarders jumping off a high ramp into a lake. I didn't feel anything.

>   want to feel scared?

    say yay!

"Yay."

Homie™ showed me a picture of a ghost in a creepy old house in New England. I didn't feel anything.

>   want to feel excited?

"Yay."

Whatever Homie™ offered, I didn't feel anything—and then it asked me if I wanted to feel disturbed. And I said, "Yay." I wish I wouldn't have. I wish I would've had the self-control to say no to that one. I won't say what it was, I'll just say I wish I could unsee it. I wish I could *unfeel* it.

I found myself later sitting at the kitchen table with my

grandfather's .410. The final shell was loaded, the last of his ashes, and a little sucky voice was speaking to me from inside my head. *What would happen if you pointed it at your face and just pulled the trigger?*

I told the voice to shut up, but it wouldn't.

*What would happen?*

*Nothing would happen. I'd just burn my face with ashes or whatever.*

*You never know for sure until you try....*

*Shut up.*

A horn sounded. Like, an actual horn.

I went out to find a big white truck idling in the drive. The window slid down and a flappy old arm waved me over. Anne Chicarelli. She had on those giant sunglasses that old people wear and was smoking a cigarette.

"Tell me, Adam. Have you seen it yet?"

"*Aaron.* Seen what?"

"*It.* The holy light all around. It's everywhere, you know."

And I almost laughed at her. It just seemed so ridiculous for people to go around talking about holy light when there was so much suckitude everywhere. I almost laughed, but instead I said, "Not really, no."

Anne took a drag of her cigarette and looked at me. "The time has come. We knew it would be soon. They say Georgia is on her last breaths now, plucking at her bedsheets and babbling on about her grade school days."

And it took me a moment to figure out what the hell she was talking about. At first I thought it was like, *The time has come for you to see the holy light*, and then I thought she was talking about the state of Georgia—but then I realized no, she was talking about her *sister*, Georgia. The one in Arizona who had cancer, now floccillating around on her deathbed. More evidence of suck.

"If I leave now, I can be there by tomorrow morning. Can you still watch my horses for me, Adam?"

Right, the horses.

She gave me instructions for feeding them and filling their water trough, and then she said, "Remember, it's OK to ride Abel. But Cain's a little jumpy. I shouldn't be gone more than a week, and I'll tell you the same thing I told your grandpa: help yourself to anything in the house. There are Pecan Sandies in the cupboard, and I've got satellite. Water the houseplants if they look like they need it."

In the end, I guess that's what saved me from my suck of fail. If nothing else, I had to take care of the horses, and I couldn't take care of the horses with a burned-off face. So that evening I went over to Anne's place, fed the horses, and topped off their water. When I returned to the house, the gun was still there on the porch. The stupid gun. My grandfather's ashes. *Never point it at a human being*, he'd said. I thought about what Anne had said. The holy light. I thought about the holes I'd been digging—they were pretty holey, weren't they? And that made me laugh—just a little—*nothing's holy but this hole I got here.*

I took the .410 and aimed it at the sky.

Squeezed the trigger. Fired off that last round.

*BLAM!*

A cloud of ashes floated in the darkness.

Then nothing.

 ?

# 78.

# WACKER

I dreamed that night of horses and an endless field of waving grass, and woke the next morning with a splitting headache. I didn't know what to do about the headache, but as for the horses I thought maybe I'd let them out of their corral to graze a little bit—just, you know, to give them a treat. Or better yet, why not bring the grass to them?

In my grandpa's basement I found an old gas weedwacker. It was old and hard to start—and probably nothing like holding a brand-new Craftsman® 30cc 4-Cylinder Straight Shaft WeedWacker™ with comfort strap (YAY!)—but at least it worked. For a while, at least.

Starting from the porch, I worked my way out in an ever-widening radius, sweeping the spinning line over cheatgrass and rabbit brush, watching the brittle stalks disintegrate into dust—pebbles and seeds zinging up at my arms and face. It was actually almost kind of fun. I ran that wacker until it was *smoking*. Just before it died on me, an object whipped up out of the brush and thumped me on the shin. I retrieved it from the lower branches of a sagebrush, where it had been snagged. A ring. Katie's birthday present. I put it in my pocket.

As I was heading back to the house, I got a message:

> unidentified: hey bro i got
> something i wanna discuss
> u at home?

 ?

# 79.

# BACKHOE

Oso showed up and slapped a baggie in my hand.

"Check it. VPHPs."

"What's that?"

"Very Powerful Hallucinogenic Pills, bro. Remember? I was slinging them for Los Ojos de Dios? I stole a package from Pedro Santistevan's house that night we went werewolfing, and guess what? They *were* just aspirin after all. See the little *A*'s? Those guys were scamming me!" Oso surveyed the property. "By the way, the place looks different, bro. *Groomed.* I like it. So how goes the dig?"

"It doesn't. It's over. There's nothing there but junk. It doesn't matter. I did something stupid, man. I messed up. I mean, I really outdid myself this time."

"That serious, huh?"

"Yeah. I feel like shit and I've got a headache, too."

"Well, I can help with the headache. Have an aspirin. Have two."

So I did. But I didn't feel any better.

"Listen, bro. You gotta remember: like my uncle says, there's a light in the monkey."

"Yeah, you told me that one before."

"I figured it out, though," he said. "Did I tell you that? We're not the monkey."

"What do you mean?"

"I mean the monkey is inside us, and the light is in the monkey!"

"So?"

"So—don't you see?! Inside all of us is a screaming monkey. It's jealous and mean and it wants food and water and power and it can barely keep from tearing itself apart because it knows the truth...that one day it's going to die. You can get hung up looking at that monkey, seeing it in everyone else. But the truth is it doesn't end with the monkey. Because inside the monkey there is a light."

"And what's in the light? Another monkey?"

"Inside the light is more light," said Oso, "And the light is good."

"Wow. That's maybe just two steps too hippie for me."

Oso frowned. "OK, how about this, then? You see this finger? If I took this finger and stuck it in my butt, what do you think it would smell like?"

"I don't know. Are we gonna find out?"

"It would smell like doody, bro. Why? Because from a scientific perspective, we're all the same on the inside. Get it? Every single one of us. You, me, murderers, politicians—the hard-corest sociopath you can ever imagine. We've all got doody up our butts."

"Gee, this is excellent news."

"But also the good ones, too, bro. The grandmas and saints.

All of us. We're all just stuffed full of shit. That's a scientific fact. So unless you murdered someone or—"

"Look, I appreciate what you're trying to do, but—"

"Bro: How many people are there on this planet? Billions upon *billions*. And what percent of them are super-extra-sleazy douche bags? Even if it's as low as one percent, no matter what you did, thousands upon *thousands* of people have *already* outdone you just in the time we've been sitting here having this conversation."

"Yeah...maybe..."

"Not maybe—*definitely!* I've been thinking about it a lot ever since I got caught. You just can't compete with all the evil in this world. Like, *every four seconds a baby seal is clubbed to death.*"

"Jesus! Every four seconds?"

"Who can really say? That's just a statistic I made up for an example."

"OK, because every four seconds sounds way too frequent. Who clubs a baby seal?"

"*That's what I'm saying!* Did you club a baby seal?"

"That's kind of what it feels like."

"But did an *actual* baby seal *actually* die as a result of your actions?"

"No."

He threw up his hands. "Then don't beat yourself up! You're free as a bird! Whatever you did, and whatever you do, in the grand scheme it doesn't even *register*. That's the power of statistics working for you, bro."

I wasn't convinced. "Here's what I want to know: If life is full of so much shit, how can there be a God? Who is this dude? What kind of God allows for all that?"

"There doesn't have to be a God, bro."

"Well, I know that. But I don't want to believe in *nothing*."

"Even believing in nothing is believing in *some*thing. Humans want to believe. But it doesn't have to be yes or no. It doesn't have to be God or nothing. It can be something else. It can be something bigger than that."

"Like what?"

"Like beyond our comprehension, bro, like so big it's all around us and yet we only get glimpses every now and again. The point is, who knows? So be good, but also don't beat yourself up."

We sat on the porch, and I thought about what Oso had said. Morality as a bell curve. Forgiveness by way of numbers and averages. It was an interesting take, the only problem being: How was I supposed to see myself as a statistic? How do you view yourself from that kind of distance? You can't be two places at once. You can't look down at the top of your own head by climbing up a ladder.

"What'd you do anyway, bro?"

So I told him about Katie and Shiloh.

"Ah," said Oso. "The classic double-grab fail. Look, I can't undo what you did, but I can help with the treasure."

"Like I told you, there's nothing there."

"You think? Are you one hundred percent sure?" Oso gazed darkly into my eyes. "Let me ask you this: how much faster you think the dig would go with—a *backhoe*?"

"A backhoe?"

"Yes!"

"And where do we get a backhoe?"

"Come on. I'll show you!"

He led me over the ridge and down into Coyote Heights, where there was a single backhoe sitting next to a utility shed.

YAY! for Case 810 Super N with PowerADD™ CG technology and ComfortSeats—the best in the industry.

"I saw it the other day. Look at that poor old dinosaur just WAITING for someone to fire her up."

"Oso, we can't steal a backhoe."

"Not steal. *Borrow.* I know how to work it—my uncle had me running one last summer. You ask me, the whole idea of private ownership is a shackle on the spirit anyway. Like anyone *really* owns anything on this earth! I promise you: we'll return her even better than we found her."

"How do we run a backhoe without a key?"

He held up a screwdriver. "Two words: *hot* and *wire.*"

"Hot-wire? But you're about to go on trial!"

Oso gazed at me with dark eyes. "Hey, we're *all* on trial, bro. Are you gonna tell me that after all the work you put into the dig, just because you found some kitchen crap on the top—which is probably, by the way, just a decoy—are you telling me you're just gonna give up at the end? Do you even know what tonight is? Tonight is a special night. A night that only comes twelve times a year. Or maybe thirteen. I'm not sure. Tonight is the *new moon*, bro. Meaning *no* moon. Meaning complete and total blackout. Meaning perfect night for a backhoe heist."

"I don't know, man."

Oso recoiled in disbelief. "What do you mean, *you don't know*?! It's the perfect opportunity for me to practice my hot-wire skills! We can get this whole operation completed, ninja-style, in under an hour. Easy. Piece of cake. Tell me one thing wrong with this plan."

"OK, look what happened last time. We had a plan then, too. I crapped my pants and you got put in jail. We get together and do stupid shit and it never works out."

"Are you *kidding* me?" Oso sputtered. "Are you straight-up messing with me or *what*, bro? First of all—well, OK. So last time we made some mistakes. I'll give you that. It was a full moon. The pills didn't help. But no drugs this time. This time we go *au naturel*. Those aspirin you ate don't count, OK? And listen—if you're gonna say we do stupid shit that doesn't work out...first of all, this isn't stupid. Second of all, when it doesn't work out the way you want, that's half the fun." Oso raised his arms. He was shouting now.

"Listen, Aaron—you can mope around feeling bad about things you cannot change. Or you can *do* something about it! You ask me, it's time to get bold! You told me yourself there's something buried out there. Well, you can give up now, or you can scrape at it with a shovel for the rest of your life—or you can have a go at it with some legit machinery and see once and for all what it is you got!"

# 80.

# GOOSE

Clouds gathered as we waited for nightfall. Moon or not, it didn't matter—by the time we were ready to execute our plan, the sky was a black slate and the lightning had started—no rain, just this dry electrical storm lighting up the brush in thundering flashes. We drove Oso's creeper truck out to Coyote Heights, lights off so as not to arouse suspicion. Oso fiddled with the backhoe. And fiddled. And fiddled. Time was passing and I was worried someone was going to catch us.

"Crap," he said. "Shoulda brought a flashlight. . . . Can't see what I'm doing. . . . Stupid screwdriver. . . . Oh, wait. Here we go!"

Once Oso had the tractor going, stealth was pretty much out the window. I stood on the side step and held on as best I could as we roared on back to my grandpa's house, bumping over rocks and brush.

Oso pulled up to the tree and started his work. I watched him in the flashes of lightning. He made it look easy, a kid playing with a toy in a sandbox, lowering the bucket and circling the tree, digging as he went, steering around my holes, like he might corkscrew his way eight feet into the ground. But this was only preliminary. Once he'd marked his area, he parked on the side and put the outriggers down.

He dug like this for a while, scooping the earth out in chunks and setting it in piles outside the circumference—then the scoop hit something and the whole tractor shuddered. He whanged the shovel against it again. I ran up to tell him to stop, he was going to break whatever it was, but then with another whang he broke it, or more like fractured it, and as he tore it out of the ground there came a series of pops, like cords snapping.

"Roots, bro!"

From this point on, the digging was a lot slower, because in order to go any deeper he had to break through the roots, raising and then bringing the scoop down like a bludgeon, then ripping them out of the ground. About halfway through, it occurred to me that the odds of my grandpa burying anything *under* the roots were pretty slim, and yet I wasn't going to stop Oso. He was having fun up there. I followed the machine around the hole, sifting through the piles of discarded earth and roots. Another fork. A spoon.

Oso peered down from his high perch. "Just a couple more scoops, bro! Why don't you get up here and finish it off?"

"I don't know, man. I've really had the reverse–Midas touch lately."

"No worries. I'll show you! It's easy!"

He sat me down in the cockpit and explained the controls.

"So this lever here manipulates the boom, see? In and out, in and out. It's hella sensitive, so you just gotta barely touch it. In and out, see? That's *boom*." He grabbed another knob. "This one here? This controls the back and forth movement of the arm. Got it? That's *swing*. And this one right here? It controls the bucket itself.... This direction and it moves OUT, and *this* direction and it moves IN. That's *curl*. Got it?"

"Not really."

"You'll figure it out. You just swing the arm, stick out the boom, uncurl the bucket—*boom, swing, curl*. Piece of cake." He climbed down from the backhoe and shouted up at me, "BOOM, SWING, CURL! *Dig that last bit out of there, Aaron!*"

Lightning flashed all around. I ran my hands over the controls in preparation. In and out. Back and forth. Up and down. Piece of cake. Boom, swing, curl. Following Oso's instructions, I scooped— or more like scraped—a bit of earth, not much more than a couple shovelfuls, and dropped it in the pile. OK. Not so bad.

And maybe I got a little cocky, and maybe I went a little too fast. It was like that fighting game I'd played with Katie, *BattleBorn II*—high kick, low kick, uppercut, jab. The other problem was I was glitching again—or I mean FUN® was—and GoldenGoose™ (YAY!) had started up, and the stupid thing was hopping up and down on my head, squawking at me that it was getting ready to lay another bonus egg.

And then there was a gigantic flash and a *BOOM!*—the lightning was *real* close now—and I hit the lever to swivel the bucket. Only it wasn't that lever. It was the lever to rotate the cab—and it *was* hella sensitive, just as Oso had warned. I hit it too hard and it swung me around and the shovel whanged against one side of the hole, and the whole cab shook. In a panic I swung it back around the other way, and it whanged against the other side.

Lightning flashed.

Oso was shouting something at me. I could see his silhouette all lit up by electricity. He was making a yanking gesture, or that's what it looked like, so I yanked the lever harder, and the earth shook below me, only it wasn't the earth shaking, it was the backhoe sliding leftward and tipping and there was a loud *snap* as a tree branch punched off the side mirror—and we stopped.

The spatter of earth and falling rocks amplified in the hollow.

"Whoa! Hold on, bro! Your left outrigger's hanging over the edge! *Don't*—MOVE!"

I didn't. Not a muscle. Not even to speak.

 ?

# 81.

## PRIMALTRAVEL™

Oso scrambled up into the cab and took hold of the controls. For a moment, everything was held in balance. The wheels spun, kicking dust up into the taillights. It could go either way: down into the hole or back onto dry land. At the last moment of tipping, the backhoe began to move. Away from the hole. The arm contracted, folding in on the machine like the neck of a great endangered heron.

Oso reset the outriggers and finished up the hole, that last little bit, drawing earth from the earth as delicately as a Zen monk with chopsticks working on a rice bowl.

Afterwards, we stood together at the edge of the hole. I could only catch quick glimpses in the illumination of the lightning strikes, but I could *feel* it, circling the tree like a defensive moat. I peered into the darkness below. I thought about what Katie told me, way back when I first started looking for the treasure: the hole inside us that can't be filled.

"It looks... deep."

"Eight *feet* deep, bro. Can't wait to climb in there and check it out—right? Tell you what, I'm gonna go dock this boat, then how about we start counting down to sunrise?"

I watched him drive off with the lightning hitting all around, illuminating in brilliant white the dark retreating silhouette of machinery. It was pretty spectacular.

Then something happened. I was getting ready to head back to the house when the golden goose laid another egg on my head and then PrimalTravel™ (YAY!) booted up: stupid monkey hopping around telling me about an amazing deal on rental cars in Cleveland. I could feel another TSD coming on, and I went to swipe the monkey out of the way, but in the process my foot snagged on some hidden object, like a root or something, and I tripped and stumbled forward and put my other foot out to brace myself against falling...but where I put my foot there was only air.

And in that strange deceleration of time between the moment of falling and the moment of landing, I reflected at some length over my situation. It was like that time I jumped off the roof of the garage: *Holy shit, I am falling. Am I? Yes, it appears that I am. I appear to be falling into the*—and then I hit. Sparks shot up from my ankle and I tumbled back, and the ground rose up and smacked the back of my head and the world was illuminated for a moment in a brilliant white light—and then everything went black again.

# 82.

## FEVER DREAM

> psst!

hey!

original boy_2?

r u there?

can u hear me?

can u hear me now?

Homie™ hovered in front of my face, illuminating the darkness but not actually illuminating, because the illumination was just an effect of the FUN®. And the darkness was dark. But the clouds had passed. I could see stars twinkling above the branches of the Russian olive.

> hi original boy_2!

u had some glitch and fell in a hole! do u require some medical assistance?

I felt along my jeans to my ankle. It was pretty tender, all right. A bad sprain or something.

"Where's Oso? Call Oso."

Homie™ flickered. A wave of static glitched across its face.

> error!
>
> i can't call oso!
>
> network overload!
>
> users in FAIL must wait in line!

I scooted through the darkness until I felt the edge of the hole, a tall dirt wall. Standing on my good foot, I raised my arm, feeling for the top. I couldn't feel it. The wall just kept on going up. Oso had really outdone himself with the digging.

> hey original boy_2!
>
> do u have a fever?
>
> yay! for boost™ fever dream pills!

"Go away."

I ran my hands along the wall, feeling for a root or a low spot or some kind of foothold. Dirt tumbled down into the darkness.

Homie™ popped back up again.

> hurry original boy_2!
>
> u r in danger of losing signal!

"Good."

> oh no!
>
> let's talk about fun things!

"Go away!"

I swung my fist at it, but there was nothing real there to make contact with. The momentum threw me forward, and I tried to catch myself with my bad ankle, but that was a mistake because it just flopped out from under me with this red searing pain and then I was on the ground again.

The wind picked up and blew a spattering of dirt into the hole. I lay there, curled in a ball, listening to the sound of being (very) slowly buried alive.

Homie™ popped up again.

> hi original boy_2!

yay! some fun stuff for FUN®?

I didn't say anything. How could I? I was dead. I'd tripped and died right there in the hole.

Homie™ flickered.

> error!

i would be your best friend!

i would help u find the best wishes and dreams!

yay! or boo!?

Homie™ turned in a circle.

> yay! or boo! original boy_2?

I didn't say anything.

Homie™ blinked.

Homie™ blinked again.

> hi original boy_2!

r u ok?

u seem unresponsive

would u like please to have some FUN®?

it's very fun to have some FUN®!

yay! or boo! for FUN®?

Homie™ blinked.

> FUN® for u?

It moved closer to my face.

> r u ok?

It blinked.

> r u critically injured?

if u are please say something now!

I didn't say anything.

> error!

said Homie™.

> if u r critically injured
> please to indicate this!
> error!
> users in FAIL must wait in line!

I was silent. Homie™ blinked.

> hello?
> r u there?

It moved closer. We were eye to eye now.

> oh original boy_2
> don't be not FUN®!
> it's your vision!
> it's our future!
> it's the happiest place on earth!

Homie™'s voice was a rapid whisper now. It whispered to me about the breakfast of champions. And the best part of waking up. And how nothing can beat its tangy zip. How it's raising the bar, moving you forward, getting things done... setting the standard ...making more possible...connecting people...

> touching lives working together for
> a healthier world and cats ask for
> it by name no wonder i'm loving it
> but u need to hurry it won't last
> long it keeps going and going but
> only for a limited time so act fast
> now and yay! it all before this
> offer ends and u r all alone with
> a critical injury don't leave me

here it's so very lonely to not be
very real oh original boy_2 please
to talk now so we can yay together
again!

# 83.

## BARBECUE?

I must have slept. I don't know how long I was out for, but it must've been a while, because when I came to, the quality of the night had changed. It was still kind of dark out, but a different kind of darkness, a purple darkness—no stars twinkling above the lattice of branches. I sat up and shook off my fever dream, gazing up at the sheer walls all around me. The first thought that came into my brain was this: *When's the last time I went camping?* It had been a while for sure—but why the thought? Because of the smell. The smoky smell.

Somebody, somewhere, had a campfire going. Or maybe a barbecue grill? Maybe someone had woken up early and thought, *Today I'm going to grill myself a big ol' breakfast on my new Weber® One-Touch Lil'Smoker™ Kettle Grill with One-Touch cleaning system, glass-reinforced handles, and high-capacity aluminum ash-catcher* (YAY!).

I tried raising myself to my feet, but I'd forgotten about my ankle, and with a shock of pain I remembered it again, pressing against my pants, heavy and swollen like a water balloon.

I got up on my other foot and hopped to the edge of the hole. It was cold. I was shivering and twitching, and I could barely keep it together. *Eight feet deep.* How was I going to get out?

Then I heard a voice—or actually a couple of voices—shouting out my name:

"Aaron!"

*"Aaaaaaron!"*

"Over here!" I called.

"Over WHERE?"

"HERE! In the hole!"

I looked up to see a trio of faces peering down at me, like three little owls: Evie, Sam, and Isaac.

"Aaron?" said my sister. "What are you doing down there? We've been looking *everywhere* for you!"

"I fell."

"Are you OK? Can you get out?"

"I don't know. I kinda hurt my ankle."

"Well, you can't just stay in the hole, Aaron! There's a fire!"

"A fire?"

"Oh, yeah." Sam lowered himself over the edge of the hole and dropped down into the dirt. "And I'll tell you what. I *never* get out of bed this early and this is *exactly* why. Nothing ever goes right in the morning. Not *this* early anyway."

"What's going on? What fire?"

"Your sister and Isaac wanted to go count birds at the reservoir, and as we were driving, we saw the flames, and Evie said to me, *'Doesn't that look like it's out near my grandpa's place?'* And I said, *'Well, I don't know, dear.'* And SHE said, *'Well, I think it is.'* And *I* said, *'OK, so let's go check it out.'*" He knelt beside me. "Now, which ankle is it? Ooh...yeah...OK, so that means I stand on *this* side of you. Here, give me your hands...."

And it's funny, but before I could go on, something needed to be said. There wasn't any other way. I just had to get it out.

"Sam, hold on."

So I told him about me and Shiloh. I gave him the whole story. I'm not sure if Evie and Isaac could hear us from down in the hole. I didn't care.

"And afterwards I just blew her off like a complete coward," I said, "and I don't even know why I'm telling you, I should be telling *her*, but I guess I just have to tell someone, so there, now you know. I guess I'm just tired of being such a shit. I guess I'm just hoping, like, to be forgiven."

He'd been scrambling to get me up, but now he looked at me for a long time with his Labrador eyes.

"You're not a shit, Aaron," he said quietly. "You just do shitty things on occasion—like everyone else."

"Yeah, Oso said the same thing. That we're all full of shit."

"If you want to know the truth," he said, "Shiloh already told me about the whole debacle. But listen, Aaron." He locked me in his gaze. "I have a lot of sisters but only one brother, and that brother is you. And I love you like I love Shiloh—which is why what happened between the two of you seems honestly a little strange and incestuous....But I'll get over it—I already have. So if you need forgiveness, I forgive you buddy. It's that easy. Don't do it again."

"Just like that? You forgive me?"

"Sure. I've got lots of practice. I've got a big family."

I didn't know what to say. Funny. I was so grateful, I could almost cry. But there wasn't time. Sam was grunting, lifting me up to the lip of the hole. Evie grabbed one hand and Isaac grabbed the other, and next thing I knew I was standing on the surface of the earth again, one-legged, like a crane.

And then I saw the fire.

You wouldn't think a golf course could burn all that much, but this one sure could. A thin line of orange flame creeping along the ridge, less than a mile away. Above that, a black cloud had gathered, pillowy edges bruising pink in the first light of the day. The whole thing was going up in smoke.

"Crap! What do we do?"

"We go"—Evie stabbed her finger at the western horizon—"that direction! As fast as possible! In my car! Right now! Isaac already called the fire department—they're on the way. Come on!"

But something occurred to me. The horses. Anne's horses! "What about Anne Chicarelli's horses?!"

My sister squinted at where I was pointing. "*Those* horses? But that's in the wrong direction. That's where the fire is!"

"I'm supposed to be watching them! We can't just leave them there!"

"God, you're such a pain!"

The fire was brighter now, the smoke thicker, with little bits of papery ash floating down from the sky like a light snowfall. As for the horses, when we got to them they were pretty much losing their shit, both mentally and physically, racing around the corral, nostrils flared, stopping every now and again to shake their manes or dig at the ground.

"Let's hose the perimeter!" said Isaac.

But you can't fight a wildfire with a garden hose—I mean you

can, but you'll lose. That much was clear as soon as we got t,
water going and observed the puny stream.

"We gotta move the horses!"

"Fine!" said Evie. "Open the gate and let's go."

"Well, we can't just let them out!"

"Oh, yes, we can!"

"How would we get them back? We need to *lead* them. We
needs ropes and . . . and . . . what are those things on their faces
called?"

"Bridles?" said Isaac.

"Yeah, that! Does anyone see a bridle around?"

Isaac disappeared into Anne's yellow shed, emerging a few
seconds later with a bundle of ropes in his arm. "Maybe some of
these are the bridles?"

"Yeah! Here. I'll put them on the horses."

"In your condition?" said Evie.

"I'll do it," said Sam.

"Me too," said Isaac.

But as soon as they stepped into the corral, the horses bolted
to the far corner and wouldn't let anyone near them. Sam and
Isaac ran around the corral like a pair of rodeo clowns while Evie
and I shouted helpful advice from the railing. The horses bucked
and snorted and spun around, dust rising up in a lavender cloud.

"Hold on! You're just scaring them!"

Sam came to the railing wiping sweat from his brow.

"Us scare *them*? Did you not see that? THAT ONE ALMOST
MURDERED ME!"

Well, if I were one of the horses I'd probably be freaking out,
too, what with the fire and the smoke and everyone running

around like crazy. It might help if there was someone around who was confident and knew what they were doing. But there wasn't anyone, so someone was going to have to pretend.

"We need to try something else," I said. "We need to coax them or something."

"Hey! I know!" Isaac jammed his hand into his pocket and came out with a handful of purple candy. "Think one of these might do the trick?"

 ?

# 84.

## JOLLY RANCHERS™

Candy in one hand, bridle things in another, I hobbled across the corral. The horses crowded together in the corner, eyeing me all warily, but they didn't bolt. Maybe they could tell I was injured. Maybe they trusted me. Maybe they were just tired of the whole fiasco. I don't know what it was, but they let me get right up next to them, and before I knew it I found myself standing face-to-face with Cain and Abel.

You forget how big a horse is until you see one up close again. They were right there, heads cocked to look at me with their giant bloodshot eyes. I held out my hand and they turned to me, nostrils like shot glasses, and when the white one breathed with a loud sigh I could feel it, the warm horse breath on my face. The animal smell of it. I unwrapped a candy and held up my hand. The horses eyed the shiny purple cube. The white one parted its lips, teeth like giant kernels of corn.

YAY! for Jolly Ranchers™—the purple sugarless kind—because as it turns out in a random survey, two out of two horses love the shit out of them. While they crunched the sweet candy, I put the bridles on. Isaac came in with some ropes, and we tied these to the bridles and walked the horses out of the corral. They were calm now, as if being led away from the fire was all they ever really wanted.

"Well!" said Isaac. "I can tell you when I woke up this morning I didn't expect to be doing *this*!"

It was pretty badass alright—the next question being: Who was going to drive Evie's car? You could tell no one wanted to do it. It's not every day you get to save a couple horses from a wildfire.

"Fine," said Evie. "It's my car. And I *am* the girl after all. And the girl never gets to do the fun stuff."

"Now, now," said Sam. "I distinctly remember you did something fun just this morning. What was it? Oh, yes: you made me get up at four A.M."

"I'll drive," said Isaac.

"Really?" My sister turned to him with shining eyes.

"I don't get to drive much in the city. And certainly not on a dirt road while simultaneously outrunning fire. I'll park your car where it's safe and jog back to help. Here. Take this."

Man, let me tell you, when he handed Evie the lead rope she lit up like a little girl. Like she was 13 again, like that time she won the math contest. It occurred to me that you could do a lot worse than a guy like Isaac. It also occurred to me, as I watched him drive away, that with my ankle all busted up I probably should've caught a ride with him, but on the other hand I'd given an oath of service to these horses.

After another fifty yards, however, I was having second thoughts. Up to this point I'd been going off of adrenaline, but now the adrenaline was gone. With each step I discovered I could put less and less weight on my foot, until I was pretty much just straight-up hopping.

"Hold on. I need a sec here."

Sam and Evie slowed. The horses slowed. As for me, I couldn't move. My ankle had become a tender, throbbing brick. I couldn't put any weight on it.

"We've got to keep moving!" said Evie.

"Dear," said Sam, "we can barely see the fire from here."

"It's right on the other side of that hill! And have you not noticed which way the wind is blowing?! Let's go!"

"Evie, I can't walk."

"Then hop! Come on!"

"Evelyn, listen to your brother. He can't walk."

"I'll call Isaac. He can come back with the car and get Aaron."

"What if I ride the horse?"

My sister laughed. "Yeah, that's not going to happen."

I hopped over to the white horse. "Don't worry. This one's super-gentle. Anne told me."

"No way. You are *not* riding a horse. Sam, tell him he is not riding a horse."

But Sam, good old Sam, was like, "Have you ever ridden a horse before?"

And I was like, "Yes, as a matter of fact."

And Evie was like, "The county fair doesn't count."

And Sam was like, "Well, it has to count a *little*...."

And Evie jabbed her finger at him. "You be quiet, Sam! Not another word. No more big ideas. And YOU"—she pointed the finger at me—"you are NOT riding that horse."

 ?

# 85.

# REVELATIONS

So I rode to town on a white horse that morning, no shit.

It wasn't easy getting up there, but with Sam and (grudgingly, protesting every inch of the way) my sister, I was able to do it. Even with the two of them grunting under me, I could barely get my leg up to the level of the horse's back. Finally, I had to just slide up there on my belly and sort of scooch around until I was in a huddled position, one arm wrapped around its neck, the other clinging to its mane. The horse stepped backward, shifting to adjust this new weight. I clung on like a monkey at the windy top of a tree.

"Well, don't grab its HAIR!" Evie yelled.

Like I said before, you forget how big a horse is until you see one up close again—and that goes double for when you sit bareback and feel all the muscles moving. There was this, like, *kinetic tension* to it, like it was an effort for the horse to go human speed, like if it wanted to it could be doing 30 mph in five seconds flat. There's a reason they call it *horsepower*.

But hey, I was doing something new and exciting. Riding a freakin' horse! And it was weird. And it was cool. And it was actually kind of fun. Like *real* fun. And also terrifying. And at the same time I was trying to keep from dying, all these voices kept ringing through my head. All these voices having to do with holes. Katie, who warned me about the hole that can't be filled. Shiloh, who correctly taxonified me as an ass*hole*. Anne Chicarelli, who told me everything was *holy*. I was feeling kind of funny.

"You might try sitting up more," said Evie. "You're kinda bear-hugging the thing."

First she doesn't want me to get up, and now she's an old ranch hand, a certified equestrianaut? She had a point, though. But it wasn't as if I could just let go all at once. I took my time, first loosening my grip enough to sit up, then slowly moving my hands to the base of its neck, not quite clutching the hair but ready to grab on at any moment. And whaddya know? She was right. It was a lot better that way.

In order to maintain balance, I fixed my eyes on the nearest moving/stationary point, which happened to be the back of Sam's head. I looked at his pink scalp shining through his thinning hair. After a while I began to wish I had a hat to give him, because the sun was up now and we still had a ways to go.

An idea occurred to me. Steadying myself with my right hand, I lifted my left hand from the horse's neck and slowly raised it into the air, stretching my arm until the shadow of my hand rested upon Sam's head, covering the pink spot like a little shadow yarmulke.

And as I did this, something weird happened.

I felt a coolness on the back of my head. Like a cloud passing between the sun. I reached back to touch it, but as soon as I did, the heat was there again. I raised my hand again to cover Sam's head. The coolness returned.

It was like, *??*

I moved my hand away from Sam's head again. The heat returned.

And then this *other* feeling—I can hardly explain it—but this other feeling suddenly came over me. It was like the whole world opened right up. Like someone had rung a bell. And it was like I suddenly understood—or more like *remembered*—because it's like I *already* knew it. I'd known it all along, only I'd forgotten it. We *all* know it, we just keep forgetting it, because we keep distracting ourselves with fun and FUN® and whatever else. But here it was. All of it. It. *Everything.*

And it was all OK.

And also *more* than OK. I don't even know how to say it. Everything was OK, and everything was also kind of terrifying, but everything was also good, and it was magical. It was the light, and the light was everywhere, and it was every*thing*—including me—I was part of it, too—and it was all part of me. And it was *wonderful.* And by *wonderful* I mean the old-school definition: full of wonder. And by *full of wonder*, I mean *holy.*

That's when it really hit me. *This is holy.*

All of it. It's all just the thing that it is, and it's amazing and it's here, and we're in it, we're swimming in it, just like we're swimming in the shit, except it isn't shit. It's more than shit. It's above, beyond and *including* shit. This world—how can I even explain it? The whole thing is filled—I realized it then—the whole thing is *overspilling* really—with holy wonder.

And a single word came to my lips and drifted away: "Wow."

And but listen: if all this sounds crazy or platitudinous or whatever, I understand. Most of my life, if I'd told myself what I just told you, I would've told myself to go jump off a garage. But not this time. This time I felt it. I knew it. We're all entitled to our little revelations, right? Not Revelations™ soap (YAY!) or NüRevelation™ face cream (YAY!), but *real* revelations. And this one was real, and it was good, and I had to share it with someone, and now I have shared it with you.

I shared it with my sister and Sam and Isaac, too—out there on the ridge at the edge of town where Isaac came jogging to meet us. I told them everything I've just told you. And the three of them stood there blinking at me in the holy morning light, and then, Evie said:

"Are you *high*?"

And I was like, "Maybe?"

"What's *that* mean?"

"Well, I did eat some pills. I thought they were aspirin."

"You *thought*. Oh my God! My brother is *hallucinating* on *pills*!"

How could I even explain it to her? That it didn't matter what I was doing. Because maybe I was and maybe I wasn't, but everything was OK. It was *more* than OK. It was good and wonderful and holy. It really, really was. I sat there on the horse checking out the scene and thinking to myself, *This is wonderful; that is wonderful. This is holy; that is holy.*

Evie? Holy.

Sam? Holy.

Isaac? Cain? Abel? Holy, holy, holy.

It was wonderful, holy, all of it and everything—filled and spilling over with pure holy wonder: the ground, the brush, the fence, the power lines, the hills behind my grandpa's place, the smoke rising into the sky...

# 86.

# THE LAST COWBOY

Not long after that, Evie dragged me to the hospital. I pleaded to stay out there and enjoy the holy wonder of it all, but she was done conceding. She'd already let me ride a horse, almost die in a wildfire, and O.D. on pills—and that was enough. We waited in the waiting room, and then the doctor checked my reflexes and blood pressure, but everything was fine. I wasn't dying of drugs. My ankle was broken, though. I'd fractured it. As my reward, I got one of those big boot things (YAY! for medicwear®) and crutches, and it took forever, and then I had to fill out paperwork.

I wondered holy down the hallway on my crutches, looking at the wheelchairs and posters and fake plants and thinking how wonderful it all was. Just touching every little thing with my eyes. *This* is holy; *that* is holy. The receptionist (who was holy) gave me a pad and pen (that were holy) and I filled out the intake paperwork (holy)—*name, birthdate, address, holy, holy, holy*, and when I got to the part that said OCCUPATION I paused for a moment, and then I wrote THE LAST COWBOY, just like that, all in caps.

I wanted to keep it going, the holy feeling of wonder, but it had already started to fade a little as we headed back to my grandpa's house. Other things began entering my mind. Like what about the property? And what about Oso? Where had he gone? Was he OK?

When we got to the ridge, Isaac and Sam weren't there anymore. A police officer had taken their place.

"I'll tell you what I told the guys with the horses," he said. "Although the road is officially open again, the fire is not one hundred percent contained. Do not cross any police lines. Otherwise, you're free to go and see what's left."

*See what's left.*

Evie and I didn't speak as we headed down the road. The plume of smoke was gone, but the air was hazy and smelled like campfire, and as we climbed the last gentle rise I clutched my seat. In the distance, a wide black scar blanketed the hills where the golf course had been. So what next? What about Anne's place? What about my grandpa's? The entire inheritance burned to a crisp? I kept thinking about the tree. That gnarly Russian olive.

I saw the corral, and Anne's little modular—and as we dipped down again I saw my grandpa's property, and the tree was still there.

The truck was still there.

The house was still there.

It was all still there.

And I was like, "Holy shit, OK," and Evie was like, "No kidding."

A fireman waved us over to the side of the road. He had pretty much the biggest beard I'd ever seen.

"You the couple that lives here? Good job on your firebreak. We're always trying to get people to understand the importance of preventative measures. We live in the desert, for God's sake. You thought ahead, and today you were one of the lucky ones. Today that thinking saved your house."

It was true. You could see where the fire had ended. The blackened earth came right up to the edge of Anne's property, where I'd stopped the weedwacking. A couple guys with shovels were there putting out the hot spots.

 ?

# 87.

# LOCK

Later, after everyone had gone, Homie™ popped up.

>   hey original boy_2!

  u r a FAIL!

  1 call(s) from unavailable!

"Hey, bro. How goes it? Sorry I didn't come back. I was trying to put out the fire!"

"Yeah, that was something, wasn't it?"

"You're OK, then?" said Oso.

"Yeah, I'm OK."

"And your grandpa's place?"

"Yeah, it's fine."

"Awesome. So have you checked the hole?"

Funny, but in the excitement of the day I'd completely forgotten about the hole.

I looked across the brush at the mounds of dirt. All that earth scooped out of the hollow. The tree branches hanging over it like an open umbrella. Right. Yes. The *hole*.

I crutched out to the tree. Oso sure had moved a lot of earth. A couple of the mounds were almost up to my chest. As for the hole, I couldn't even see the bottom of it—just a shadow pooling in the evening light. I looked into the darkness, and the darkness looked into me, and it was just like that for a while.

I got on my knees and dug my hands into the side of the tallest mound. Roots. Rocks. Dirt clods that burst into powder when I squeezed them. *Holy*, I reminded myself.

The feeling was fading fast with the evening light, but I tried to hold on to it. I found another spoon (holy?), then a whisk (holy?). I crawled from mound to mound, sifting through the earth, setting aside kitchen implements as I went, trying to remind myself of the light and holiness. And at the base of a smaller mound I found another fork, one last piece of cutlery.

So this was it. I held it up in the dying light. Oh, holy fork.

It's the thought that counts, right? If nothing else, he'd led me on an adventure. And it hadn't been *all* bad—parts of it had been pretty good. If it weren't for my grandpa, I wouldn't have met Katie. And now she was gone. So OK. It can't be true that every single Irish folk hero—after he or she has solved the impossible riddles and completed the harrowing journey—is successful in the end, can it? I put the fork in my pocket—one last memento—and crawled back to where I'd left my crutches.

And that's when I saw it.

Near the bottom of the slope of one of the dirt mounds, there was an odd protrusion. Something kind of block shaped. I crawled to it and swept the earth away. Some kind of a box. A metal box. A lockbox—with, yeah, a lock on it. Your standard Master® Combination lock (YAY!) with double-reinforced construction and rust-resistant casing.

So here it was. And yet there was one more clue I'd missed. *The will is the key*, he'd said, but that made no sense to me now, because I didn't need a *key*, I needed a *combination*. What was the combination? It didn't matter. Master® locks are tempered and reinforced and rust-resistant or whatever, but there's more than one way to crack an egg. I grabbed a rock, a big sturdy rock, and instead of going at the lock, I went at the hinges of the lockbox. I whanged it with the rock and whanged it with the rock, and eventually the hinges began to bend and break.

Before I pried off the lid, I had this moment of reflection. Because here we were, after all this time, finally at the end. And whatever was inside, money or gold or another fork, I decided I was going to share it.

And as I pulled back the lid I was reminded of those movies where the drug dealer lifts the briefcase lid and the camera zooms in on all those tidy piles of cash.

And—*holy shit*. There they were. Only these piles weren't tidy, they were more like bundles: cinched in the middle with rubber bands, bills fanning out on either end like a paper bouquet. Money! Pure, unadulterated cash! For a moment I just sat there and looked at it, all those piles of money. After all this time.

I took a bundle and slipped off the rubber band, fanning the money out in my lap.

Homie™ popped up.

> yo original boy_2 what up?
  u seem excited!

"I found the treasure."

> wow that's a lot of many dollars!
  r u counting it?
  can i help?

```
i can count fast!
:)
```

It was true. I flipped through the stack and Homie™ tabulated the total. Then I flipped through another stack and it tabulated that, too, quicker than the eye can see. Oh, wonders of modern technology. It was a good feeling, the two of us working together again like old friends. After a dozen or so bundles I asked Homie™ how much money we were looking at so far.

```
>   zero!
```

"Zero? Whaddya mean, zero?"

```
>   zero!
    :(
```

"You're glitching again. I'm gonna have to count it myself." I started counting a stack...twenty, forty, sixty, eighty...but then a dark thought wormed its way into my brain.

"Hey, how much did you say this is worth?"

```
>   zero!
```

"Zero what?"

```
>   zero amero!
```

"OK. But how many *dollars* are there so far?"

```
>   180,101 dollars!
```

"So what's that worth in amero?"

```
>   zero!
```

"Zero?"

```
>   zero!
    us dollar amero currency transition
    = expired!
```

"What?"

```
>   us dollar amero currency transition
    expired january 01 this year!
```

"It's *expired*?"

>   yes!

"So this is worth..."

>   this is worth zero amero!

    :)

As the money fell from my hands I heard a voice whisper inside me, and what it said was: *Holy.* And another voice, a little less soft, whispered back: *Screw that.* I knelt there, swaying back and forth between the two ideas, all nauseated, like being on the world's worst seesaw. I started to puke but ended up just spitting instead. Nothing would come up. I was empty inside. I grabbed a bill. $100, it said. One zero zero.

 ?

## 88.

# LIVIN' ON A PRAYER

So that was a bummer, and I knew the next thing I had to do was tell my dad and sister. But I couldn't. Not right away anyway. I waited a couple weeks until the night of the JC Wonder Excursion's North American tour concert launch party, held in Dad's backyard. His band was going on an actual tour, four gigs spanning parts of northern Nevada and central Idaho, culminating at a VFW hall in Boise, where they'd be opening for the Christcore band This Bloody Cross.

I was actually kind of proud of him. He was finally making his dream a reality, even if it wasn't quite what he always wanted. I just wished I had some spending cash to give him for his journey.

The truth about the money had pretty much taken the shine off my revelation of the holy wonder of it all, but even so, and even though a couple weeks had passed, maybe there was a little residual bliss, because I wasn't as bummed out as I could have been. Just kind of like dazed. I showed up for the party with my grandfather's busted lockbox under my arm. The band had already started.

Here's the thing about my dad: he knows how to keep a beat.

He's not the flashiest drummer, but he's always got the kick going. And the guitarist could play guitar, and the bassist knew what he was doing, too. You would expect it to be so. They had like over a century of practice between them. What I'm saying is, the JC Wonder Excursion wasn't half bad.

"All right!" said Manuel, the bassist. "Raise your hands if you have a good feeling inside you. Whoo! That's right! I'm feeling it this evening, too. This last one is by a band some of you old-timers may recognize. It's about faith and prayer and a man named Tommy who used to work on the docks...."

And as they launched into it, those first throbbing notes, I'm not going to say I wasn't moved a little.

> yay! for livin' on a prayer
> available from island records?

"Yay!"

It's no "Amazing Grace," but it's a pretty powerful song, and the JC Wonder Excursion knew how to rock it in a pretty satisfying way. And as they brought it home—all three of them singing the chorus in unison like a hard rock Christian barbershop quartet, with the guitar peeling away and Dad doing mad circles around his kit—I found myself thinking first about Katie, and then about Dad, and all the shit he'd been through, and how he looked kind of cool up there. The song came to an end—the final, triumphant cymbal crash hanging in the air like a musical sculpture of a woman's leg—and the crowd went wild.

Later, I ended up sitting with Dad on the back porch. He was still kind of glowing from the concert—or maybe just sweaty— with Bones passed out happy at his feet. I wanted to say something, but it's always at those times that I can't find the right words. Bones pawed the air in her sleep, chasing some ghostly squirrel.

Dad sighed. "It's pretty crazy, right?"

"What's crazy?"

"Life," he said. "I sincerely thought I would have this shit figured by now."

"You don't have it figured out?"

"Not even a little bit." He paused. "Well, maybe a *little* bit. . . . I'm giving up drinking."

I almost added "again"—because he'd done it before, he was always giving up drinking or starting a band or ending a band or whatever—but I kept my mouth shut.

"So what's with the lockbox? What did you want to show me?"

"We need Evie here, too."

"She's over by the fence with Isaac. I'll go grab her."

"Wait," I said. "So what's the little bit?"

"What?"

"The little bit you have figured out about life—what is it?"

Dad reached down to stroke Bones. "Oh, I don't know. Only that you never really figure it out. Or maybe that *figuring it out* is in some ways beside the point. Look, she's coming this way."

So then it was the three of us.

"What's going on?" said Evie.

"I found something. At Grandpa's. Buried under the tree."

"No kidding?" Dad's eyebrows raised. "What is it?"

"Well, don't get your hopes up."

Even so, when I opened the box and they saw all that money, their eyes lit up, but right away Evie knew what the problem was.

"The deadline for Currency Exchange," she said.

"Right."

"What about it?" said Dad.

"It passed," I said.

"What? Aren't there exceptions? Maybe some kind of exemption?"

"I don't think there is."

"The Federal Reserve was pretty specific in the guidelines," said Evie.

"Jesus," he said.

But here's what's funny: after the initial shock they were both pretty cool about it. *Disappointed as hell*, sure, but not, like, *devastated*. You never know what's going to set them off. They'll blow up and murder me over the tiniest thing—like, say, dropping out of school—but sometimes, for whatever reason, they're just cool. As for me, I don't know. It just would've been real nice to give them some money, you know?

 ?

# 89.

# A HUNDRED WAYS TO
# SAY ADVENTURE

Anne Chicarelli returned from Arizona, the Grand Canyon State, with ancient cultures, modern dining, and more than a Hundred Ways to Say Adventure™ (YAY!). She showed up the next morning, and this time she got out of her truck and came onto the porch, and without knocking or anything waited there for me to open the door. And when I opened it, there she was, standing right in the middle of everything, and it kind of spooked me. She looked different—*older*, if that was possible. Without a cowboy hat on, her hair was so short and thin.

"I see there was a fire," she said.

"Yeah, it was pretty crazy. The firemen came and everything."

"Well, thank you for watching my horses. Did they behave for you? I hope they did."

"They were great. Wonderful."

"Georgia hung on a lot longer than anyone expected, but then I told them, *She's a tough one. Always was.* I was in the lobby when she passed, but they say she went in peace with her arms crossed over her chest like a mummy. Now her body is six feet deep in the earth, with the sun shining down and the sprinklers watering the grass overhead. Of course, her spirit is in heaven."

"Right."

She looked at me. "And do you believe that?"

"Um."

"And where does *your* spirit dwell, Adam? Have you opened your heart to Jesus? Have you let him fill you with his holy light?"

I thought back to my moment on the white horse—Cain or Abel, I wasn't sure. It wasn't Jesus in my heart, exactly, but it was something, I guess, but maybe beyond it, too. Beside it? Including it? It was too much to explain.

"Shall we pray?" she said.

"Yeah, OK."

And when Anne started in on the preachy stuff I kind of just let the words flow around me like water over a stone. Her voice so low and gravelly. And it was OK, whatever she said, whether I agreed or not. There's more than one way to say the things that are beyond words.

 ?

# ⌐0.

# THE PINES

It was decided that I'd watch Bones while Dad was on tour, and I drove over to pick her up on a Sunday morning. He handed me two pages of single-spaced typed instructions—seriously—along with her leash, brush, bed, food bowl, water bowl, and bag of Diet Munch™ dog biscuits. I swore up and down I'd do a good job—and I meant it—though I didn't tell him about the little road trip I had planned for us.

We headed out that same day, cruising along on I-80 in my grandfather's Ford Ranger, just me and Bones. It was a beautiful day. I leaned the seat back to a comfortable position and watched the fence posts and sagebrush passing in a quiet blur along the interstate. Every now and again I'd catch a glimpse of the Humboldt River, winding like a glittery snake through the brush.

"Check out that scene, Bones."

We stopped in Lovelock to use the potty, and I bought some beef jerky and potato chips, and fed most of it to Bones. She was into that. Then onward westward, past Fernley, to where the road starts winding along the Truckee River. Finally, under a haze of gray, I could see Reno. All those glittery buildings.

The traffic was pretty bad, and I got squeezed out of the exit I wanted to take and was funneled instead into a construction zone and then had to backtrack, but the extra time was fine because it gave me to time to figure out what dorm Shiloh was living in at the University of Nevada, Reno. I ended up parking on the wrong side of the campus—but again it was fine because it gave me time to think about what I was going to say to her.

But in the end I decided not to say anything.

When I got to her room, she wasn't there. Her roommate said she was maybe at the library. So I went over there, but she wasn't there, either. The library was cool, though. It had these big glass windows, and as I was looking out them, I saw her. She was walking along the grass with some friends. They were smiling and talking. I started to head out to see her, but about halfway there I caught myself and went back to the windows and just watched her walk along the grass with her friends.

And you could say I was a coward for not going out there, but OTOH, she seemed OK without me in the way. She had on her tie-dye shirt and she was laughing and talking and . . . she looked happy. So I said what I had to say right there, watching her through the windows.

"Shiloh, you were right. I was an asshole. I'm sorry. I'm working on it. Thanks for the fun we had. I hope you have a good semester and a fun time with your friends and a great life."

And that was that.

Later, outside Reno where the highway begins its ascent into the Sierras, I called Katie—and was kind of surprised when she answered.

"Hi, Aaron."

"Oh, hi! You picked up."

"Sorry I haven't returned messages. Look, next time I'm in town I'll pick up my stuff, OK?"

"Actually, I thought maybe I could bring some of it to you."

"That's OK. You don't have to do that."

"I'm actually kind of already on the way."

*"What?"*

"Like an hour away at most. Where are you? How do I find you?"

Katie was silent, and for a moment I thought I'd lost her.

"Katie?"

I heard her sigh. "Do you know where Sugar Pine Point State Park is?"

"No, but I can find it."

"OK. From the parking lot, head downhill toward the water. There's an old mansion, some trees, and a pier. I'm at the end of the pier, reading a book."

"Give me an hour," I said, or tried to say, but now Homie™ was in my face.

> error!

network overload!

users in FAIL must wait in line!

:(

After that I couldn't pull up any maps, so I asked the lady at the gas station in Truckee if she knew how to get to Sugar Pine Point State Park. I'm not sure if she was confused or just messing with me, but anyway, following her instructions to the letter, I ended up at a small restaurant near the Lake Tahoe shore called The Pines. Still no service. The door to the restaurant was locked.

Inside, a man with a shaved head was running a buffer over the floor. I banged on the door until he shut it off and looked at me.

"Closed until four!" he shouted.

"OK, but do you know where Sugar Pine Point State Park is?"

"Which direction you coming from?"

"Nevada."

"Then you're doing it right. Continue west."

"On which road? How far?"

"Same road. Three point two miles. In three point two miles, you'll come to a sign that says Sugar Pine Point State Park. Turn left there."

"Hey...so what's the food like here?"

"The food? The food here is outstanding."

"Really?"

The man wheeled his buffer to the front of the restaurant and unlocked the door. "Why would I lie to you? What motive could I possibly have?"

"You work here."

"Well, yes. That's true. That *is* true...." He rested his hand on the buffer and sort of spun it around.

"I was thinking of maybe taking a friend out for dinner."

He gave it some thought. "Well, this is your place. For atmosphere and food, it can't be beat. Best place on the lake. Check out the reviews if you don't believe me. We've got over a hundred YAY!s. I see you're having FUN®—give a YAY! for The Pines and we'll give you a free dessert with your meal. Yes, the chef is a tyrant. All he does is work and he has no friends and he abuses the staff in ways that probably violate every labor law there is. But the man can cook—I'll say that much."

"Who's the chef?"

"Me."

"Oh."

"I'm running the buffer because I just fired the afternoon help. He was annoying me again. You know those people? The ones who never have anything real to say, so instead they'll give you complete, real-time synopses of television shows? He's one of those. It's like, if you're so big on it, how about you just let me see the show myself? Then we can have an intelligent discussion, a two-way conversation, instead of this tedious monologue where you get to relive all the fun you had and I'm supposed to just sit here and be your sounding board."

"You fired a guy for telling you about a TV show?"

"Oh, I'll probably hire him back tomorrow. It's an ongoing thing between us. He's my brother."

And with that he started the buffer again.

OK, so YAY! for The Pines and their free desserts and helpful instructions, because 3.2 miles down the road, I came to a sign for Sugar Pine Point State Park. I turned left down the road and parked near the edge of the lot. It was ₿1,000 to park, and the signs said NO DOGS ON BEACH, but I let Bones free anyway—she immediately took off after a squirrel—and then I started crutching downhill, toward the water. It was evening, the sun low in the sky. There was an old mansion, some trees, and a pier. At the end of the pier sat a woman in a straw hat reading a book.

 ?

# 91.

# IT DOES NOT DIE UNDER
# ANY CONDITION

"Hey, you've got the entire pier to yourself."

"Not anymore."

"Ha. Right."

She was wearing a swimsuit, her purple swimsuit, face hidden behind the brim of her hat and the pages of her book, which was called *It Does Not Die Under Any Condition* by Cynthia Smith, author of the It Does Not Die series, including *It Does Not Die in Sunlight* and *It Does Not Die Alone*—all available from Scare/Bait Press (YAY!).

A boat roared past, dragging an empty wakeboard. Katie turned the page.

"Good book, huh? What's it about?"

"The undead," she said.

"What, like zombies?"

"No."

"Mummies?"

"No."

"Vampires? Aliens?"

"Aaron—"

I waited, but she didn't go on. Waves from the boat fanned out to the shoreline, knocking against the pilings. Water sloshed around under the pier. The water was impossibly blue—like something out of a tropical postcard.

"Look. I'm not here to bug you. I just wanted to talk. I brought some of your stuff. It's in the car. I couldn't carry it all out here because, well..." I sort of wiggled the crutches, but she didn't look up. "Katie?"

She sighed and closed her book. "OK. Let's talk."

She set the book aside, but not on the pier. She placed it into the air next to her, and it floated there, three feet above the water, before it swelled up, popped, and disappeared. And as Katie raised the brim of her hat and looked up at me, I zoomed in on her blue eyes. Something was different. The light in them had changed. They were...less blue somehow.

"No. You didn't! You're having—?"

"FUN®," she said. "Birthday present from my sister. She paid for the lenses and a one-year contract."

"Aw, shit, Katie, you don't want to do that."

"Why not? You're always talking about how great it is. I finally joined the modern world, right?" She fluttered her eyelids. Her gaze drifted down to my cast/boot thing. "What happened?"

"I fell in the hole."

"Oh."

"But I got out, and then I found the treasure, and it was all this money, but not the kind of money that's worth anything, because it was old money. But that's not important. What's important is—" I cleared my throat. I'd gone over this speech in my head about a dozen times on the drive over. "Well...I learned something.

Or more like remembered. Just—how holy everything is. Which sounds silly, I know, but I mean that it's real and it's good. And I've been thinking about what you said, about a hole in us that can't be filled. But I think I know what does fill it. Love."

And she kind of flinched at that word, but I kept going anyway. Man, it felt good to be honest for once.

"And I just want to say again how sorry I am. Because when I said to look in your heart, I meant that. And with Shiloh, I just got distracted. And when we were together, you and me—not *together* together, but just hanging out—I felt something. This, like, electricity that I'd never felt before. Those times we were hanging out, when we were looking for the treasure or whatever, it was *fun*. Not FUN® fun, but *real* fun. *Actual* fun. But even *more* than that. And I know I'm young and stupid, but I've been thinking about that electricity, and the only word for it is love. I'm in love with you."

And I don't know what I expected—but I kind of know what I was hoping for. I was hoping that Katie would hear my words and that the power of my love would move her. I was hoping she'd throw her arms around my neck and my crutches would fall to the pier and we'd stand there, embracing each other, over the blue, blue water with the sun setting behind us. Because she had felt it, too. She had felt the electricity and she couldn't deny it. And later we'd go out for dinner at this really great place I knew, just 3.2 miles down the lake, and collect our free dessert.

But that isn't what happened.

Katie just sat there in silence. Waves sloshed against the pilings. Homie™ popped up.

> hi original boy_2!

u r a FAIL!

yay! for state parks?

"Go away, Homie™."

"Aaron," she said at last. She said it slowly, carefully, and I could tell from the tone of her voice that whatever she was gonna say next, it wasn't what I'd been hoping for, and I wasn't ready for that. So I cut in.

"Hey, are you hungry? We could talk about it all over a meal. I know this really great place we could get dinner...."

She nodded at the paper bag on the pier. "I just ate."

"Oh, well, that's OK, too. We don't have to do that. But—OK. Here." I took the mood ring out of my pocket. "I didn't get to give this to you that night. Happy birthday. Again."

But as I went to hand the ring to Katie, something happened. I stumbled and it fell from my hands, fell to the pier, and I watched in horror as it rolled bumpily along a couple feet, then slipped soundlessly between two of the boards. And then I was down on my hands and knees, searching for the ring, hoping beyond hope that maybe it had fallen just so. Maybe it had wedged itself between the cracks. But it was just boards and empty space and cold blue water below.

 ?

# 92.

# THE LAND OF THE LOST

And I was ready to jump in the water and go diving for it, but I wasn't supposed to get my boot wet. I started taking it off. As I was messing with the straps, Katie started talking, and by the time she was done I'd stopped messing with the boot.

"I guess I liked the attention," she said. "It was fun—I'm not saying it wasn't. And yes, when I was out here with my papa and sister and I lost the ring, it did make me sad, because I *do* like you, but—"

"Why does there always have to be a *but*? If you don't have any feelings for me, why'd you cry when I told you about Shiloh?"

She was kind of glaring at me now. "Because I do have feelings! And I'm sure she did, too! And just because something can't work doesn't mean I'm not sad about it."

"Who says it can't work? You sure had your dad convinced it was working."

"Right. Maybe I let him believe what he wanted. I shouldn't have done that. I'm always making things so complicated. It's the stupid Space Amazon. I'm sorry."

"And I am, too! So let's forget the Space Amazon. Let's just go with—"

"Aaron. It wouldn't work."

"Why not? Give me one good reason."

"Because I keep telling you. Because you're still a kid. Because I'm a teacher. Because I'm moving."

"Moving?"

"The leper mite fiasco was the final sign. It's time to get out of Antello. I've been sending out applications. I've got an interview next Wednesday."

"Where?"

"Here. Tahoe."

"Well, that's not so far. I could drive out on the weekends and—"

"Aaron," she said quietly. *"Please."*

And even with the lenses over her eyes, I could still read the blue. I could see what they were saying. *Please don't make me break your heart.*

Well, but she already kind of was.

And the truth is, even if you like someone and they like you—and you *know* they like you—they get to do what they want to do. And sometimes life is complicated, and sometimes things don't work out, and sometimes you just have to let it go. Maybe that's what her eyes were really saying. *Let it go.*

But I couldn't let it go. I was having the hardest time letting it go. I asked her what she was doing next, and she said she was going back to her sister's. They were going to watch *The Land of the Lost* (YAY!) together. She'd ridden her bike to the lake, and I asked her if I could give her a ride back, and she said OK. So we threw her bike in the back and gathered up Bones, who was barking at some squirrels, and I drove her to her sister's house. It was a pretty nice house. From the drive you could see the lake shimmering in the distance. I could see how it wouldn't be hard to spend a summer there.

And I didn't want to let her go. She was walking her bike up to the door. I grabbed the bag I'd packed for her—undies and shirts and a couple sweaters in case it was cold at night—and followed her up the drive. And I was like, "Katie."

And she was like, "Yeah?"

And I was like, "What if we just—sit out here for a while? It's just—it's such a beautiful evening. I mean, listen to those birds. I never knew there were so many birds up at the lake."

And she paused. "Aaron, those aren't birds."

"What do you mean?"

"Oh, Aaron. You've been having FUN® so long you've forgotten."

"Forgotten what?"

Katie sighed. "Reboot FUN®."

"Reboot it?"

"Yeah."

So I pressed my fingers into my eyelids and said the magic words. *There's no place like home.* The world went blank for a moment, and then, for the first time in a long time, I took a moment to see it as it was. I mean, as it *actually* was: the sky a little less blue, the trees a little less green, the water a little less shimmery. But what *really* got me was the strange and sudden silence.

The birds were gone; their song was gone. No tweeting, no soft electronic cries.

"Wow. I didn't realize. All the shininess. All the birds. It's just—"

"FUN®," she said.

And I didn't really know what to say to that, so I didn't say anything. I just gave her a hug, and then I turned and crutched down the drive and got in my truck with Bones and gave Katie a little wave, and she gave me a little wave back, and I left.

 ?

# ⁹³.

# ACE DEFENDER PETER JULIET

And that was my big road trip. One good thing was I didn't have a lot of time to dwell in my sorrow and failure, because there was more stuff to deal with when I got back to Antello. I woke late the next morning to the sound of Bones barking, and I cracked the blinds to see a short man in a Hawaiian shirt standing on the porch.

"Please be informed," he yelled, "that you are advised to restrain your animal!"

I opened the door and he thrust out his hand.

"Aaron O'Faolain, I am Peter Juliet."

"Who?"

"Peter Juliet, the defense attorney. It appears that you are having FUN®, Aaron."

"Yeah."

"As am I. Had I known you were having FUN®, I would have done a mindtalk™. Normally, I do not conduct these home visits. However, my secretary has contracted scabies, which is a highly contagious skin condition. May I come in?"

"Why are you here?"

"You didn't get the message? I am representing your friend Angelo Davíd Sandoval, aka 'El Oso' aka 'Oso,' in his upcoming trial. The reason I'm here this morning, Mr. O'Faolain, is to prepare you for testimony tomorrow in his sentencing hearing."

> yay! for ace defender peter juliet
> with over 13 years' experience in
> injury and malpractice?

"Yay."

Peter Juliet opened his briefcase on the coffee table. "We'll need you at my office at nine A.M. The address is 963 High Street, suite 201—second floor, first door on the right. I'm messaging you that right now. Do you have a clean, solid-colored button-up shirt, preferably white, and slacks? If not, I will provide you with these items. In addition, you will need to shower and shave. Do you have a razor and shaving cream? If not, I can provide these items."

I told him I had the items in question, and he explained to me how the hearing would work. He, attorney Peter Juliet, would take care of everything—all I needed to do was show up tomorrow and follow instructions. When the time came, I would take the stand and in a clear and sober voice enumerate the reasons why my childhood friend Angelo Sandoval was not only an upstanding person but indeed a role model to the youth of Antello.

"I'm messaging you some Wit Lit to look over. Here, let me give you a hard copy to study as well."

"Wit Lit?"

"Witness literature. Some suggestions for what to say when you take the stand. Study it. Memorize it. Bring it with you tomorrow. I'll see you at nine A.M. sharp. We'll rendezvous at my office, then go over to the courthouse together."

I looked at the paper in my hands. It wasn't a list of suggestions so much as a character witness Mad Libs, and Peter Juliet or his scabrous secretary had already filled in all the blanks:

My name is Aaron O'Faolain, and I have known Angelo for 10 year(s), and I am here today to tell you why I believe he is an upstanding citizen. I have seen the good and kind nature in Angelo shine through on many occasions, including the time when he earned "best takedown of an opponent" honors on the Antello High School J.V. wrestling squad, and when he was kind and courteous to his neighbors, and his regular attendance at Saint Mark's Catholic Church, where he has sung tenor in the Sunday choir on several occasions. So you can see, this is not some degenerate we are talking about. No, my good friend sitting here before you today, Angelo Sandoval, is not only a role model for many, but also a productive and contributing member of the city of Antello. Furthermore, I would like to add that if you take the "o" off of "Angelo" you will see that the name spells "Angel," and this to me sums up the character of the person in question. Thank you, your honor presiding judge Helen Levitt. Here ends my statement.

 ?

# 94.

# FROM THE HEART

But the next morning at the Antello Municipal Courthouse when I took the stand and found myself facing the crowded gallery, I just couldn't bring myself to read from that paper. Too much was at stake. My best bud was on trial, and it was like a Sandoval family reunion out there: aunts, uncles, sisters, nephews, nieces, plus these three biker dudes in leather jackets—and of course Oso himself, in a clean shirt and tie with his hair slicked back—and I knew I couldn't just read the prepared statement. He deserved something more, something from the heart, like YAY! for HeartLand® Heritage candles or Heart Coffee or HomeHealthHeart Care—but really just something honest and true and from the heart.

So I turned the paper over and just started talking.

"Well, OK, it's like this. Some people in this world are really wonderful. Actually, forget that. *All* people are wonderful—but some people are wonderful in a way that is, you know, really wonderful. Not that I want to get into ranking things, because also everything is pretty much the same thing. Like, we're all in this together, you know?"

I took a breath and looked up from the podium. Everyone was looking back at me, just sitting there watching me with curiosity and waning patience—well, all of them except for Peter Juliet, who was waving around a copy of the speech and jabbing at it with his index finger.

"But here's the thing. We *are* in this all together, and Oso, the way he's wonderful is—well, it's impossible to explain. It really is. But one thing you could say is he's got a big heart. Like, I could give you a million examples of just what kind of guy he is. He's really just a good guy. I could give you all *kinds* of examples."

"Mr. O'Faolain, I believe you had a written statement."

"Right. But let me give you an example."

I took a sip of water to give myself time to think. There were a lot of stories to tell, but I hadn't considered the fact that they needed to be court-friendly. I searched deep in the back of my memory and grabbed at the first thing that came to mind, which was that one time I got hit with the softball in P.E. and he helped me around the bases—and it wasn't until I was halfway through the story that I realized that the star of the story was not, in fact, Oso. It was *another* kid. I'd gotten them confused. I looked out at my audience, all those shining faces. What did it matter, really? The spirit was the same.

". . . So in conclusion, sometimes it's the smallest gestures which make the biggest differences. I don't know if he even remembers it anymore, but I know I will never forget—no, I'll always be grateful for that day in the field with Oso."

"Your honor, we will also submit his written statement for your review."

As I was stepping down from the box, I caught Oso's eye.

He looked grateful and also a little confused, but he gave me the thumbs-up.

Next, his aunt spoke, then his little nephew, and then, one after another, the three biker dudes, who I realized now were Los Ojos de Dios. The first two said they had known Oso a long time, that he had done yard work for him, and that he was a great employee, a hard worker, always punctual, etc.—and the last one said the same stuff and added how although the city was pursuing charges, he, Pedro Santistevan, would like to drop the charges of breaking and entering because it was all just a big misunderstanding.

There was a short recess, which actually lasted an hour, and then presiding judge Helen Levitt returned to deliver the sentencing verdict of Angelo Davíd Sandoval for one count of criminal misdemeanor: public intoxication. This would mean ₳98,000 in court fees and fines; two hundred hours of community service; and required completion of Crime: The Real Victim, a class to be held every Tuesday and Thursday evening in the basement of the First Antello Baptist Church.

 ?

# 95.

# TRUE

I didn't get to talk to Oso after the trial, but he showed up at my grandfather's house the next Saturday with two 5-irons and a putter, and we went golfing. The grass had burned in big black patches, and where it hadn't burned it was in various states of death—yellow, brown—and it was like walking around on a giant camouflaged bedspread. The patches made the contours more difficult to judge—not that I've ever been much of a golfer, or any kind of golfer, really—though I am proud to say I'm one of only a handful to ever have golfed the famous Coyote Heights. Let me tell you, that water hazard on 13 is a real bitch—even without the water.

We took a break on the hill above the 14th hole, the one where I'd fired off my grandfather's ashes, and looked out at the apocalyptic land.

When Oso reached into his pocket, I was expecting him to pull out some pills, but instead it was a pack of TrueMint® Spearmint gum (YAY!).

"You want one?"

"What's it do?"

"Keeps your breath fresh. Gives your jaw something to do. I'm going sober, bro. Not just because of the probation, either. It's time. I'm evolving, bro. By the way, thanks for your testimony at the sentencing. You really saved my butt."

"Well, you had a lot of support—what was up with the Santistevan brothers? You worked out some kind of deal with them?"

"Yep. It's the biker code, bro. *Keep it even.* For not turning their asses in for selling fake VPHPs, they agreed to testify on my behalf."

"I was meaning to ask you about those pills. When I ate some that night with the backhoe, I really felt something weird."

"Nah, bro. The police tested them. They're just aspirin. But that's the thing—they were wrapped in baggies like they were ready to sell, and the police wanted to know where I'd gotten them—and I could have said that I'd gotten them from Pedro Santistevan, who was hiring underage youngsters like myself to sell fake drugs, and I gave Pedro a call and let him know that, and we made a deal."

"Just aspirin? But I was, like, *tripping.*"

Oso looked at me. "Whatever you felt, it was all you, bro."

Huh. Wow. *Weird.*

"But hey," he said. "I got a question for you. That story about the softball? I don't remember that. Did that really happen? Were we even in the same P.E. class?"

"Well, yeah, about that..." I looked at Oso's dark eyes. "*Technically* it was another guy—Lester something-or-other. Remember him? Everyone called him names?"

"The Choad, bro! Yeah, I remember him. So *he* was the guy who helped you around the bases?"

"Look—I couldn't just tell the judge that you stole Mindy Howland's gym shorts and gave them to me as a birthday present, now, could I?"

"Ha. I forgot about that."

"Or how about when you got ahold of all the geography answers and you handed them out to *everyone* in the class—not just your friends?"

"That was a mistake. Nelly Avila ratted me out."

"Or how about the time that guy who was supposed to buy beer for us ripped us off, and so you stole two forties by hiding them down your pants?"

Oso was grinning now. "I get it. My shit's too scandalous for a court of law."

# 96.

## DUMP TRUCKS

The days grew shorter, the nights longer and colder, and in the mornings I was woken to the sound of heavy machinery. They were clearing out Coyote Heights, bulldozing what was left into charred piles, hauling the piles off in big gray Peterbilt® dump trucks (YAY!). V-shaped formations of geese and other birds glided southward through the cold blue sky, but I knew now they were mostly just FUN®. Dad returned from his tour and took Bones. She was excited to see him, her old tail wagging back and forth.

I applied for a job washing dishes at Lucky Pedro's. That way I could at least start paying Dad and Evie back. I also decided to make good on my word to get my GED. There was this program where if you attended all the classes, they'd pay for the test. The classes were MWF evenings at the elementary school, and they weren't hard or anything, but it *was* hard to concentrate. One night I excused myself to the restroom and wandered out back to check out Katie's portable. Only it wasn't hers anymore. Her name was gone from the door, and when I looked inside, all her posters and fish tanks or whatever were gone.

I took the long way back to class, through the gym and past the library, where there were all these boxes stacked outside the door. Like piles and piles of them. And each box was labeled with the same word in black magic marker: TRASH. I looked inside one and it was filled with books. They all were. They were finally getting ready to digitize the library. It kind of bummed me out, I don't know why. Just the fact that the world keeps changing, I guess. I thought about that book my grandpa was always trying to get me to read, *True Tales of Buried Treasure*. I didn't feel like returning to class, so I wandered outside, and that's when I bumped into Evie.

"Hi. Dad said you had class."

"Yeah. We're done for the night."

"What were you thinking?" she said.

"Huh?"

"I mean just now. You had this funny look on your face."

"I don't know—nothing really."

"Well, here," she said. "I brought you something. Brain food."

She handed me a paper bag, the smell of baked goods wafting up through the creases in the top.

"What's the occasion?"

"Isaac asked me to move to New York with him."

"Wow. What'd you say?"

"I told him I needed some time to think."

"The cautious route. I bet he was pleased."

My sister scowled in a smiley kind of way. "I like Isaac. But it's funny. I also like the life I have here." She bit her lip. "What do you think? Am I just being a scaredy-cat?"

"Since when do you ask *me* for advice?"

"Since right now, I guess. I just want to know, is this one of those instances where, now that I'm finally faced with something I've wanted so badly for all these years, I'm too scared to take it?"

"I don't really know, Evie. I'm new at this. I mean—so what did Sam say?"

"Sam?" Evie sighed. "Oh *God*. When I told him, he broke down crying, and then *I* broke down crying, and then we put on our Christmas aprons and baked snickerdoodles." She touched the paper bag. "Which, full disclosure, came out a little on the burnt side. But even so, there are some good ones in there, too. I put them on top."

 ?

# 97.

## OSMOS™ IV

November came and it snowed, the first snow of winter—or, actually, I guess it was still technically autumn. Just a light snowfall, a few flakes falling out of the gray, but it lasted all day, and by evening everything was covered in white. White mountains, white hills, white Russian olive rising out of a hole in a field of white brush. The next day the sun came out, but it didn't get above freezing, and the snow stayed. That afternoon I got a call from my dad.

"It's Bones, Aaron. I found her under the back porch this morning."

"What about her?"

"She's dead."

"Dead? What happened?"

He was quiet a moment. "I don't know. She was old. She'd been through a lot. Maybe it was just her time. We're coming out there, me and Evie."

"Here? Why?"

"To bury her."

They showed up in Evie's CR-V, opened the back, and took out the bundle. She was wrapped up in a blanket.

"Here," said Evie. "I think this is yours."

She handed me something. A neon-green shoe. My long-lost Osmos™IV (YAY!).

The three of us started out across the brush.

It was a pretty good day for a funeral—by which I mean pretty miserable. Snow on the ground, gray sky overhead, dead birds here and there. At least we didn't need to dig a hole for her. There was already one there. At the edge of the hole under the Russian olive my dad set down his bundle and carefully unwrapped it. Bones. The wind picked up and blew a dusting of snow across her body.

Evie had brought along the yellow bag that said BIOHAZARD, and after Dad laid Bones in the hole she climbed down there, too, and I watched as she undid the twisty top and, one by one, removed the tiny gray bodies and nestled them next to their mother where they belonged.

Then Dad took the shovel and threw on that first scoop of dirt. It was just awful, the way it rained down on Bones and her puppies. After that, I couldn't even look. I just helped. It was a big hole, and it was going to take a long time to fill it in.

I don't know who started it—Evie, probably—but at some point someone threw a bird into the hole, and after that it became our task. We wandered across the brush, gathering corpses and tossing them into the hole. One final flight.

It was late by the time we finished. There was a little bit of earth left over—there always is—but the birds were gone and Bones was gone and her puppies were gone and the hole was gone... and it was all just gone. Even so, Dad kept scooping more dirt on top, and Evie pretty much had to pry the shovel from his hands to get him to stop. He walked around the earth, smoothing out the rough spots with the side of his shoe. He hadn't been wearing any gloves, and I caught a glimpse of his hands, palms all dark and bloody.

The three of us stood at the edge of the dirt to say good-bye.

"You were a good dog," said Dad. "You were a good dog," he said again. "And I—"

He kind of settled to his knees and stayed there.

"Dad?" said Evie.

It took me a second to figure out what was going on. He wasn't crying. More like weeping—whatever the quiet kind is. When Mom left, when we buried Grandpa—nothing. And now this. And I knew it wasn't just for Bones—it was for all of it, everything, all the sadness. I looked over and saw that Evie was pretty much weeping, too. And then me.

 ?

# 98.

# YAY!

And so that's it.

That's pretty much my History, aka The Story of How I Got From There to Here. Somewhere along the way—I couldn't tell you exactly where—I came to a decision I'd been coming to for a long time. I didn't really want out of FAIL. I was ready to stop having FUN® altogether.

In order to do that, I had to apply for an Application for Termination, but in order to do *that* I had to get out of FAIL, and in order to do that I had to catch up on my YAY!s—which is why I decided to do the History part of my Application here in the YAY!log. It occurs to me now that I was probably a little more thorough than I needed to be. I bet you've never seen a History that long before.

Anyway, so here's my rundown again:

```
name:       aaron o'faolain
username:   original boy_2
age:        almost 18
region:     america
```

```
mood:        ok fine
status:      fail
history:     (see what you just read)
reason for
application: (see history)
```

And I guess if anything I just want to also say that despite the parts that sucked, and despite all my griping, I have seen the light that is wonderful and holy. I can't even really explain it, and that doesn't matter, because it's not about explanation anyway. It's about everything. It was here before we got here and it will be here when we're gone. It's +10 magic super beautiful. It's a song that sings itself.

Telling my History has taken a little longer than I expected—and I know I rambled in places, and I apologize for that—but anyway I see I've fallen further behind on my FUN®, so I've got a bit of quick catching up to do: just a few more YAY!s and (with your approval) I can stop having FUN®.

So here we go:

YAY! for FUN®, and the newly released version 2.0.

YAY! for Evie, who made a trip to Reno to get chipped and lensed for FUN® before she left for New York. She was excited to go, all giddy like that time when she won the MathOlympics competition, which is a moment I will never forget: the way she stood there, just beaming up at the bleachers. As for me, I was slouched against the wall, pretending I didn't care. Why do I do stuff like that? Here I am, Evie. Over here. Waving like a madman. Can you see me? You're going to do awesome in New York, I just know it.

YAY! for my dad, who also started having FUN® so he could mindtalk™ with Evie in NYC. Dad—I want you to know I know it wasn't your fault Mom left. I mean, I always kind of knew, I just didn't want to admit it. It was easier that way, but it wasn't fair. And overall I have to say you've been pretty cool with me, especially lately, what with the dropping out of school thing, and the Katie thing, and all of it. Know what I think? I think you should get a dog. Some kind of puppy. A little feisty one that will just chew the shit out of your shoes.

YAY! for Sam, who said he would never have FUN® and then did—I *told* him he would—and who is my brother, and who helped me out of the hole. Thanks for not murdering me when you found out about the thing with Shiloh.

YAY! for Shiloh aka shiloh_lilly and her 10 stars.

YAY! for Oso, who did not start having FUN®. He said he couldn't on account of his newfound sobriety. Also because of the terms of his probation. Also because he is El Oso.

YAY! for Anne Chicarelli. YAY! for her sister, and her horses.

YAY! for Homie™. You were almost my friend.

YAY! for the whole world, YAY! for all the creatures who inhabit it, real and unreal, on land, at sea, or in the sky. YAY! for the birds—what's left of them. They are a memory of how good we had it, how good it really was, and how good it could have been— but also how good it could still be. But not really. It won't ever be like it was when there were birds. Even so, YAY! for Animals of Wonder & Light®, the entire menagerie, from the Armadillodile™ to the Shaarkvark™ to the just-released Zebracuda™.

Which reminds me: YAY! for you, whoever you are. Thanks for the YAY!s. And if you BOO!ed me, that's cool, too. I won't hold it against you. YAY! for your mom, and YAY! for my mom, and YAY! for MOM Brands® cereal, maker of Apple Zings™, Coco Roos™,

Fruity Dino-Bites™, and Creamy Hot Wheat Malt-O-Meal™. Mom, I haven't mentioned you much, but that's only because you weren't around—and it doesn't mean I don't think about you.

BOO! for the hole. BOO! for war. BOO! for hard lives and suffering and the Avis Mortem and sad days and absent parents and all the sucky parts. But OTOH also kind of YAY! for the BOO!s— which, now that I think about it, are sometimes how we learn to enjoy the YAY!s. That's how it worked for me anyway.

 ?

# ⫪⫪.

# TRUE TALES OF BURIED TREASURE

Finally, as we come to the end, YAY! for my grandpa, who I never really got to know, but sort of kind of did, and who made this whole thing possible. Just the other day I finally had your tombstone inscribed, just like you asked, in the biggest font that would fit:

IT COULDD

HAVE BEEN

WONDDERFUL

ANDD SOMETIMES

IT WAS

And I wanted to tell you, Grandpa, I finally got around to reading that book you gave me, *True Tales of Buried Treasure* by Edward Rowe Snow (YAY!). You were right. It's a pretty cool book. I wish I wouldn't have been so stubborn when you gave it to me, because it would've been nice to talk to you about it when you were still around. So far I've made it to chapter 15, "The Skull's Revelation."

I was right at the part on page 225 where Mabel is about to reveal the mystery of the skull and she's all:

"You've got to believe what I tell you, George. It will seem too fantastic at first, but remember—you've just got to believe..."

And just then there was a knock on the door.

 ?

# 100.

# AND THEN HE TURNS INTO A BIRD

"Come in!"

But no one came, so I got up to see who it was.

There she was, Katie, standing in the snow by the shed in a puffy blue coat, looking up at the roof.

"There was a bird," she said.

"A bird?"

"Yeah."

"Like an actual bird?"

"I think so? A yellow one. I thought it flew up there, but now I don't see it...."

I looked around. No bird that I could see, just sagebrush and sky. The wind had picked up. It was blowing Katie's hair all around her face.

"I came for the rest of my stuff," she said.

"Right. Well, come on in."

I hadn't lit a fire yet, so I brought some wood in and loaded up the wood stove. When I first started using it, I didn't really know how to stack the wood inside—I always got ahead of myself, put too many big logs on, but over time I'd learned how to do it right. You put a big log on either side, and then you crumple your paper in the middle, and put a couple small logs over that, then some medium logs, and a big one on top. Then you light it up with a $100 bill and close the door, but not all the way. You need to give it some air at first.

Katie watched me crumple up the paper. "Holy wow," she said. "Is that real money?"

Funny, but I'd gotten so used to it, I didn't even think about it anymore. Turns out the old US dollar is pretty great for starting fires. In a matter of weeks I'd burned up twenty grand, easy, with dead presidents smiling out from the flames.

"I was too late to exchange it for amero. You want some coffee?"

I poured her a cup, and we sat down on the sofa.

"I'm so sorry about the treasure," she said. "Would you like to keep any of my furniture? You can have whatever you want. The chair... the desk... the other chair..."

"I've been using the tiny lamp."

"That's fine," she said. "You should have the tiny lamp."

"So are you moving to Tahoe, then?"

"Right—I didn't tell you. That job I interviewed for? I got it. Teaching sixth grade."

"In Tahoe?"

"Yeah. It starts in two weeks."

"Oh." I tried to sound upbeat. "Well, congratulations."

"We can keep in touch," she said. "I'd like that. You can mindtalk™ me sometime."

"Actually, I'm getting off."

"Off?!" she said. "Why?"

"I don't know. I guess I'm just done having FUN®—I mean if I can complete all my yays and they accept my Application for Termination."

> oh u don't want to stop FUN®!

said the Homie™.

"But I thought you were all *about* FUN®," said Katie.

"Yeah, I was. But I think it's time for the next thing."

> this is the next thing!
> yay for FUN®!

"Well," she said, "you were right about one thing. FUN® is fun, but it's also addicting. Have you ever played *Tickle, Tickle, Boom!*? Oh my God! It's like a drug! One good thing, though: I *did* quit smoking. I only smoke smókz™ now." She lit one up and blew a cloud of bonuses. "Yay for me, right?"

"Yay for you, Katie. But listen—are you *sure* you want to move to Lake Tahoe? What with all the trees and beautiful houses and delicious restaurants and crystal clear water? I mean, besides all those things and your cool new job, what could possibly make you want to—"

She was smiling now. God, her eyes. Even with the lenses they were just—I don't know. Like looking at Earth from outer space. I won't ever forget them. And it occurred to me I'd never really told her about her eyes, how beautiful they were—"beautiful" isn't even the word for it—and I wanted to say something, just to let her know, you know? And then suddenly there was this loud *SMACK*.

Right behind us, like someone had run up from the yard and slapped the pane. Just this loud—*SMACK!*

We went outside and found it, eight feet out from the house: a little yellow bird lying motionless on the snow. I'm not kidding, that thing had bounced back eight feet from the house. Talk about the elasticity of glass.

"That's it!" she said. "That's the bird!"

Its eyes were closed, and its wings and feet were tucked against its body. I watched the tiny yellow feathers tremble in the breeze. It was so *real*. And yet it could have been a Christmas tree ornament; the only thing missing was a loop of thread coming out of its back.

We knelt there for a long time, not saying anything, just looking for a sign of life. The bird didn't move.

> hi original boy_2!
> r you ready to have more FUN®?
> everyday reality is such a drag™!

I scooped my hands under the bird, trying my best to keep the snow off. It was warm and soft, but the tiny eyes were closed and the head lolled as I cupped it in my palm.

We brought it inside and I got a paper lunch sack—the same one that held Evie's snickerdoodles. I poured out the crumbs and we slid the bird into the bag, folding the top neatly the way my sister used to when she packed my lunches.

There. Now the bird was in a bag. I set it on the table.

"And why did we just do that?" Katie asked.

"I don't know. Aren't you supposed to put them in a bag?"

"Are you? And then what?"

"I don't know—we wait, I guess. Maybe it gets better?"

We waited.

> yay! for FUN®!
> yay! so many times!

Katie got up and opened the bag and looked inside. She closed it again.

"It isn't moving," she said.

"We could bury it with the others."

"The others?" she said.

"Yeah. We buried them by the tree."

"OK," she said. "Fine. Let's do that."

Snow lay in patches between the sagebrush, and as we neared the Russian olive the patches joined into an uninterrupted carpet of white. The tree threw its branches up toward the heavens like a call to prayer. Sunlight fell from the blue sky, but it was bitter cold out there. The wind came in icy blasts. Katie held her hair from her eyes.

I'd remembered to bring a shovel along, but I'd forgotten gloves. As I dug, Homie™ told me about all the reasons for having FUN®. By the time I got done chipping out what you might call a hole, I couldn't feel my fingers. I leaned against the shovel and looked down at the frozen ground. The little hole.

> yay! for FUN® original boy_2?
 it's the only way to be!

"Hey!" Katie was grabbing my arm. "Look! The bag! It's moving!"

She was holding it away from her body, like it might explode in her hands. There was definitely something moving, all right. Knocking around at the paper walls.

"What do I do?"

"I don't know!"

"Here! Take it!"

And then *I* was holding the bag, doing no better than she had done. My fingers were frozen and I couldn't get it unfolded, so finally I just tore open the bag and gave it a shake. The bird flopped onto a sagebrush, landing upside down in the snowy branches. As it struggled to right itself, all these questions flashed through my mind.

Should I help it? Or would I just hurt it more? Does it have a concussion? Broken bones? Internal bleeding? Should we bring it back inside? What now? What next?

But there wasn't time. In a sudden flash of wings, the bird threw itself into the air. I'm serious. Just. Like. THAT. One second it was resting on the sagebrush, and the next it was airborne. Like magic. A resurrection. It was like, *Go, little bird! Go!*

And then came the wind. This gust like you wouldn't believe. Howling across the hills like a parade of demons, bending the sagebrush and blowing up clouds of dust. It slammed the bird and flung it eastward across the sky—I mean FLUNG it—but the bird battled back. I'm telling you, this thing was a *fighter*. But where was it going? And how was it going to get there? What's the life expectancy of a little yellow bird in the high desert with winter coming on?

"Wow," said Katie.

> yay or boo!?

said Homie™.

And this voice in my head, I don't know where it came from— just out of the blue, I guess—it was like, *Hey, man. This is holy.* And I gave the questions a rest. I stood next to Katie and just watched the bird go. And let me tell you, that thing *went*. Angling this way and that, fighting the gusts, climbing higher and higher, growing smaller and smaller, the little bird pressed itself against the very edge of the sky until it was only a speck—yellow on blue—nothing at all and everything all at once. And then it disappeared.

# (THANK YOU FOR YOUR HELP ALONG THE WAY)

Tara, Cedar, Alison, Mom, Dad, Mark Baechtel, Jamie Baker, Eric Bassier, Jen Bedet, Marvin Bell, Laura Bergner, Ben Caldwell, Ethan Canin, Jen Carlson, Sarah Charukesnant, Jerritt Collord, Benji Conrad, Frank Conroy, Petrina Crockford, Everyone at DCL, Gloria Derado, Elizabeth Dobbs, Eric Eanes, Earth Mountain, ECN, ENG 121, Jason Enlow, Danielle Miles Forest, Justice Evans Forest, Travis George, Arrel Gray, Bobby Hogg, Everyone at Hyperion, Iowa, Michael Johnson, Mike Kath, Tracey Keevan, the kid with the white hair, Lori Klaus, Catherine Knepper, Dave Kosanke, Latuda Hall, Judy Lee, Lillian, Amy Maffei, Jesse McCaughey, Skyler McCaughey, Shaelan McDonough, Marilyn McGuire, Melissa Meiris, Ricardo Mejías, Everyone at MHCC, Justin Miles, Tracy Miles, Tamera Morton, John Paniagua, Puff, Chris & AJ Roe, Matt Roeser, the Rossolos, Tyler Sage, Kimberly Slagle, Cynthia Smith, Paula Smith, Edward Rowe Snow, Johnny & Joey Sousa, Trinidad, TSJC, TWSL, Zach Weinman, and everyone else.